THE DAY WITHOUT YESTERDAY

By

William Rossbach

"I am haunted by a conviction that the nihilistic philosophy which so-called educated opinion chose to adopt following the publication of the Origin of Species committed mankind to a course of automatic self destruction. A doomsday was then set ticking."

Sir Fred Hoyle
British Astrophysicist

Chapter One

Branch Nichols had no interest in solving the world's oldest riddle—the reason for a 4,000-year-old, 6 million-ton stack of limestone blocks. He just wanted to get in and get out. The quicker the better.

A flash of lightning penetrated the thick darkness as Branch shut the passenger side door and switched on his flashlight. He walked along the sandy shoulder of the road stopping several feet beyond the rear of the small Chinese sedan, his rented gray Chery Car.

Branch strained his eyes, waving his flashlight. His lean six-foot frame silhouetted against the distant glow of lightning. His dark hair half covered his ears and hugged the collar of his black leather jacket. He pushed a thick clump to one side of his forehead.

His concern had grown throughout the day. And though he was determined to do what he came for, he had one overriding thought:

Coming here was a real bad idea.

Just then lightning flashed and revealed a figure approaching.

Behind Branch, the driver's side door slammed shut. Branch's friend, Roddy, a portly Hispanic came around the rear of the car and zipped his charcoal windbreaker. The forty-eight degree temperature was cooler than normal for mid-May, even at 4 a.m.

"Ya know..." Roddy said.

He didn't get a chance to finish. A bolt of lightning shattered the air. In that momentary eruption of light, they saw a man. Thunder grumbled as Branch aimed his flashlight.

Roddy sucked in his breath at the sight. The man had a deep scar beneath his right eye, and the mauled left socket contained a mismatched fake eyeball. He carried an unlit lantern.

"You are early," the man said.

"Too early?" asked Branch.

"Follow me."

The man walked into the darkness as lightning flashed again, this time without the noisy display. The brief light illuminated the Great Pyramid of Giza and their new acquaintance walking toward it. A drizzle started.

"I thought it never rained here," Roddy said.

"About twice a year," said Branch.

"What are the odds we'd have rain on our one and only visit to this place? And where did you find Quasimodo, anyway?"

"One hundred eighty-three to one, and I met him in Cairo on directions from Benjamin."

Branch aimed his flashlight at Quasi and followed him.

"I'm sure you have a good reason for this Halloween excursion," Roddy said, as he trailed Branch. "I'm not too sure about Quasi. He doesn't look like a guy we should trust."

Despite Roddy's reluctance, he trusted Branch. They'd been friends since childhood, and he knew his buddy as well as anyone, not that anyone truly knew Branch.

Quasi stopped at the entranceway to the Great Pyramid and spoke with a slightly built Egyptian soldier.

Roddy grabbed Branch's arm. "The military. What now?"

"Relax."

When they caught up, Quasi rubbed his thumb over his first two fingers. Time to pay.

Branch was ready for this and, reaching into his shirt pocket, pulled out a five-dollar bill and handed it to the guide. The guide, in turn, passed it along to the soldier.

Roddy kept his flashlight on the currency. He leaned over to Branch and whispered, "Is that all you're gonna give him?"

"Trust me," whispered Branch. "Five dollars is a large bribe in this country. At least it is when you're only sneaking into a place where tourists aren't allowed."

"Everyone's allowed in the Pyramid."

"Not where we're going."

The soldier stepped away, kept his back to them as Quasi turned on his battery operated lantern and entered the Pyramid.

That's when Branch noticed several rings, several inches in diameter, hanging from Quasi's belt.

Before following, Branch glanced over his shoulder.

Roddy said, "You're not getting spooked again are you?"

"I'm telling you: we were being shadowed this afternoon."

"Yeah. One of your old buds from the CIA."

"He wasn't my bud, and you know I never worked for the CIA."

Branch entered the Pyramid with Roddy right behind him.

"But you knew him."

"I knew *of* him."

"A terminator," Roddy said, with a smirk.

"We didn't call him that, but yeah."

With Quasi leading the way, Branch and Roddy climbed tunnel steps that had stood for nearly five millennia. The climb was long and steep. Reaching the top, they ducked to enter the chamber, empty except for an open sarcophagus made of granite.

Branch surveyed the walls as Quasi stood by the entrance and Roddy peered into the granite coffer.

"Nobody home," Roddy said.

"This was never a tomb," Quasi said. "You can't believe everything you read."

Branch was becoming antsy. "I don't see it. These walls look solid. Where's the exit?"

"No exit," the guide said.

"You told me you'd give us access to an underground tunnel."

"That is in the Queen's chamber. This is the King's chamber."

"Take us to the Queen's."

"Queen's chamber is off limits to tourists."

"We're not tourists." Branch was perturbed, but now he realized he was being held up.

"I paid you. Twenty dollars, yesterday in Cairo, remember?"

The Egyptian folded his arms and stared Branch down with his one good eye. Clearly, he wanted to be paid again.

Branch exhaled, wrinkled his forehead, and pulled out his wallet. He drew out a five and handed the money to the hold-up man, who took it and held it up to the beam from Roddy's flashlight. "This is fine for low-level guards, but my services are worth ten times this."

Branch ripped the bill from the Egyptian's hand and stuffed it in his wallet. He yanked out a fifty, and handed over the much larger chunk of currency.

"Queen's chamber is this way," Quasi said, as he ducked through the doorway.

Branch and Roddy followed Quasi about half-way down until the guide turned left onto a walkway. Branch had barely noticed it on the upward climb. Quasi turned left again and entered another chamber. He stepped to the far wall as Branch and Roddy came in behind him. He removed a six-inch diameter ring from his belt. A screw protruded from one side.

Quasi knelt on one knee and inserted the screw in one of the stones. He turned the ring clockwise forcing the screw into the hole. Quasi attached three smaller rings to the big one. Each of these had a three-foot cord attached with a padded ring at the other end.

Quasi held out two of the rings. "Take these," he said.

Branch and Roddy each took a ring. Quasi stood from his kneeling position. "Pull," Quasi said.

"You have to be kidding," said Branch. "That block must weigh about three tons."

"This one is much lighter. Pull."

All three of them took firm hold of the rings, set their feet, leaned away from the stone wall, and pulled. The easy movement seemed miraculous to Branch as the giant stone slid across the ancient limestone floor.

When the stone block had cleared the wall by a couple of feet, Quasi stopped pulling. "Enough," he said.

Branch and Roddy relaxed.

"Why is this one so light?" Branch said.

"Hollow," said Quasi.

Roddy scratched his head. "How'd they do that?"

"Don't know," Quasi said. "Before my time."

Branch went to the opening, bent over, and aimed his flashlight in.

"At the bottom of stairs," said Quasi, "you will find three tunnels."

"We have a map," Branch said.

Quasi grunted. "We will push the stone back when you return. Don't get lost."

"Bread crumbs," Roddy said. "That's what I forgot."

"Don't worry," said Branch. "We'll get out okay."

Branch entered the opening and after a few steps, came to the stairs. Roddy trod behind him on the steep descent of the narrow stone stairway. When they reached bottom, Branch estimated they were fifty feet underground.

Branch took out a map and studied it. "This tunnel," he said, pointing.

They crept along the narrow passageway.

"Smells like a wet dog down here," Roddy said.

They'd gone 100 yards when they reached a chamber the size of a two-car garage. The tunnel continued on the other side of the chamber.

"Where do you think that goes?" Roddy said.

"Sphinx, I imagine."

Roddy and Branch stepped into the empty room.

"What we need is on these walls," Branch said. He shined his flashlight from one end of a wall to the other, revealing carved inscriptions.

"Right," Roddy said, as he dug out a camera from his inside coat pocket. He turned to the wall behind him and began flashing away.

"Let's make this quick and get out," Branch said, as he too fetched a camera from a jacket pocket.

"What are you worried about? No one but Benjamin, Quasi, and the Egyptian guard even know we're here."

Outside the Pyramid, two black Nissan Cubes slithered along the side of the road and stopped behind the Chery Car. The lights went off, then the engines. Lightning burst through the heavy darkness as all the doors opened. The drizzle became steady rain, pelting the eight men who exited the cars.

Brussel stood at the front of the Mini MPV. He was a man without a smile, a man without a conscience, and so far as anybody knew, a man without a first name.

Mitch Wallach stopped next to him as he always did. Wallach had soft, boyish features and throwback granny glasses. His look contrasted Brussel's severe cheekbones and leather-like skin. But in their respective talents, each was a perfect complement to the other.

Brussel was more lethal instrument than human being: cunning, brawn, a knack for weaponry. Plus, he was smart, something for which many failed to give him credit. An often-fatal mistake. You couldn't hide from him. That's what Brussel had Wallach for.

Mitch Wallach had a talent for finding things—and people. As a private detective, he was the best, and he made a good living. But the money was hundreds of times better working for Brussel.

Brussel's cell phone rang. The ringtone came from Chopin's "Funeral March."

"Yeah," Brussel said with a growl. "We have the writer and the bodyguard trapped underground. We need only wait for them to come out." Brussel listened to the caller, and then answered. "As you wish. We'll go down and get them." He shoved the phone back in his coat pocket.

The other six men looked toward Brussel, waiting for instructions. All eight wore wide brimmed hats and white calf-length trench coats.

"We got cold and we got rain," said Wallach, "but why these coats? We look like the James gang."

"Who?" Brussel asked.

"You know, Jesse James."

"Works for me." Then, pointing to the first two in line, Brussel said, "You two, stay with the cars. The rest, come with me."

The six of them started across the sand toward the Pyramid. Each man had a flashlight in one hand and a gun in the other.

Branch and Roddy finished taking pictures.

"What do you think all this stuff says?"

"Don't know," Branch said, as he shoved the camera into his pocket.

"Are we done here?" Roddy asked.

"Yeah, let's get back and help Quasi replace the stone."

Quasi was no longer in the Queen's chamber. Brussel and his men climbed through the hole and went down the stairway. Brussel was quick to give orders. "You two go down the left tunnel, you two down the right." His men reacted swiftly. Brussel forged up the middle with Wallach close behind.

Branch and Roddy entered the tunnel and stopped at the sight of two flashlights beams.

"The next tour is coming through," Branch said.

Bright flashes accompanied the sound of gunshots and both Roddy and Branch dropped to the ground.

One of the gunmen placed his flashlight under his right arm while still holding the gun in his right hand. He put his free hand into his left front pocket and grabbed a seven-inch Cobra two-way radio from inside his trench coat.

"We've got them," the gunman said.

Roddy and Branch turned their flashlights off and lay motionless on the tunnel floor.

"What do you think?" Roddy said.

"I think we better run."

The two of them jumped to their feet, turned on their flashlights and started running, with Roddy in the lead. They ran into the chamber, heard gunfire behind them, and kept going into the next tunnel.

Branch was right on Roddy's heels. "You want to shift it into second Roddy?"

"Hey, my wife feeds me better than the pharaohs. You should get a wife."

"If I were gonna find one, I would've found her by now."

They came to a stairway and began what was now an arduous climb for them. The stairs took them about thirty-five feet closer to the surface. They ran until they reached a T-junction and had a choice to go right or left. Roddy tried to catch his breath as Branch shined his flashlight one way and then the other.

"Check your map," Roddy said.

"Doesn't cover this part," Branch said, turning to the right. "Come on."

Roddy staggered along trying to keep up. They entered a small room, which seemed to be nothing more than a storeroom for statues, with no exit except the way they came in.

Roddy was panting. "Okay, General Custer, what now?"

Branch waved his flashlight around the room. He trained the light on two small stone sculptures of an Egyptian guard.

"Grab a statue," Branch said. "Turn off your flashlight."

"Gotcha."

Roddy immediately grasped Branch's plan. They each picked up a statue, flicked off the lights, and stood on either side of the doorway. They didn't have to wait long. Seeing no lights ahead of them, the unsuspecting pursuers ran into the room. Branch hit the first in the back of the head as he ran by, knocking him forward onto the floor. Roddy whacked the second one on the forehead, knocking him backward.

Branch and Roddy took the guns from their two victims.

Roddy shined his light on the gun. "The full-size Jericho 941; Israeli; sold in the U.S. as the Baby Desert Eagle."

"And I need to know this, why?"

Roddy shrugged. "Just showing off."

Roddy's guy groaned. He reached in his pocket, removed a vial, and shook it.

"Good, there's some left."

"What's that?" Branch aimed his light. "Aspirin?"

Roddy placed the vial in the hand of the guy he'd hit. "They're gonna need that."

Guns in hand, the two retreated. When they passed the tunnel from the Pyramid, they saw beams of light. They kept running until they entered a circular room with large stone columns all the way around. They crossed the room and entered a broad chamber with even larger columns.

Branch slowed and walked to the middle of the room. He made a u-turn and began climbing a stairway alongside a wall. Roddy was not far behind. At the top of the stairs was a short porch and another wall. Branch looked for a way to get to the other side as Roddy finished the climb and sat on the stone porch.

After catching his breath, Roddy said, "I see you found us another dead end."

"Where you find a stairway, you usually find a door."

"The bad guys should be here pretty soon. They can help us look."

As Branch continued searching for a way out of their predicament, he heard the sound of footsteps. Beams of light shot through the doorway. Branch ran his fingers over every inch of the wall at the rear of the porch, the wall next to the porch, and the ceiling. Nothing. They turned off their flashlights.

Four men burst in below them. Branch and Roddy crouched away from the steps.

Brussel surveyed the room. No exits. He aimed his light up the stairs but couldn't see his prey. He motioned to one of his men to go up.

The gunman went to the staircase and crept upward.

Branch knew they'd have to reveal themselves soon and considered surrender. That option didn't seem like a good idea since their immediate termination seemed inevitable. The man on the stairs was about half-way up, and Branch decided to act.

"Nobody up here," said Branch. "Honest."

The man on the steps started shooting. Branch waited until after the third shot, rose up, and fired two shots. He hit the man, who fell off the steps and onto the floor below. The other three fired their weapons and Roddy returned fire. The men below ran to the columns to take cover. The three kept up a steady barrage of lead as Branch and Roddy crouched low, getting off the occasional shot, until...

"I just fired my last round. I got no more bullets," Roddy said. "How about you?"

"Same. We should have taken some clips from those two guys when we had the chance."

"Think we could call a time out and get those clips now?"

The shooting from below had continued unabated.

"Stop firing!" Brussel shouted.

The shooting stopped. Branch and Roddy sat, leaning against the wall, waiting for the ultimatum they knew the gunmen were about to give.

"Guess this is it," Roddy said. "I should've listened to my wife: *Don't hang around with Branch. He'll get you into trouble.*"

"She's been saying that for twenty-five years, since high school."

"And she's been right for twenty-five years."

Brussel stepped out a little way from the column he was using for cover. "Come down and we'll talk."

"What are you offering?" Branch asked.

"I might let you live."

"What do you think of his offer?" Branch asked Roddy.

"He didn't mention money, new car, paid vacation, nothing."

"We still gotta surrender."

"Yeah, been real good knowing you, Branch."

"Hey, Roddy, I'm trying to be positive here."

"Me too."

Branch sat up straight. "Here's our guns." Branch tossed his to the floor below and so did Roddy. With leaden movement, they got to their knees.

Brussel, Wallach, and the remaining gunman came out from behind the columns.

As Branch and Roddy started to stand, the wall behind slid sideways. They turned on their flashlights and aimed them at the new opening. There stood Quasi.

Quasi shook his head. "I leave you two alone for a little while."

Roddy turned toward the waiting thugs below. "Never mind."

Branch and Roddy jumped to their feet and sprinted through the doorway. Quasi yanked a lever and the door slid shut.

Quasi said, "Sorry about hitting you for the extra fifty dollars."

"Don't mention it," Branch said.

"I just don't know what came over me."

Quasi led, carrying a small satchel hung from a strap over his shoulder. After several steps, he opened a door and stepped aside to let Branch and Roddy go through. He followed them and closed the door behind him.

The rain pelted them.

"Where are we?" asked Branch, who noticed Quasi was keeping one hand inside his partially zipped jacket.

"Between the paws of the Sphinx," Quasi answered. "This way."

Quasi led them up a short flight of steps, returning them to ground level.

"Be careful," Quasi said. "Two men guard your car."

"We could use your help," Branch said.

Quasi removed the satchel strap from his shoulder with his free hand and held it out to Branch. "Take this."

Branch took the satchel. "What do I do with it?"

"Take it to Dr. Von Brunner in Switzerland to receive the first piece."

"What piece? And why me?"

The caretaker looked at Branch in the dark and the rain and the soft glow from the flashlights that bounced off their jackets. He spoke, for the first time, in an earnest and gentle voice. "It's been exactly 4,700 years since the Great Pyramid was built. The time is right." Quasi said nothing for a few moments as Branch stared at him, and then, "Recovery of the key has begun."

As his one good eye rolled upward and closed, Quasi dropped to the ground.

Branch and Roddy crouched on either side of him. Branch unzipped Quasi's jacket. He took the Egyptian's wrist and moved his hand down to his belt, revealing a blood-stained shirt.

Roddy put his hand to Quasi's neck and checked the carotid artery. "No pulse."

"We can't just leave him here," Branch said.

"The sun is coming up in..." He hit the button on his watch to make it glow. "One hour and forty minutes. Astronomical twilight is approximately 79 minutes. So we're gonna start losing the cover of darkness in just twenty-one minutes."

"Yeah, we better go retrieve our rental from those two goons," Branch said, as he put the strap over his head and hooked it on his shoulder.

The two men stood.

"You got a plan?" Roddy asked.

"Don't I always?"

"Unfortunately."

Branch headed in the direction of the road with Roddy right behind.

As they crept to the edge of the road across from the three parked vehicles, they saw the two men standing between the Chery Car and the Nissan Cubes. They were facing away from Branch and Roddy, keeping watch on the Pyramid.

"Get your camera out," Branch whispered, as he got his from inside his jacket.

"You want to take their picture?"

"Sort of. Here's how it's gonna go: flash, gun, nose job. What do you think?"

"I think we need a better plan. It's not like we're in a Hollywood action movie. This has to actually have a chance to work."

Branch gave him a cocky smile. "Trust me."

Roddy shook his head. "That's my problem; I always do."

Roddy took out his camera, and the two sneaked across the road. They closed in on the two trench-coated guards one cautious step at a time. Branch and Roddy each held his camera at eye level with his left hand and reached out with the right. They tapped each of the men on the shoulder.

The surprised sentries spun around. Branch and Roddy clicked their cameras' shutter buttons, causing the lights to flash just inches from the eyes of the two men.

Blinded, each of them covered his eyes with his left hand, reached inside his coat with his right, and pulled out a Jericho 941.

Branch and Roddy grabbed the pistol barrels and jerked them upward. The two men cried out in pain at having their index fingers—their trigger fingers—yanked in an unnatural direction and broken.

Branch and Roddy tossed the guns aside and with extreme prejudice, each smashed the palm of his hand against the nose of his chosen chump.

The two abused sentries, cupped their left hands over their noses as they stumbled backward and fell to the ground.

Branch and Roddy ran to the Chery Car and stopped cold as a flash of lightning revealed movement at the opening to the Great Pyramid.

Brussel led as Wallach and a third man followed.

Behind them, the two that had been rendered unconscious carried the one that Branch had shot.

Brussel, Wallach and the third man started to run.

"Here they come again," Roddy said.

The two jumped into the rental. Branch reached into the back seat and retrieved a laptop. Roddy began digging in his pocket for the key.

"I had it," Roddy said.

"You lost the key?"

Roddy fished it out with a grin and held it up. "Gotcha!"

"Just drive."

Branch flipped the laptop open while Roddy attempted to insert the key in the ignition. He missed and knocked the key from his hand. Branch powered up his computer as Roddy fished around on the floor.

Branch, calm as ever said, "Is there a problem?" He looked out the window at the three men approaching, the darkness just beginning to break. "They're gonna be strapping on our seat belts in a matter of seconds."

"It's gotta be here."

"If you lose that key, it's gonna spoil our friendship."

Roddy found the key. "Got it." He held it up with a big smile.

"Can we go now?"

"Testy."

Roddy inserted the key, started the engine, and made a u-turn. The two ducked low as Roddy pressed hard on the gas.

Brussel, Wallach, and the other gunman arrived at the roadside, panting. They took aim and fired. The two hapless guards with their bloodied noses—guns now held in their left hands—came up shooting, as well. All five kept up a steady stream of bullets, pummeling the side and rear of the Chery Car, and destroying every single window.

When the shooting subsided, Roddy peaked over the dash. He slowed to make a right turn and then pressed hard on the accelerator.

"Ten miles to Cairo," Roddy said. "Hope you enjoyed our tour of the Giza Plateau."

"Up until you had the key mishap."

"It was your plan."

"Don't change the subject."

Roddy, more relaxed now, nestled in the seat. "I like their coats. How 'bout we get those for ourselves?"

Branch clicked on the Bluetooth icon. "Give me your camera. I'm sending our snapshots to Israel, to an expert on Hebrew. He's a friend of Benjamin's."

"Hebrew inscribed on an Egyptian structure?" Roddy said.

"Benjamin believes that what we now call Hebrew may have been the original language spoken by everyone on earth, before the flood. If you believe in that sort of thing."

"I do," Roddy said. "Why don't you?"

"Don't start." Branch let the laptop rest on his knees as he picked up Quasi's satchel from the floor. "Let's see what we've got in here." Branch opened the satchel in the faint predawn light.

Roddy glanced at it as he drove.

Branch reached in and pulled out a smooth, polished stone-like square, a half inch-thick with four-inch sides. The outer edge was a frame three-eighths inches in width. The square stone had a one-eighth indentation inside the frame and the inner part of the frame had three and a quarter inch sides.

"What do you think it's for?" Roddy asked.

"We'll find out when we go to Switzerland. First things first. Let's get to Jerusalem."

"Okay, Israel, here we come. Hey, do you think the rental agency will notice the bullet holes?"

Chapter Two

Red Barrows took long strides, ahead of the others, up the hillside under the morning sun and spotted the cave. It was just as the local boy had described it. He was becoming almost giddy at the thought of being not only vindicated, but revered.

Barrows knew he was a better archeologist than what most people seemed to think. He would prove them wrong. *Them*—who wouldn't accept his dissertation till after four years of agonizing research and countless rewrites; *them*—who wouldn't give him tenure at the university; *them*—who wouldn't award him grant money for this dig. Thank God for Roger Darkin, his current benefactor.

Barrows glanced over his shoulder at the two interns who didn't seem concerned about keeping up. Jerry Justice and Julie Johnson weren't holding hands but their arms kept brushing against each other as they walked. They never seemed quite willing to admit to a romantic attraction that even a blind man could see. The two interns were his favorite students. He called them "the JJs." Barrows smiled as he looked forward again—in time to avoid tripping over an inconveniently placed igneous rock.

Behind the JJs their Turkish guide led two fully loaded camels. Supplies on one and tools on the other.

They traveled at the southern base of Little Ararat, also known as Mt. Sis, the smaller sister of Mt. Ararat to the north. To the east and a bit north sat the city of Yerevan, capital of Armenia. Five miles due east was Iran.

Barrows had been made aware of a certain cave in a roundabout way. He'd heard of it from a close friend, who had a student who went on a tour of Christian sites in Armenia and took a side trip into Turkey. The student had learned of the cave, and something astounding inside, through a chance meeting with a boy on the street.

Barrows' pace quickened as he neared the entrance to the cave. He didn't break stride as he reached behind to pull the flashlight out of the side pocket of his backpack.

Entering the cave, which allowed him plenty of headroom, Barrows panned his light—the fifteen foot span—from side to side and crept into the darkness. He stopped as he realized he was holding his breath. Barrows exhaled and began to breathe naturally, continuing forward, panning the walls near the floor with his light. He heard his two interns talking as they neared the mouth of the cave.

Where is it? Shouldn't be too much farther. The boy who'd made the discovery said he walked only a short way into... *There! There it is.* Barrows stepped toward the small opening in the wall. He crouched low and bent over, aiming his flashlight into the tunnel. *Can't make out a thing.* Frustrated, Barrows rose up and relaxed his weight on one knee.

"The secret tunnel?" Jerry said, as he and Julie sauntered up behind him. "I feel like the Hardy boys."

"Except one of us is a girl," Julie said.

"I'm sure this is what we came to find," Barrows said over his shoulder. "But smaller than I anticipated."

"I couldn't even fit," Julie said.

"The boy who went in must've been a lot smaller than us," said Jerry. "I guess this means we dig."

Barrows stood. "Let's grab the pickaxes."

Julie set her backpack on the floor of the cave. "I'll get the camera out."

Barrows and Jerry had been hacking away, on and off, with their pickaxes for a couple of hours. They'd made the tunnel wider and higher and had almost reached the other end of the four-foot-long opening. Julie sat on her backpack. She held the digital camcorder and watched her professor and sort-of boyfriend dig away. She'd recorded some of the digging and was waiting till the two had broken through to pick up the action again.

"Why don't you guys take another break?" Julie said.

"We're almost there," Barrows said, as he knelt on his right knee, reaching in with his right hand to pick away at the left side of the tunnel. They'd long since discarded the large picks they started with to widen the initial opening. Now, they reached in with smaller ones.

Jerry worked on the right side reaching in with his left hand. The two had developed a well-coordinated effort. They took turns swinging the small picks without ever hitting each other's tool.

"You're like a man possessed, Professor," Jerry said.

"You don't know what I've had to endure being a Christian in a profession dominated by evolutionists. They would never take me seriously because I went on record as a believer in the Bible. I had to. My wife, my parents, everyone would disown me if I did otherwise. However, if this find is everything I think, not only can I accept evolution, but I'll be famous as the one who proved it." He stopped digging and looked at his students. "Of course, you two will share in that."

"Professor," Julie said, "I'm not a Christian. I've never even read the Bible. But I'm wondering: do you genuinely want to give up your Christian faith?"

"Yes," Barrows said. "It's caused me nothing but problems."

"But, Dr. Barrows, couldn't you just become a theistic evolutionist?"

Barrows laughed. "Indeed, not. Those are the silliest people of all. Both Christians and evolutionists who know better know you can't have it both ways." He jabbed at the tunnel wall all the harder.

Barrows and his young intern had broken through to the other end of the tunnel and Barrows was eager to go in. He grabbed his Pelican xenon rechargeable flashlight. A costly item. He'd paid over a hundred dollars, but Barrows wouldn't apologize for spending so much on a teacher's salary. This expedition was going to make his career, and he wanted to have the best equipment for such a momentous undertaking.

Jerry stuck his shovel into the tunnel to scoop up some more rocks. "Let me finish up here," he said. He dragged a shovel full to the mouth of the tunnel, lifted, turned and flung the dirt onto the pile nearby.

Julie snapped a picture of him in action with her camera. "Hmm! Manly shot. Might need a frame." Jerry smiled and tried not to blush.

Julie reached for the camcorder—Barrows' $5,400 Canon XL. *Not going to apologize for that either*, Barrows thought. Though he'd let his secretary know that it had been marked down from 7,000.

"Okay," Julie said, "I'm ready to record history in the making."

Red Barrows, with xenon rechargeable in hand, crawled into the tunnel as Julie aimed the camcorder. When Barrows entered the chamber, he rose up on his knees, so the camcorder now videoed him from the waist down.

Barrows cried out. "This is amazing! It's everything I hoped for. Come in here, both of you."

Branch and Roddy caught a morning flight to Israel. Upon arriving at their hotel, Branch called Dr. Meir and set an appointment. It was mid-afternoon when they set foot on the campus of the Rothberg International School, a division of the Hebrew University of Jerusalem. The school sits on Mount Scopus, in the northeast corner of the most conquered city in the world. Mount Scopus was a favorite launching point for invaders due to its fabled view of the city.

When Branch and Roddy went through the door marked with Dr. Meir's name, they found a curly redhead behind a desk. She wore khakis and sat with her feet on the chair. She propped a book with Hebrew on the cover on her knees, hiding her face.

"Pardon," Roddy said. "Americana. You speakah any English?"

Branch turned his head and gave Roddy a frown. Roddy raised his hands in a helpless gesture.

The girl lowered her book, revealing a freckled face with black, horn-rimmed glasses. "Better than y'all." Her accent was from the *deep* South.

Branch grinned at a stunned Roddy.

"Arkansas?" Roddy said, as if he could guess by her accent which state south of the Mason-Dixon she called home.

"Alabama," she replied.

Roddy said, "We're here to see —"

"Are you Nichols and Rodriguez?" she asked.

"We are," said Branch.

She put her feet on the floor and laid the book on the desk. Hitting a button on the intercom, she said, "Professor, your three o'clocks are here."

A soft voice came across. "Send them in."

Freckle Face gave them a tight-lipped smile as Branch and Roddy strolled into Dr. Meir's office.

The room spoke of organization, carefulness, and attention to detail. Branch surveyed the lack of clutter: every book sat neatly on a shelf, except for a few precisely stacked at the corner of the desk.

Branch also noticed the back of a large padded chair facing toward a window. It over-looked Jerusalem. *Nice view.*

Dr. Meir came around his desk and extended his hand. After the three had introduced themselves, Dr. Meir said, "Let's get right to it. I've been studying the pictures you sent."

The professor went across the room to a computer.

"Can you read it?" Branch said.

"Some. Much of the writing is unmistakably ancient Hebrew. But the rest," he said, as he clicked again, "must be an older form of the language."

"What can you tell so far?" Branch asked.

"Seems to be about the beginning of man, of history and culture, of the very existence of man. And this is interesting. Appears to be scientific references."

"Science in a pre-ancient Hebrew inscription?" asked Branch.

Meir tugged at his goatee. "It's the speed of light."

Roddy appeared puzzled. "You think the ancient Egyptians knew the speed of light?"

A woman's voice interrupted. "The pyramids and Sphinx stood long before the Egyptians came."

Branch and Roddy glanced around the room but saw no one.

Like a jack-in-the-box, a young woman popped up from the big chair by the window. She was pretty, petite, and blonde.

"Linda," said Meir. "I nearly forgot you were here." To Branch and Roddy he said, "This is Linda Chapel, my niece. She's an archeology writer."

"I was doing research at the National Library," Linda said. "And I dropped by for a visit."

Branch eyed the uninvited listener. On any other day, he'd have plenty of time for someone this attractive, but right now Linda's presence annoyed him. "Sorry to disturb your visit," Branch said. "Could you drop in later?"

"Nope." She offered him a warm smile. "I find this fascinating."

Roddy stepped toward her. "What'd you say about pyramids before Egyptians?"

"Years ago," Linda began, "a geologist discovered evidence of water damage. He concluded the pyramids and Sphinx had been under water at one time. The geological community scoffed at him. Years later, about 200 geologists went to Egypt to study the pyramids and realized he was right. Water damage."

"So," said Roddy, "they agreed the pyramids used to be under water?"

"No," Linda said. "The official word is heavy rain. Over a period of hundreds of years."

"That's right," Dr. Meir said. "Can't have the pyramids under water. That conjures up images of Noah's flood."

"Yeah," said Linda. "Some people become upset when any of the sciences gives support to the Bible."

Branch folded his arms in front of him and said, "This is educational but we're doing our own research here. Perhaps you'd like to return to the library."

"I'd like to know more about this," Linda said, pointing at the computer monitor. "What do you think, Uncle Dagan?"

"I think that I'll need more time to study this," Dr. Meir said.

"We'll keep in touch," Branch said. "We're going to Switzerland to drop off something with a Dr. Von Brunner, just as soon as we find out what city he's in."

"He's in the city of Saint Gallen," Meir said.

"And that's perfect," Linda said. "He's an expert on the speed of light, one of the few who believes it's not constant, but slowing down. We should leave right away."

"We?" said Branch. He turned to Dr. Meir. "What difference would a change in the speed of light make?"

"The question of speed is related to dating methods," Meir said. "It could mean that the Earth is a lot younger than many scientists currently believe."

"Exactly," Linda said. "If it could be proven that the speed of light isn't constant but has slowed over time, findings from popular dating methods would shrink. It could mean the universe has been here such a short time that the debate over evolution would end."

"The science establishment would be turned upside down," Meir said. "Thousands of careers would be ruined."

"People shot at us," Roddy said. "Is it that important?"

"I don't know," Meir said.

"Okay," said Linda. "Let's head for Switzerland."

Branch ignored her and shook Dr. Meir's hand. "Thanks, Dr. Meir. We'll keep in touch."

Branch went for the door as Roddy shook Dr. Meir's hand.

Coming out of Meir's office, Branch nodded goodbye to Freckle Face. She lowered her glasses enough to fully reveal her piercing blue eyes.

Roddy was close behind. He bowed his head and pretended to scratch his forehead, covering his view of Freckle Face.

Branch held the door for Roddy. Linda hurried across the room to catch up. Branch shut the door in front of her.

When they got to the street, Branch hailed a taxi.

With amazing stealth, Linda appeared right next to them. "So, where are you guys staying?"

"Scopus Hotel," Roddy said.

"Should've left you with the pharaohs," Branch said to Roddy.

Once they were in the taxi, Branch slammed the door before Linda could get in. As the taxi pulled away, he heard Linda shout, "Guess I'll just catch up later."

At the hotel, Branch got on the phone and made reservations for a flight to Switzerland. He scribbled the flight number on a piece of paper and left it on the bureau, near the bathroom.

Later, a knock came at the door. Roddy was waiting for the coffee pot to fill.

"Aren't expecting anyone, are you?" Branch said.

Roddy shook his head. "Must be for you."

Branch went to the door and peered through the peephole at an empty hallway.

As he opened the door, Linda slipped past him into the room.

She saw Roddy at the little kitchenette. "Coffee? Could you please pour me one?"

"Miss Chapel," Roddy said. "Nice of you to drop by."

Branch frowned at Roddy who smiled and shrugged.

Linda sat in a wide overstuffed chair. "This is a great room. You guys must be loaded."

"Did you come to say goodbye?" Branch said.

"I came to find out what flight we're on."

"Listen," said Branch. "We spent part of last night dodging bullets, and we don't even know for sure why they attacked us or who they were."

"I don't care. I'm coming."

Branch was frustrated and reaching his limits of gentlemanly conduct. He put his hands on his hips and said, "No. You. Are. Not."

Linda curled her legs up on the chair and stared down, pouting, at her tightly folded hands.

Roddy brought her a mug of coffee. "Cream and sugar?" he asked.

"Yes, thank you, Mr. Rodriguez."

"My first name is Chico but my friends call me Roddy." He started toward the kitchenette, stopped and turned to face her. "If you don't mind my asking, why are you so determined to go with us, Miss Chapel?"

"Linda, please. I believe you guys may be on to something special."

Roddy drifted over to the counter and picked up a bowl of sugar and tiny pitcher of cream. On his way back, he said, "Has to be more. What makes this so important to you?" Roddy placed the cream and sugar on the end table next to the chair.

Her face flushed with anger. "It's my dad," she said. She sat up straight, put some sugar in her coffee, and poured cream in.

"Go on," said Roddy.

She stirred her coffee with the spoon from the sugar bowl. "He was a teacher. A university professor."

"What did he teach?" Branch asked.

Linda said, "Geophysics. He taught geophysics. He was one of the best. Everyone said so. His students; other teachers."

"What happened?" Roddy asked.

She directed her eyes at Roddy and then at Branch. "One day he committed the unpardonable sin. He dared to question evolution. No. More than question. He said the theory wasn't possible."

Branch was dubious which must have shown because Linda sat up straighter, drilling him with her eyes.

"Listen," she said, "my father made an honest study of the facts and came to a logical conclusion. What more would you expect from a scientist?" She took a deep breath, trying to collect herself, and went on. "Nothing happened right away. Not until he started teaching his students what, to the rest of the faculty, amounted to heresy."

Linda sat staring at nothing for several moments, then put her head down.

Roddy went to the bed and sat on the edge. "Please Linda, go on."

"He lost his job," she said, without looking up. "And then they put him on trial. At least, that's what I call it." She raised her head. "They took away his degree. He had a Ph.D."

"They can do that?" Roddy said. "I never heard of that."

"Yes, they can! Turns out it's not such an unusual thing. Many other teachers have lost their degrees for daring to question the state religion."

"What?" said Branch. "Religion?"

"They teach it in the schools," Linda said, "as if it were a fact, even though there's no actual hard science to support it. It's a faith-based belief. A religion."

"Yeah, well uh, look, I'm sorry about your father," Branch said. He folded his arms and went on, "But you cannot go with us."

Roddy stood and went to the counter.

"You guys married?" she said. "Not that I care. I'm just curious."

Branch relaxed a little and went along with the change of subject. "Not me. Roddy's the responsible one."

"Responsible?" Linda said, her eyes flickering with amusement.

"That's what my wife always says," Roddy told her as he crossed the room with two more coffee mugs.

"Ah," she said, smiling.

Roddy handed one of the mugs to Branch.

"So," said Roddy, "tell us about the rest of your family."

"I have an older sister. My mom died when I was young. How about you?"

"Two sisters," Roddy said, "Both older. Still have both my parents."

Linda considered Branch. "What's your story, Mr. Glum?"

Branch smiled in spite of himself and began: "I was orphaned at three. A friend of my dad's, Benjamin Rydal took me in and raised me. He's the one who gave us our contact in Cairo."

"And is this what you guys do with your time, skulk around ancient ruins?"

"Not exactly," Branch said. "Roddy was a sergeant in the Army Rangers. He retired after twenty years and now works as a freelance bodyguard."

"No one needs more guarding than Branch," Roddy said.

"What about you?" Linda said to Branch.

"I'm retired from a former occupation. You don't need to know anything about me."

"Sure I do. What were you, a spy?"

"Close," Roddy said.

"Not even. If you must know, I worked for a secret government agency that didn't involve spying."

Linda looked quizzical. "Is it one of those, 'I could tell you but I'd have to kill you things.'"

"I wouldn't have to kill you."

"So?"

"Look, after I quit there, I went back to college and studied investigative journalism. Now I write. When I have time."

"A writer, huh? So we have something in common."

"Go figure."

Roddy peeked at his watch. "Hey buddy, we gotta be leaving pretty soon."

"Right," said Branch. "Miss Chapel, we're gonna be—"

"Okay. I just want to go to the bathroom first." She jumped up from her chair, went to the bureau, and set her mug down right next to the piece of paper with the flight number written on it. "This is fun. I've never been to Switzerland."

She trotted off to the bathroom and closed the door behind her.

"That does it," Branch said. He went to the kitchenette, opened a drawer, and pulled out a knife.

"Little extreme, don't you think?" Roddy said.

Branch went to the window and yanked on one of the cords. He was able to pull most of it free, and then cut the cord with the knife.

"Hey, Amigo," Roddy said, "I'm thinking the hotel management might not approve?"

"They can put it on the bill." Branch retrieved the paper with the flight number and stuck it in his shirt pocket; then grabbed a chair and set it in the middle of the room. "When she comes out—"

"Oh no, Branch, we can't do that."

"She's like glue. We're gonna un-stick her."

The toilet flushed, and moments later Linda emerged from the bathroom.

"Miss Chapel," Branch said. "Sit in the chair."

She focused on the cord in his hand. "You wouldn't."

"No. Roddy will." Branch handed the cord to Roddy and headed toward the bed. "Tie her up while I finish packing."

"Why me?" said Roddy.

Branch stopped at the bed. "You know all about knots. You were in the Army."

Roddy pondered that for a second and then shook his head. "That's the Navy."

Branch shrugged. "Close enough. You," he turned to Linda, "get in that chair or I'll put you there myself."

Linda glowered at Branch as she stomped over to the chair. She sat down hard. "Okay," she said, putting her hands behind the chair. "Tie me up."

"You're giving up?" Roddy said.

"You're two great big, strong men, so I'll go quietly."

Roddy aimed a petitioning look at Branch. "Amigo?"

Linda scrutinized Branch. "Did I mention courageous and noble?" She tilted her head to one side. "No; I didn't. Forget it."

"She's not bullet-proof," Branch said. "We can't let her take the risk."

"Alright," Roddy said. With a noticeable lack of resolve, he began to tie her to the chair.

Linda said, "I've a right to make my own decisions about risk, don't I?"

"Not today," Branch said, as he shoved clothes into his black leather valise.

"What if I have to go to the bathroom?"

"You just went."

"What if I have to go again?"

"Hold it."

Roddy finished tying her up, and Branch finished packing. Roddy's brown leather roundhouse duffel bag was already sitting by the door.

"What if no one comes to untie me?"

"The maid will come in the morning," Branch said, as he selected two cloth napkins from a drawer.

Branch went and stood by Linda. "Open wide."

She clamped her mouth shut.

Branch balled up one of the napkins and handed it to Roddy. He put his hands to Linda's sides and tickled her.

She started to giggle, but she kept her teeth clenched together. Branch continued the tickling as he said, "You like being tickled, don't you? You love it. Admit it."

Though she couldn't stop giggling, she stared daggers at Branch and said, "No!"

At that moment, Roddy shoved the napkin in. Branch wrapped the other one over her mouth and tied it behind her head.

Branch grabbed the valise. Roddy went to the door, picked up his duffel bag, and opened the door.

"Sorry," Roddy said, staring at Linda tied to the chair.

Linda stared hard at Branch.

Branch studied Linda with a mocking smile. "Anger becomes you. In a cute sort of way."

He turned and went out the door.

After leaving the elevator on the ground floor, Branch stopped by the front desk.

"Tell me," he said to the man behind the desk, "is there any maid service now?"

"Not before morning," the desk clerk said. "Sorry."

"That's fine."

Benjamin Rydal was in his senior years, gray-haired, with a distinguished appearance. People often asked for his autograph, mistaking him for Morgan Freeman.

Benjamin sat at his computer looking at Branch's image coming from the Tel Aviv Airport. Branch set his coffee cup down and took a bite out of his hamburger. Benjamin smiled as he noticed a McCafé kosher sign, behind Branch, next to a McDonald's kosher sign.

"I wondered if you two were ever gonna get around to letting me know how things are going," Benjamin said. "Other than by terse email."

"We didn't know much for sure. You were right about the Hebrew, though. I left digital copies with Dr. Meir."

"He's a capable man. Now what about this physicist you mentioned in your email?"

"The caretaker at the Pyramid gave us something to give to a Dr. Von Brunner. It was his dying wish."

Benjamin was thoughtful for a moment and then he said, "Good luck to you both."

"We've got a plane to catch. We'll check in from Switzerland."

"All right," Benjamin said. The image of Branch on Benjamin's screen disappeared. He pushed himself away from the desk and turned his wheelchair at a right angle. Benjamin sat staring toward the book-lined walls of his immense study. There were thousands of books all around him, but he wasn't looking at them. He was staring into the unknown future.

"Godspeed."

Branch closed his laptop. Roddy sat across from him, cell phone in hand.

"I love you too, honey," Roddy said. "Branch? Branch who...? Yeah, I'm with Branch.... Trouble...? No, we're not in trouble.... What do mean, not yet?"

Branch was grinning by now.

Roddy looked at his watch. "Gotta go, sweetie. I'll call from Switzerland. Bye." Roddy clicked his cell phone off.

"Everything okay?" Branch asked. "Did she give you permission to go to Switzerland?"

"Shut up," Roddy said, smiling. "She's mad at you."

"Come on before we miss our plane."

They picked up their stuff and headed for their gate.

Walking down the aisle, Branch noticed the plane was only about half full.

When they got to their seats, they found a smallish person curled up under a blanket.

Branch checked his tickets to be sure and then said, "Hey you, that's our seat."

Roddy said, "Probably some kid that didn't want to sit with his parents."

"He's in our seat."

"That's okay. I want to sit by the window anyway."

"The sun's about to set," Branch said.

"You can still see stuff."

Roddy moved in past the squatter and sat by the window. Branch sat in the aisle seat.

One of the attendants started giving her little talk as the plane taxied toward the runway.

Branch removed a book from his carry-on; a biography of Dr. Wolfgang von Brunner. He'd been fortunate to find the bio at a downtown bookstore on the way to the airport. He opened it and started to read.

Soon they were high in the air, moving away from the lights of Israel.

A familiar but muffled voice said, "I love taking off in airplanes, don't you?"

Branch took his eyes off the book and looked down at the blanket.

Two smooth white hands pulled the blanket down revealing its occupant. Linda.

"You?" Branch said.

"Isn't this a coincidence?" she said as she sat up in her seat. "You're going to Switzerland. I'm going to Switzerland."

"How'd you get out?"

"Maid came in."

"There were no maids. I checked."

Roddy put his nose to the window. "I see the Mediterranean."

"I'm thinking about throwing you in," Branch said.

Roddy cupped his hands to either side of his face to shield his eyes from the overhead light—and probably Branch.

Branch stared at Linda.

"I have three brothers," Linda said. "They were always tying me to a chair. I got quite good at escaping."

"You have one sister, no brothers."

"I think I spotted some sharks," Roddy said.

"At 10,000 feet?" said Branch. "Look, Linda."

"Miss Chapel to you."

Roddy pressed his nose harder against the window. "Could be dolphins."

Linda pulled a book out from underneath the blanket. "I'll just read my mystery novel. I won't be any trouble at all." She opened her book.

Branch noticed the cover. "Good author?"

"Chandler Ross? He's the best." She nestled in her seat and started to read.

Branch lay against his seat. "What's happening with the human race when you can't trust your best friend to tie a girl to a chair properly?"

Linda chuckled as she continued to read.

Roddy was still stuck to the window.

Branch pushed his seat back into a reclining position. *Terrific. This is all I need. As if I didn't have enough trouble already.... But what I don't understand is why I'm feeling glad that she's here.*

Chapter Three

The plane arrived in Zurich in the early morning. The three caught a train from the airport heading east for Saint Gallen and their hotel. The one-hour ride through hills and forests kept Linda's full attention. Unfortunately, for Branch, she thought he should enjoy the view too. Linda kept nudging his shoulder telling him to "look at that," when all Branch wanted was to read his book.

"So," she said, "you've been reading that book since we left Israel. What have you learned about Professor von Brunner? Brilliant, isn't he?"

"Maybe so, but he's an outcast from the scientific community."

"That's what happens when you dare to tell the truth."

When they arrived at Saint Gallen, they switched to the orange Trogenerbahn narrow-gauge train. It took them up a steep hill leaving the main part of town far behind in the valley.

Before boarding the Trogenerbahn, Linda had time to grab some brochures. On the trip up the hill, she regaled her two traveling companions with more than they ever wanted to know about Saint Gallen.

"Did you know," said Linda, "that Saint Gallen was founded by a monk? He's remembered today as St. Gallus. Legend says he stumbled into a briar patch and took it as a sign from God. He built a hermitage with the help of a bear."

"A bear?" said Roddy. He shook his head. "I'm Catholic and I don't even believe that."

"People choose to believe in lots of things. Like aliens from outer space. Ask yourself, Roddy, why does anyone believe anything? It fits their agenda; they're just comfortable with it because that's what they grew up with; or because they want to. Anything that can be interpreted as indicating little green men becomes proof."

Branch stopped trying to read the biography.

"You're convinced aliens are a myth, are you Miss Chapel?"

"Yes, I am."

"Ever hear of the Men in Black?"

"Ever hear of Leprechauns?"

Branch just shook his head and went back to reading his book.

However, he couldn't focus. He started thinking about the danger they might be in. Branch kept glancing up from the book, looking at Linda. Could he protect her? Branch closed the book, held it tight in his hands and considered the petite girl next to him. He lived in a world that, by contrast, made hers seem so innocent.

The train took them to the last stop where they found a quaint inn with a difficult German name, quickly forgotten.

Branch gave his name to the desk clerk who turned away to search for a key.

"You did tell him two rooms, didn't you?" said Linda.

"Don't worry," Branch said, with a mocking smile. "You'll have your own little Shangri-La, Goldilocks. So the Big Bad Wolf can't get at you."

The clerk returned and handed Branch two keys. Branch, in turn, handed one of the keys to Linda.

"Here, said the beast to the beauty."

She took it. "An actual key, not a swipe card."

"Quaint, huh?"

Branch picked up her bag along with his own.

Linda adopted a lecturing tone. "You mixed four characters and one place from four different stories. Three children's and one grown-up."

Branch stared in consternation for several moments. "So?" he finally said, as he turned and took long strides to the elevator.

She scurried behind him. "Well, you can't do that."

Roddy came along behind them.

When they got off the elevator, they found Branch and Roddy's room.

"Yours must be the next one down," Branch said. He set Linda's bag on the floor and put his hand on Linda's shoulder.

"If you need anything," he said, "let us know." He gave her—what he was sure was—the most charming smile of all the smiles in his repertoire.

"Listen," she said, with a mocking smile of her own, "I'm sure you're used to having the ladies fall all over you, but let's get one thing straight. My reason for being here is scientific. Trust me...." She took hold of his wrist and removed his hand from her shoulder as if it were some nasty thing that might contaminate her. "You have zero chance here."

She reached down, picked up her plum-colored London Fog 17 inch cabin bag, and headed down the hall. After shoving her key in and opening the door, she took one last look at Branch. "Humph!" She disappeared into the room and slammed the door.

Branch turned to see a grinning Roddy.

"Shot down," Roddy said. He took the key from Branch and stuck it in the keyhole.

"I wasn't in flight," Branch said.

Roddy opened the door and started in. "Good for you to get shot down for a change."

Branch followed Roddy in, holding his hand up in a pleading gesture. "I wasn't even on the runway."

The next morning, the three met in the meal hall. Everyone was served a breakfast of scrambled eggs, thick bacon, potatoes, toast, coffee and juice. The atmosphere at the hotel was warm and cozy.

Branch was impressed the hundred-year-old building was in exceptional condition.

Linda entered in true morning person style, as, through bleary eyes, Branch watched her bounce to the table. Linda sat next to Roddy, across from Branch.

"This place is neat, isn't it guys?" She didn't wait for an answer. "The inn is run by an elderly couple. Mrs. Steinholtz told me the story of how they met here when they were kids trying to earn money to help their families. So romantic. They saved their money and bought this place, so they could always live here where they met. Isn't that wonderful?"

"Yes, Linda," said Roddy. "It is."

She looked at Branch for a response. Linda was sure she could see a faint glimmer of amusement in his eyes as he chewed on a piece of bacon.

"So, Mr. Glum, what time do you wake up?"

He managed a slight pseudo-smile and bit off another piece of thin hog meat as the left side of Linda's mouth edged outward.

"Ah, well, I shouldn't disturb you while you're at the trough." She turned to Roddy. "So how did you guys get involved in this thing with the Great Pyramid?"

"The reason was born sixty years ago," Roddy said. "The story begins with Branch's grandfather, Jeremiah Nichols, a Bible scholar. He was convinced the Great Pyramid was a source of scientific knowledge. He asked his friend, Stone Rydal, Benjamin's father, to go and search."

"Why him?"

"He was an archeologist."

"A brave, adventurous one," Branch said. "My grandfather could never forgive himself." Branch returned to his food.

"Don't stop. Tell me what happened."

Branch swallowed, sipped some coffee, and went on. "He took his twelve-year-old son, Benjamin, with him. They found what we found. They didn't have cameras, so they copied on paper the writing on the walls. Jeremiah heard about their find and became excited. He called a friend, an evolutionary biologist named Chuck Windar. Jeremiah was sure this would prove the earth was only 6,000 years old."

"Did they have proof?"

"We don't know. A couple days later, six men showed up at Stone Rydal's house with guns and grenades."

"Grenades?"

"We figure they knew Stone's reputation and decided overkill was the best approach. Anyway, a fierce, running gun battle ensued. Stone owned a genuine nineteenth century Colt 45, and he was good with it. He and Benjamin had to dodge grenade explosions, enduring numerous injuries. Stone killed two of the attackers. Benjamin got his dad's shotgun and saved his dad's life at one point. One of the gunmen had gotten the drop on Stone while he was reloading. Benjamin blew him away, but the recoil from the shotgun knocked him against a wall. He was dazed. When he shook the fog loose, he watched his father and another man shoot it out at close range. Emptying both guns, they shot each other to death.

"Benjamin spotted another gunman, placed the butt of the gun against the wall to absorb the recoil, and fired. He missed, jumped to his feet, and ran for his life. The sixth man, he thinks, was the one who threw the grenade that blew him out a window, landing him twenty feet from the house. The two surviving gunmen left him for dead. Benjamin survived but lost the use of both legs."

"Wow, that's so sad. What about Benjamin's mother?"

"She died giving birth to Benjamin. My grandfather finished raising him along with his own son, Tyler, who was fourteen at the time."

"Jeremiah's wife, your grandmother. Tell me about her."

"Years later she went missing for a few days. When she returned, she claimed aliens had abducted her. She was never quite right afterward and passed away in a mental institution."

"Oh, that's terrible."

"No one was sure what happened to her."

"So, whose idea was it for you guys to go to the Pyramid?"

"Branch insisted he had to go," Roddy said. "And I insisted I would go with him."

"Benjamin had been talking me out of going all my life," Branch said. "He had a recent, sudden change of mind."

"Why?"

"Don't know. And there's more to the story."

Branch picked up a slice of Greek toast and took a bite. He poured some more coffee into his cup and reclined in his chair as he ate.

Linda motioned with her hands signifying he should hurry up.

Branch smiled at her anxiousness, swallowed his toast, and sipped his coffee.

"Okay," he said. "Here's what happened next. My father, Tyler Nichols, grew up, got married, and became an investigative journalist."

"Like you," said Linda.

"Whatever. When I was born, my mother suffered the same fate as Benjamin's. So I started life half-orphaned already."

"Oh, I'm sorry."

"She had health issues no one knew about before the pregnancy. She had a choice to abort or die in childbirth."

"She must've been a wonderful person."

"Yes," he said, nodding, "she must've been." He looked thoughtful for a moment. "Anyway, my father was pursuing research on Area 51. According to a letter he sent Benjamin, he was on to something staggering to the imagination. My father had to go, regardless of the danger."

"What was it?"

"Not sure. My father's body was discovered in the Mohave Desert, riddled with bullets. He was found alive and told the man who found him that Area 51 was a hoax, and a cover-up."

"What exactly did he mean?"

"We never found out. But then he said something that didn't seem to fit. He told the man he'd also discovered evidence for a recent creation." My father's last words were, 'The answer is in the pyramid, grand...' He had more to say but never finished."

"Pyramid grand. Grand Pyramid, right?"

"Guess so."

"You're right. That's odd since the Great Pyramid is like eight time zones away."

"Nine."

"Had he been to the Pyramid before maybe discovering the same thing you did?"

"Don't know, but he'd studied ancient Hebrew. That's the way he liked to read the Old Testament."

Branch went back to eating while Linda pondered all she'd heard. Roddy was getting seconds from the girl serving the tables.

Finally, Linda spoke up. "How old did you say you were when your father died?"

"Three. So I don't remember him. Benjamin took me in and raised me, just as my grandfather raised him."

Linda's expression went numb. "Benjamin's father died because of those inscriptions, and now my Uncle Dagan has them."

"He knew the risk," Branch said. "He's an old friend of Benjamin's and he was willing to accept that risk."

"I'll call him and see if he's alright."

The three continued eating with occasional small talk. Branch wondered why he'd opened up to her the way he did. He'd never told anyone his family history before. Even Roddy, whom he'd known all his life, learned most of the details from Benjamin.

After breakfast, they strolled outside wearing light jackets.

Branch studied a map.

"We go down the hill to the first left and follow the road into the mountains."

Linda took out her cell phone. "Just give me a minute. I'm calling Uncle Dagan. He should be in his office by now."

Branch and Roddy went across the lot to the edge of the mountainside overlooking the sun bathed valley, and the city of Saint Gallen.

"Breathtaking," Roddy said.

"I agree."

They heard a shriek behind them, and turned to see Linda holding her phone to her ear. She appeared to be in shock.

"Oh my g..." she said. "And then you..." She stood rigid, listening. "But you're all right..." She listened again. "Yes, I'll be careful. Talk to you later."

Branch and Roddy had walked to her side and waited for her to say something.

"Two goons with guns came to Uncle Dagan's office demanding the pictures from the Pyramid."

"I hope he just turned them over without an argument," Branch said.

"One of them laughed at his secretary's accent. Called her a Cracker. She kicked him in the gut, and the guy doubled over, Uncle Dagan pushed the other guy into him, and he and his secretary ran. When the police arrived, the computer hard drive was gone along with his CDs."

"I'm glad he's all right," said Branch. "We're fortunate to still have our cameras with all the photos we took."

Roddy said, "When we get back to our room, we better start making some copies."

Branch nodded.

"I'm thinking," Linda said, "anybody we involve will be put in danger."

"I thought of that too," said Branch. "The very reason I did my best to leave *you* behind. I called Dr. von Brunner to give him a chance to reconsider. He told me the risk doesn't matter. In fact, he's eager to meet with us."

They climbed into the little blue Golf 4x4 they were borrowing. Roddy moved the driver's seat back as far as it would go but still had difficulty grabbing the seat belt.

"We couldn't find a smaller car?" Roddy asked.

"Their perfect for these narrow mountain roads," Branch said.

Linda leaned forward from the back seat. "Don't complain. It was generous of the Steinholtzs to lend us their car."

They drove down the steep winding road, made the left, and found themselves on what appeared to be a one-lane road.

"Hope no one is coming from the other way," said Roddy.

"You mean like that guy," Branch said, as a car rounded the next bend and came straight toward them.

"What do I do now?"

"Just pull to the right."

"What right?"

"Go on. You've got a little room."

The other driver moved to his right as Roddy also veered right, coming close to the edge, with a 100-foot drop. They passed with only inches to spare. The other driver smiled and gave a little wave. Linda returned the smile and waved.

"Nice job, Roddy," Linda said.

"I can do this. I'm just glad they drive on the right side in this country. I let Branch take the wheel when we go to countries where they drive on the wrong side."

They admired the snow capped peaks and a narrow waterfall as they drove. Finding the spacious hillside house was easy. They parked in the rear, according to von Brunner's instructions, and walked to the front. After knocking and a brief wait, a small elderly man with collar length, white hair opened the door.

"Come in," he said. "You must be the Americans." He had a thick German accent.

His home looked like the aftermath of a hurricane. A scattering of books, folders, and papers filled the room. Items of clothing were in the mix. Two shirts, a jacket, several orphaned socks and a Chicago Cubs baseball cap.

"Boy," Linda said, under her breath, "their fans are everywhere."

Von Brunner led them to the kitchen and cleared a few things off the table. A video screen sat on a counter against the wall.

"Watching some TV?" Roddy said.

"My surveillance monitor. I watched you coming." He went to a coffee pot next to the monitor. "Sit," he said. "I made some coffee."

"This is a lot of house for one man," Linda said.

"I like to pace when I'm thinking. I can walk for miles. But who wants to go out walking when it's cold or raining. With this house, I can do all my walking indoors."

They sat round the table as von Brunner poured coffee.

"I understand you're curious about the speed of light. You want to know why I think light is slowing down? I'll tell you. The measurements of the speed of light throughout history show a decrease of half-a-percent over the last 300 years." Von Brunner slid the coffee pot into the coffee maker. "You can connect the measurements. Drawing a line on a graph produces a curve which reaches the speed of infinity at 6,000 years ago."

"Six thousand years?" Linda said. "Just like Bishop Ussher. He came up with the same result using genealogies in the Bible."

"Sunday, October 23, 4004 BC," Branch said.

Linda brightened. "Right."

"And Sir John Lightfoot went even further, saying creation took place at nine o'clock in the morning." Branch shook his head. "Let's keep it real. Let's stick to science."

Linda appeared miffed but said nothing.

Von Brunner grabbed his side and showed pain.

"Are you all right Dr. von Brunner?" said Branch.

"It passes." He let go of his side after several moments and sat in a chair at the table. "Evolutionists make criticisms, of course, but so far no one can prove the findings wrong."

"I understand," said Branch, "that the speed of light has something to do with dating methods and their accuracy."

"Yes, the accuracy of radioisotope dating relies on a constant rate of decay. I'll give you an example. Uranium-238 decays into lead-206."

Roddy leaned forward. "You're saying uranium turns into lead, and what's important is how long this takes to happen."

"Correct. Now the half-life of uranium-238 is supposedly 4.5 billion years. What do we mean by half-life? We're talking about the time it would take for half of a given number of uranium-238 atoms to turn into lead-206.

"Now, if we assume a constant rate of decay, we're talking about Uniformitarianism, the foundation of all dating methods. If this proves not to be true, if the speed of light has decreased, the same would be true for the rate of mineral decay. Dates set at billions of years could become no more than a few thousand."

"But," said Branch, "what about Einstein?"

"Einstein's theory of relativity would be out the window."

"I thought modern science had proven relativity."

"Those same modern scientists claim proof of evolution. They have proven nothing. Scientists' knowledge of the universe is increasing. This is causing more of them to question both special and general relativity." He paused and looked thoughtful. "You know, it's really all about time. Which, in actuality, is an illusion."

"What do you mean?" asked Branch, becoming intrigued.

"First off, you have to realize creation is comprised of matter; which is comprised of energy; which is comprised of information. These exist in a state of flow we call time. What *is* time? I referred to it as a state of flow, and time flows forward. You cannot have an infinite regress in time. To accomplish this, time would have to move backward. But, since it moves forward, this illusion we call time must have a starting point at which all things came into being. Time, matter, energy, and of course the building blocks—information—such as DNA. This was the first day, the day before which all the things that make up our reality didn't exist."

Roddy set his mug on the table, looking thoughtful. "The day without yesterday."

"Exactly. Now we still haven't defined what time is or how it works. I've come up with a way to visualize the passage of time. You may be aware that a movie is really a series of pictures. Twenty-four pictures or photos run through the projector every second. When we see them on a screen, we experience the illusion of movement. But what we're really watching is a series of photographs.

"Each frame passes in front of a light and is projected onto a screen. Think of that projected frame as a moment in time. As a new frame passes in front of the light, we experience a new moment in time. The previous frame is now part of the past. The next frame is the future. But the light is constant. It doesn't go into the past with the previous frame, and the light doesn't move to the next frame, the future. The future moment must come into the light. In other words, it is always now! Creation is recreated from moment to moment, but with change, with the appearance of movement. From the past to the future. But as we now understand, it is always, ever, and only *now*."

Linda sat, transfixed. All she could utter was, "Fascinating."

"It is quite fascinating," said Branch. "But it's theory. Dr. von Brunner, the main reason I came here was to give you this." He took the little platform, which Quasi had given him, from his jacket pocket, and set it on the table.

"Ah, you have it. Young lady," Dr. von Brunner said to Linda, "would you bring that to me?" He pointed to a small box on the counter near the coffee pot.

Linda retrieved the box and set it on the table in front of von Brunner. He flipped the lid open and revealed a tiny pyramid shaped object, about an inch-and-a-half on all sides. It appeared to be made of the same material as the platform. Von Brunner took it out, pushed the box aside and, holding the tiny pyramid, extended his hand toward the platform.

When the platform was still several inches away, the piece jumped from his hand, and onto a corner of the platform. They all stared in amazement. Branch picked it up and tried to pull the little pyramid free, but it stuck hard.

Von Brunner spoke. "I'm a member of a clandestine order known as the Pyramidions, started by Shem, son of Noah. The key had been given to him by his grandfather, Lamech, before the flood."

"You're serious?" Branch said.

"Quite. We hold the greatest Pyramid secret of all, only to be revealed at the right time. The order was almost exterminated around A.D. 1000 when it was infiltrated. Within forty years, the status quo was restored, and I'm sure phony members are no longer an issue.

"But for safety's sake, someone with special knowledge was able to separate the pieces, and no one Pyramidion is allowed to have more than one piece, or even the knowledge of who has the rest."

"Do you know where to go for the next piece?" Branch said.

"Not I, you. I will tell you who to contact."

"No," said Branch, standing. "This isn't our project. We just came to drop off the platform of whatever this thing is."

"The 4,360 years of waiting are ended. You've been chosen to assemble the pieces. This is why the caretaker gave you the platform which holds the pyramid, which is the key."

"Key to what?" Linda asked.

"I'm not sure. No one person possesses all the knowledge we have. This is a safety measure in case we're infiltrated again. My contact in the Pyramidions is a computer programmer living in the Bahamas. His name is Ackerley Smith. He has his own 120 acre island."

"I'm sorry, Doctor," Branch said. "We can't help you. We need to go, now." Branch set the platform on the table.

Von Brunner glanced at his monitor. "We have more guests." He rose from his chair.

Linda caught her breath when she looked at the monitor. The men approaching the house were carrying guns. "Those aren't guests."

Roddy frowned. "The trench coat gang. How'd these guys find us again?"

"Credit cards, cell phones," Branch said. "Dr. von Brunner, I don't suppose you have any guns in the house."

"Yes, come this way."

The frail little scientist hurried down a hallway, toward the rear of the house. Branch and Linda immediately followed von Brunner.

In his study, von Brunner stooped in front of a large safe and unlocked it. He opened the door and stood up.

"Help yourself," von Brunner said.

Branch went to the safe, crouched, and withdrew an automatic weapon. He stared for a moment before looking at von Brunner. "You have an Uzi?"

Von Brunner shrugged. "I like to hunt."

Branch turned around and looked for Roddy, who hurried through the door.

Branch gave him a sarcastic smile. "We're not keeping you from anything, are we?"

Roddy just smiled, and Branch tossed him the gun, then reached in the safe and pulled out a ludicrously large handgun.

Branch said, "This is a breech-loading hand cannon chambered for rifle cartridges."

"Seven millimeters, ten-inch barrel," von Brunner said. "Watch the recoil. Last time I fired the thing, I wound up on my fanny."

Branch handed clips for the Uzi to Roddy and grabbed a box of ammo for himself.

"Sorry, Linda, we don't have one for you."

"That's okay. I'll just scream at them."

The sound of the front door being broken in startled them. Branch stepped over to the professor's desk and tipped it over. "Get behind this," he said to Linda and von Brunner.

The two did as they were told while Branch and Roddy went down the hall a little way and then separated. The house was a maze of hallways. Branch thought maybe they could get them in crossfire. He peeked around a doorway and spotted two of the intruders.

They saw him too and opened fire. Bullets splintered the molding on the doorway. Two bullets cleared the opening and a vase exploded; then a goldfish bowl. Branch watched two fish squirm on the floor, hoping he was not about to meet the same fate. He heard the Uzi and knew Roddy had them pinned down. The intruders were trapped in the living room.

Branch reached around the doorway and fired into the room. The gun produced powerful recoil causing the shot to go high. It hit a mirror, scattering fragments all over the room.

Wallach cried out in pain.

Branch was feeling confident now. "Looks like we've got you surrounded and out gunned."

Roddy yelled, "Do you want to surrender?"

A long pause followed. Branch figured they must be discussing their options. Then something bounced down the hall, stopping in front of the doorway. A grenade.

Branch jumped to his feet and ran. The blast twenty feet behind almost knocked him down. *What kind of assassins carries grenades?* As he continued to run, he heard another explosion. Roddy.

He rounded a corner. A pile of rubble lay before him. Branch's eyes darted in their unblinking sockets as he made a visual search through a thin cloud of dust, but he saw no sign of his friend. "Roddy." No answer.

He was about to begin digging when the pile of plaster and wood moved. Roddy poked his head out. "Hey, did you notice they have grenades?"

"No, I missed that. Quit playing in the rubble and let's get out of here."

Roddy stood and hurried after.

Branch dashed into the study. "We have to leave," he shouted. He reached the overturned desk, but no one was behind it. Roddy stopped at his side.

Branch looked for an exit, but the only one was the doorway he'd just come through. "How could they have gotten out of this room?"

Roddy was quizzical. "Rapture, aliens, who knows?"

"You're a help." Branch yelled, "Linda, Professor, where are you?"

"We're up here. On the second floor." Linda's voice was muffled.

"Second floor?" Branch said.

"Second floor of heaven?" Roddy asked. "Or a spaceship?"

"Will you give it a rest?"

Just then, a bookcase swung out. Linda peeked from behind. "Come on you guys; this is neat."

Roddy chuckled. "A secret passageway."

"You gotta be kidding me," Branch said.

They followed Linda behind the bookcase, closed it, and went up a narrow staircase. At the top, they found a room with lots of overstuffed furniture. Von Brunner sat in an easy chair, sipping a bottle of cognac. He wore a set of padded headphones that threatened to swallow von Brunner's small head.

"Professor," Branch said.

Von Brunner saw Branch out of the corner of his eye. He pulled the left headphone away from his ear. "Mozart. Relaxes my nerves."

"We need a way out of here," Branch said.

"How are we doing, gun battle-wise?" von Brunner said.

"Bad news about your goldfish," Branch replied.

"Aw, Copernicus and Galileo. Too bad."

Von Brunner set his cognac down, took off the headphones and rose from his chair, putting his hand to his side and wincing. Linda moved toward him with concern, but he waved her off. He kept his hand on his side as he walked.

Branch's voice exuded urgency. "Professor, we need to get to the ground outside?"

The noise of shattering glass punctuated the exigent plea. A grenade lay on the floor. Roddy knew they only had about four seconds to react. He grabbed a couch and swung it around ninety degrees. Branch dove over, as Linda, von Brunner, and Roddy went to the floor behind the couch. The grenade exploded, sending bits of the floor in all directions.

Von Brunner was still holding his side as he got to his knees. "This room has a door to an outside stairway."

They all rose and headed toward the back. Von Brunner was shuffling along at a good pace. He opened the door and stepped out.

"Wait," Branch said.

He hurried to catch the little professor. A shot rang out and von Brunner fell to the porch. Branch ran out, aimed his formidable weapon, and fired at the shooter on the ground.

The shot knocked the gunman off his feet.

Branch stooped to check the professor's wound. "Looks serious," Branch said. "I'll carry you."

"It's all right, I was dying anyway," von Brunner said. "They saved me from months of suffering."

Linda got on her knees and put her hand on his forehead. "We can help you."

His eyes went vacant. Branch closed the lids and grabbed Linda's wrist. "We have to go."

"We can't just leave him."

"We can't help him now and we don't have time for anything else."

He raised her up and started down the stairs with Linda in tow.

A new threat appeared on the ground. Before Branch could react, Roddy fired his Uzi from the porch above and eliminated the gunman.

The three of them hurried down the stairs and jumped into the Steinholtz's Golf 4x4. Linda crouched on the floor in the back. Branch and Roddy put their windows down. Roddy shifted into drive with his foot on the brake, put his right hand on the wheel and hung his Uzi out the window with his left. Branch stuck his seven-millimeter hand cannon out the window.

"Ready?" Roddy said.

"Hit it," said Branch.

Roddy gunned the engine and the car shot up the drive. Two hit men stepped into their path. Branch and Roddy began firing, and the two men dove for their lives in opposite directions. Roddy took a hard right and sped down the road. Branch hung out the window, facing toward the driveway just as the gunmen were getting ready to shoot. Branch opened fire and the two dropped for cover.

Branch turned to Roddy. "At least we left that artifact behind. Now it's no longer our responsibility."

Roddy looked at him while keeping one eye on the narrow road. He smiled.

Branch studied him a moment. "You didn't."

Roddy took the platform with its attached pyramid out of his pocket.

"Wonderful, Roddy," Branch said, with all the sarcasm he could muster.

Linda got off the floor and sat on the edge of the seat. "You two work well together. I'm so happy to be part of the team."

"Team?" Branch said. He rolled his eyes, let out a groan, and gazed out the window.

They returned to the hotel and Roddy inspected the car for bullet holes. He was relieved to find none this time. Linda returned the keys to Mrs. Steinholtz and said she was sorry they weren't gonna be around for lunch. Branch called Benjamin to tell him they needed to change their identities. Benjamin told him to go to London, and he would have someone meet them with new passports, credit cards, and cell phones.

The three went to their rooms.

When Branch and Roddy entered their room, they froze. The aftermath of a whirlwind greeted them. Clothes were strewn across the floor and furniture; mattresses were flipped over; even the lining in the suitcases had been ripped out.

"You see the cameras?" asked Roddy.

"No, I don't."

"What do you think they were looking for in the suitcase linings?"

"Hard copies of the pictures we took."

"They're thorough," Roddy said, nodding in approval. "Gotta give them an A+."

"You would."

Linda burst into the room. "My room's been..." She stared at the mess.

"Ransacked?" Roddy said.

"Uncle Dagon gave me copies of the pictures you guys took. I had hidden them in the lining of my suitcase. Now they're gone."

Branch raised an eyebrow—surprised by her foresight.

"Now we have nothing," Roddy said.

The three boarded the Trogenerbahn and rode down the mountain.

Linda said, "Do you think they'll follow us and catch us?"

"I don't know," Branch said, "but we're getting out of Switzerland as fast as we can, go to London, and then try to become invisible."

The rest of the ride was quiet and solemn. They made their flight without any trouble and were on their way to London. If they could sneak in and out of England, they'd head for the Bahamas, and the next link in the chain.

Chapter Four

Strolling through Heathrow airport, Branch said, "We're taking a tour on the Thames River."

Linda hopped up and down on her toes a couple times and said, "Oh good, I love boat tours."

"I consider a river ride to be the best way to take in a city."

"As long as we're not being shot at."

Roddy asked, "Aren't we on a mission?"

"Yes," Branch said. "The boat will take us to the Mayflower Inn in Rotherhithe, a district of London. Benjamin has sent someone to meet us. He'll give us new identities so we can't be followed this time."

On the tour boat, the three stood by the railing watching London go by. The temperature was about the same as in Saint Gallen, but here the weather included clouds and dampness.

"Why do they call it the Mayflower Inn?" Roddy asked.

"The Mayflower set sail from a point nearby," Branch said.

Linda said, "Rotherhithe is also significant for the ten-foot skeleton dug up in 1717."

Branch frowned. "Sounds like an urban legend, another Goliath tale."

"Other skeletons," she explained, "dug up in the U.S., are in the eight to twelve-foot range. A group of soldiers at Lompock Rancho, California unearthed the bones of a twelve-foot tall man in 1833. Diggers found skeletons measuring from eight-and-a-half feet to ten-feet long in the Humboldt lakebed in California back in 1931. Archaeologists in Brewersville, Indiana, discovered one measuring nine-feet, eight inches.

"In other parts of the world, skeletal finds of ten to thirteen feet aren't uncommon." Linda had entered an enthusiastic soapbox, teacher mode. "Skeptics dismiss the story of Goliath because they don't believe in giants" Linda said. "How tall *is* a giant? The Bible says Goliath was six cubits and a span. A cubit is a foot-and-a-half and a span is nine inches, making him nine-feet, nine-inches tall." Linda put her hands on her hips and squared her small shoulders. "So," she said, "you cannot dismiss the possibility of a boy fighting a giant named Goliath based on height."

Branch had folded his arms as he leaned against the railing. "Well, shame on me," he said with a smirk.

"Yes, shame on you," she said as she smiled.

They disembarked and took the short, late morning walk to the inn. It was a small, white, two-story building with a hanging garden in front. The place was only half full. The three weary travelers ordered coffee and sandwiches.

Sitting at a table in a corner, Branch swept the pub with a cautious eye looking for what he was not sure. A middle-aged man approached wearing a gray suit and carrying a briefcase. He extended his hand to Branch.

"I'm agent Luke Cardwell," he said with a British accent. "MI6."

"What can I do for you?" Branch said, as he shook Cardwell's hand.

"I came here to do something for you. Benjamin Rydal would like us to make you invisible."

"Sit down."

Branch introduced Linda and Roddy. When the waitress came by, Cardwell told her he wanted nothing.

He extracted an envelope from his briefcase. "I have driver's licenses, credit cards, and passports for all of you." He passed the envelope to Branch.

"I don't need to know whom you're hiding from," Cardwell said, "but I am curious."

"Brussel," said Branch.

Cardwell shifted in his chair and wrinkled his brow. "Ah. The international legend."

"Please tell me he's not still working for the company."

"Oh, I can tell you, the CIA wants nothing to do with him. Brussel became a rogue agent twelve years ago. When the agency discovered his extracurricular behavior eight years ago, he disappeared. A brutal contract killer now, Brussel has been linked to dozens of assassinations. We think there's a pattern. No one is sure."

"What can you tell us for sure?" asked Branch.

"What I can tell you is the secret agency you once worked for was part of the pattern."

"What kind of work did you use to do?" Linda asked.

Branch didn't answer, so she pressed.

"How secret?"

"I was a UFO hunter."

Linda gaped at him in astonishment. "Men in Black?"

"A super-secret branch. In fact, being on the outside now, I haven't had contact with any of them since I left."

Branch turned to Cardwell "You said the agency *was* part of the pattern."

Cardwell appeared reluctant to answer, but in a careful tone he said, "The agency no longer exists." He stared at Branch for a few moments before he finished. "They're all dead; murdered."

The shock hit Branch hard, and he felt his focus on reality slip out of gear for a moment, and then return. Branch finally blinked, as he stared at Cardwell.

"The entire agency? Over a hundred people?"

"A hundred thirty-two. The agency was top secret, but it's still a nightmare keeping it all out of the media."

"Why?" Branch said.

"They were onto something others didn't want anyone to know about."

"What others? Who?"

"We're not sure."

"Or won't tell."

"We don't know, but if you find out, please keep us informed." Cardwell leaned forward with cold eyes. "If you encounter Brussel," Cardwell said, "kill him. And anybody with him."

They got on a Thames tour boat and rode in silence until Linda finally spoke.

"I'm sorry about all those people you worked with."

"I got out years ago," Branch said. "We were just chasing ghosts. What seemed like real leads turned out to be more myth than reality. What appeared mythical at first often turned into something that might be real, but we never found a lasting trail to follow."

At the airport, they used their new identities to book a plane to the Bahamas. Linda sat between Roddy and Branch as usual, with Roddy's nose stuck to the window—as usual. Linda took out a book and started to read.

"You finished the other book?" Branch said.

"Yes, this is another Chandler Ross mystery novel. I just can't get enough. He's so good."

Branch put his seat back to rest his eyes. He pondered the loss of an entire agency he spent years working for. He thought about the acquaintances and friendships he once had. What had they finally found that caused their complete annihilation? And what about he, Roddy, and Linda? Could they continue to out-maneuver such a powerful entity, one with seemingly unlimited resources?

The three landed in Nassau late in the day. They took their carry-on bags, the only luggage they had and started for the exit doors watching for their contact. Branch had phoned ahead on his secure new cell phone and set up a meeting with Ackerley Smith. Nearing the doors, Linda pointed and said, "Must be our guy."

Branch spotted a tall, thin, not quite middle-aged man, sporting a tan and carrying a sign that read, *Pyramid Gang*.

"So much for a low profile," Branch said.

Roddy chuckled. "I like this guy already."

Reaching the man with the sign, Branch said, "Hello, I'm Branch Nichols."

Smith took Branch's outstretched hand. He turned to the others. "And you must be Roddy and Linda." They all shook hands.

"Come on," Smith said. "The taxi will take us to my plane."

They rode to a dock where Smith had his seaplane moored, a Cessna A185F. They got into the air and headed for Smith's private island.

When she'd had enough of gazing out the window, Linda began her interrogation. "You're a computer programmer, Mr. Smith?"

"Yes, and call me Ackerley."

"So, Ackerley, would you mind giving us a brief history of what you've done?"

"Not at all. After I graduated from ITT Technical Institute at Oxnard, I did some government work. Later, I entered the corporate world. After that, I developed some games for kids, educational games."

Branch said, "I don't suppose you could tell us anything about the government work you did."

"As a former employee for the government talking to three strangers, no. It's top secret. But as a Pyramidion talking with three fellow searchers for the truth, yes, I can tell you anything. The project I worked on involved virtual reality, creating what appears to be real but isn't."

He began his descent toward the island.

"I never learned the intended use," Smith went on. "That was on a need-to-know basis, and they didn't feel I needed to know." After a short pause, he added, "I once overheard someone say, 'Send this off to NASA.' I'm not sure what he was referring to. Whether it was my work or something else."

"You do think it was significant, though?" Branch said.

"When I asked later, I was told to forget it and not ask questions."

The island came into view: sand, palm trees, and a sand-colored, two-story beach house with a giant telescope sticking out of one end.

Smith landed his seaplane next to the dock and they walked to his Jeep.

Roddy was impressed. "An actual 1940 Willy's Jeep."

"Right," said Smith. "The car that won the war. Jump in and we'll go to the house. My wife was planning to have a meal ready for us."

They rode over several sand dunes getting to the house. Smith introduced them to his wife, Miranda. Linda asked if she could help in the kitchen. She added that after being in the company of men for the past few days, she was ready for some girl talk.

On the way, Linda took in the wrought-iron furniture and cedar ceilings. She stopped by a mantel over a stone fireplace and perused some photos. They were pictures of Ackerley standing next to battered cars. She shook her head in wonder and went on.

They feasted on shellfish, yucca, black-eyed peas, and mangoes. They shared small talk and watched the sun go down beyond the huge bay window. Afterward, Smith invited them to his living room. The five of them relaxed and enjoyed the night breeze coming in over the balcony.

"Now," said Smith, "you found some ancient writing below the Great Pyramid of Giza. And you're curious about why the speed of light is mentioned."

Branch nodded.

"The whole of the cosmos," Smith began, "is winding down. This is how we know the laws of thermodynamics. The speed of light is winding down too, which is a good barometer of how far we have come since the beginning of the once perfect creation."

"Ackerley, tell us what you can about Shem and the Pyramidions," Branch said.

"He started the Pyramidions to protect the key until the time for its reassembly was at hand."

"Key to what?"

Smith shook his head. "I don't know... There's also a legend that he built another pyramid in some other part of the world but we don't know where."

Branch opened his carry-on bag and took out the platform with the tiny pyramid stuck to the corner. "But this is part of it?"

"Ah, the MacGuffin."

"What's that?" Roddy asked.

"A term coined by the master of suspense himself, famed film director Alfred Hitchcock. It's what everyone is chasing after."

"He gets credit," Branch said. "But it's possible he appropriated the term from a screenwriter named Angus MacPhail."

"Is that so?" Smith said. "Interesting."

"What's it really called?" Roddy said.

"You can call it the tiny pyramid. Or the key."

Roddy nodded. "I like MacGuffin."

Smith went to a table and picked up a small box. He returned with it and stood near Branch. "I took this from the safe when I knew you were coming." He opened the box and revealed a tiny pyramid just like the first one.

Branch held out the platform. Smith picked up the tiny pyramid and it jumped from his hand and onto the platform. The new piece sat against a corner flanking the first piece.

"That's spooky," said Roddy.

"Don't ask me how," Smith said. "I've no idea."

"Where do we go next?" Branch asked.

"You must visit a man named Wile E. Coyote."

Roddy grinned. "No kidding; that's his name?"

Ackerley smiled. "A former code breaker for the CIA. He lives on a yacht in Chicago during the warmer months."

Branch put the platform with its two pyramids into his carry-on.

"Ackerley, what do you think the key is for?" asked Branch.

"I believe it will unlock the reason for the Great Pyramid. Shem said Noah was the builder. Just as the Ark of the Covenant, Noah's ark, and the temple in Jerusalem were, it was built under God's direction, according to God's specifications."

"I'm sorry," said Branch. "I don't like to criticize anyone's religion, but I have a hard time with claims that are well, outrageous."

Linda frowned at him, but Ackerley studied Branch for a few moments, and then with a slight smile, he said, "Come with me. All of you."

They followed Ackerley to the spacious balcony. The night sky was dotted with hundreds of stars.

"Magnificent, isn't it?" Ackerley said. "What do you see? Lots of tiny lights on a spring night? Mighty balls of fire? I'll tell you what I see. A giant computer programmed to get an answer to a question."

"What question?" asked Roddy.

"I don't know. Miranda is an astronomer—with a hand gesture he indicated the telescope, at the end of the house, aimed at the sky—and together we're trying to decode the universe. Which is made up of matter, energy, and information."

"Von Brunner made the same point," Branch interjected.

"We know information is fundamental. We believe all that we call reality is subject to a single programming rule."

"Sounds radical," said Branch.

"Not anymore. Many others have come to the same conclusion. But this implies a cosmic programmer. Since mainstream science is still held hostage by evolutionists, you're not likely to hear about it much. But that won't stop us from doing our own investigation," he said, as he looked toward his wife.

"Most people don't realize," Miranda began, "our position in the galaxy is the best possible location we could have to study the stars. The universe is, in fact, designed for scientific discovery."

"Yes," Ackerley said, "information always has purpose. A computer program, which is information, is written with purpose. It solves a problem or manipulates a system. A manufacturer creates a slogan, also information, to get you to buy his product. Life itself has been written. We start with the syntax, the genetic code in DNA. Next, we go to semantics where DNA information is read and understood. This brings about action, the pragmatic stage. Here, protein blends in living cells; it puts the complete life form together with all its biological functions. Everything in existence requires some form of information at the beginning. And every form of information has a sender, a creator."

Miranda took over. "If the universe has been programmed, we should be able to learn its meaning, its purpose. And perhaps ours, as well."

"Fascinating," Linda said. "And I'm intrigued by what you said about the earth being in an ideal location to study the universe. What exactly makes that so?"

"Well, it has an awful lot to do with Sir Edwin Hubble's dirty little secret."

"Hubble?" Roddy said. "Isn't there a telescope in space named after him?"

"Yes. Hubble discovered that the distance to the edge of the universe was about the same in any direction."

"So we're at the center of the universe?" said Linda.

"Right," Miranda said. "Hubble was beside himself when he realized the truth. He warned the astronomical community never to admit this to anyone. We're supposed to tell people the universe would appear the same no matter where you are. This, of course, makes no logical sense."

"Why didn't Hubble want astronomers to say we're at the center?" Roddy said.

"Because that's the kind of thing you expect to hear from us ignorant Bible-thumpers," Ackerley said.

Everyone laughed except Branch, who was deep in thought. Then he said to Ackerley, "I'm having a hard time believing a man of science would be so dishonest about science."

"Oh, you'd be surprised how much dishonesty abounds in the scientific profession."

Linda yawned and looked at Miranda. "I think I'm ready to crash and burn."

"We have a room prepared for each of you," said Miranda. "You're welcome to stay and visit with us for several days if you like."

"We appreciate the offer," Branch said. "I think it's best if we leave in the morning. Thank you for your hospitality."

The next morning, Miranda made breakfast and the three prepared to leave with Ackerley.

Two black helicopters approached the beach on another part of the island. They carried beneath them two shiny new black Range Rovers, with tinted black windows, attached to giant magnets. The helicopters lowered the Rovers onto the beach. The window on the passenger side of one of them opened. Brussel's granite-like face appeared, and his hard eyes surveyed the area. The copters detached the cars from the magnets and flew away. Brussel raised his window.

Ackerley put the top down on the jeep. Linda rode in front, while Branch and Roddy rode in back. Miranda waved goodbye as they pulled away.

Smith drove over the dunes, one after another. When he mounted the last one, he stopped cold. The two black Range Rovers sat between them and the seaplane.

Ackerley didn't know what to make of the sight. "How in the world did they come to my island?"

"I suggest we get out of here fast," Branch said.

"You don't think they're friendly?"

All four windows on the passenger side of the two vehicles came down. The occupants extended handguns and automatic weapons through the open windows.

"Guess not," Ackerley said.

"So much for disappearing," said Roddy.

"Must be a leak at MI6," Branch said.

Ackerley made a sharp turn and jammed the gas pedal as the men in the Rovers opened fire. He sped into the palm trees, weaving in and out.

Ackerley punched a number on his cell phone. "This is Ackerley Smith. I'm under attack on my island." After a moment, he said, "This is no joke. Send the Coast Guard."

"U.S. Coast Guard?" Branch said.

"They have a presence here."

"I hope we don't reach a dead end," Roddy said.

"Don't worry; I know every pebble of sand on my island."

Branch realized Ackerley was making only left turns.

"We're gonna wind up where we started," Branch said.

"That's the idea."

"You sure you know what you're doing?"

Ackerley said, "If I were them, I'd follow with one car and have the other one stay put. At least until the driver determined which direction would be best to cut us off."

"And your plan is to make it easy for them?"

Ackerley flashed a confident smile as he glanced over the seat. "Trust me, I've done this before."

"You've what?"

"Is it my imagination," Roddy said, "or are we slowing down?"

"Have to give them a chance to catch up," Ackerley said.

"Catch up?" said Linda. "I thought we wanted to get away."

At that moment, one of the Rovers came over a dune behind them.

"Ah," said Ackerley. "There they are." He immediately accelerated.

They didn't have to drive far before they met the other Rover. Ackerley floored the gas pedal. The Rover took off in a new direction making it obvious they intended to intercept. In doing so, they had to drive on the opposite side of a dune, which blocked the Willy's from view.

Ackerley glanced at his mirror. "They're keeping pace. Have to admire the driver's ability."

Linda gave him a look that said, *Are you nuts?*

The second Rover raced out from the other side of the dune and bore down on the Willy's. Ackerley looked in his mirror at the pursuing Rover, then at the other one.

"Now would be a good time," Ackerley said. He yanked the wheel to the left in time to avoid being cut off.

The Rover turned in the new direction, aiming for the Jeep. The pursuing Rover came into view. Neither driver had time to react. The pursuing Rover rammed the other Rover and both came to a halt.

The Willy's Jeep raced away. "Yeah," Ackerley shouted. "Still got it."

"You said you've done this before?" Branch said.

"Used to drive in demolition derbies. I used to win a lot."

Branch and Roddy exchanged a look.

Roddy peeked over the back seat. "I thought I noticed a chain saw in here."

"Yes," said Ackerley. "Why?"

"How fast can you get to the other end of the island?"

"It's about four miles. Not long."

They sped across sand and between palm trees for the next eight minutes.

Finally, Roddy said, "Drive right past that palm tree and over the next hill."

Ackerley did as Roddy told him.

"Okay, stop here," Roddy said. Roddy got out of the Jeep, went to the rear and reached into the space behind the back seat. He moved the luggage around and found the chain saw. Roddy yanked it out and ran between the tracks of the Jeep, over the hill.

The other three looked at one another, then got out of the Jeep, ran to the top of the hill and lay down.

Roddy stood by the palm tree he had asked Ackerley to drive past. He pulled the cord on the chain saw which started and gave a loud whine.

The other three lay on the sand watching.

Roddy began cutting through the tree.

With only a little left to go, he stopped and sat down, holding the chain saw as it idled. He heard the approaching Range Rover. Roddy sat listening as the sound of the Rover grew louder. When it appeared, Roddy waved, and the Rover sped toward him. Holding the chain saw in one hand, Roddy put the spinning blade to the tree and cut away. The Rover was getting near when the palm tree started to fall.

The other three on the hill watched, open-mouthed as the tree fell toward the Rover. The driver jammed the brake, but he was too late. The tree hit the Rover right in the middle, denting the top and smashing the windshield.

Roddy turned off the chain saw, got to his feet, and ran hard up the hill with the others cheering him on.

The four men, wearing bright, multicolored shirts, were unable to open the doors. They broke what was left of the windows and climbed out of the Jeep. Wallach wanted to shoot but had missed his chance. The quarry dropped out of sight on the other side of the hill.

———

Roddy was laughing, and so were the others as they reached the Jeep. Roddy tossed the chain saw into the back, and they all got in the Jeep. Ackerley gunned it, spitting sand from the back wheels. They headed down a slope to the beach and stopped. Looking ahead and behind they couldn't spot the other Rover.

They heard a loud ping, then another, and another.

"Something's hitting the Jeep," Ackerley said.

"Bullets," said Branch. "Up there." He pointed to a cliff where the Rover sat, with Brussel and three others aiming their guns.

Ackerley jammed the accelerator. "We're sitting ducks."

Wallach and the other three lined up behind the car and pushed the fallen palm tree. It was too heavy to lift off the car, but they were able to push one end toward one side of the car as the other end twisted toward the other side. Finally, after a lot of grunting, the men forced the tree to slide off the car. The end opposite the one they were pushing landed on the car's hood.

The Jeep headed down the beach away from the shooters. They sped toward a fallen tree. "From our last hurricane," Ackerley said. "No way around." He looked over his shoulder. "If we do a one-eighty, we'll be right under their guns." When they reached the tree, Ackerley brought the Jeep to a halt. They got out and hid behind the Jeep.

"Even if we got away from here without being shot," said Ackerley, "it's a small island with little cover. They'd hunt us down."

The firing stopped, and Linda peeked over the hood of the Jeep.

"Get down, Linda," Branch said.

"What's that man holding?" Linda asked.

Wallach and the other three pushed the palm tree off the hood and onto the sand.

Wallach looked up the hill where their quarry had escaped. With a gruesome grin, he said, "These people are gonna die today." He tugged at the material of his shirt. It was a light orange with dark orange veins, sprinkled with white foliage. "It's their fault I had to come down here and wear this abomination."

Branch peered over the Jeep. "RPG. Run!" They all jumped up and ran toward the beach.

The man on the hill fired the rocket-propelled grenade launcher. It went over the Jeep and hit the fallen tree. The four dove to the ground as fragments of the tree splattered across the sand.

Branch examined the cliff. "A rifle with a telescopic sight."

They all looked at the cliff and noticed one of the men taking aim, not knowing which one he picked as his first victim.

"This just gets better and better," Ackerley said.

A faraway explosion shook the air, followed by an explosion on the cliff beneath the Rover and shooters. Branch and the others turned their attention to the ocean where they spotted a Coast Guard Cutter. The cutter fired again. This time the shot sailed over the Rover and into the trees.

"They've got their bearings now," said Ackerley.

They watched the four men hurry to the Rover and then speed away.

"Come on," Ackerley said. They all ran to the Jeep and climbed in.

Brussel's Rover sped up to the beach near the seaplane. Wallach's Jeep was waiting. Wallach stood beside it holding his computer. On hearing the Coast Guard gun, they'd returned. Brussel's car stopped near Wallach's, and Brussel motioned for Wallach to get in. One of the men in the back seat slid over to make room for Wallach.

"Can you get a message out?" Brussel asked.

"I cracked his wifi password before we set down on the beach," Wallach answered.

"Send him an email," Brussel said to Wallach. "Tell him we failed again."

"This is getting repetitive," Wallach said, as he took his laptop out and opened it.

The helicopters returned and lowered the magnets to the Rovers.

Ackerley and company stopped a quarter of a mile away and watched the helicopters raise the Range Rovers off the beach. They rose high into the sky. A loud blast sounded, and seconds later one of the Rovers exploded.

"It's the Coast Guard," Ackerley said, pointing.

The cutter sliced through the waves.

The copter swayed as its cargo was blown to pieces. Its flight path steadied and it trailed after the one carrying the other Rover.

Inside the Rover, Brussel said, "Good thing you switched vehicles."

Wallach said, "He sent us a reply. It says, 'Guess I should have hired better killers.'"

Brussel managed a faint smile. "Have to like an employer with a sense of humor."

Branch, Roddy, and Linda returned to the Nassau airport and under police protection, boarded a plane for Miami.

On the plane, Branch explained, "We'll use cash and take a bus. That way we won't have to show any identification. And, of course, we'll throw away our now useless cell phones."

"I have to call Christine," Roddy said.

"You can use a land line at the airport."

When they landed in Miami, Roddy used a pay phone to call his wife and ran out of quarters before they finished talking. *As if I wasn't in enough trouble already.*

Linda called her mom and learned that her cat had desecrated the carpet again; no doubt, Linda was sure, to get even with her for being gone. *Cat logic!*

Branch called Benjamin and told him the new identities hadn't worked. Benjamin assured him things would get much worse. He was now convinced someone in the Pyramidions also wanted them dead. He believed the three of them were marked for termination even if they gave up looking for answers.

"Come to Pennsylvania. Use a bus and pay cash like you planned. We'll regroup and try to figure things out from here."

Branch knew that getting Benjamin's input was the smartest thing he could do. He purchased the bus tickets and spent the entire trip pondering the likelihood of a fake Pyramidion. Someone was somehow tracking them via other members of the clandestine group. Branch wondered whom he could trust besides Roddy, Linda, and Benjamin.

Chapter Five

Benjamin Rydal's chauffeur met Branch, Roddy, and Linda at the bus station. He drove them to Benjamin's mansion in the secluded hills of northwestern Pennsylvania.

They enjoyed a meal prepared by Benjamin's chef. They shared the full details of their adventures with Benjamin, who listened, and then took time to get to know Linda.

"I hope these two haven't been too much trouble for you," Benjamin said.

"Roddy's been nice."

Roddy nodded in appreciation as he continued eating.

"Mr. Nichols hasn't been a total pain in the neck."

Branch gave her a mocking smile. "And you likewise, Miss Chapel."

"And I've had my mystery novels to read. They're good company."

"Ah, mystery novels. You have a favorite author?"

"Yes, Chandler Ross."

Benjamin glanced at Branch and back at Linda.

"He's the best," Linda said. "Nothing like a Chandler Ross mystery. I would love to meet him someday." She stared at Branch. "I bet Chandler Ross is intelligent, charming, and gallant."

Benjamin was amused. He looked at Branch and said, "You haven't told her."

Branch had an unrepentant smile as he turned up the palms of his hands. "I just was never able to determine the right time to share that."

"Share what?" Linda said, looking at Branch and then at Benjamin.

"Branch, here, is your favorite author. Chandler Ross is his pen name."

Branch grinned at Linda's flustered gaze. How could her favorite author and Branch Nichols be the same person? She wanted to grab Branch by the throat. "You let me go on about... and you never said... and I fed your already overblown ego."

"You never heard me complain."

Linda's eyes narrowed as she stared silent curses at his gloating countenance.

"Well," said Benjamin with a smile, "perhaps we should retire to my study."

Benjamin rolled away from the table in his wheelchair as the others rose; Roddy was still eating as he stood.

The study was the size of a one-half gymnasium; part library, part office; a train set sat in one corner of the room.

"Wow," said Linda, "do you think you have enough books?"

"Probably not."

Roddy went straight for the train set. He found an engineer's hat, put it on and sat at the controls.

Linda sat on a loveseat, and Branch sat at the other end. She rose, went to an overstuffed chair, sat, and curled her feet up under her.

"Let's go over the facts you've accumulated so far," Benjamin said. "And see what we've got."

Branch started. "We found inscriptions on the wall in some form of pre-ancient Hebrew language. Since we no longer have pictures of the inscriptions, I think we should go back down."

"Can't," Benjamin said. "The Egyptian government increased security and no one is getting near."

"I guess they don't want anyone to know what we found either," Branch said.

"No, they don't. Egypt has a proud heritage, and they don't want inconvenient anomalies getting in the way."

"All right," said Branch, "we can be sure our discovery is important to someone. Or there wouldn't be all these attempts on our lives." He stood and started to pace. "We know what Dr. Meir said about proving the speed of light has slowed over time. He said, 'The science establishment would be turned upside down. Thousands of careers would be ruined.' Von Brunner became an outcast for what he believed."

"But is that enough to want people dead?" said Benjamin. "I don't think so."

"Ackerley Smith said the universe was like a giant computer programmed to find the answer to a question."

"And his wife, Miranda, told us the earth is in the perfect position to study the universe." Linda said. "Right at the center, she said."

"So what might we learn about the whole of creation that certain people wouldn't want known?" Benjamin asked. "And, who are those people?"

"I guess that's what we need to find out," Branch said. "As well as discovering what phenomenal secret the Pyramidions preserved for over 4,000 years."

"Seems to me," said Linda, "everything will lead back to the Pyramid, the place where all this started."

"I think you're right, Linda," Benjamin said. "Which is fitting. Ever heard the Great Pyramid described as a Bible in Stone?"

Branch frowned but Linda was intrigued.

"No. What does it mean?" she asked.

"Prophecies are believed to be embedded in its stone structure. For instance, in the king's chamber, the only thing you'll find is an empty sarcophagus symbolizing the empty tomb of Christ."

Branch said, "You can read in anything you like."

"Perhaps," said Benjamin.

With a sardonic smile, Linda said, "Don't pay any attention to Mr. Mopey."

"I thought I was Mr. Glum."

"That too. Go on, Benjamin."

"One of the most remarkable things about the Great Pyramid is the top. Isaiah, chapter twenty-eight, verse sixteen talks about laying a cornerstone in Zion. Zechariah, chapter four, verse seven reads, 'He shall bring forth the headstone.'"

"Headstone, not cornerstone?" Linda said.

"Right. In Psalms, chapter one-eighteen, verse twenty-two we read, 'The stone the builders refused is become the head of the corner.' Jesus refers to that verse in Matthew chapter twenty-one, verse forty-two. Also, chapter four of Acts, verse eleven says, 'This Jesus is the stone rejected by you, the builders, which has become the head of the corner.'"

Linda said, "And you think a connection exists between those verses and the pyramid."

"Head of the corner is often translated cornerstone," Benjamin said. "But a cornerstone is at the bottom of one corner of a building. Construction starts with that. With a pyramid, however, the headstone, or capstone, goes on after construction is completed. But the headstone doesn't conform to the rest of the pyramid. The capstone is made first, becoming the foundation for the rest of the pyramid. The pyramid must conform to *it*. The pyramid is the only edifice in the world with this unique feature."

"Wait a minute," said Roddy. "I saw the top of the pyramid during one or two of those lightning flashes the night we went. Seemed to me the top was flat."

"Right," Benjamin said. "The headstone was never placed on the pyramid. Cast aside by the builders, to quote a phrase from Scripture."

"What else?" Linda asked, her eyes wide as she leaned forward from her seat.

"Isaiah, chapter nineteen, verse nineteen says, 'In that day there will be an altar to the LORD in the midst of the land of Egypt, and a pillar to the LORD at its border.' Isaiah, chapter nineteen, verse twenty reads, 'It will be a sign and a witness to the LORD of hosts in the land of Egypt.'"

Linda asked, "How can this altar or pillar be in the midst and on the border at the same time?"

"Excellent question. The latitude and longitude of the Great Pyramid breaks up the land surface of the Earth into roughly equal quarters. That puts it in the midst. As for the border, Egypt was originally two separate kingdoms. They were referred to as upper and lower Egypt, and not united until 3,000 B.C. The Great Pyramid is right on the border. In fact, Giza is Arabic for border."

"So," Linda said, glancing toward Branch, "what do you think?"

"I think I'd like something—I don't know—scientific?"

"Don't have much use for the Bible, do you?"

Benjamin said, "I have Branch's grandfather, Jeremiah Nichols, to thank for my appreciation of the Bible. Somehow, though, I was not able to pass that on to Branch. But I do have some science or at least some mathematics to go along with my lecture."

Linda turned to Branch. "Pay attention, cowboy."

Branch gave her a tight-lipped smile. "I'm on the edge of my couch, salivating in expectation."

Linda laughed and turned toward Benjamin.

"All right, Linda, tell me, do you know what pi is?"

Before she could answer, Roddy turned away from the trains and said, "You mean like apple, cherry, and banana cream?"

"No, Roddy," Benjamin said. "This is p-i, not p-i-e. But thanks for the effort."

Linda was pounding her head with the palm of her right hand. "I hated math. Let me think."

Her eyes brightened. "I remember. Pi is the ratio of the circumference of a circle to its diameter, and the number after the decimal goes into infinity."

"Right. Now take the distance around the base of the pyramid. Divide that by twice the height of the pyramid. And you get the value of Pi to the nearest one ten-thousandth. What makes that even more astonishing is until recently we weren't able to calculate Pi to that level of accuracy."

Linda turned her attention to Branch and said, "You getting this?"

Branch was reclining against the back of the couch with his eyes closed as he let out a loud snore.

Benjamin had a hint of a smile as he went on. "Here's another one. The builders used a measurement called a pyramid cubit. The base length of the pyramid is 365.242 pyramid cubits, which is exactly the average number of days in a year."

"What are the odds?" Linda said.

"Astronomical," said Benjamin. "Entire books have been written on the mathematical wonders of the pyramid. As well as the pyramid's relationship to Scripture. There's just too much to discount."

Linda turned toward Branch with a what-do-you-think-about-that expression on her face.

Branch peeked out of one half-opened eye. "Hey, I'm keeping an open mind."

Linda turned away and said to Benjamin, "You know, what you said about there being too much to discount reminds me of evolutionists. With some of them, no matter how many embarrassing facts you throw their way, they stay committed."

Benjamin said, "Branch might be convincible. But some people who, clinging to their naturalist worldview will never be convinced. And that reminds me of a story." He smiled as he rested his arms on the arms of his wheelchair, raised himself up a bit and leaned forward. "A psychologist had been treating, for many weeks, a patient who had convinced himself he was dead. The psychologist pointed out that the medical evidence showed he was alive, and in perfect health. The patient refused to be convinced, saying medical evidence could be misinterpreted.

"The frustrated psychologist finally had an idea. He asked his patient, 'Do dead men bleed?' The patient replied, 'No, of course not.' The psychologist pulled out a pin and pricked the patient's finger.

"To the patient's dismay a small drop of blood appeared.

"'See! You're bleeding,' the psychologist said, sure that he'd proven his point. The patient replied, 'Wow! I guess I was wrong. Dead men do bleed!'"

Linda laughed, "Yeah, sounds like an evolutionist. I guess they don't mind looking ridiculous."

"Oh, they mind. In fact, an evolutionist would have an answer. He would say you can draw blood from a fresh corpse, which is true. This of course ignores the fact that the patient had been coming to the psychologist for weeks and, so, the corpse wouldn't be fresh. But whenever the issue is brought up, the evolutionist would say 'We've dealt with this before. Let's move on.' They still look ridiculous but they're not fazed. They'll continue to pretend they have provided an answer to the problem.

"The same with the Big Bang Theory and secular models for the formation of the solar system. They are aware of serious problems. But they'll create assumption upon assumption to explain away any scientific evidence that destroys their worldview."

Branch decided he'd endured enough evolution bashing for one evening. He stood and said, "I suggest we turn in now and get an early start in the morning."

"Chicago?" Roddy said. "Best place in the world to get a good meal."

"We'll continue to travel by bus so we can pay cash and stay under the radar."

"Nonsense. Take my Mercedes," Benjamin said. "I'll give you plenty of cash so you can buy gas and everything you need."

"All right," Branch replied.

"Thanks for everything," Linda said. She kissed Benjamin on the cheek and left to go to her room.

"Someone will wake you for breakfast," Benjamin told her.

"Goodnight, everyone," said Linda.

After she was gone, Branch said to Benjamin, "I think we should ditch her. No one knows she's here. She'll be safe, and Roddy and I will go it alone."

"All right," Benjamin said, "if that's what you want."

Branch and Roddy each went to bed with the intention of rising well before sunrise.

Branch and Roddy sneaked out the next morning. Benjamin's maid had peeked into Linda's room and reported, "She's buried under the covers."

The two guys loaded their stuff into the trunk of the dark blue Mercedes, climbed into the front seat, and drove away.

They were half way to Pittsburgh on Interstate 76 when Roddy asked, "I wonder what that blanket is covering up in the back seat."

Branch looked over his shoulder at the blanket. He shook his head. "Couldn't be."

"Couldn't be what?" Roddy said.

"Nothing, I'm having Déjà vu."

"Again?"

Branch gazed at Roddy and said, "Never mind."

A familiar voice emanated from under the blanket.

"I love car rides."

Branch watched as the blanket was peeled away by two small, smooth hands revealing Linda.

"Isn't this amazing? You're going to Chicago. I'm going to Chicago."

Roddy had a massive grin as Branch turned to him.

"Don't look at me," Roddy said.

Branch turned to face Linda. "How—?"

"I figured you couldn't be trusted, so I put some stuff under the blanket on my bed, went out to the car, crawled in, and spent the night. Now I'm gonna read my book." She sat up straight and produced a Chandler Ross novel from under her blanket.

"Good choice of reading material," Branch said with a smirk.

"Not every day you get to critique an author's work right to his face, or at least the back of his head."

Branch's smirk faded.

"For instance, right here on page fifty-six when your lead character says—"

"Oh, no," Branch said.

Roddy laughed.

They drove down the interstate as the sun rose from behind. Branch knew big trouble lay ahead. Moreover, one little trouble was right behind him. Linda kept up a running critique all the way to Chicago.

Linda wanted to go to the Field Museum of Natural History when they arrived in Chicago. Branch was not in favor, but Roddy thought a tour of the museum would be "neat." They arrived at 4PM, an hour before closing.

"I love museums," Linda said as they entered. "Let's check out the evolving planet exhibits."

Branch and Roddy followed her. She seemed to be on a mission.

"I brought you guys here to show you what we're up against. Get to know the enemy. Be amazed by the smug, arrogant rhetoric of the closed-minded people who still control the scientific establishment. And the minds of millions of young people in schools run by leftwing fundamentalists."

"Do you need a soapbox for this?" Branch asked.

"No," she said with a sweet smile. "I'll be fine."

They approached a crowd of people who were looking toward a platform. A man with his chest thrust out, wearing a satisfied smile and black-rimmed glasses stepped to the front of the platform and spoke.

"I'm Dr. Roger Darkin. Thank you all for coming to the unveiling of this historic discovery."

Behind Darkin was a platform set at a forty-five degree angle covered by a tarp. Branch noticed the other end of the crowd was filled with members of the news media, holding microphones and cameras.

"You'll all be glad to find I'm a short-winded person," Darkin said.

The crowd laughed.

"So I'm tossing the speech I had prepared," Darkin said, "and going right to the introduction of the discoverer himself. Please welcome Dr. Redmond Barrows."

The crowd applauded. Cameras flashed as Red Barrows stepped forward and Darkin went down the steps at the side of the platform.

"This is an exciting day for the human race," Barrows said. "We found the proof we have searched for, proof we were always sure we would find someday. And now there can be no question that the evolutionary model is the correct one."

Branch glanced at Linda who was wearing her most serious frown, the one she usually directed at him. She began taking advantage of her thinness, slipping between people to get closer to the platform.

Barrows went on: "Now I would like to unveil the greatest archeological find of this young millennium: Ararat Man."

A rope attached to the tarp pulled it away, revealing a skeleton lying on a surface made to appear as stone. The crowd reacted with astonishment while Linda tried to get nearer.

"Here you can observe," Barrows said, "just as we found it, a creature who was part man and part ape. As you can see, our friend here had the skull and rib cage of a *Homo sapiens*. He had the arms and legs of a *Pan paniscus*, called a Bonobo, an almost extinct form of chimpanzee. They are found today only in the Democratic Republic of the Congo, also known as Zaire. The Bonobo is the nearest still existing relative of humans.

"The Bonobo often walks upright, and they have sex facing each other. These are two human characteristics, but it gets even better. Whereas other animals only engage in sex to reproduce, the Bonobo does it for fun."

Branch watched the reporters, with big smiles, write furiously. It was always exciting news when the news contained the magic three-letter word. This almost ensured they wouldn't question the validity of the find. Why ruin a terrific story?

"This, then, is a true Hominid, a genuine missing link," Barrows said.

Linda raised her hand.

"Ah, a question?" Barrows said.

"I'm Linda Chapel, freelance archeology writer. How do you know this wasn't put there for you to find?"

"A hoax, you mean? I can assure you that isn't the case. The entrance to the chamber containing the skeleton needed to be enlarged before any of us could enter. The boy who found the skeletal remains is only seven, and just small enough to crawl in."

"And you trust this boy?"

Barrows stared at her for a moment, pondering his answer. Then he smiled and said, "Silly me. I should have realized that Turkish children are internationally notorious for creating archeological hoaxes."

Everyone laughed. Except Linda.

"I appreciate your excitement over this curious find. But I'm confused."

Barrows smiled condescendingly. "Perhaps I can enlighten you."

"Well, if the hole was only big enough for a seven-year-old to crawl in, how did Ararat Man get in there?"

All eyes were on Barrows, who appeared stunned. Barrows jaw seemed to move while his mouth failed to open. His countenance went from deer-in-the-headlights to panicked, darting eyes as journalists stared, waiting. Branch shook his head. The fool was so giddy over his find he hadn't bothered to ask the obvious question.

The silence was broken by Darkin: "Little Ararat is a volcano."

All eyes now turned toward Darkin as he stood by the steps to the platform. "Our friend lying on the stone slab probably died from heat or smoke inhalation, and the volcanic rock formed around him."

Eager for the missing link to be genuine, members of the audience nodded their acceptance.

Regaining his composure, Barrows said, "I'm guessing this find is tremendously upsetting for you. I can understand your consternation. You're a Christian, are you not?"

Linda didn't react, so Barrows went on. "I too am a Christian. One who believes the Bible and evolution can be reconciled. We realize today that Darwin was wrong. Evolution did not happen gradually. We now know change came about through what scientists refer to as Punctual Equilibrium. In layman's terms, hyper-evolution, large jumps, as we see in our distinguished ape-man."

"Thank you for your inquiry, though, Ms. Chapel," Darkin said. "It's essential for us to deal with all the tough questions. People need to be sure this find is genuine, and I believe there can be no doubt about the validity of Ararat Man." Darkin turned toward Barrows. "Thank you Dr. Barrows. You've given a spectacular gift to the world."

Darkin began to applaud, and the rest of the crowd joined in.

Barrows stepped down from the platform and shook hands with Darkin.

Branch saw Linda fuming. She looked as though she wanted a piece of Barrows, and maybe Darkin. And anyone else who got in her way. Branch decided it was time to leave. He muscled his way through the crowd and grabbed Linda's arm.

He started pulling her, but she resisted. "Come on," he said, "the museum has a rule against punching out professors."

"No, they don't. Let me go. I'm gonna eat his bacon."

"You're gonna what?" he said with a grin.

"Oh shush," Linda said, as she became more docile, allowing herself to be led. "I was trying to sound tough."

"Oh," he said, amused by her effort.

The JJs were standing near the end of the platform. As Branch and Linda passed by, Jerry spoke to Julie loud enough for Linda and Branch to hear. "Some of these Christians are so backward." Julie smiled but seemed embarrassed when Linda shot the JJs a menacing glance.

Linda started pulling away, and Branch was now almost dragging her. "Come on Rocky," he said.

"Did you hear what he said?"

"Let it go. Aren't Christians supposed to turn the other cheek, offer the right hand of fellowship and all that?"

"I'd like to give him the right hand of fellowship. Resulting in a fat lip." She fumed for a few moments as they walked, and then, "Imagine, calling me backward. He's the one who believes in evolution."

They were soon joined by Roddy. "Hey, pretty cool name for a missing link, isn't it—Ararat Man."

Linda stared at him. "*Et tu*, Roddy?"

"Well, it's just a bunch of bones anyway. Some from a human, some from a chimp."

"Of course," said Linda. "I bet they took two skeletons and put bones from each one together so they could claim to have found a missing link."

"You were not observant," said Branch. "I read some signs while Dr. Barrows was giving his pompous speech."

"You thought he was pompous? I thought he was pompous! I'm sorry. You were saying."

"According to the signs they videotaped the whole excavation. They did find those bones in a space where the entrance was not accessible by anyone larger than a seven-year-old."

"Still a hoax."

To avoid driving in Chicago's dense traffic, and having to find their way around, they took a taxi. They left Benjamin's Mercedes at the museum parking lot. The Burnham Park Harbor, where they'd find the next piece, was close by. The three all sat in the back seat with Linda in the middle. They rode in silence for awhile until Roddy spoke.

"Linda, if you don't mind my asking, why are you so sure the exhibit's a fake?"

"Roddy, if there was one missing link, there'd be more, millions more. They'd dominate the fossil record."

"So you're sure this one isn't real."

"Roddy, listen," Linda said, as she turned to face him. "The history of evolution is riddled with frauds. For instance, in 1922, Henry Osborn, the director of the American Museum of Natural History made a find in western Nebraska. He claimed he found a fossil molar tooth from a creature who was part man and part ape. So ecstatic were the evolutionists, who wanted it to be true, that a picture of the whole Nebraska Man was drawn. The artist even included his habitat, and his wife and children."

"Amazing," said Roddy. "How could they do that from one tooth?"

"They couldn't. It was a combination of arrogance and imagination. And imagine their embarrassment when it was finally proven the tooth came from a pig!"

Roddy laughed. "A pig? No kidding?"

Branch was looking out the back window. "I'm not sure, but I think maybe someone's following." Roddy turned to look, and Linda scrunched down in the seat.

After a moment, Branch said, "Never mind. I'm just being overly vigilant. No one knows we're here. Go on with your little spiel, Linda." Roddy faced forward, and Linda sat up.

"Piltdown Man," Linda went on, "was discovered in Sussex, England, in 1912. It was considered to be one of the most significant fossils allegedly proving evolution. Forty-one years later the skull was shown to have been chemically treated to make it appear older, and someone had even filed down the teeth."

"Okay," said Branch. "So there's some dishonesty among scientists. Besides, that was a long time ago."

"But it's typical, and that kind of thing still goes on. I'm sure you both know about Lucy."

"The ape-woman," said Roddy.

"The museum in St. Louis had a replica of Lucy built, based on the bones they have. They gave Lucy human-like hands and feet but with a lot of extra hair. Turns out, Lucy has the wrist and big toe of a chimpanzee. The director of the museum is aware of this, as well as the fact that Lucy isn't even female. But the exhibit cost them seventeen million dollars. So he refuses to make the necessary changes, which, of course, would render it worthless."

Branch glanced at her. "I don't think we can write off the whole idea of evolutionary fossils just because some of them are fakes."

"If the evolutionists had anything genuine they wouldn't get so excited every time there's an alleged find. And the science text books wouldn't be filled with lies and frauds which are the only support they have for evolution."

Roddy said, "Lying always ends in people getting hurt."

"You couldn't be more right," Roddy. "Have either of you ever heard of Ota Benga?"

Branch and Roddy looked past Linda, at each other, and then shook their heads.

"He was a Pygmy living in the Congo at a time when Americans were unaware of these little people. In 1904, he was captured by an evolutionary researcher and taken to America, to the Saint Louis World Fair. He was displayed as 'the closest intermediate link to man.' Two years later he was taken to the Bronx Zoo and put on exhibit with apes. The zoo's director gave speeches bragging about the magnificent 'transitional form' he'd acquired."

"Must've been such a nightmare for him," Roddy said.

"He committed suicide. He had a wife and two children. And considering how he'd been treated, I guess you might say his name was ironic."

Roddy watched Linda, waiting for her to finish.

"In his language, Ota Benga means friend."

They again rode in silence.

Chapter Six

That evening, they ate a meal at the Cafe Spiaggia—an Italian restaurant on North Michigan Avenue. After some shopping by Linda at Bloomingdale's, also on Chicago's Magnificent Mile, they took a taxi to the Burnham Park Harbor.

At the water's edge, they found a man with wild curly hair. Branch was sure the man's lively colored shirt would make a Hawaiian blush.

Branch asked, "Are you Wile E. Coyote?"

"That's right, and I suspect you're the Pyramid Gang."

"Indeed we are."

Roddy said, "Is that your real name?"

Wile chuckled. "Yes. Most people call me Wiley."

They all shook hands, and Wiley escorted them into his dinghy. They rode between the north and south moorings and took a left down a path between boats. Wiley's was on their left. It was much bigger than most and parked at the end of one of the rows of transient docking.

On the yacht, they made themselves comfortable below deck. They sat in a circle, with Branch and Linda all but hugging opposite ends of a sofa. The four of them drank strawberry smoothies. A desk sat across the room, and a downward spiral staircase occupied a far corner.

"So Wiley," Branch said, "tell us about yourself."

"I used to work for the CIA. Before I realized they were evil." Wiley spoke in a hyper-urgent manner, using his hands as if trying to shape each word. "I was a code breaker. One day I intercepted what I believed was coming from a UFO."

"Why did you think the source was a UFO?" Branch asked.

"It was coming from 10,000 miles up, so I checked, but no planes were flying in the vicinity. While attempting to decipher the message, I was taken aside and warned not to continue. I wanted to know why and when I kept pressing for answers they gave me two options. I could retire and live a comfortable life. Or be terminated."

"Unusual options," said Branch.

"My employer liked me. I chose door number one and asked for a yacht." He spread his hands indicating they were sitting in it. "I requested beach front property in southern California for the colder months, and a half million dollars a year. To my amazement, I got everything I asked for."

"Guess he liked you a *lot*," Roddy said.

Wiley shrugged. "He's also married to my sister. You don't want to cross her." He evoked smiles from his three guests and even a slight titter from Linda.

"Anyway, since then I've been working at my hobby full time."

"What is your hobby?" asked Linda.

"The study of numbers in Scripture and their significance."

"Oh?" she said, perking up. "Tell me about it."

"Here we go," Branch said, under his breath.

"The number seven, for instance," Wiley said. "It's the number for perfection or completeness; used like no other number. In the Bible, seven appears 287 times; that's seven times forty-one. The fractional part, seventh, is used ninety-eight times; which is seven times seven times two. And seven-fold shows up seven times. When you add the number of times used for each number, you get 392. That's seven squared plus seven to the third power. You also have seventy which is found fifty-six times, and that's seven times eight. Seventy in combination with other numbers is in scripture a total of thirty-five times, seven times five."

Branch looked at his watch.

Wiley went on: "In creation it's fascinating to note that there are seven continents and seven colors in the rainbow. There are seven basic musical notes: do, re, me, fa, so, la, and te. In science, the periodic table contains seven rows of numbers. Between acidity and alkalinity the pH value is seven.

"I could go on and on about the ubiquity of this number, such as the fact that the international code for direct calls to Russia and Kazakhstan is seven."

"Wait a minute," Branch said. "How relevant is that?"

"Just wanted to see if you were paying attention."

"Busted!" Linda said. "Caught paying attention after feigning lack of interest."

Wiley continued. "The number seven permeates Scripture. Beginning with Creation's seven days and ending with Revelation's seven seals. The number six represents the weakness of man or the manifestation of evil. I'm sure most people are familiar with the number 666, the number of one of the beasts in Revelation. But I doubt that many are aware the number for Christ is 888. Eight represents new birth or new beginnings. Like seven, three represents completeness or perfection. Which might be why there are three eights for the Christ, and three six's for the beast.

"You mean Antichrist, don't you?" said Linda.

"How many times do you think the word Antichrist appears in Revelation?"

"I don't know. I never counted."

"I can tell you exactly. Zero! Antichrist is found in John's epistles four times but not in Revelation. It's one of the two beasts that has the number. Along the way some joker decided the two were one and the same. But this isn't so."

"Interesting," Linda said. "I'm fascinated. Tell us more about numbers."

"All right, here's an intriguing one. Eleven is the number of disorder and judgment. In Exodus, Moses pronounced eleven judgments on Egypt."

"Wait a minute," said Roddy. "I thought there were ten."

"I'm sure most others would say the same. But the encounter at the Red Sea was the eleventh and final judgment."

Roddy smiled and nodded.

"Next we could mention the curse on Canaan, son of Ham, when Noah became angry with Ham," Wiley said. "Canaan had eleven sons. The number of sons is significant. Jacob had twelve sons and Jesus had twelve apostles. Twelve is the number for governmental perfection. But I digress." Wiley waved his hand. "Back to eleven. The 254th day of the year is September 11. If you add two, five, & four, you get eleven. September 11 to December 31 is a span of 111 days."

He glanced at Branch who was shaking his head with a look of mild disgust. Wiley smiled and went on. "Flight 11 hit the World Trade Center first and the plane had a crew of 11. New York was the eleventh state to sign the constitution. And the World Trade Center was built over a period of 11 years."

Branch twisted in his seat. "A lot of coincidences, nothing more."

"Maybe so," Wiley said. "But it *is* interesting."

"I suppose, but we came here to retrieve the next piece of our little pyramid."

"I thought we agreed to call it the MacGuffin," Roddy said.

"Yes, of course," Wiley said. He went to a safe in the corner. After a few flicks of the dial, he cranked the handle and pulled the door open. He reached inside and retrieved a lock-box. It measured about twelve-inches wide, by four-inches high, and eight-inches deep. After setting it on top of the safe, he went to the nearby wall. He took several books off the shelf and knocked on the wall: first, three times, then twice and four times. A four-inch square swung open from the wall. Wiley reached in and retrieved a key.

He went to the lock-box and opened it with the key. He took out what looked like a small jewelry box with a digital display. He started punching numbers.

Roddy was amused. "Should we come back tomorrow?"

Wiley smiled and said, "No. Almost done."

The box opened, and Wiley took out a piece similar to the other two pieces of the pyramid, except larger and differently shaped.

Branch dug the platform with its two pieces out of his jacket pocket. He started to move toward Wiley when Wiley's piece jumped from his hand. It stuck to a corner of the platform, joining itself to one of the others.

"Wow!" said Roddy. "They never jumped so far."

Wiley said, "I think the pulling power increases exponentially as the pyramid grows in size."

"We better be on our way," Branch said.

As Branch turned an open can of gasoline sailed through the door, into the cabin. A shotgun blast blew out a window at the port side, then another, followed by a third window. An open can of gasoline was hurled through each of the windows.

Wiley ran to a closet. "I have guns."

"I would suggest fire extinguishers," said Branch, pointing to the sofa.

Branch, Linda, and Roddy ran for the sofa. As if with one mind, they jumped on, pushing it over, with the back of the couch crashing to the floor. The three crouched and dragged the cushions over them.

Wiley looked over his shoulder as he opened a closet door. As he did so, the flaming ejection of a flare gun shot through one of the blown out windows. Wiley shut himself in the closet as the flare ignited the gas. A loud whoosh and an inundation of flames flooded the air, stealing the oxygen and replacing it with smoke.

Wiley came out of the closet, carrying two fire extinguishers. He tossed one to Branch as Branch stood. Roddy came up from the floor and caught the other when Wiley tossed it. Fresh air rushed in the windows as the smoke left. Branch and Roddy went around the ends of the sofa and attacked the flames as Wiley went in the closet.

A few moments later, Wiley emerged with a paper bag and two hand-guns. "We need to go downstairs."

Roddy and Branch cleared a path to the staircase, with everyone now coughing as they fled to the lower level.

The air was breathable. Roddy and Branch set the fire extinguishers down, and Wiley handed them the two guns. Wiley was still holding the paper bag. Branch scanned the room for—he didn't know what. A long couch sat against a wall and on the other side of the room was a giant wide screen TV panel.

Linda said, "I don't see another exit."

"We're all out of exits, I'm afraid," Wiley said.

Their situation was dismal, but things got worse as automatic weapons fire tore through the ceiling. They all scattered. Roddy and Branch began a rapid-fire assault on the unseen shooters. The sound of yelling and running followed.

Branch again made a helpless survey of the room. He shook his head. *We seem to be in a rut when it comes to hopeless situations.*

Roddy went by his side. "Trapped again, amigo."

Branch trained his eyes on Wiley. "What's in the bag?"

Wiley reached in and pulled out a hand grenade. "Three of these."

"Good," Roddy said. "If things go from hopeless to more hopeless, we can use them to commit suicide."

Wiley shrugged. "The evil guys have them. I know. I've heard stories."

"Me too," Branch said. "Give me that."

Wiley tossed the grenade, and, pulling out another, tossed it to Roddy, who said, "You keep your grenades in a paper bag?"

Wiley took the last grenade out. "Made from recycled paper. Pays to be responsible." He folded the bag and laid it on an end table.

Branch went to the couch and flung the seat cushions aside. "Take that end of the couch," Branch said to Roddy. "We need to make a canopy."

Roddy and Branch lifted the corners from the bottom and dragged it several feet away from the wall. They tipped the couch and laid it on its back, then grabbed the legs and pulled up, so the couch was resting upside down. Branch knelt on one knee and rested the couch on the other knee.

"Everyone crouch against the wall," Branch said.

They all lined up as he said, between the couch and the wall.

"Now what?" said Wiley. "We're still trapped." He pointed to the ceiling with smoke beginning to come through. "And the fire will be here any minute."

"On three, we'll pull the pins and take out the wall," Branch said, indicating the one with the TV screen.

"Sure, why not?" Wiley said, flippantly.

Branch counted, "One, two, three."

They pulled the pins and tossed the grenades at the wall.

Wiley said, "You realize, of course, we're below sea level."

They all looked at one another, suddenly aware of the obvious.

"Too late for a recall," Roddy said.

"Scrunch!" said Branch.

They each made themselves as small as they could while Branch and Roddy pulled the couch over them.

"I hate this," said Wiley. "My TV screen does Blu-ray and 3-D."

They all covered their ears. The thunderous explosion from the three grenades was followed by a mini-tsunami. It raised up the couch and flooded the underneath in a split second. The four were slapped against the wall. But the couch deflected most of the water's force and spared them from being crushed like empty eggshells.

The four pushed the couch off and swam for the hole. The water was dark and cold. Branch could hardly tell where Linda was next to him, but he stayed as close as he could. Coming up for air, they turned around to see the top of the flaming yacht as it sunk. The four gunmen were all either swimming to their dinghy or climbing in.

The yacht finished sinking, and the last of the fire was doused. The attackers were barely visible.

The four escapees continued to swim for the wall at the north end.

Branch was the first one up. He grabbed Linda's hand and lifted her onto the embankment. Roddy had a little difficulty getting his portly frame up and over, but managed. He then helped Wiley out of the water.

Wiley was gassed and trying to catch his breath. He wheezed, "I have… a safe house… not far… we can walk."

"We'll drive. Our car is at the Field Museum," said Branch.

"Better," Wiley said.

"Let's go before our friends come looking."

Wiley struggled to get to his feet.

Linda was shivering. Branch took off his jacket and put it around Linda's shoulders. Even though the jacket was wet, she was impressed. "Thank you."

The walk to the car took less than ten minutes, but being soaking wet, and with the temperature in the mid-50s, it seemed longer. Wiley's safe house was a room at the Blackstone Hotel. The drive was less than a mile. They brought dry clothes in with them so they could change after they showered. Linda went first while the three men talked.

Wiley had wrapped himself in a blanket and curled up in an overstuffed chair. "Your next contact is Dr. Peter Reed, an astrophysicist in Santa Fe, New Mexico. He works at Los Alamos."

Branch was concerned. "Wiley, are you sure you're gonna be all right here?"

"Of course. Not even my former employer knows about this place. I keep it under an assumed name. Besides, you have the pyramid piece now, so they'll have no interest in me."

"They certainly are interested in us," Roddy said. "They just keep coming. No matter how well we hide, they find us."

"Which raises a question," Branch said. "How'd they locate us this time? No way could they have known we were in Chicago, let alone on Wiley's boat."

"Unless someone spotted you," Wiley said.

"Exactly what I was thinking. We did spend time at the museum and a restaurant."

"And Bloomingdale's," Roddy added.

"Yeah, lest we forget the obligatory shopping excursion." Branch glanced toward the bathroom where Linda was taking a shower. "Probably her fault we were spotted."

"Come on, now," Roddy said. "You know you like her."

"She's become tolerable."

Roddy shook his head with a look of mock disgust.

They showered, put on fresh clothes, and had their wet ones laundered. Later, they stood in the lobby of the Blackstone, ready to leave. Roddy and Wiley shook hands.

"Watch your backs," Wiley said. "I think there might be an infiltrator in the Pyramidions."

Branch and Linda faced each other as Linda glanced at Branch's jacket slung over his arm. "Thanks again for the use of your jacket."

He nodded.

"It was gallant of you."

He smiled, slightly.

"Who knew?" she said.

"Guess I'm not all bad."

"Not quite."

They climbed into the Mercedes and headed southwest, toward New Mexico.

They drove just over three hours until they reached Springfield at 2AM. Branch felt more secure having put some distance between them and their pursuers. He also took solace in the fact that Brussel and company had no way to determine which direction their quarry was headed. Unless, of course, they found Wiley and tortured him into telling what he knew. Branch chose not to share that possible scenario with Linda.

Sitting in his motel room, Branch sat on the edge of his bed pondering recent events. Could this Ararat man be the missing link the evolutionists had been looking for? Was the Earth really at the center of the universe? He broke from his reverie and glanced at Roddy when his friend laughed at something his wife had said. They were visiting on Skype. Roddy was beginning to feel guilty for being gone so long, but Christine was a most understanding wife. Roddy was lucky to have her, and for that reason, Branch liked her. She, however, considered him a rogue.

Branch began to wonder what Linda thought of him—deep down, that is, when she wasn't giving him a hard time. He frowned. *Why should I care? She's a pain in the neck.*

They spent the next night in Oklahoma City and went on to Santa Fe in the morning. They arrived at Dr. Reed's house on the outskirts of town in the late afternoon. Branch parked the Mercedes a quarter of a mile away.

It was too warm to wear his jacket, which lay on the console between the front seats. Branch took the tiny partial pyramid out of the pocket and gave it to Linda to put in her purse.

He was becoming ever more wary and told Linda to stay in the car while he and Roddy went to the house on foot. Branch and Roddy retrieved two Glock handguns stashed in a secret compartment under the floor of the trunk.

Roddy and Branch approached the adobe ranch house from opposite sides with almost no cover, a boulder here, a cactus there. They'd be spotted if anyone was looking out a window.

Branch sidled up next to the building gripping his Glock. He sneaked up to a window and peered into a bedroom. Through an open door, Branch saw part of someone in the next room, in a chair, at a desk.

He crept to the rear and found the door wasn't locked. His eyes darted around the kitchen as he entered. He moved toward the next room as he now felt perspiration sliding down one side of his face. Branch exited the kitchen and was now standing behind the man at the desk. The man was working at a computer.

The front door burst open and Roddy dove into the room. He hit the hardwood floor on his right shoulder, rolling over, and coming up on one knee. He held the Glock tight in hand.

"Nice shoulder roll, Mr. Rodriguez. And you, Mr. Nichols," the man said without looking over his shoulder, "may enter too. The shoulder roll is optional, but I must warn you I haven't swept in over a month."

"Dr. Reed, I presume," Branch said.

"The one and only."

Branch stepped toward Reed while he said to Roddy, "Go wave Linda in."

Roddy stood and brushed off his right shoulder. "Over a month, huh?" He brushed the floor dust off his knee.

"Sorry, I guess I should have just invited you in." He pointed to monitors mounted on the wall. "I saw you coming."

"The Swiss Doc had those, too," Roddy said.

"Careful alertness is a must for a Pyramidion," Reed said. "Especially these days."

Roddy went out the front door.

"Sit down, Mr. Nichols. I'll be with you in a moment. Just finishing my blog for today."

Branch sat in a stuffed chair as Reed typed away on his computer. After a minute or so he swung around in his swivel chair. His white hair and yellow shirt contrasted his sun-bronzed face and arms.

"Sorry about the entrance," Branch said, "but we've been stalked by a persistent handful of gunmen."

"Brussel and Mitch Wallach."

"You're familiar with them."

"You shouldn't worry about them so much as the one holding their leash."

"And he is...?"

Roddy and Linda entered.

"Hello, Miss Chapel."

"I hope these two didn't startle you, Dr. Reed."

Roddy and Linda sat on a sofa.

"No. I enjoyed watching them. Stealthy move behind the little cactus, Mr. Rodriguez."

Roddy gave an embarrassed smile.

"You were saying," Branch said, "you know who controls Brussel?"

"Darkin. Third-rate biologist."

Linda said. "I'm sure he engineered the fraud at the museum, too."

"They have a convincing find, Miss Chapel. Although from what I've been reading on the internet, there's one loose end."

"What's that?" Branch asked.

"A small Christian TV station sent a news team out to interview the boy who found the bones." He paused, adding drama to the moment. "The boy and his entire family have disappeared. Without a trace."

"So, the plot thickens," Linda said.

"Yes, and the plot will thicken for the three of you in ways you can't imagine. You'll be on a thrill ride, yes, but your journey will also take you into a reality few are aware of. You'll see what the world has become. You'll discover the cruel consequences of the nightmare religion known as evolution."

Reed's three guests sat transfixed. They wondered just how much trouble they'd gotten themselves into.

Branch was as usual, skeptical. "You seem to have a lot more knowledge about all this than any of the other Pyramidions we've met. Why?"

"I'm a member of the Leadership Council. I need to tell you things so you'll begin to realize whom you're up against. First, you need to know the truth about NASA."

"Oh, come on, Dr. Reed," Branch said. "Are you going tell us about some conspiracy theory involving rocket scientists?"

"The rocket scientists are pawns of NASA, which is itself a pawn in a much larger fabric of intrigue. Their mission is to prove evolution. Which is the reason NASA exists."

"You're serious?" Branch said.

"They need to prove the existence of life on other planets as the source of life on this planet. Darwinism has become untenable. So they now want to make people believe aliens seeded the Earth and gave evolution a kick-start."

Linda scooted forward on the sofa and leaned toward Dr. Reed in her most urgent sermonizing pose. "But that's dodging the issue. They still have to explain where the aliens came from. The questions are still the same. How did life start? How did the universe get here?"

"Perhaps not. They'd create a stall mode, claiming we can't be sure of the answers until the aliens come and tell us."

"They're still dodging the issue."

"That's what evolutionists do best."

Branch was doubtful but curious. "How are they gonna accomplish their plan?"

"I'm not sure, but something's going on that involves computers. You'll want to track down a programmer named Harlan Wilson. He worked at NASA for several years before he left. Reason unknown. Whereabouts unknown."

"How do we find him?" Branch asked.

Reed shrugged. "You're resourceful. You'll find a way."

Thanks a lot.

Roddy spoke up. "How's a biologist have his own hit-man? Aren't they pretty expensive?"

"Darkin is a millionaire, born into money. An only child. His father was a wealthy entrepreneur, his parents died when he was young. He had three uncles—all childless—who were also successful and wealthy. After Darkin finished college, they started dying off rather fortuitously, and he got everything."

"I get the impression you think he had something to do with their deaths," Roddy said.

"I have no proof, but I'm sure he's the one Brussel and Wallach are working for."

"If he's a millionaire, why does he work? I wouldn't." Roddy grinned.

"Even the wealthy take on careers. He was interested in science, and biology was all he had brains for."

"Don't you gotta be smart?"

"Physicists have a saying: Physics is the only real science. All the rest is stamp collecting."

"And you're one of the real scientists."

"Astrophysicist. Or as I sometimes like to say, glorified physicist."

"Don't be modest," Branch said.

"I'm an intellectual reprobate. Physicists possess bigger brains than everyone else and, therefore, bigger egos. Unlike most others, I'm willing to admit to this glaring fault."

Branch said, "So why is Darkin trying to have us killed?"

"Not sure, but he'd like to get his hands on the little pyramid you're putting together."

"They were trying to kill us at Giza even before we had the platform for the pyramid."

"True. The inscription you photographed on the wall must be something they don't want known. But I believe putting the pyramid together is more urgent. So, without further ado, the next piece is in that potted plant." He pointed to a pot with several cactuses.

"Shouldn't you hide it better?" Roddy said.

"I learned from Edgar Allen Poe—the original mystery writer—and his story *The Purloined Letter*."

"Hidden in plain sight," Branch said.

"Right."

Linda took the platform, with its adhering pieces, from her purse and held it out toward the cacti. From across the room, the piece jumped from among the plants and onto the platform.

"Now, that was scary," Reed said.

The new piece was shaped like the first two and took over the fourth corner of the platform. Linda put it back in her purse.

"Five more pieces and you'll have a complete pyramid," Reed said. "You'll need to go to California next. My niece, Wendy is an assistant curator at the Natural History Museum of Los Angeles. She can tell you where the next piece is hidden."

"She doesn't have it?" Branch asked.

"No. She told me it's with the Egyptians."

Roddy said, "We have to go back to Egypt?"

"No. Somewhere in the U.S. but I don't know what she means by the Egyptians."

"What's her address?" Branch said.

"She wants you to come to the museum so she can show you what Darkin has hidden. You won't be disappointed, I promise."

"Can you tell us what it is?" Linda asked.

"And spoil the surprise? Wouldn't think of it."

"Dr. Reed," Branch said, "you told us you're one of the leaders of the Pyramidions. Doesn't that make you a distinctive target?"

"Yes, I know far too much for my own good, and I think they're getting close to finding me. Don't worry, though, I have an exit strategy."

"Are you sure it will work?" Roddy said. "Can we help?"

"It's foolproof." Reed said. Then he pushed himself up straight in his chair, and with his elbows still on the armrests folded his hands as he leaned forward just a bit. "Now I want to share something with you that has me concerned if you don't mind."

"Go ahead, Dr. Reed," Branch said.

"What if I told you that NASA might be right?"

"Come on," Linda said, "you don't really think we're being visited by aliens from some other world, do you?"

"A friend of mine went missing. He was investigating Area 51 and wound up in Hinsdale County, in southwestern Colorado. I can't imagine why he would go there. His last text message said he'd made a discovery that'd change all the rules. He hasn't been heard from since."

"Is he reliable?" Branch said.

"Depends on your definition of reliable. His name is Warren Hanley."

"Hanley? Loose cannon, shaggy blond hair?"

"That would be him."

Branch looked at Linda and Roddy. "I used to work with him." He turned his attention to Reed. "I thought he was dead with everyone else."

"Hanley got out three days before the mass assassination." Reed opened a drawer and took out something that resembled an iPod. "In case you want to look for him, take this. It's a tracking device. He had a GPS installed in his wristwatch."

Branch took the device. "Thank you. I would like to find Hanley. He's not only a friend, but the only other survivor from the agency. Maybe he has an idea of what they were on to. How was he traveling?"

"He flew a plane to Lake City and landed just west of town. He walked to the Jeep rental place and headed into the mountains."

"Thank you, Dr. Reed. We'll be going now." He turned to Roddy and Linda. "I suggest we look for Hanley, first, before going to California. Lake City is around 300 miles from here, about a six hour drive."

Linda said, "How do you know that, just off the top of your head?"

"I've been there. Investigating my father's murder."

"Didn't you say he was found in the Mojave?"

"When he left Area 51 in Nevada, he was headed to Lake City, Colorado."

Branch turned to Reed and shook his hand. "Thank you."

Reed said, "Good luck finding Hanley. Tell that unguided missile I said hello."

"Will do," Branch said.

The three headed out the door, but Branch stopped and turned around to face Reed. "Are you sure you'll be all right? You can come with us."

"I'd only be a hindrance. Besides, I have my foolproof exit strategy."

The three climbed into Benjamin's Mercedes and drove away. Reed waved goodbye and went inside.

Roddy was driving, and Branch rode shotgun. Linda curled up in the back seat. "Wake me when we arrive," she said.

Branch sat up straight. "Turn around, Roddy," he said with urgency.

"You forget something?"

"Turn around," he shouted.

Roddy slammed on the brakes and whipped the car around in a hard U-turn.

"Floor it."

Roddy hit the gas.

Linda sat up and leaned forward. "What wrong?"

"I just figured out his exit strategy."

They were barreling toward Reed's home when a massive explosion ripped through the house. Flames swelled and pieces of adobe battered the car as Roddy brought the Mercedes skidding to a halt.

They just sat for a while and watched.

Chapter Seven

The three drove north into Colorado, into Hinsdale County.

Linda was reading a brochure she'd picked up at the last gas station. "Hey, guys, listen to this. Hinsdale County has been designated as the remotest place in the contiguous U.S. Hinsdale County is one of the few places left where you can be more than ten miles from a road. It says here 95 percent is federal land and much of the county is still unexplored." She folded up the brochure and leaned toward the front seat. "This is the place farthest from civilization of anywhere in the lower forty-eight states."

They drove into Lake City, which is surrounded by many 14,000 ft. peaks of the San Juan Mountains. They found Farabee's Jeep and Polaris RZR "RaZoR" Rentals. The trails were rated by four classifications. The first three were Easy, Moderate, and Challenging. Hanley had taken a RaZoR since he wanted something for the fourth—rated Difficult. The description for this one was: "Experienced 4-wheelers only. Solo travel not recommended. Vehicle damage possible..." Branch decided against doing the same. He asked where someone might land a plane on the west side of town and got directions.

Driving through town, Branch didn't see a single building over two stories. Unless you counted the steeples on two of the churches he saw. They found the Cessna 172 parked in an open area just big enough for takeoffs and landings. It was a four-seater, so Linda sat behind Roddy.

"How safe are we in this?" Linda asked.

"Don't worry," Roddy said. "More Cessna 172s have been built than any other plane."

"I'm only concerned about this one. And our pilot."

Branch turned with a smile. "Hey, I hardly ever crash."

"Yeah." Linda sat back and fastened her seat belt.

They flew over the mountainous terrain, following the GPS signal.

"We're way off the trails," Roddy said. "And there's no place to land when we do find him."

"One conundrum at a time," Branch said.

"So," Linda said, "you're perplexed and confused but won't admit it."

"I protest," said Branch.

"Protest what?" Linda said.

"Perplexed and confused have the same meaning."

They'd been flying for an hour when they spotted a curious anomaly.

Branch said, "The flat, white area below doesn't seem right. It's large enough to land. What do you think?"

"The GPS signal is right below us," Roddy said. "Doesn't make sense. Why don't we see him?"

"Let's find out." Branch started his approach.

Linda said, "You think this is a good idea? I mean, how could anything so vast and flat be here, anyway?"

Branch didn't bother to answer, but went ahead and landed.

When they'd all climbed out of the plane, Branch said, "Not rock; not dirt. I don't know what we're standing on."

"Must be about twenty acres' worth," said Roddy.

They walked in three different directions, not quite knowing what to search for until Linda cried out. "Here! I found something."

Roddy and Branch ran to where Linda was standing. "Look," she said, pointing.

Branch and Roddy squatted and took hold of handles indented in the surface. They pulled open a hatch revealing a three foot wide, seven foot long opening with metal stairs beneath.

"A stairway inside a mountain," said Roddy. "A little unusual."

Branch took the GPS tracker out of his pocket. "He's down there, or at least his wrist watch is." Suddenly, the signal stopped. "That's not good." Branch looked at Roddy, knowing he didn't even have to ask his friend if he wanted to continue on.

He knew they both would search for Hanley until they found him, but he was sensing danger. "We better move ahead carefully." He glanced at Linda.

Roddy considered Linda, as well. "I think you should stay here, Missy."

"No way I'm staying here alone," Linda said. "I'm going, too. Although, we can skip the 'ladies first' amenity this time."

Branch stepped down onto the first step and started his descent. He found a large open space, about a half acre, with doors at three of the walls.

He had to go down about three stories to a concrete floor. Roddy was right behind him, and Linda was close behind Roddy. Branch peeked over his shoulder and saw that Linda's eyes were wide with apprehension.

"We'll split up," Branch said.

"Each of the three walls has one or more doors," Linda said. "So, what are we saying? We each pick a wall?"

"No. You stay with me," said Branch.

"Gotcha!"

"You're not gonna argue?"

"Nope."

Branch smiled as he turned away. *Why couldn't it always be this easy?*

He and Roddy gave each other a good luck nod as they parted ways.

Branch picked a door at random to open. No locks, no alarms. *They aren't expecting any unwanted visitors.*

They went down an empty corridor and decided to turn left. Going through another door, they entered what appeared to be a lounge area. It had vending machines and several small tables, each surrounded by chairs. They started to walk across when they heard a voice.

"Can I help you?"

Branch and Linda turned and in a shadow in a corner of the room they spotted a man sitting in an easy chair, smoking a cigar. The man put out the cigar in a floor stand ash tray, stood, and stepped toward them.

Branch was relieved since the man appeared unintimidating. He was elderly, unarmed, and had a gentle way about him. "I'm Holloway, head of security. What brings you here?"

Branch said, "We're looking for a man who hunts UFOs. Got any around?"

"UFOs, or UFO hunters?"

"Either one."

"You're interested in flying saucers. Would you like me to show you one?"

Branch and Linda exchanged a quick glance, and then Branch said, "Sure."

"Follow me," he said.

Branch and Linda followed him out a door, up one corridor, and down another. Holloway talked in a low voice on a BlackBerry as they walked.

"You get a signal here?" Linda said. "Who's your provider?"

"Has a special technology. I could get a signal from the center of the Earth."

When Holloway opened another door, he led them into another hangar-like area.

They stopped cold. Branch's eyebrows rose and a wide smile ensued. Linda took a step back and placed her fingertips over her mouth. Her eyes blinked twice and segued into an open stare. Holloway observed them as his eyes squinted with a twinkle of mischief.

Sitting in the center of the hangar was what could only be described as a flying saucer. Standing over twenty feet high, the anomalous craft stretched sixty feet in diameter at the middle. It looked like something you'd see in a comic book. Like an upside-down bowl on top of an upside-down plate. With that resting on top of a plate, right side up, on top of a bowl, right side up. That's how Branch had always described the popular version of a UFO.

"Unbelievable," Linda said. "This can't be real."

"Typical reaction," said Branch.

"Extraterrestrials aren't visiting our planet. So this is a—"

"Fraud?" Holloway said. "No, the spacecraft is real, but you're right about the extraterrestrials. None has ever visited from another planet, and I'm pretty sure none ever will."

Branch stared quizzically. "So you're saying..."

"Built right here by humans. Mostly German ingenuity."

"I hunted these things for fifteen years," Branch said. "I had begun to think maybe the whole idea of flying saucers was a myth." Branch gazed in wonder like a small boy. He'd finally found what he'd always believed was the ultimate prize. "What's the history on this?"

"Work started on them in the 1940s right after the war. The incident in 1947 near area 51 was a crash of one of the experimental saucers."

Linda said, "Not a special type of weather balloon used for spying on Russia?"

Holloway laughed. "You'd have no way to guide them over specific targets. You're talking about random photos taken over thousands of miles of terrain. Would the cameras even work in such extreme cold? And how good were the lenses seventy years ago?"

"What about the cover-up?" Linda asked.

"They dropped hints about an alien space craft and let the public run with the idea. A fake alien—a little green man—was created. Hospital personnel, who were in on the subterfuge, pretended to make an attempt to save said alien. A random nurse was allowed to get a peek at the spectacle. After she spread the story, she was disposed of."

"What about abductions?" Branch asked.

"Every now and then, someone's kidnapped, and later convinced they were abducted by aliens."

Branch tensed, realizing his own grandmother had been a victim. Though he'd never known her, he still wanted to get his hands on somebody.

"Why is such a thing even necessary?" Linda asked.

"Preparing the way for the future. When terrorism has run its course, just as the cold war did, a threat of alien invasion will do quite nicely."

"For what?" Branch said.

Holloway hesitated, giving only a hint of a smile.

Branch said, "You look like the proverbial cat subsequent to the canary acquisition."

Finally, Holloway said, "I wouldn't want to spoil the surprise."

Branch wasn't sure if Holloway was trying to sound ominous or if he knew something that might change the world.

"Thanks for the tour," Branch said. "We'd like to collect our friend now and be on our way."

"You don't think I can let you go, do you? You've been to the honeycomb. Besides, your plane is already being disposed of."

"No offense, but you don't strike me as being all that dangerous."

"No offense taken. But you need to check out the gentlemen behind you."

Branch and Linda turned around and met two of the largest human beings they had ever seen. They were well over six feet, and each had a body like Mr. Olympia.

Branch turned back toward Holloway. "These aren't the biggest goons you could find, are they?"

Holloway seemed to consider the question for a moment, and then, "No, but they'll do."

Holloway walked between Branch and Linda. "Follow me," he said.

Branch thought discretion over valor would most likely be the better choice and started to follow. Linda grabbed Branch's arm with both hands and walked with him. Branch glanced down at her, more than a bit surprised.

"Don't read anything in," she said. "I'm just terrified."

"We've been in trouble before."

"Not the same. When you're dodging bullets, you don't have time to be this scared. Right now, it's all about suspense. I don't do well with suspense in real life. Just novels."

After several turns, Holloway led them down one final hallway and stopped at a metal door. In front was a security man of normal size. The guard removed a key from his belt and opened the door.

"Go right inside," Holloway said.

They entered with Linda still clinging to Branch's arm.

In a corner, sitting on a cot, Branch spotted a thick head of shaggy blond hair. The owner was reading a Clive Cussler novel, *Sahara*. The man on the cot lowered the book and smiled. *Hanley.*

"Branch, you loser, what are you doing here?"

"I'm part of a rescue party."

The door slammed shut behind them.

Branch went to his old friend, who stood, and they shook hands.

Hanley leered at Linda. "Yeah, she can rescue me, anytime."

"This is Linda."

"Yours?" Hanley said, looking at Linda's hands still clinging to Branch's arm.

She released her hold. "I'm not anybody's."

Branch said, "You've seen the saucer?"

"Been inside. Checked it out. Even found a manual for take-offs and landings, weaponry, and a recipe for sushi."

"Well, you got a lot farther than we did."

"Holloway caught me playing Captain Kirk, introduced me to the steroid twins, and here I am. As you can see, we have plenty of cots to go around and a bathroom," he said, pointing. Hanley stared at Linda. "In case you want to freshen up."

Linda surveyed the bathroom from where she was standing. "The one without the door."

Hanley scrutinized her. "You're a complainer, aren't you?"

She stared, tight lipped and squinting hard as if she could do him harm with just her gaze.

Hanley held up a broken wrist watch, solving the mystery of the discontinued GPS signal. "Either of you know the time?"

They heard a thud, as though something, or someone, had hit the door.

"Guess we can leave, now," Branch said.

A few moments later, the door opened.

Roddy entered, "Someone order a pizza?"

"You brought Roddy," Hanley said. "Outstanding!" He walked over and shook hands with Roddy.

"What took you?" Branch said.

"Sorry. I found a kitchen, and I was hungry." He removed a partially eaten sandwich from inside his jacket. "So, I put this together." He took a bite. "The food here is terrific."

Hanley put his hand on Roddy's shoulder as he looked back at Branch. "You guys are some rescue team. One gets caught because he can't take his eyes off the girl, and the other stops off for lunch."

Hanley hurried out the door, stepping over the unconscious guard.

Branch noticed Linda staring back at him, and said, "I don't know what he was talking about." He hurried out the door.

As Linda hurried past Roddy, she mumbled to herself. "A cowboy and now a gunslinger." She went out the door.

Roddy glanced around the empty room. "You're welcome." He followed the others out.

When they came to the flying saucer, Hanley stopped and gazed in wonder. "I'm gonna put my name on the license plate."

"Another time," Branch said. "Right now, we need to get to your Jeep so we can escape."

"Oh, they confiscated my ride, and if we try to climb down the mountain, they'll catch us or kill us for sure."

"We need a way out of here."

"You're looking at it."

"The saucer?"

"You remember I was in the space program, don't you?"

"I remember you were kicked out of the space program. With extreme prejudice."

"Yeah, but not before I learned how to fly a space shuttle. The controls in this are real similar."

Hanley charged up the stairs to the opening at the side of the bottom half of the saucer. The others went up after him. Once they were all inside, Hanley pushed a button, which closed a sliding door. The wall was an array of consoles, screens, and light panels filling the entire perimeter of the ship. A padded bench went around, as well. In the middle of the cabin was a circular staircase.

Hanley led as all four went up the stairs to the top level. They found a half-dozen seats. One was at a set of controls at the front of the ship. Two more seats sat on either side and behind the first. Three more sat behind them.

A window went all the way around.

Roddy peered down to the hangar floor. "Hey, gang, we got some admirers."

Hanley fiddled with controls. "Do they happen to resemble Holloway and company?"

"Sure do. He's just standing there with arms folded."

"He thinks we're trapped, that we can't fly this thing."

Linda stepped next to Hanley. "Please tell me you can."

He stared her in the eye. "I can fly this. Probably. Maybe. I mean it's not exactly... Look, let me work here. I'm figuring things out."

"Have you figured out how to get the ship out of here?" She stepped to the window and pointed at the ceiling of the hangar.

"One thing at a time."

Roddy stood at the window smiling and waving.

Branch said, "Roddy, stop antagonizing them."

"What? He's waving back."

They heard a sound below. Branch ran to the staircase. "The hatch is opening up."

"They're using an override," Hanley said. "I'll fix it. But first, hit that button," he said, pointing.

Branch pushed the button and a panel slid open. He reached in and pulled out an automatic weapon. "Roddy," he said and tossed the gun to him.

"Ruger 1022," Roddy said.

Branch took out another. "Let's get down there."

The two went down the spiral staircase and took positions on either side of the hatch.

"Here they come," Roddy said.

"We don't need to shoot them," Branch said, "just scare them off."

"Right."

They opened fire in the direction of three security men, who fired back as they ran for cover. Roddy and Branch ducked as bullets sprayed into the cabin, pinging off consoles and shattering one of the screens.

"Maybe you should explain the rules to them," Roddy said. "I'm pretty sure they were trying to hit us."

Upstairs, Hanley typed in data, flipped switches, and checked gauges. Several lights started flashing, accompanied by a low hum. "We have ignition. Or whatever it's called in one of these things."

Hanley continued to work, and Linda went to the window on the other side to check on Holloway. The sound of gunfire from below continued at a steady pace.

"Let's try this," Hanley said, as he flipped another switch. Almost immediately, sunlight flooded the cabin.

"Holloway seems to be panicking," Linda said. He's waving his arms and yelling. Some nerdy-looking guys in white coats are running around."

Linda rejoined Hanley, who pointed up. She gazed at the rising roof.

"I found the garage door opener," Hanley said.

"I'm impressed."

"Enough to give up your boyfriend for me?"

"My what?"

"Come on. I've seen how you look at Branch."

"Look at... I don't look... I mean, we're just... that's absurd."

Hanley grinned. "Yeah, you're head over heels. Excuse me; I need to close the hatch downstairs so we can leave." Hanley went back to work.

"Fine. But just so you know, nothing is going on between Mr. Nichols and me."

"So I've got a chance, then."

"Even less chance than you have of getting us out of here."

"You kidding? I'm on a roll."

"Really? Well, I've got grim news, your garage door is closing."

Hanley directed his attention upward and indeed, their escape portal was shrinking.

"Nuts."

Down below Roddy and Branch each fired off a shot every few seconds. They just wanted to keep the security personnel away from the stairway. But that didn't last long.

"Hey, amigo," Roddy said, holding up the magazine from his weapon, "I'm out. How about you?"

"Yeah, me too. Should have brought a couple of refills, I guess."

"Maybe we should start thinking ahead."

At that moment, the sliding door began to shut.

"Always in a nick of time," said Roddy. "What are the odds?"

Hanley shouted from above. "Get up here, quick. We need to take off right away."

Roddy and Branch dashed up the spiral stairs.

Branch took the seat next to Linda, and Roddy sat in the middle seat behind them.

Hanley worked the controls. He turned to the others and with more swagger than a pirate, he said, "Buckle up, and get ready for the ride of your lives."

They all strapped on their seat belts. Hanley made a few more adjustments.

Roddy surveyed the ceiling outside the craft. "Our escape route is getting pretty tight."

"Thanks for the heads-up, Roddy," Hanley said, with a roll of his eyes.

"No problem."

"Here we go." The hum had become louder. Hanley pulled back on a lever; the hum increased, and then. Nothing. It stopped. "No, no!"

Hanley played with the controls some more but seemed confused.

"Our exit is almost gone," Roddy said.

"I'll get this, don't worry."

"Too late," Linda said.

Hanley glanced up. "We just need to reopen it."

The screen above the keyboard turned to a light green and dark green letters appeared. They read: AN AUTOMATIC INHIBITOR IS TRIGGERED IF ANYTHING GETS IN THE WAY OF THE SAUCER. YOU HAD ONE CHANCE TO ESCAPE AND YOU BLEW IT. TIME TO GIVE UP.

"Holloway, you bum," said Hanley. He typed on the screen: OUR RIDE HAS TEMPORARILY BROKEN DOWN. I'LL HAVE IT FIXED IN A MINUTE. Hanley fumbled with the controls.

Holloway wrote back: NOT GOING TO HAPPEN. THE HANGAR HATCH IS SECURELY LOCKED. YOU CAN'T OVERRIDE.

Hanley wrote: BUT I JUST OVERRODE THE INHIBITOR. WATCH THIS.

Hanley started working the controls with a new vigor.

"Shouldn't we be discussing terms of surrender?" said Roddy.

"Not today," Hanley said.

The saucer began to hum again. Hanley moved the lever and the ship tilted upward reaching a forty-five degree angle. They each rested against the backs of their seats.

Linda's eyes grew wide with panic. "Mr. Hanley, I don't think suicide is our best option."

"Trust me," he said, with a mock evil grin. Hanley reached forward and flipped three switches. Next, he stretched his arm until his hand hovered a couple of inches above a large red button. He looked over his left shoulder at Branch.

Branch's left elbow was on the armrest, with his head resting against his left hand. "You're certifiable. You know that, don't you?"

"Thanks, Branch. You've always been there for me."

Linda had reached full panic mode by this time as she gripped the armrests. "Branch, aren't you gonna tell him to stop?"

"Nah, he wouldn't listen."

Linda turned to Roddy, who nestled in his seat, rested his head against the back, and laid his arms on the armrests. "These chairs are so comfortable."

Linda peered back at Branch, who held out his hands, palms up as if to say, *What do you want from me?*

Linda turned her attention back toward Hanley, who was looking ahead, out the window, at the hangar ceiling. "Prepare to be amazed," he said.

His hand came down on the button as Linda screamed, "No!"

Three bay doors opened on the front lip of the saucer. Cylindrical objects rose out of each one. They rotated, firing bluish, clear pellet-like projectiles at the ceiling. The sound of rushing wind filled the air.

The ceiling exploded in a mass of wreckage that pelted the saucer. The debris bounced off the window, which, for the moment, seemed impenetrable.

Outside the saucer, security men ran in all directions, seeking cover. They dove behind or under anything that appeared protective.

Holloway stood stone-like, a graven image standing against the chaos of his little kingdom.

In the saucer, Hanley raised his hand from the red button and the firing ceased, with debris still falling. "A little more off the top," Hanley said. He pulled back on the lever again and the saucer tipped back some more. He pressed down on the red button and the pummeling commenced once more, ripping the ceiling apart.

After ten more seconds of that, Hanley released the button. Above them was a gaping hole.

"You do nice work," Roddy said.

"Thanks."

Hanley reached to the keyboard and typed, SO LONG, HOLLOWAY. THANKS FOR THE ACCOMMODATIONS.

Hanley did some typing on another keyboard and flipped a few switches. He grabbed a lever like a computer's joy stick, and yanked back.

They shot out of the hangar, climbed high above the mountains and leveled off, heading west.

Back at the hangar, Holloway, stalwart and angry, held up his BlackBerry and typed.

In the saucer, Holloway's message appeared on the screen. YOU'RE DEAD. YOU REALIZE THAT, DON'T YOU?

Hanley said, "Holloway. What a kidder."

"That take off was amazing," Branch said.

"Yeah, we hit 2 Gs coming out of there."

"I didn't feel a thing. How'd we do that?" Branch said.

"The saucer is probably using some form of zero-point gravity to fly. Might have been discovered by Nikola Tesla eighty-years ago. Who knows? But what I think is that the same technology is used inside the craft. It—how should I put it?—makes us impervious to gravity from outside the craft."

"I want to know more about those guns," Roddy said.

"They use some sort of microburst pellets. Like putting a windstorm in a Gatling gun."

"Where are we going?" asked Linda.

"Where would you like to go? We're cruising at a modest speed of around a thousand miles an hour in case you want to sightsee. We'll be over Utah in a few minutes and over Nevada in twenty minutes."

Branch got up and started toward the window. "You could take us back to Lake City. We can pick up our Mercedes."

"No kidding. You're tooling around the country in a crummy old Mercedes?"

"The best we could get on short notice."

"No Rolls Royces available?"

"It's Benjamin's car."

"Oh." Hanley's demeanor changed. "How is Benjamin?" he asked.

"Doing well," Branch said.

"Good," he said, nodding. "Give him my best."

"Stop by sometime and do so yourself."

Hanley's face lit up as his mischievous grin returned. "Say the word and I'll turn this baby around and take us to Pennsylvania."

By this time, Linda and Roddy had gone to opposite sides to watch the scenery stream by. They enjoyed the view for the next twenty minutes while Branch and Hanley did some catching up. One of the topics they discussed was the question of why their former agency had been wiped out. Hanley was sure the UFO hunters were getting too close to the truth. But, ever the rebellious loner, Hanley decided to quit the agency and do his own search. Ten days later, he discovered the saucer site.

Roddy was excited. "I love to fly and be by the window."

Linda turned toward Roddy. "It's 360 degrees of window! If you use your peripheral vision, you can see where you're going and where you've been at the same time."

Branch slapped the side of his face and said, "Wow, isn't that something?"

Linda stifled a grin, and said, "Shush, you." She turned back to her sightseeing.

Hanley said, "You're all having entirely too much fun." His countenance became serious. "I think that's about to change, though."

"What's up?" asked Branch, as he leaned forward.

"Air Force, dead ahead. Coming this way. Better strap yourselves in, everyone."

Roddy and Linda hurried back to their seats.

"I wonder where they came from," said Branch.

"We're over Nevada now. I bet they're from Edwards Air Force Base."

"That's in California. What are they doing here?"

"No doubt we can thank Holloway," Hanley said.

"You think the Air Force is in on this whole thing, too?" said Branch.

"No, but if they shoot us down, they'll cover it up. That's all Holloway needs. Hang on."

Hanley took a sharp turn to the right. The two jets sped past them, turned left, and soon caught up.

"They're fast, aren't they?" said Roddy. "SR-71 Blackbirds."

"That's right," Hanley said. "Fastest air-breathing aircraft in the world. They'll do over 2,000 miles per hour."

Linda said, "But can't this saucer fly faster?"

"No doubt, but I searched and the owner's manual is gone. I never had a chance to finish reading."

"So, what exactly are you saying, hotshot?"

With an air of frustration, Hanley said, "I'm saying I don't know how to get the darn thing out of first gear."

A light flashed, so Hanley flipped the switch. A voice came from the speaker.

"Repeat, identify yourself."

Hanley searched the panel near the speaker. "This looks good." He pressed a black button. "We heard you have amazing hamburgers on this planet. Could you direct us—?"

The pilot cut him off. "You will follow us and be shown where to land. If you do not comply, we'll shoot you down."

Hanley turned to the others. "The Air Force has no sense of humor."

"Isn't that why they kicked you out of the space program?" said Branch.

He grinned. "Among other things." Hanley turned back toward the controls. "We'll just have to lose these guys."

Linda leaned forward on her armrest. "I thought you said you didn't know how to make this thing go any faster."

"I don't. But we can out-maneuver them. They can only change directions so fast and then it becomes dangerous. If they incur as much as 7Gs, they'll be rendered unconscious while we won't feel a thing."

"What is a G?" asked Linda.

"The gravitational force exerted on the body." Hanley pressed the black button. "We'll be saying so long now guys. If you're ever on the planet Zeno—."

"Incoming!" Roddy said.

They all turned to see missiles coming at them from behind.

"Never really in trouble," Hanley said, as he turned forward and tried to reset the controls before impact.

Too late. Both missiles exploded against the saucer. The saucer was bounced and rocked so hard that only their seatbelts kept the four of them from being thrown at the walls like helpless rag dolls.

Hanley only needed a few moments to recover as he finished resetting the controls. He grabbed hold of the joy stick and executed a sharp left turn. The jets continued on but for only a second, then they tilted left and began a far more gradual turn.

"I'm gonna hug the ground, get under their radar, and try to lose them."

"Houston, we have a problem," Roddy said.

"What?" Hanley said, as he turned his body. Roddy pointed toward the back with his thumb. Black smoke was trailing from the saucer.

"This can't be good," said Hanley.

"It gets worse," Linda said, pointing toward the spiral stairs. Smoke was coming up from the lower half of the ship.

Hanley said, "I think we have oxygen masks under the seats." He reached down, hit a button, and out popped a mask. He put it on while the others released their own masks.

The saucer sailed along the ground with Hanley dodging boulders. This became difficult as the smoke filling the cabin grew denser.

"Maybe we should land," said Linda. "How are you gonna fly when we lose all visibility?"

"I'm planning to fly by instruments alone," Hanley said.

"You know how to do that?"

"I'm learning as we speak."

"Hope you're a fast learner," Roddy said. "Because I'm blind here."

"Finally, we're on autopilot. The ship should go over hills and any other obstacles on its own... I think."

"Where exactly are we?" Linda said.

"Over the Mojave National Preserve."

The saucer sped along at a few hundred miles per hour, navigating its way over and around trees and hills, and finally, a nice flat desert. But trouble was right behind them.

The saucer was shaken hard by another missile blast. Linda screamed. They felt as if the saucer was trying to retch them from their seats.

"How'd they find us without radar?" Hanley said.

Linda leaned toward him. "Maybe all the black, billowing smoke we're trailing behind us."

"Well, that's cheating." Hanley fiddled with the controls. "That last hit wrecked something important. I can't slow down to land. We're gonna try a mobile set-down."

"Mobile set-down?" Linda said.

"Albeit, rather harshly."

"You mean crash and burn?"

"Are you always this much fun on trips?"

Hanley spotted something on the console. "What's this?" He flipped the switch. A sucking sound initiated, and the smoke started to clear. "Who knew?" He reset the controls to take it off autopilot and grabbed the joystick. He took a right turn.

They all ripped off their oxygen masks.

Branch said, "Did the space shuttle program train you for this?"

"No. You're not concerned, are you?"

"How do I look?"

"Terrified."

"Shows, does it?"

"Hang on." The ship whisked across the desert floor as Hanley started his approach. He got the saucer low to the ground and began skimming. Each time the ship grazed the ground, they were jerked forward.

Branch said, "What happened to the zero-gravity thing that kept us from being affected by the outside gravity?"

"Must be broke, too," Hanley replied, in a most cavalier manner. "Exciting, huh?"

They continued to bounce along, scraping up desert soil and brush as they skimmed the floor. Finally, the saucer skidded to a halt with desert dust swelling up.

The four hapless occupants sat motionless for a moment, and then remembered to start breathing again.

Linda caught her breath at the sight through the window of the black smoke rising up from the rear of the spacecraft.

Branch realized he was gripping the armrests so tight his hands had turned white. He relaxed and leaned back in the seat.

Roddy dug a candy bar out of his jacket and started taking the wrapper off.

"Thank you for flying Crash-way Airlines," Hanley said. "According to my calculations, we're near Baker Airport. We can charter a plane."

"Good," Branch said. He turned to face Linda and Roddy. "We'll fly to Barstow and take the Greyhound to Los Angeles."

"You have business there?" Hanley said.

"We're gonna meet someone at a museum."

"Okay, well, let's start hoofing it."

When they disembarked from the saucer, they searched the sky for the two persistent Blackbirds. But the planes had gone.

They tramped across the Mojave Preserve to the Baker Airport. The "Pyramid Gang" filled Hanley in on all they'd done and learned so far. At Baker, they found someone to fly them to Barstow.

They were just about ready to leave when Hanley said, "You three have a pleasant trip. This quest you're on sounds dangerous and exciting, so I wish I could go with you. But I need to check in with an old friend at NASA. Something he said to me one time about South America has finally clicked and I need to find out what he knows."

"You sure you don't want us to drop you somewhere?" Branch said.

"I have a ride." He shook hands with Roddy. "Keep my boy out of trouble." Roddy smiled and nodded. Hanley shook hands with Branch. "Watch out for my girl." Branch gave a nod and an almost imperceptible smile. Linda rolled her eyes. Hanley went to Linda, and in a most charming way, he said, "It's been wonderful meeting you, and sharing an adventure."

"It was a memorable experience." Linda did her best not to show it, but she was a bit saddened by his leaving.

The three climbed into their chartered plane, waved goodbye to Hanley, and set out for Barstow.

At Barstow, they got on a Greyhound Bus and headed for Los Angeles. When they arrived, they decided to buy new clothes since everything they weren't wearing was still in the Mercedes. They were running low on cash since most of that had been left in the car as well. But Benjamin had given Branch a debit card to get more cash when they needed some. The money was in a numbered account in the Cayman Islands, so using the card wouldn't be dangerous.

They rented a motel room so they could clean up, and Branch called Wendy, Dr. Reed's niece to set up an appointment with her at the museum. Roddy called his wife. It had been a while, and he got quite an earful. But after she got it all out, she told him she loved him and to take care.

Afterward, Linda said, "Maybe you should go home and see her."

Roddy answered, "When I was in the Army, I was gone for months at a time. So she's used to it."

"You should head for home, anyway."

Roddy stared at his shoes. "Yeah, I know. But who would look out for Branch?" he said, raising his head. "And you?"

"I absolve you of any responsibility."

"I'll make it home soon," he said, with a smile. "Besides, absence makes the heart grow fonder. At least, I hope it does."

Chapter Eight

They arrived at the museum in a rented Nissan Altima. Branch looked in all directions with a vigilant eye as they walked toward the entrance.

The three entered and stopped just inside the door. They surveyed the entrance area, looking for anyone who might be an employee. They didn't notice the girl coming to them from the side.

"Hello," the girl said. As they all turned toward her, she said, "You must be the Pyramid Gang."

"That's us," Branch said.

"Do you have it?" she said.

"The MacGuffin?" said Roddy.

"Right here in my purse," Linda said.

"I'm Wendy. Come with me," she said. They all followed.

"We're sorry about your uncle," Linda said.

"Committing suicide wasn't like him. I find it hard to believe."

"But we saw the explosion," Roddy said.

She nodded.

Wendy looked to be early twenties, probably just out of college. She wore a light blue smock over her street clothes. Her name was on the front, and the museum's name was on the back. The smock had large pockets at the waist and what appeared to be a map stuck out about an inch above the left pocket. Wendy led them to an elevator, and they went down to the basement. Leaving the elevator, they entered a large room.

She began to give them a sort of tour. "This room is full of Egyptian artifacts."

"What's over there?" Branch said, pointing to a door.

"The mummy room. We have quite a collection, but no one gets to see them or anything in this room. The curator and assistant curators, like me, are sworn to secrecy."

"Why," said Roddy. "The Egyptians aren't a secret. Egypt's full of them."

"But none of this stuff came from Egypt."

She let that revelation hang for a moment, not wanting to satisfy their curiosity too soon.

"Then where?" asked Linda.

"Right here in this country. The Grand Canyon, to be exact."

"You're pulling our leg, right?" said Branch.

"I was told you're the skeptical one. Come here; I want to show you something."

They followed her to a glass-covered case, which contained a page from an old newspaper. The title read: EXPLORATIONS IN GRAND CANYON. Subtitles included: *Mysteries of Immense Rich Cavern* and *Remarkable Finds Indicate Ancient People Migrated From Orient.*

"The explorer's name was G.E. Kinkaid, who some have called the real Indiana Jones. Today, that whole portion of the northern part of the Grand Canyon is off limits to hikers. Kinkaid found an underground network of tunnels filled with Egyptian artifacts. The stuff in this room is a sampling. The mother lode is hidden away in some deep dark subbasement at the Smithsonian."

"The Smithsonian is hiding stuff?" said Roddy.

"The Smithsonian has thousands of so-called anomalous artifacts. They are things that don't fit with the popular version of Earth history. And because they don't fit, they're kept hidden. Changing the accepted story of the way things were is a no-no."

"She's right," Linda said. "I remember what happened to a geologist named Virginia Steen-McIntyre. Her dating of a Mexican site was too provocative. As a result, she was fired. Her career ended, and the date for the site was reset to fit prevailing history, the story the powers-that-be want told. It's just like the travesty my father endured."

"So, the geologists in charge lied?" said Roddy. "And then fired this lady for telling the truth?"

"Yes, they did," Linda said.

"That's not right at all."

"And you don't hear about that kind of thing much for two reasons," Wendy said. "First, most people, whether geologist, archeologist, historian, or whatever, will lie. They'll agree with conventional wisdom rather than risk their careers. Second, when they do stand up for the truth, and lose their job and perhaps even their degree, it's not considered newsworthy. The news media is owned and controlled by people you don't even want to know about."

"You sound like your uncle," Branch said.

"He told me a lot of things he thought I should know. By the way, Linda, I wanted to tell you how sorry I am about your father. I know he was one of the brave ones who told the truth and paid the price."

"Thank you," Linda said. "I think maybe things will change. There's a brilliant movie out about such people."

"I know. *Expelled: No Intelligence Allowed.* Wonderful documentary."

Branch was getting antsy. "We should get going. Can you give us the next piece to the puzzle."

"I'm sure my uncle told you that it was entrusted to the Egyptians."

Branch took a quick look around the room.

"Not here," she said. "You have to go to the Grand Canyon, to the pyramid."

Incredulous, Branch said, "A pyramid in the Grand Canyon?"

"Ever the skeptic, aren't you, Mr. Nichols? You only have to go inside and find the space between the stones, just above the doorway."

"I'm less skeptical," a familiar voice said. Darkin stepped out from behind an exhibit as they all turned to face him.

"How'd you get in here?" Wendy said. "I didn't hear the elevator or the noisy door to the stairway."

"We've been waiting for you. When we saw the so-called Pyramid Gang approaching, we came down ahead of you. I knew this was where you'd bring them."

Brussel, Wallach, and two other gunmen stepped out into the open.

"As you can see, I brought backup," Darkin said. "And had we missed you, all the airports in southern California, both private and public, are being surveilled. So you weren't going to escape."

Linda grabbed hold of Branch's arm.

Branch remained calm as he said, "You know, Brussel, we have to stop meeting like this."

"I'm sure this will be the last time," Brussel said.

Darkin stepped toward Linda and held out his hand. "If you'd be so kind as to hand over the MacGuffin."

Linda hesitated, looking at Branch, not wanting to accept failure after they'd been through so much.

"Hand it over to them," Branch said.

Linda opened her purse and took out the partially constructed pyramid. Darkin reached over and yanked it out of her hand.

Branch said, "You're the Pyramidion infiltrator aren't you?"

"Yes," Darkin said, "but not deep enough. Imagine, all the time the one-eyed caretaker in Egypt had the platform for the rest of the pyramid. I expected someone important."

"Everyone's important," Roddy said. "In the eyes of God,"

"You don't say," said Darkin. "One wonders why he allows so many important children to suffer starvation."

Wendy folded her arms. "God gave this planet to us with the understanding we would take care of one another. Children go hungry because mankind doesn't do enough to care for its own. You can't blame God."

"You'd think God would, at some point, intervene."

"He did," Linda said. "Two thousand years ago. But as long as people like you continue to deny him, all forms of suffering will continue."

"Makes me want to pass the hat."

Darkin put the MacGuffin into a side pocket of his suit jacket.

"Now we need to dispose of the four of you."

Brussel cocked the hammer on his gun.

"Not here," Darkin said. "Take them somewhere far away."

"We have our tours now. People everywhere," Wendy said. "You think you're gonna get us out without lots of screaming from me?"

"I'll help," said Linda.

"Good plan," Branch said. "Would've worked better, though if you two hadn't told them."

Linda's countenance changed to *uh oh.*

"We'll wait till the museum closes," Darkin said. "The curator is one of mine. He'll get us out after everyone is gone and the doors are locked."

Brussel spoke. "You mean we have to stand here and wait for two more hours? Can't we lock them somewhere? What's that room?"

Wendy flinched. Her eyes darted a glance at the door to the mummy room, then at Brussel. Wide-eyed, she whispered, "That's the mummy room. Please don't lock us in there." In a whiney voice, she said, "It's, like, really creepy and stuff. Dead guys in dirty band-aids. I don't ever go in that place."

Darkin went to the door and peeked in. "This is the only way out."

"Hey, I'm hungry, anyway," said Wallach. "Let's stick them in the room, for now. We can come back and kill them after dinner."

"Sounds good," Brussel said. "I don't like to kill on an empty stomach."

"All right," Darkin said, his ire growing. "You guys better finish them this time. You've certainly had enough chances. Give me your keys."

Wendy handed the keys to Darkin.

"Okay, everyone," Wallach said. "Into the mummy room. No pushing or shoving. Let's make this orderly."

Wendy was first, but she stopped at the door. Branch went ahead and opened it. He went in, and the others followed.

When they were inside and the door shut behind them, they heard the sound of Darkin turning the lock.

"Trapped," Roddy said to Branch. "A familiar predicament."

"Not for long," Wendy said, her eyes all a glint.

She went to the wall opposite the door and turned to the perpendicular wall, where stood a coffin-like case. Wendy opened the case, revealing a mummy. She tipped the bandaged remains toward herself and reached behind. "Fortunately, he's one of the light ones." A sliding door opened beside her. She removed her hand and pushed the mummy back in and closed the case.

Roddy said, "You handled the mummy without any show of fear."

"They're harmless. They're all dead. I love it here." She started through the open door.

"I don't believe this," Branch said. "You have a secret panel?"

Wendy stopped and over her shoulder she said. "Pyramidions are an endangered species. A good exit plan is a must. The secret to our survival is to ensure nothing is ever what it seems."

The others followed her into the hall. Wendy went to a fire alarm and pounded three times on the wall, next to the alarm. Nothing happened. "Put in by a man." She turned to Roddy. "Would you do that for me?"

Roddy was confused, but went ahead and pounded three times on the wall in the same spot. The fire alarm opened out like a door.

"Thank you," Wendy said, and she pushed a button inside the wall. The sliding panel closed, and she shut the fire alarm door. "Okay, let's go."

Branch watched her scurry down the hall. She was perky for someone who had, moments ago, escaped death.

Wendy led them through a maze of tunnels. "These passageways are for employees only. The secret door, of course, was not in the original building plans. It was installed in one night while everyone was gone."

"But why have one?" Branch said. "And why there?"

"I've been spending a lot of time in the Egypt room, studying artifacts. I'm an Egyptologist. I'm not supposed to be snooping in the Egypt room, so if I hear the elevator or the noisy door to the stairs, I can exit through the secret panel. That pesky little fire alarm door has been a problem, though. Last time I took a sledge hammer with me."

Outside, Darkin and his four henchmen walked toward the parking lot. Wallach appeared thoughtful.

Darkin said, "Why so pensive, Mr. Wallach?"

"I was thinking about the girl. The one who works at the museum."

"Did you want to take her home with you?"

"I didn't mean that way, although she was cute. It just seemed kind of strange."

Brussel muscled past the other two goons. "What did?"

"One minute she's waxing eloquent about God. The next she's talking like a dim-witted Valley Girl."

Recognition registered on Brussel's face. He launched himself back toward the museum, followed by the others.

On the other side of the building, the Pyramid Gang and Wendy hurried to the parking lot. Wendy's late model, red convertible Audi R8 Spyder was parked there.

"Awesome wheels," Roddy said.

"This is what you get when you've got no family but lots of inherited wealth."

"I have the opposite," Roddy said.

"I'd gladly trade," Wendy said.

"Our car is right over there," said Branch.

Wendy took the map out of her pocket. "Here. Use this to find your way around the Egyptian part of the canyon. The map is hand drawn, but accurate. No published maps since they won't let anybody go there. Also, the map shows a labyrinth of underground tunnels. Not sure if you'll need that." She looked across the parking lot. "Ah, I see our friends are headed back in already." She ran toward the museum.

They watched her go, wondering what she could be up to. Branch opened the map.

"Oh, my," said Roddy, staring at the map. "The plot thickens."

Brussel bolted into the Egyptian room from the stairway, his three cohorts right behind. He tried the door to the mummy room, but found it locked. Frustrated, he waited for Darkin. Moments later, the elevator door opened. Darkin stepped out and strolled up to the others, keys in hand.

"Don't worry, they can't get out." Darkin unlocked the door as Brussel and his men drew their guns. Darkin stepped back, and his band of thugs charged in.

They searched the room. Darkin stood, dumfounded.

Brussel was livid now. "Open every one of these coffins. Make sure they're not hiding in them."

They ripped open each of the cases, and found only mummies hiding in them.

Finally, Darkin said, "At least we know where they're going. Get to the canyon, and make sure they join the pharaohs in eternal glory."

The door slammed, and they heard the sound of the lock turning.

Wendy put the key in one of the pockets of her smock and smiled at the pounding and yelling of Brussel and company from the other side of the door.

She turned and crossed the room to several rows of shelves. She reached past an eight-inch statue of Akhenaton and pushed on a spring-loaded door at the back. Reaching in, she pushed a button. A picture of the Grand Canyon on the wall next to her opened out from one side. Wendy let the door at the back of the shelf close and opened the picture out, revealing a safe. She punched in five numbers and turned the handle. Inside was a blue 4 by 10 envelope. She put it in a pocket on her smock, closed the safe and the picture, and left.

Branch's eyes grew wide. "Tyler Nichols."

"Your father's signature?" Roddy said.

"Seems so." Branch experienced a sudden epiphany. "Pyramid, grand. Those were his dying words. I always assumed he was referring to the Great Pyramid of Giza, but he meant the pyramid in the Grand Canyon."

"Maybe it's Shem's pyramid," Linda said. "You remember. The one Ackerley told us about."

Branch nodded. "Could be."

They studied the map until Wendy returned.

Branch said to her, "My father's signature is on here."

"I know. After he drew the map, and passed it along to my grandfather, he went back to the Grand Canyon pyramid to hide the fifth piece of the pyramid key. He also wanted to take pictures. Of what, I'm not sure. My grandfather never saw him again."

"Why hide the piece in the pyramid?" Branch said.

"My grandfather had become quite paranoid and wanted the piece hidden where no one would find it."

Linda was quizzical. "So, are you telling us Branch's father was a Pyramidion?"

"No, but he was one heck of an investigative journalist. He uncovered the Pyramidions and also claimed to know the location of manmade flying saucers."

Branch said, "How can you know for sure my father hid the piece before he was captured?"

"I don't, but the successful completion of the pyramid key depends on you finding the fifth piece."

Roddy was anxious. "Hey, does anyone remember we no longer have the MacGuffin. Even if we find the next chunk, we got nothing to stick it to."

"We'll have to deal with that later," Branch said. "We can't let Darkin get his hands on it."

"You have some time," Wendy said. "Can't be sure how much, though."

"What do you mean?" asked Branch.

"They went back to the mummy room." Wendy held up a key. "I grabbed a spare and locked them in. The door can't be unlocked from the inside. They could be there for days before anyone goes down, and forget about cell phone reception."

"Which is good since we'll have to drive, with the airports being watched."

"Better hurry. If they get out and call ahead before you arrive..."

"Yeah," Branch said. He turned to Linda. "Maybe you should—"

"Un uh," Linda said. "No way I'm not coming. This is an archeologist's dream."

"Okay, okay," Branch said, having resigned himself to the inevitable stubbornness he'd come to know. And put up with, along with his particularly frustrating inability to lose her.

"You'll go in by helicopter," Wendy said. "A pilot named Jake Bond will take you. He's a bit of a rogue, the kind of person we need for this mission."

"How'll we know him?" Branch asked.

"He'll know you." Wendy hesitated before she spoke again. "I have some bad news to give you before you leave."

Branch responded with a look of amusement. "Why am I not surprised?"

"I can't tell you how to find the sixth piece. My contact has disappeared."

"Who was your contact?"

"Jeremiah Daniels. He's an odd fellow. Calls himself an astrotheologian."

"Pardon me," Branch said.

"He has Ph.D.s in astronomy and biblical studies. He says God's entire plan for man was written in the stars at the moment of creation. It's nothing new but he's the foremost expert." She opened the door to her car, reached in, pulled out a packet of papers and handed them to Branch. "Here, this is everything I know about him. Maybe you can track him down. Assuming he's still alive."

"Are you gonna be all right?" Branch asked

"Don't worry about me. Even Mr. Wallach won't find me."

Branch reached out his hand. "Thank you, Wendy."

Instead of taking it, Wendy took the blue envelope from her pocket and placed it in Branch's hand. "One last thing."

Branch took the envelope. "What's this?"

"A prophecy from a seventeenth century Turkish monk. He was staying at the Sümela Monastery which is built into the side of a cliff facing the Altindere valley. He never fit in and, after several years, he left because of his disgust for the pagan nature of their devotion to the Virgin Mary."

Linda chimed in, "Who, of course, didn't stay a virgin after the birth of Jesus."

Branch gave her a sidelong glance.

Linda went on, "The Bible tells us Jesus had brothers and a sister."

"Thank you for the commentary," Branch said.

"No problem."

Branch looked back at Wendy. "You were saying."

"Well, the monk, named Gazanfer, spent the next seventy years traveling the seven cities in the Book of Revelation. The seven churches of the Apocalypse. He'd become obsessed with prophecy and prayed for understanding of the end times. He finally despaired of ever hearing from God and, at the age of 100, he left Ephesus. He headed for the coast and took a boat to the Island of Patmos where John received the Book of Revelation. Legend says Gazanfer fell into a deep sleep and had a vision. The content of the envelope is what he was given."

"Why are we being given this?" Branch asked.

"In the hope that you may be able to decipher its meaning."

"The last thing we need is another mystery to solve," Branch said. "But you did save our lives."

"I hope you can unravel it."

"Don't worry," Roddy said, "Branch is good at solving mysteries." To Branch: "Go ahead and open it."

Branch stuck the envelope in his pocket. "We'll deal with it later."

They drove up Interstate 15 to Las Vegas, where they switched rentals, but not before Branch changed names. He acquired a set of false IDs from a shady character he knew—Linda chose not to ask questions—and rented their next car using his new alias. When they arrived, they went straight to the visitor center. Linda insisted, much to Branch's consternation.

"I'd like to meet with our contact as soon as possible," said Branch.

"Come on now. You know how I feel about brochures," Linda said.

Linda shopped while Branch and Roddy gazed out the windows, hoping not to spot their favorite pursuers.

Linda finished, and the three went to the Grand Canyon airport, and stood where Wendy had told them to wait.

A voice behind them said, "The Pyramid Gang, I presume."

They all turned to see a thirty-something man standing there. He was handsome, Linda mused, wearing dark sunglasses and holding a half-filled martini glass.

"Branch Nichols," said Branch, as he extended his hand.

"Bond, Jake Bond," the man said, with a British accent, and shook hands with Branch.

"Chico Rodriguez," Roddy said, as he shook hands with Jake.

"Roddy, isn't it?"

"Yes."

Jake turned to Linda. "And you're Linda Chapel." He took her hand in, what Linda thought was a gallant manner.

She pointed to his martini glass. "Shaken, not stirred?"

"Ginger ale. Didn't have to do anything."

Brussel, Wallach, and six of Brussel's most contemptible assassins stepped down the ramp of their chartered plane. Each had a white trench coat over his arm.

"You think we beat them here?" Wallach said.

"Maybe, but if they do get to the pyramid they won't be getting out.

"I've had it with their uncanny string of luck."

"I know how you feel. I have to kill someone soon. I've never gone this long."

"I realize the temperature gets pretty cool here but did we have to drag out these trench coats, again?"

"I like the look. Too bad we couldn't wear them in the Bahamas or California."

"Please don't bring up the Bahamas. I'm trying to forget those shirts with the nightmare colors."

They continued on without spotting their quarry walking toward Jake's helicopter.

Flying over the Grand Canyon, Linda was happy to have a brochure to read. "Hey guys, listen to these names. The Tower of Set, the Tower of Ra, and Osiris Temple. Why would sites in the

Grand Canyon have Egyptian names, unless…" She let the implication hang without bothering to state the obvious.

Jake spoke over his shoulder. "The official word is that explorers just liked using Egyptian names. Now I ask you: how naïve do they think people are?"

"The official word on cultures is isolation," Linda said. "It's the belief that people didn't move around much thousands of years ago. And certain individuals don't want to rewrite the history books."

Jake said, "Don't dare mention to anyone connected to the Grand Canyon, in an official capacity, that Egyptians once lived here. You'll receive a condescending laugh."

"Well, Egyptians left their mark in Australia," Linda said. "So, why not here?"

They flew in a roundabout fashion, so no one at the airport would observe them heading in the direction of the off limits area. When they landed, they weren't near a pyramid or anything else that appeared Egyptian. Just a lot of rocks and dirt, with the only vegetation being the occasional cactus. One of them was a flowering cactus with a bright pink flower opened wide like a bowl. Linda had to get a closer view. Roddy crouched next to her.

"Isn't it beautiful?" said Linda. "So gloriously pink."

"Got some little yellow thingies at the center."

Branch left Jake and the helicopter and joined his two companions.

"Jake's gonna wait here. He says if others come, they'll land close to the pyramid and shouldn't be able to spot him. Here, Linda, put this flare gun in your purse."

The three began to hike in the direction that Jake had pointed. They approached what appeared to be a partition with one part of the wall set back farther than the rest. They turned into the narrow opening, followed a curve for about forty feet, and exited into a large open area.

Set against a cliff that rose a good hundred feet, was a pyramid, five stories tall. They stopped and stared in awe.

"Jake said this was the only way in on foot," Branch said. "Anybody with a helicopter will land here."

"Doesn't seem to be any guards," said Roddy.

"Jake told me all guards are posted on the outer perimeter. They don't expect anyone to get this far."

They walked across the open area to the entrance of the pyramid. They stood for a few moments taking it all in.

"Seems to be made of limestone," said Linda. "Like the pyramids in Egypt."

Branch searched the sky. "Let's get what we came for."

The three entered into a chamber of about 160 square feet. They all stopped at once and stared at the most anomalous thing they never expected to find.

"Can't be," said Linda.

"I think it is," Branch said.

"How about that?" Roddy said. "An elevator. Wonder where it goes."

A voice from the shadows said, "Down, fifteen stories." Three gun wielding Neanderthals stepped out.

Two of the gunmen were about Branch's size, but the other was enormous.

The man who spoke before spoke again. "So nice of you to stop by."

Branch whispered to Roddy, "Godzilla is yours. I'll take Chatty Cathy and his sidekick."

"Thanks, amigo," Roddy whispered back.

"No problem."

Branch reached out to push Linda back behind him.

"This your pyramid?" Roddy said.

The three said nothing as they continued to step closer.

"Is that where the tour begins?" Branch said, pointing to the elevator.

The three captors stopped. Chatty was a few feet in front of Branch, and Sidekick was at Branch's left side, close enough to shake hands. Godzilla stood in front of Roddy.

Chatty said, "Yuk it up. When Brussel gets here, the fun's over."

"You invited him, too?" Roddy said. "Outstanding."

"Yeah, we hang out with him all the time," said Branch.

Chatty said, "I'd kill you right now, but Brussel insisted on having the pleasure."

"Too bad he'll be too late," Branch said.

"Too late for what?"

Branch glanced at Roddy who returned an ever so slight nod.

"To witness what a wonderful job you've done," said Branch. "Up till now."

Chatty's perplexity showed as he tried to grasp what Branch was hinting at. Then it hit him. And so did Branch, kicking the gun out of Chatty's hand with the size twelve hiking boot on his right foot. At the same time, he used his left hand to grab Sidekick's gun, breaking the man's trigger finger.

Meanwhile, Roddy kicked the gun out of Godzilla's hand and, with everything he had, punched the oversized thug in the gut. Which seemed to have little effect.

Branch was holding the barrel of the gun in his left hand and tried to put the grip into his right hand. But Sidekick swung his foot up in time to knock the gun away. Branch grabbed the ankle of his attacker with his left hand, just as Chatty lunged toward him. Branch shot his right fist at Chatty's nose knocking him backward.

Though off balance, Sidekick tried desperately to get his hands on Branch, who still had Sidekick's ankle. Branch flipped him up causing him to fall on his back and hit his head on the stone floor, knocking him unconscious.

Roddy was in a boxing stance, rotating his fists. Godzilla smiled and started toward Roddy. The outcome of what would follow didn't seem promising. Roddy knew he might have only one shot at winning, and decided to take it.

"Sorry about this," Roddy said and kicked hard against Godzilla's kneecap. The giant's eyes bulged as he bent over to grab his knee. Roddy boxed his ears three times. Godzilla was disoriented. Roddy grabbed his arm, pulling him forward, and then shoved him from behind, forcing the man to bang his head against the stone wall.

Godzilla was dazed, but still on his feet. He turned around. Roddy cocked his head to one side and put his hands on his hips. *What do I have to do*? Finally, the big man fell down, unconscious, into a sitting position against the wall.

Meanwhile, Branch was dealing with Chatty, who, nose bleeding, was now in a rage. He charged at Branch and grabbed him by the upper arms. Branch grabbed hold of his assaulter's shirt, swung him around and rammed him into the wall. When his head whacked against the stone, he dropped his hands from Branch's arms. Branch stepped aside as Chatty fell forward, slamming his forehead on the stone floor.

Linda was standing in front of the entrance with unconscious men on either side of her. She stared at Branch with admiration. "That was impressive," she said.

Branch gave just a hint of a smile. A cocky, self-satisfied smile, in Linda's opinion. As she realized what she was doing, she turned to Roddy. "You too, Roddy. You were fantastic."

"Let's get the fifth piece and get out of here," Branch said. He moved past Linda to the entranceway. Just above it was the gap between the stones. Branch reached up and shoved his hand in. "I can't feel a thing."

"Maybe it's too far back," Linda said. "I have smaller hands. Let me try." She stepped just below the gap as Branch moved aside. After a moment, she turned to Branch. "I'll need a lift."

Branch got behind her, put his hands on her waist, and lifted her with little effort. Linda shoved her hand in.

"I've got something." She pulled her hand out, and Branch lowered her to the floor. She turned around to face him. "Hmm, strong." She was doing it again! Flustered, she held up the piece. "Shaped like a little, tiny pyramid." She could feel the blood rushing to her face, and hoped the light was too dim for anyone to tell.

Roddy was ginning at Branch.

"We better go," Branch said.

"Should I put this in my purse?" Linda said, refusing to look at Branch.

"Yeah," Branch said. "Come on."

He started through the entrance but stopped short. Roddy and Linda came behind him.

"Guess who," Branch said.

They peered into the Arizona sunlight. Brussel, Wallach, and their six colleagues were climbing out of two helicopters. Wearing white trench coats, they headed straight for the pyramid.

The three went back inside.

"Guess we're gonna have to take a ride," Branch said.

"My prayers have been answered," said Linda. She ran ahead of them to the elevator. She found four buttons next to the doors. They were marked open, close, up, and down. She pushed the button marked open and the doors slid to the sides. Inside the ten-by-ten compartment was another row of buttons, next to the door.

They went inside, and turned around in time to see their old acquaintances entering. Roddy smiled and waved. Brussel glared back.

Roddy said, "I don't think he likes me."

"I'm not gonna like you either if you don't hit the close button," Branch said.

"Testy." Roddy pressed the button. After a moment, he said, "This is some elevator. Doesn't even feel like we're moving."

"We're not."

"Try the down button," said Linda.

Roddy reached for the button. "You gotta push a lot of buttons to go any—Whoa!"

The elevator shot down, as they felt their stomachs relocate in their upper esophagi.

As their anatomy began its return to normal positioning, Roddy said, "I like that look. The trench coats. What do you think?"

Branch shook his head with an air of mild disgust.

The elevator reached bottom, the doors opened, and the three stepped into a tunnel. They stood on a stone floor that met with stone walls. A wood ceiling stretched across the twelve-foot wide tunnel, eight feet above the floor. Incandescent lights were spaced at about twenty-five feet along the ceiling.

The elevator doors closed and they heard it leaving.

"Our ride is over here," Branch said.

Linda and Roddy turned and faced a parking area that had been cut into the wall. A row of four-wheeled vehicles sat at the front.

"They look like all-terrain vehicles," Roddy said. "A cross between a golf cart and a dune buggy. I'm gonna call them golf buggies."

Each one had a flatbed cart attached to the rear. "We won't need that," Branch said.

Roddy unhooked a cart while Branch got behind the steering wheel, and Linda sat next to him. Roddy unplugged the electric charging cord suspended from the ceiling, and jumped in the back seat. Branch moved the buggy into the tunnel.

"Okay, which way do we go?" Branch said to Linda.

Linda looked up the tunnel one way and then down the other. "What I wouldn't do for a brochure with a list of must-see sites, and a map, right now."

"How about the map in your purse?" Branch said. "Will that help?"

Linda forgot she was carrying the map they'd gotten from Wendy. She mustered as much dignity as she had left after repeated embarrassments. Then opened her purse and took out the drawing made by Branch's father. She kept her gaze down, not wanting to meet Branch's, and unfolded the map.

Roddy leaned forward to check it out too.

"There's the pyramid," Linda said. "And now we know this is an elevator shaft."

Roddy pointed, and said, "That's the 'You are here' spot. Until we go somewhere else, of course. And then we'll be there."

"That's helpful," Branch said, evenly.

Linda pointed. "We should go that way."

Branch yanked on the steering wheel and floored the gas pedal. The hybrid cart accelerated to full speed, about thirty miles an hour, in a matter of seconds.

"Probably," Linda said. "I mean, I'm not sure," she continued, glancing at Branch.

Branch gave her a stern look, complete with an undercurrent of mild rage.

"Here comes the next tour," Roddy said.

The eight hunters charged out of the elevator and took aim at their prey.

"Incoming," Roddy said.

They crouched low, using the backs of their seats for protection. Bullets pinged off the golf buggy and tunnel walls as Branch followed a welcome, but all too gradual, curve in the tunnel.

Finally, they were out of sight of their pursuers and relaxed a little.

They reached a fork, and, without asking this time, Branch took the left fork.

Soon, they stopped at an intersection. Roddy leaned between Linda and Branch. "The choices are piling up," he said.

"You notice a difference in the tunnels to the right and left?" Branch said.

"Concrete walls instead of stone. Wood ceilings, but the wood looks different."

"I'm guessing they're recent additions used to connect the other tunnels."

"Shortcuts."

"Should we take one?" Branch said, looking at Linda.

She cocked her thumb to the right and Branch made the turn.

They didn't have to go too far this time before they came to a chamber that covered several acres. It was a natural cave of solid rock. Stacks of wooden crates stood everywhere.

Branch reached over and tugged on the map to get a better look. "This map shows other caves connected to this one but with no other exits."

"Maybe your dad didn't have a chance to finish," Roddy said. "Or maybe exits have been added since the map was drawn."

Branch spotted someone coming into the cave. He was riding a golf buggy and pulling a flatbed cart carrying a wooden crate. A forklift was approaching from another direction. Branch drove between some of the stacks of crates and parked in a corner.

"We need a new map," Branch said, in a low voice.

"We should ask someone for directions," said Roddy.

"Before we leave, I'd like to know what's in these crates," Linda said.

"Let's find out," said Branch.

They all left the buggy and went to the nearest crate.

Between two of the boards was a one-inch wide crack. Roddy and Branch, sneaking their fingers in the thin break, grabbed one of the boards and started pulling. Hard enough to force the nails out, but not so hard that they made noise.

After two minutes of careful tugging, the board came free. They all peered into the crate.

"Not enough light," Branch said. "Can't tell what's inside."

Linda opened her purse and fished out a tiny flashlight.

"You have a flashlight in your purse?" Roddy said.

"In case I can't find my keys. You guys have pockets, so everything's easy to find. When you have a purse, things get lost."

"What if you can't find your flashlight?" Branch said, with a straight face.

Linda stared at him for a long moment, and then, "Don't get me riled; I have a pretty good right hook."

Branch put up his hands in self-defense.

Linda shined the light into the box. "An Egyptian vase. Now, why are they crating up Egyptian artifacts?"

"And do they plan on taking them somewhere else?" Branch added.

"Smithsonian would be my guess," Linda said. "Wendy was not the first person I've known to tell of secret history being held hostage in their subbasements."

"Nothing we can do about this now," said Branch. "Our first priority is to find our way out. Linda, stay here."

"And if you find a way of escape?"

"We'll come back. For a while, at least, you won't be dodging bullets."

Roddy and Branch left her and entered stealth mode as they moved among the crates.

Linda looked with curiosity in all directions and spotted a tunnel. She ran toward it, stopped behind a crate, and peeked out. No one was around, so she ran across an open space to get to the passageway.

Meanwhile, Roddy and Branch crept up to where the two men they'd seen were working. The forklift driver was placing the crate on top of another crate. The buggy driver turned his vehicle around and headed back the way he came.

Roddy and Branch snuck up on the fork lift driver who was backing away from the stacks of crates while letting his forks down. He stopped and checked his watch. "Break time."

Suddenly, he realized he wasn't alone. Roddy was standing next to him.

"As long as you're on break, anyway, maybe you could help us."

"Who are you? Where did you come from?"

Branch approached him from the other side. "We're a couple of tourists, and we've lost our way."

"Yeah? Well, I'm gonna help you find your way to a holding cell."

"Hey, this guy's scary," Roddy said.

"I'm terrified," said Branch.

The driver flashed a self-assured smile. "You guys should know that I'm a fifth degree black belt in karate."

"No kidding?" Roddy said. "That's impressive. So, you can break stuff with your bare hand."

He nodded, brimming with confidence. "Yes, I can."

Roddy directed a sidelong glance at Branch. "Should we flip for him?"

"Why bother? You always win."

Roddy took out a quarter and flipped it. "Heads I win tales you lose."

Branch frowned.

"Tales. You lose." To the driver he said, "Come on down."

The driver jumped down from the lift truck. He peeked over his shoulder at Branch. "Don't run away. I'll be with you in a second."

Branch smiled.

Driver turned to Roddy, who was in a boxer's stance, rotating his fists.

"You gotta be kidding me," Driver said.

"It's my style. Don't make fun."

Driver swung his leg up at Roddy's head, and Roddy fended it off with his forearm. Driver spun around and took a swipe at the other side of Roddy's head. This time Roddy had to duck, and the guy's foot swiped his ear.

But as his foot came back down, Driver was left vulnerable for a split second. Roddy took advantage, drilling his right fist into the man's left cheek, knocking him backward.

The guy could take a punch, though. Staying on his feet, he charged Roddy, who backpedaled as the man attacked him with a flurry of kicks and punches.

Roddy held his own until he found an opening he could exploit. He jabbed at the man three times on the jaw. Now, somewhat dazed, Roddy's attacker was ripe for pruning. Roddy shot his right fist at the man's nose, knocking him to the floor.

The martial artist lay on his back, staring up at Roddy.

Roddy relaxed a little. "I took up boxing in the army."

The man wasn't finished, though. He jumped to his feet and charged Roddy again. This time, Roddy didn't use his fists.

Instead, he grabbed the man, turned his body, flipped the man over and slammed him to the floor. Roddy pounced on him, hooking one arm under his victim's neck. He moved the other under the guy's leg sliding his hand up onto the back of his waist. Roddy pulled up on the man's lower body, pinning his shoulders to the floor.

Branch got down on his knees like a referee and counted, "One second, two seconds, three seconds. Pinned!" Branch tapped the rock floor and got to his feet.

Roddy stood up, too. "And I was a wrestler in high school. State champ. Light heavyweight."

"You got lucky," the beaten fork lift driver said, as he got to a sitting position, and moved away, backing up to a crate.

"It's been said that, 'Someone with only a year of training in boxing and wrestling can easily defeat a martial artist of twenty years experience. '"

"Oh, yeah? What idiot said that?" the man said as he stood.

"Bruce Lee," Roddy replied.

"The famous martial artist? I don't believe you."

"You got beat," Branch said, as he grabbed the guy by the shirt. "Now, tell us how to get out of here."

"I forget."

"Memory loss can have painful consequences." Branch said.

The forklift driver charged at Roddy, who ducked down, putting a knee and a fist to the floor. The driver tripped over him, flew forward and hit his head on a crate, knocking himself unconscious.

Roddy stood back up. "These guys keep banging their heads. It's like a pattern."

"And convenient. We don't have to deal with them if their unconscious, or take time to tie them up, and gag them."

"Good point."

"Time to split up. We can cover twice as much ground," Branch said. "I'll follow the guy on the cart."

"Golf buggy."

"Yeah, right. You go the other way."

After giving each other a good luck nod, they went in opposite directions.

Linda was perusing the chamber she'd discovered at the end of the short tunnel. The walls were covered in inscriptions. Just like the ones Branch and Roddy photographed fifty feet beneath the Pyramid of Giza. She continued to wander finding more tunnels and more chambers. They contained many artifacts, vases, statues, and even mummies.

Linda was having the time of her life. Then she remembered she had a camera in her purse. She rummaged through her 'magic bag,' as her father had often called it, and dug out her camera.

Happy as a shopper at a close-out sale, she started snapping pictures of everything.

Branch had come upon an arsenal and a complete map, on a wall, of the underground labyrinth. He was amazed at the number of tunnels and chambers. Getting to this place hadn't been difficult. He felt fortunate that there were few workmen around and that he was having little trouble staying undetected.

Branch commandeered two machine pistols and a satchel full of extra clips. He studied the map, noticing how far they'd come in relation to the rest of the tunnel network. They'd explored only a small part.

Roddy had found the kitchen. He was building a sandwich on a sesame seed bun and talking to himself.

"Roast beef, leaf lettuce, a slice of tomato, onions, mayonnaise, and now I'll top it off with some bacon." He put the top bun on, and, for a moment, admired his handwork. "I never knew the Egyptians ate this well." He picked up the thick sandwich and took an enormous bite.

He swallowed the first bite, frowned, and set the sandwich down. "I'm so selfish. I need to take care of my friends, too." His countenance brightened. "Two more sandwiches coming up."

Branch slunk back the way he'd come, thinking it was all just too easy and wondering when their pursuers would catch up. But he figured they'd have to split up at the four-way intersection. Meaning, Branch and his companions wouldn't have to confront more than two of them, at least, not at first.

Branch reached the room with the crates, and since no one was around, he trotted to the nearest stack. He looked over his shoulder and saw a golf buggy coming carrying two men. Branch ducked behind the stack of crates.

The golf buggy stopped only a few feet to the other side of the crates. The one riding shotgun spoke first.

"We should have kept going, instead of doubling back."

"There are too many tunnels," the driver said. "We might as well do a more thorough search of this area."

Branch backed away and went deeper into the stacks of crates. He carried the guns and ammo but hoped they wouldn't be necessary.

The two searchers began cruising.

Branch crept through the piles of crates back to the golf buggy they'd left in the corner. He was upset, but not surprised that Linda was not there waiting, as he'd instructed. He set the ammo and one of the guns on the floor by the front seat. He heard a noise and whirled around, with his gun at the ready.

It was Roddy, eating a monster sandwich. "Glock 18," Roddy said, pointing with his sandwich. "You couldn't find something better?"

"You've gotta be kidding me," Branch whispered.

"Hey, all this adventure makes me hungry," he whispered back. Then he held up a bag. "I brought some for everyone. By the way, why are we whispering?"

"Bad guys are on the prowl."

Roddy went around to the right side and got on the seat. He peeked in the bag Branch had left on the floor. "Extra clips for the guns. This is an exciting new turn. Thinking ahead now, are we?"

"I bet we won't need them now that we have them."

"Come on, have a sand—Hey, where's Linda?"

"Don't know." Branch noticed a flash coming from a tunnel. "She did *not* flash a camera."

"Yeah, I think she did."

"No, she didn't."

Another flash came from the tunnel.

They heard shotgun's voice. "I think a camera flashed in that tunnel."

"See?" Roddy told Branch.

The driver said to his colleague, "Could you be any louder?"

"Just drive?" shotgun replied.

Roddy nudged Branch with his elbow. "They sound like us."

Branch got behind the wheel of the buggy, backed up, and turned around. He headed straight for the tunnel.

Linda strolled out looking like a satisfied tourist. Roddy removed a bottle from his bag.

"Get in," Branch demanded.

"Testy," Linda said. "Roddy, what's with the bottle?"

"Sparkling grape juice."

Branch turned to face Roddy. "Are you serious?"

"Occasionally."

"I want some," Linda said, as she hopped on the back seat.

Driver and shotgun moved into sight at the end of the row of crates.

Branch did a hard right, and drove between crate stacks as the two men drew their guns.

Branch weaved in and out as he negotiated the irregular pathways among the stacked boxes. Roddy was pouring sparkling grape juice into wine glasses. "Plastic," he said. "Unbreakable. I think." Roddy tossed a sandwich onto Branch's lap and gave Linda a glass of juice and a sandwich.

"Thank you, Roddy," she said. "I'm famished."

Roddy poured one for Branch and held the glass out to him. Branch gave him a look.

"Come on," Roddy said. "You can drive with one hand."

Branch took the glass. When he reached the end of the cave, he turned right, then right again. "We've gotta figure out how to lose them."

"By doubling back?" Roddy asked.

"Giving myself time to think," he said and took a sip of juice.

Their two pursuers were moving with them, just a hundred feet away. They started shooting whenever there was a gap between crates.

Half way across the cave, Branch said, "I hate to interrupt your meal but are you gonna shoot back any time soon?"

"The problem is these Glock 18s are difficult to control. They're small, light, and fire real fast."

"Meaning?"

"Meaning, I'm not gonna have any better luck than they are. You notice how far they're missing us by?"

"We've gotta do something. Brussel and the rest will be here soon."

"We could draw them into an ambush."

"I'm listening."

Branch lost Driver and Shotgun, then came to a stop. Roddy got on a fork lift and repositioned a stack of crates, just so.

Next, they went looking for their adversaries. When they found them, Branch shot out into the open and zipped right past the two before they'd time to react. Driver made a u-turn and took off after them.

Branch did some weaving, which made it impossible for their followers to get a clean shot. Branch and company reached the place they'd prepared. He took an extra wide turn around the corner. The two men behind them made a much sharper turn.

With no time to react, they smashed into the crate Roddy had left for them. Both men were propelled forward into the crate. And knocked unconscious.

Branch backed and turned, until they sat perpendicular to—and facing—the other buggy. All three were eating sandwiches and drinking sparkling grape juice.

They sat, while feasting, looking at the motionless gunmen, and finally Roddy spoke. "Bad guys hit their heads again."

Branch put his sandwich back on his lap, but held onto his glass as he turned the wheel and drove away.

After they drove into a tunnel, Roddy said, "You know the way out?"

"I found another elevator."

Linda leaned between them. "If you need me, I'll be on the floor."

"You drop something?" Roddy said.

"Look behind us."

Roddy and Branch turned and saw three golf buggies with six bad guys in them.

Roddy put his sandwich in the bag, handed his glass to Linda, and took up one of the Glocks.

"Shoot out one of the tires," Branch said.

"I'll be lucky if I hit one of the buggies."

The shooting began in earnest as Roddy and the guy riding shotgun in the first buggy exchanged fire. Bullets pinged off the buggy, the floor of the tunnel, and the walls.

Roddy ejected a clip and reloaded.

As the buggy zoomed through the tunnel, Roddy continued to fire, as did the gunman behind them.

After Roddy had spent another clip, he ejected it and pulled a fresh one out of the satchel.

"This is embarrassing," Roddy said.

"Don't worry," Branch said. "I promise I won't share the particulars of this episode with anyone."

Roddy turned around and took careful aim as the trailing gunman continued to shoot at them. He squeezed the trigger. The semi-automatic fired in quick succession. Bullets bounced helter-skelter off the floor of the tunnel. Finally, one hit the right tire of the pursuing buggy.

When the tire blew, the buggy jerked to the right and smashed into the side of the tunnel.

Brussel and Wallach whipped around the disabled buggy and continued on, followed by the other buggy.

"How much further?" Roddy said.

"Almost there. Get ready to run." Branch turned and looked down at Linda on the floor. "How are you doing?"

"Not too bad. Careful on the turns, all right? I don't want to spill any juice."

Branch kept the pedal to the floor. The tunnel walls whisked by as it twisted one way and then the other. Every time Brussel and Wallach spotted their prey, they pumped out a steady barrage of bullets. But thanks to the winding corridor, these intervening moments of gunplay were brief.

The Pyramid Gang reached the elevator. Branch ran to it, sandwich in one hand and glass in the other, and kicked the open button with his boot. The doors parted. Meanwhile, Roddy gathered up the guns, ammo, and his bag. Linda got to her feet and ran for the elevator.

Brussel and Wallach sped around the last turn just as Roddy dashed into the elevator, right behind Linda.

Linda hit the close button with her elbow, and, as the doors shut, they heard the sound of bullets ping off of them.

Branch studied the meal in his hands for a moment. "I can't believe I ran in here holding these."

"And you didn't spill a drop," said Roddy. He took another bottle out of his bag. "More?"

Branch frowned. "Why not." To Linda: "Would you please do the honors?"

"Of course." With a glass in each hand, she managed to stick out her left index finger and push the up-button. Roddy checked his watch.

They all felt as if they shrunk six inches when the elevator shot up.

On the way, Roddy held out his bag and said. "I have a surprise."

"What, dessert?" Branch said.

He removed his surprise from the bag. "Homemade bomb. Look, C4, digital timer, and all the wires are red, so they don't know which one to cut. Not that they'll have time."

The elevator came to a stop. Roddy checked his watch again.

Linda hit the open button and Branch stepped out.

"Hold the button down a few seconds, missy," Roddy said.

She did so while Roddy set the bomb down. Then he tossed the satchel with the ammo, the two guns, and his bag out of the elevator. He held the sandwich in his mouth, took his glass from Linda and with his free hand he picked up the bomb.

Branch stood holding his sandwich in one hand and glass of juice in the other. "Need help?"

Roddy set the glass down, took the sandwich out of his mouth, and flashed an amicable smile. "I'm good. Enjoy your meal."

He set the timer. "It should go off about one second after the doors start to open. Okay, missy."

Linda took her hand off the button and jumped out. Almost immediately, the doors started closing. Roddy flipped a switch on his bomb and tossed it in the elevator.

They picked up their stuff and started walking, leisurely, to the cave entrance.

"It's never taken me this long to finish a sandwich," Roddy said. "So many interruptions."

As they walked into the sunlight, they heard the muffled sound of the explosion fifteen stories beneath them. Branch used his handheld transceiver to radio Jake to come get them.

After Jake told them he was airborne, Branch fired the flare gun, which Linda had put in her purse, at the blue sky.

"I'm glad we finally got those guys," Roddy said. "You think we got them? I think we got them."

"I hope so," Branch said. "I certainly hope so."

Branch stopped and set his glass on a boulder, reached in his pocket and took out the envelope Wendy had given him. He opened it, took out the note, and bit into his sandwich.

Roddy and Linda waited as Branch read what was on the paper.

"Well?" Linda said.

Branch showed them the note and they read:

NDDGMR 23. Add four of what Hebrew has not, two of one, plus two others, then reverse, and follow—in their proper places—with two of the only number not in Gregory's dates.

Roddy's forehead developed deep furrows. "What are the odds we'll figure that out?"

"I'm stumped, for now," Linda said.

Branch put the note back in the envelope and stuck it in his pocket. "I should've left it alone. I'm gonna lose a lot of sleep over this."

The sound of Jake's helicopter announced his arrival. He landed near them, and as they were boarding smoke poured out of the cave entrance.

Jake pointed and said, "Do you folks realize there is a sizable billow of smoke emanating from the cave from which, I'm assuming, you just left?"

Roddy said, "Yeah, pretty much standard procedure with us."

Chapter Nine

Jake returned them to the airport, and they drove their rental to Lake City, Colorado, where they picked up Benjamin's Mercedes, and then they drove cross-country to Pennsylvania. They needed to regroup, to figure out a way to find the next contact, and plan how they might recover the MacGuffin from Darkin.

Their feelings were mixed at this point. They'd survived, which alone was an outstanding accomplishment. And though they finally stopped their persistent tormentors, they'd hit a wall. For at least the time being, they didn't know where to pick up the trail.

They also had no idea where the trail led. What was the MacGuffin for? Why the cryptic responses from Dr. Reed, and his niece Wendy? And why did Dr. Reed tell his niece things he didn't tell them?

Perhaps he was afraid he might scare them away from completing their quest.

When they arrived at Benjamin's house in the country, he greeted them on the porch with an elated smile. They could see how happy and relieved he was that they were all safe and well. Linda kissed him on the cheek. Roddy and Branch shook his hand.

"Let's go inside," Benjamin said. "I'm sure you have lots to tell me, and I want to hear every word."

They went straight to the study. Entering the room, Branch glanced at the fireplace and the couch facing it. He remembered the many winter nights when he was growing up, sitting by the fire. Benjamin would tell him stories of adventure. Branch realized the couch symbolized something he'd lost somewhere along the way. The need for a home, and to be part of a family.

Linda passed him on her way to the other couch. She was beautiful and amazing.

Roddy took his seat at the train set, donning the engineer's hat. Benjamin parked his wheelchair across from the couch where Linda sat.

Branch went to the couch and was about to sit by Linda, when he thought better of it and went to the end, instead.

Benjamin noticed her disappointment.

Branch said to Linda, "I'll give you your space."

"Yeah, all right," she said, as she dipped her head forward, hiding her face with her hair.

Branch didn't miss that. Had the rules changed, and if so, why wasn't he notified? He gave her a sidelong and confused, glance. *Women!* A guy had to be a mind reader to know where he stood.

"I'm glad you're all in good health," Benjamin said. "I'm disappointed you were unable to find out why a pyramid was built in the Grand Canyon, or why the Egyptians were so far from home."

"Tour guide's day off," Branch said.

Benjamin smiled. "Too bad. We need to deal with more pressing concerns, anyway. Like finding the next contact and retrieving the, uh, whatchamacallit."

"MacGuffin," Roddy said from his stool by the train set.

"Thank you, Roddy," Benjamin said over his shoulder. He turned back to the others. "Now, after doing some research, I've found the location of Professor Darkin's home. He teaches in Cambridge, but, like a lot of teachers, he lives in Maine. Kennebunkport, to be exact."

"Wonderful," said Branch, with a frown. "I finally have an excuse to go to Maine. Seems like a long way to drive to work."

"Hour and forty minutes, but he's only at the school three days a week and his chauffeur drives." He could tell Linda was eager to talk. "Linda, do you want to share something interesting?"

"I took pictures. One of the caves had inscriptions like the ones at Giza."

"I'm aware. Your uncle contacted me right after you sent the pictures to him, and I look forward with anticipation to what they might reveal." He turned his attention toward Branch. "You said in your terse email you had an extraordinary story to tell me, but you were saving it so you could watch the expression on my face. Okay, tell me about the flying saucer."

Stunned, Branch stared at Benjamin. Linda stared, and Roddy turned from the train set.

"How could you know?" Branch said. "We didn't tell anyone."

A familiar voice emanated from near the fireplace. "Sorry to steal your thunder, old buddy."

They all turned toward the couch by the fireplace. Rising to a sitting position was a grinning, shaggy-headed, Hanley. "Looks like the team's back together again."

"I thought you were gonna go to South America," Branch said. "What stopped you, and what do you mean by team?"

"Already been. Nothing could stop me. And it's a collective entity working toward a common goal."

"Why did you go? How come you left so soon? And what common goal?"

"I was looking for flying saucers. My departure involved a small army commanded by an eighty-nine-year-old Nazi, and a car chase or two. There was gunplay, but with little collateral damage. Now, do I get to join the Pyramid Gang, or not?"

Branch stared at his friend for a moment, with all other eyes in the room staring at Branch. Finally, he said, "Welcome to the collective entity."

Benjamin and Roddy applauded.

Linda giggled.

Hanley rose and shook hands with Branch and Roddy, and he kissed Linda's hand. Then he sat in an overstuffed chair.

Benjamin said, "Warren was telling me about flying saucers. He believes they are in the jungles of South America, but he hasn't seen any."

Linda started, "So, Mr. Hanley—"

Cutting her off, he said, "Warren. Please."

"Yes, well, anyway, why did you expect to find flying saucers in South America?"

"An acquaintance once told me he believed that by the end of World War II, the Germans were quite advanced in saucer technology. And that a core of military leaders and scientists escaped to South America just before the Allied takeover. I didn't think much of it until I saw—and even flew—a flying saucer. I thought, *What if this guy is on to something?* So I went to Brazil to find out for myself."

"But didn't find anything?" Branch said.

"They're hiding something, and as long as I'm allergic to that many bullets at one time, it can stay hidden." Hanley leaned back into his overstuffed chair, ready to give up being the center of attention.

Branch pulled from his pocket the piece of paper Wendy had given him. Handing the scrap to Hanley, he said, "Here, why don't you use your oversized brain to figure this out?"

"Oversized brain?" Linda said.

"Inside joke," Hanley said. "Pay no attention." Hanley studied the note on the paper.

"What is it?" asked Benjamin.

Branch said, "An alleged prophecy from a former monk."

Hanley read aloud, "NDDGMR 23. Add four of what Hebrew has not, two of one, plus two others, then reverse, and follow—in their proper places—with two of the only number not in Gregory's dates."

"What do you think?" Benjamin said.

"Not the foggiest," said Hanley, handing the paper back to Branch.

"Didn't make any sense to me," said Benjamin. "Now, about the MacGuffin," Benjamin said to Branch. "What do you think your next move is?"

"Well, seems to me four separate missions loom ahead of us," said Branch. "We need to track down Harlan Wilson, the programmer from NASA. Find out how they intend to fake proof of evolution, and why the late Dr. Reed thought it was crucial to expose NASA. Jeremiah Daniels, the astrotheologian. He's our next contact, so we assume he's got the sixth piece. Then, of course, there's Roger Darkin. His home in Maine might be the most likely place for him to hide the MacGuffin. I also think someone needs to go to Turkey and track down the boy who found the missing link. With Darkin being mixed up in the Ararat Man charade, a whole lot more may be at stake than creating a provocative museum exhibit."

"Perfect," Hanley said. "There are four of us. We'll each take a mission."

"Split up?" Branch said.

"Right. We'll accomplish our tasks four times as fast."

"I don't think splitting up is a good idea." He glanced at Linda and then back at Hanley. "No reason to hurry; no ticking bomb."

Benjamin said, "I realize you're concerned about Linda's safety. But since you've eliminated your pursuers, you'll all be under the radar. In fact, I found a way to guarantee it. As for the ticking bomb, we can't assume anyone or anything will be available for you to find whenever you get around to it. And Darkin won't stop searching for you, or the contacts with the other four pieces."

"Right," Hanley said. "We can't be sure where Darkin hid the MacGuffin, so we should bend every effort toward finding it."

"You said it yourself, Branch," Linda added. "Dr. Reed was a Pyramidion who thought finding Harlan Wilson and exposing NASA was necessary to the cause. Though we haven't yet discovered what the cause is. I think going our separate ways is a good plan."

Roddy brought the Lionel, standard gauge, Union Pacific Challenger, with its trailing cars, into the station and to a halt. Roddy then turned to the others.

"Benjamin, you said we could stay under the radar. How?"

"Any of you familiar with Whisper Systems?" They all returned blank looks, so he went on. "They're not far from here. Based in Pittsburgh. They've come up with a way to encrypt phone calls and text messages. I acquired five Android smartphones that include the RedPhone app for calls, and TextSecure. One Android for each of us."

"How about GPS?" Hanley asked.

"Removed. From all the phones. So, no one can find you, and with encryption, no one can decipher your communications.

"What about passports and other identification?" Branch said.

"New ones for all of you. This time, I went as deep undercover as is possible to go. I secured them from an organization you don't need to know about, but I guarantee there are no leaks."

"So what's my new name?" Roddy said.

"You'll all keep your first names, but each of you will be using the same last name. Eckstein."

"Chico Eckstein," Roddy said. "Got a nice ring."

They all laughed.

"Was this chosen at random?" Hanley said.

"No," said Benjamin. "Eckstein is German. Eck means corner and stein means stone."

"Cornerstone," Linda said. "How appropriate. Although, technically, a pyramid has a capstone..."

"Spare us," Branch said.

"Cornerstone, or capstone if you prefer," Benjamin said, smiling at Linda, "will serve as a code name if you need to contact one another in case of an emergency."

"So, who goes where?" Linda said.

"Why don't you track down the astrotheologian?" said Branch.

Linda opened her purse and took out the packet of info Wendy had given them. "Already been studying this. Jeremiah

Daniels is an enigma, to say the least. He's an eighty-two-year-old marathon runner, hang glider, and motorcycle enthusiast. Got his masters in mechanical engineering at Johns Hopkins, and a master of divinity at Wheaton. Was the pastor at five different churches. Kept being driven out for teaching science in Sunday School."

"Why?" Benjamin asked.

"Some believed he should only teach the Bible."

"So where might Reverend Daniels be?"

"He might be anywhere. He might be nowhere. He's like a puff of smoke. But I have a hunch that I'd like to follow. He's a regular attendee at a Christian summer retreat in Michigan. It's called Maranatha Bible and Missionary Conference. Their summer program doesn't start until late June. But according to a notation from Wendy, he always said he might like to be a year 'round resident."

"Okay, what about you, Branch?" said Benjamin.

"I'd like to track down Harlan Wilson, but I'm not sure where to start."

"Why not start at his last known place of employment?"

"NASA? Sounds more like a job for Hanley."

"Don't look at me. I'm *persona non grata.*"

"All right, then, I'll go," Branch said. "Which leaves Maine and Turkey."

Hanley said, "Darkin's house may be guarded by security men, most likely carrying pictures of all of you. I'm still unknown to him."

"Good," Branch said. "Roddy, I guess you're going to Turkey. Do you think you can track down the boy who discovered the ape-man?"

"Just call me Sherlock Rodriguez."

"Do you have a plan, Sherlock?"

"I knew a guy in Army intelligence. He works for the CIA now and last I heard, he was stationed in Turkey. But first, I need to go home and visit my wife."

"Fine. Call as soon as you're on your way, as soon as Christine says you can come out to play again."

Roddy just grinned at Branch.

Benjamin said to Hanley, "You're gonna be in the neighborhood of your alma mater."

"Couple states away but not a long drive."

"Which school?" asked Linda.

"M.I.T. Studied to be an engineer in aeronautics and astronautics."

"They kicked him out, too," Branch said.

"Did they now?" said Linda.

"Many times," Hanley said.

"You were kicked out more than once?"

"Yeah."

"How'd you get back in?"

Hanley, for the first time, seemed embarrassed, and not wanting to answer.

"Well?" Linda said, folding her arms.

Hanley said nothing, so Branch helped him out. "They couldn't bear to lose him. So they kept giving him another chance."

"And they did this, why?"

"His I.Q.," Benjamin said.

"Yeah," said Hanley. "Nobody knows what it is."

"I don't follow," Linda said. "What do you mean?"

Benjamin was smiling like a proud papa at Hanley. "He means his I.Q. is so high it can't be measured."

Linda lowered her voice an octave. "You guys *are* putting me on, right?"

Hanley said, "Proves God has a sense of humor. Putting a brain like mine in a guy like me."

"What's the highest I.Q. that can be measured?" Linda said.

"Two hundred and forty," Benjamin said.

Linda said to Hanley, "Did you graduate?"

"Yes, a couple years ahead of Branch. M.I.T. is where we first met."

"I was majoring in writing and humanistic studies," Branch said. "We were chasing the same girl and got to be friends along the way."

"What happened to the girl?" asked Linda.

"I graduated," Hanley said. "Never saw her again. I thought she was gonna marry Nichols."

"She told me goodbye and left school the same year as Hanley," said Branch. "I thought she eloped with him."

Hanley said, "It wasn't until years later, when we both went to work as UFO hunters that we discovered the truth. She'd dropped off the edge of the planet. We decided to check with the university, but the school has no record of her ever having been there."

"How strange," Linda said. "What was her name?"

"We knew her as Midnight Jones, a philosophy major," said Branch.

Hanley said, "Maybe I'll stop by and check out our old bench."

Branch gave him a look.

"Hey, I'm a hardcore nostalgic," Hanley said.

"Which is a contradiction in terms," said Branch. "You never got over her."

"Don't be ridiculous."

Benjamin said, "Warren, while you're there, I want you to do something for me."

"Yes sir," Hanley said, with genuine respect, even sitting up straight when he said it.

Linda was surprised and impressed.

Benjamin went on, "I need you to look up Professor Lyle Wentsler. He teaches Cultural Studies at Harvard. Be careful though; that's where Darkin teaches Evolutionary Biology."

"Like I said before, he hasn't seen me. Probably isn't aware that I exist. Unless he has a hotline to my old buddy Holloway."

"Anything is possible," Benjamin said. "When you see Lyle, tell him Operation Bilderberg is on."

"I will."

"Can't you just email or call?" Branch said.

"Too risky."

"Snail mail?"

"Even that's compromised."

Branch wanted to learn more but didn't press.

They all talked about their adventures over dinner; then went to their rooms. Later that evening, Linda happened to meet Hanley in a hallway.

"We really should stop meeting like this," Hanley said.

"Couldn't agree more," said Linda, leaning away from him and against the wall. "Besides, we haven't been meeting at all; like this or otherwise."

"And why not?" Hanley said, putting his hand above her shoulder and leaning in.

"Are you always this forward with the ladies? And does it ever work?"

"Yes. Is it working now?"

She said nothing for a moment, and then: "You've been acquainted with Benjamin for a long time, true?"

"That's a non-answer. Means I have a chance."

"You must know Benjamin pretty well. You seem to have a lot of respect for him."

"He's the closest thing to a father figure I've ever had, and I've never met anyone more deserving of respect. Why?"

"Your attitude toward him doesn't fit the image you project. Perhaps there's hope for you, after all."

"Well, let's not get carried away."

"You made a reference to God as creator. Was that just rhetorical?"

"No. Unlike your boyfriend, I do believe in God."

"I can't say that with your attitude and behavior that you strike me as being a believer."

"Like the words of the song, 'I gotta be me.'"

"That song was sung by a member of the infamous Rat Pack. Yet, somehow"—she squirmed a couple inches further from him—"I don't think you're quite the rogue you... make as if."

"What an awkward end to a sentence. Perhaps you're flustered. I have that affect on women."

"I'm so glad one of us thinks so."

Hanley grinned.

They didn't notice Branch standing at the end of the hall.

Chapter Ten

Benjamin's chauffeur took them to the airport. They'd begun referring to themselves now as the Family Eckstein. They entered one another's numbers into their Android phones.

They said their goodbyes at the airport, with the guys all shaking hands. Roddy and Linda hugged, Hanley kissed Linda's hand. Branch started to move in for a hug, stopped, backed off, and took Linda's hand. They wished each other well.

Hanley got on a plane for Boston; Linda caught a flight for Muskegon; Branch headed for San Francisco; and Roddy went home to Missouri.

Hanley rented a car at the airport and drove to Cambridge, to M.I.T. The campus had undergone construction since he left. The new architecture was considered creatively modern, he guessed. Creatively berserk was a better description. One of the buildings appeared to be falling down. *Apropos.* The design said volumes about modern art and architecture.

He went to the bench he used to sit on with Midnight. Hanley considered her to be the most brilliant, interesting, and beautiful girl he'd ever met. And while women in general could be aggravatingly mysterious anyway, she was the most enigmatic person he knew. That alone made her intriguing enough for him to want to find her again.

He got up from the bench, took one last gander at the so-called modern architecture, shook his head, and left.

He drove up Interstate 95, through New Hampshire, toward Kennebunkport, Maine, and Roger Darkin's home.

Leaving San Francisco, Branch drove down Interstate 280 and up Route 85. He went to the NASA Advanced Supercomputing (NAS) division at Ames Research Center, at Moffett Federal Airfield. He asked about Harlan Wilson, and was told they didn't know his whereabouts. But if he wanted to, Branch could talk to someone who had worked with Wilson.

Branch was led to an office by an officious, albeit cute, young secretary named Janie. She gave him a running commentary on the work done at Ames.

"Pleiades is the name of our supercomputing powerhouse. It's the sixth most powerful computer in the world. For more than twenty-five years, the NAS Division has given scientists and engineers the resources and simulation tools they need to conduct vital missions. This enables them to make scientific discoveries that profit the whole human race."

She went on with her spiel without letup until they came to a door with a name plaque that read Smith Underwood.

"I hope you don't mind me rattling on the way I did."

"Not at all, Janie. I feel well informed now."

"I'm proud of what goes on here. Besides, my last job was tour guide. Old habits."

"Tour guide? For NASA?"

"No, no. Walt Disney Studios in Burbank."

"Oh."

"Well, you can knock on the door. If you need anything, I'll be at my desk." She scurried away.

Branch knocked and a voice told him to come in. Branch entered and closed the door behind him. Underwood had a spare office. Few books, no plants, and raised blinds on the window, which eliminated 50 per cent of the wall behind the desk.

Branch approached Underwood as he was typing at a computer. Branch waited for him to stop, and extended his hand.

"Hi, I'm Branch Nichols. Hope I didn't catch you at a bad time."

"Smith Underwood," he said, rising and shaking hands. "Have a seat. I'm catching up on email. Nothing of pressing importance. Just staying in touch with our alien friends on the dark side of the moon."

Branch returned a blank stare.

Underwood chuckled. "My peculiar sense of humor," he said, with a wave of his hand.

"I'm sure some people would think you were serious."

"Yes, I'm amazed at what some people are willing to believe. Now, how can I help you?"

"I'm trying to track down Harlan Wilson."

Branch noticed a reaction, albeit a subtle and brief change in countenance. Underwood carried on as though unfazed.

"Ah, Harlan. Well, he's been absent for a couple of years now. Went out to lunch one day and never returned."

"Doesn't sound good. Was he in any kind of trouble?"

"I wouldn't know. He wasn't the type to get into trouble."

"Are you at all familiar with the term Pyramidion?"

Again, a flash of change in his demeanor. "No. I'm not."

"You're not," he said as if agreeing, rather than questioning. He was sure Underwood knew more than he would admit. Perhaps he was afraid.

Underwood opened a drawer and pulled out a business card. "If you find Harlan, I'd like to know how the bum is doing." He began to write on the back of the card. "I'll put my home address and phone number on here." When he finished writing, he handed the card to Branch.

Branch took the card and glanced at it. He put the card in his pocket and shook hands with Underwood. "Thank you for your time."

Branch went to his car, took out the card, and read the back. *Meet me at the Lion & Compass for lunch at 11:30.* Branch spotted someone, who seemed to be looking at him out of the corner of his eye, walking across the parking lot. *I'm becoming overly vigilant.*

He took out his phone and got directions to the restaurant.

Branch put his phone back in his pocket and surveyed the parking lot. The man was gone. *Probably nothing.*

Branch arrived at the restaurant at 11:30. He sat in the parking lot, watching for Underwood. He only had to wait a few minutes.

He and Underwood walked together. "I like the tropical setting," Branch said.

"The *New York Times* said the 'Lion & Compass is to the Silicon Valley what Sardi's was to the theater district.'"

"So the food is good."

"Culinary oasis."

"Seems odd to pick such a popular spot for a clandestine meeting."

"Exactly. No one will suspect."

They were the first diners since the restaurant had just opened for lunch. They were given a table by a window.

When the maître d' left, Branch leaned toward Underwood. In a conspiratorial whisper, he said, "Why the intrigue?"

"You asked about someone who was working on a project no one—including me—is supposed to be aware of."

"I thought you two worked together."

"Officially, yes and on certain simulation projects. But he was involved in something he didn't want to be part of and that's why he left. By the way, how do you know about the Pyramidions?"

"I was volunteered to acquire the pieces to a tiny pyramid, a key of some kind. Are you familiar with that?"

"Yes, I'm Harlan's backup if something happens to him. The piece would then fall to me."

"Harlan has one of them?"

"Yes, but you must be aware, the chain has been subject to disruption. I'm not sure if you'll be able to locate all nine."

"Don't each of you have at least two contacts."

"Yes, at least two and the pieces have been passed along from keeper to keeper for thousands of years. But the truth is we're now being hunted down."

"So where's Harlan?"

At that moment, a waiter came to take their order. Underwood ordered a turkey and Havarti cheese on Milton's multi-grain bread. Branch ordered a cheeseburger.

The waiter left and Branch stared at Underwood, waiting.

Underwood leaned in. With people starting to enter the restaurant, he glanced to one side to make sure no one was close enough to hear. Then he turned his attention toward Branch.

"You're gonna have to take a *very* long trip, Mr. Nichols"

"Where to?"

"You'll find Harlan Wilson at Hell's Gate."

Bullets zinged by, ripping at the door jam, and popping a couple of vases at the far side of the room. Hanley had tripped an alarm, and now Darkin's formidable security team was chasing him through the mansion.

He returned fire as he darted to the other side of the doorway and slammed the door shut.

A volley of bullets punctured the handcrafted mahogany. Some lodged deep into several first editions on the bookshelves.

Hanley ejected the empty clip and inserted a new one. He had armed himself when he overwhelmed a guard who patrolled the grounds at the rear of the estate.

Hanley ran across the room toward an open door. He turned and fired a couple of shots through the closed door to keep his pursuers at bay a little longer. Then he went into the next room and shut the door behind him. He discovered a key in the latch, so he locked it.

He took in the new surroundings. It appeared to be a study, which had a large desk, featuring some books, papers, and a twenty-inch laptop computer. Hanley went to the desk and flipped open the laptop. The computer's wallpaper was a picture of the Great Pyramid and Sphinx behind a dozen icons.

Hanley clicked on the "My Documents" icon. The file opened and he perused it for a few moments; then closed it. He closed the laptop and opened the desk drawer on the right, then the middle, and finally the one on the left.

"I don't believe this." Hanley reached into the drawer and grabbed the MacGuffin. "This is too easy."

The door flung open, followed by the well-polished shoe of an angry, hulking security man, who subsequently sprayed the room with bullets from an automatic weapon.

Hanley ducked behind the desk. "Spoke too soon."

"Are you under attack?" Roddy said to his wife, Christine, as she slapped at a fly on her leg.

"Everything's okay, sweetie. He's in retreat."

They sat on reclining lawn chairs, on Roddy's boat. Christine wore a conservative one-piece bathing suit. Roddy had on shorts, and an unbuttoned shirt. The boat floated across Table Rock Lake. Roddy's house in nearby Kimberling City was not far from Branson—home to numerous musical performers.

Lots of retirees lived in the area. Roddy often said one of the things he liked about living here was that when he retired, he wouldn't have to move.

Christine peered at Roddy through her sunglasses. "So, tell me more about this pyramid society with the MacGuffin. Are they gonna save the world, or what?"

"Don't know yet. The MacGuffin is some kind of key to something. Been waiting for over 4,000 years to be reassembled."

"And you're going to Turkey to hunt for the boy who found the so-called missing link?"

"Yeah, it's amazing how so many people will jump on a single artifact."

"I've been listening to the news. This Ararat Man, or Bonobo Man, as some people are calling the skeleton, is the man of the hour. He's become the Holy Grail of evolution."

"Which is why I have to leave soon."

"Summer and Autumn will be home from college in ten days."

"And I look forward to seeing the girls. The sooner I go, the sooner I'm back."

When Linda arrived at the Maranatha Bible and Missionary Conference center, she couldn't pass a barrier requiring a code. She parked in the Bible retreat's main lot, and started walking. She found the sidewalk that went down to the beach on Lake Michigan.

She met a middle-aged woman in a pink sundress coming from that direction.

"Can you help me? I'm looking for an elderly man named Jeremiah Daniels, who might be living in this area."

"I don't recognize the name."

"He's in his eighties. Likes to run, hang glide—"

"And ride motorcycles?"

"Yes."

"Sounds like Reverend Wildman. Or "wild man," as some like to call him. He lives down the road about halfway to the beach." She described the house to Linda.

Linda walked about an eighth of a mile until she found the house.

After knocking on the door, she turned to admire the surrounding scenery with its many evergreens and oaks. The area included a nearby forest, and the beach, which she still couldn't see.

After several moments, the door swung open. An elderly, but robust, white-haired man stood in the doorway.

"Hello, young lady."

"My name is Linda Chapel. Are you Jeremiah Daniels?"

"I'm sorry. Someone must've given you the wrong address. My name is Wildman."

"Are you a Pyramidion?"

His countenance changed and he seemed confused, not sure how to answer.

Linda said, "I'm looking for the sixth piece to the pyramid key."

Stepping back, he said, "Come inside."

Hanley was crouching behind Darkin's desk as bullets skidded off the top. He crawled around the corner, dove out onto the floor and fired repeatedly. Three security men ducked out of the doorway and back into the adjoining room.

Hanley got to his feet and ran to the window. He dove through it, and because he was on the third floor, which was not as wide as the bottom two floors, he landed on the roof. He rolled over a few times and stopped himself from going off the edge.

He stood and ran along the shingled rooftop, looking for a way down. He heard an automatic weapon firing from the ground. He located the man shooting at him and fired back.

Hearing the sound of a bolt being cocked, Hanley turned and shot in the direction of the guard behind him. The guard ducked back inside.

The man on the ground was trying to un-jam his weapon. Hanley stood, ran, and jumped through a window and onto the floor. Bullets from below strafed the colorful *Ali Baba and the Forty Thieves* wallpaper.

Hanley started to get up, stumbled forward, and then got to his knees. He was next to a child's bed with the name Roger on the Headboard. Beneath the name was the inscription, Born March 5, 1964. Hanley glanced around the pristine room as he got to his feet. Toys stood on the shelves. A Frisbee, Tonka Trucks, Matchbox Cars, a Mr. Potato Head.

Hanley shook his head as he got to his feet, and chuckled. *Who maintains their childhood room for forty-five years after they've outgrown it?*

He ran across the room. This time, he opened the window, peered out, and seeing no one, stepped through and onto the roof. Hanley ran along the edge until he found a thick stand of bushes. He dove off the two-story rooftop, stretched out, turned over in mid-air, and landed in the bushes on his back.

He rolled out of the bushes and into a standing position on the ground. He looked around and then trotted off into some nearby trees, heading toward the rear of the estate where he'd left the car.

Jeremiah had ushered Linda into his living room, and they were now sipping tea.

"Everything you've told me, Linda, about Wendy and the rest, convinces me you're telling the truth. I'll give you the sixth piece before you go."

"Jeremiah, I was curious. You've been asked to leave five different churches."

"Asked? I got booted, thrown out with extreme prejudice."

"For teaching science in Sunday school?"

"I taught the kids scientific reasons why evolution could never happen."

"And some parents complained."

"Some parents think all their children need is the Bible. If they memorized enough Bible verses, they'd be prepared for anything, or so the parents thought."

"But you disagreed."

"Someone did the research and wrote a book called *Already Gone.* Today, 70 per cent of children raised in Christian homes leave the church when they reach their twenties. This even includes children who were home schooled. They are making this decision while still in high school, in middle school, even as early as grammar school."

"And it's because of evolution?"

"If the first chapter of Genesis falls, the rest of the Bible falls with it."

"Where are you going?" the lady at the ticket counter asked Branch.

"Hell's Gate."

The ticket agent slid her glasses down to the end of her nose and peered over them. "Excuse me."

"Hell's Gate, Australia."

"I'm pretty sure we don't have any flights that land there."

"Get me as close as you can."

"I'll see what I can do."

She began punching keys on her computer.

Hanley had made the trip down Interstate 95 in just over an hour, which, he was sure, had to be a record. He drove back to MIT to find Professor Wentsler. He wasn't at his office, so Hanley went to his home. He knocked on the door and after a moment, Wentsler answered.

"I'm Warren Hanley. I'm here as a favor to Benjamin Rydal."

"Please come in." He locked the door behind Hanley and motioned for his guest to sit. The precise gesture was like a conductor getting just the right nuance from the violin section.

"How is Benjamin?" Wentsler said.

"Doing well."

"I'm glad you returned from Maine unscathed."

"Actually, I acquired quite a few cuts... Wait, how'd you know—?"

"I have my sources. It's remarkable you were able to gain entrance to the house. Even more remarkable that you got out alive. Were you successful in your venture?"

"Piece o' cake."

"But you said you were cut."

"I changed my shirt after the bleeding stopped."

"Ah, yes. All's well that ends well, I suppose."

"I need to pass along a message from Benjamin. He said to tell you that Operation Bilderberg is on."

Wentsler nodded. "Thank you, Mr. Hanley. That's good news."

"I don't suppose you're gonna tell me what it's about."

"I'm sure Benjamin will fill you in when the time comes."

"Then I guess I should be leaving."

At the door, Wentsler opened it, and Hanley came alongside.

"Now, I'm afraid I have some bad news to share," Wentsler said. "Your image, no doubt was captured by security cameras, cuts and all."

"I'm not gonna worry about that."

"It gets worse. I couldn't contact Benjamin to warn him about sending people, for fear of compromising him. I'm being watched around the clock, and now our adversaries know you too. And *that* you *should* worry about."

"Deep doo-doo, huh?"

"Exactly."

"And, exactly, who are these people?"

At that moment, Wentsler glanced out the door. "Watch out!" he cried, as he pushed Hanley out of the way. Wentsler whirled halfway around and crashed on the carpet.

Blood poured from Wentsler's chest.

Hanley grabbed the door, slammed it, and dove to the floor. Several holes rapidly appeared in the door. He checked Wentsler's carotid artery and found no pulse.

Hanley jumped to his feet and ran to the rear of the house. Looking out a window, he saw no one. He opened the door and moved onto the back porch, scanning the bushes and wood fence.

Seeing nothing, he ran to the gate and opened it. He did another visual check, and, satisfying himself that there were no snipers, he started to run.

Chapter Eleven

Roddy sat on the couch in his home as Christine brought two eight-ounce bottles of Coke. She sat next to him and handed him a bottle. She leaned into to him.

Roddy was always amazed anyone so beautiful would fall in love and marry him. Especially someone with such a warm heart.

Growing up, he and Branch agreed the hottest girls had the coldest hearts. Christine was the exception and ever since they met, she and Roddy had been best friends.

She referred to Branch as Roddy's other best friend. She'd long since given up trying to convince him to replace Branch with another, other best friend.

"So, you'll be leaving for Turkey in the morning?"

"That's the plan, and I appreciate that you're not giving me a hard time."

"I'd really like to. But on the bright side, Branch won't be present."

"Aw, come on," he said, with a smile. "You know you like Branch."

"Especially when he's not around."

Roddy's Android jingled to let him know he had a text message. He took the phone out of his shirt pocket. "Hey, look who finally decided to contact me."

"This is exciting," Christine said, deadpan.

Roddy read the message. "On my way to Hell's Gate?"

"He's going home?"

"Be nice... He says here that it's in Australia."

"Good. Far away from Turkey."

Linda rested on a bench which rested on a porch. She sat with her legs tucked under, looking out toward Lake Michigan. Jeremiah sat on the bench, as well.

He was eighty but looked hardly more than sixty. Jeremiah was vigorous and alert, with thick white hair reaching his collar.

"What did you teach the kids in Sunday School, Jeremiah?"

"I taught, among other things, the laws of thermodynamics. I always started with them when I had a new group. There are four, numbered zero to three."

"Zero?"

"Yes. The most fundamental law wasn't known until after the other three were discovered. Since the number one was already taken, the new, albeit preceding law, was given the number zero. The Zeroth Law is simple. It says heat won't flow between two things that are the same temperature. Easy so far, wouldn't you say?"

Linda nodded and smiled.

"Now, law number one says you cannot create heat and you cannot destroy heat. Heat will only do one of two things: flow from one place to another, or take on a new form."

"I don't understand," Linda said. "If you light a candle, doesn't the candle create heat?"

"No. The process of burning merely sets it free. The candle already contained the heat, but in a different form. Chemical energy. The amount of heat is unchanged, just somewhat disorganized.

"Now, on to the Second Law. First, we must deal with the concept of entropy. This is a gauge for the distribution of heat, a measure of how much energy is not available in a system. Put another way, we're talking about a change from order to disorder. Whenever heat flows from something hot to something cold, there will be more entropy. If heat were to flow from a cold place to a hot place, there would be less entropy.

"The Second Law declares that in a closed system, we will always see increasing entropy. A closed system is one that can receive no heat from outside itself. The universe is, therefore, a closed system.

"The Third Law states no process can be reversed. This is because for heat to be converted without waste, the temperature of the exhaust would have to be absolute zero. So, an efficiency rating of 100 per cent isn't possible. Every process adds to entropy. So order in the universe is on an inescapable path toward disorder."

"Can you nutshell all this for me?"

Jeremiah laughed. "Okay. In an attempt to simplify all this, someone described the three laws this way: 'The First Law says you can't win. The Second Law says the best you can do is to break even. The Third Law says you can only break even at absolute zero.'"

Linda said, smiling, "Clever, but I'm still not sure I understand the laws, or how they affect everyday life."

"Not to worry. Let's take a walk on the beach and have dinner. You must stay here tonight, and tomorrow I'll continue with my lecture. I'll make you an expert before you leave."

She laughed. "I don't know about that, but I would like to stay and visit with you some more."

The next morning, Hanley sat on the edge of the bed in his motel room. He'd left his rental car behind, and called the agency to let them know where to pick it up. He'd gotten a room for the night, but still had no transportation. He also hadn't contacted Benjamin. Hanley dreaded having to tell him about his friend's death.

He got his Android phone out and said, "Call Dad." Benjamin answered after the second ring.

"Hello, Warren."

"Benjamin, I have good news and bad news."

"Start with the good."

"I paid Professor Darkin's home a visit and recovered the MacGuffin."

"Well, what do you know? I'm amazed you got it back so quickly."

"Darkin wasn't expecting anyone to get past his security, both coming and going. The thing wasn't even locked up. And his guards need some serious target practice."

"You did a good job, Warren. Now tell me the bad news."

"I went to visit your friend, Professor Wentsler. A hit man showed up just as I was about to leave... I'm sorry, Benjamin."

"Lyle murdered? I knew he was being watched, but assassinated. Doesn't make sense."

"I don't think he was the target. I think your friend took a bullet for me."

"You must've been followed all the way from Maine."

"Yeah, until the episode at Wentsler's, I was asking myself if the raid on Darkin's house went a little too easy."

"Dodging bullets is never easy. Darkin simply got careless."

"So what about the message? He never had time to pass it on to anyone."

"Don't worry. I'll make other arrangements. How about you? What is your next move?"

"I need to catch up with Linda. She's holding the fifth, and possibly the sixth, piece to the puzzle."

"I'll pray for a safe journey, but watch your back."

"I will."

Branch didn't usually suffer from jet lag, but the trip was long. And he didn't relish the idea of taking an extended ride in a Jeep to a remote part of Australia's last frontier. It was one of the oldest scenery-rich terrains in the world, complete with bits of prehistoric rainforests. They used to blanket the region.

It was the middle of the night but the waxing moon lit up the landscape nicely.

He appreciated the flora, fauna, rare birds, and some spectacular rock formations. Which added to its uniqueness. But he still didn't like having to drive out to the middle of nowhere to find this computer geek.

Harlan Wilson was one of the elites of the elite of humanity's brain trust. His whole life had been the active fulfillment of his destiny. He was one of the movers and shakers in man's striving toward scientific accomplishment. Now he was hiding on the edge of creation.

Underwood had told Branch much about Harlan Wilson and in radiant terms. Branch had become eager to meet the man. Almost as eager as he was to get this trip over with.

He followed Underwood's directions and came to a spring with a mini-rainforest nearby. In the shade, he found a twenty-by-twenty-five foot adobe hut.

Branch knocked on the door, and in a moment, it opened. The man standing in the doorway was holding a book entitled *The Joy of π*. He didn't have the pasty skin one might expect with a computer geek. Instead, he had the bronzed appearance of someone who was living not far south of the equator.

"Can I help you? Are you lost?"

"My name is Branch Nichols—"

"Thank God, you found me. Come in. It's almost my bedtime but I hate having to waste three hours a night sleeping, anyway."

Branch was a little surprised, but only a little. After all the surprises he'd had in recent days, why shouldn't an expatriated NASA nerd, living in the closest thing to a temporal void, be darn-near expecting him?

The candlelit living room and kitchen were mated and occupied most of the meager space. A bathroom and tiny bedroom took the rest. A cubist painting by Picasso hung on a wall.

Harlan noticed him looking at it.

"Yes, it's genuine."

Branch gave a polite nod. He had no interest in the alleged art of self-involved, womanizing, mad, socialist painters.

They sat in two easy chairs, which rested in opposing corners of the living room.

Branch said, "I was told by Dr. Peter Reed and Smith Underwood you were involved with a good deal of NASA's digital skullduggery."

"How is Dr. Reed?"

"I'm sorry, but he's now the late Dr. Reed."

"You don't say?"

"Self-detonated explosion."

"Blew himself up, did he?" Wilson was pensive for a few moments. Then, looking as though he'd just resolved an issue in his mind, he said, "Peter always did have a flare for the dramatic."

Branch wasn't sure how to respond to Harlan's casual reaction and simply nodded.

"I imagine he wanted me to tell you all about my work at NASA. I'm an astronomer as well as a computer geek. Also, you'll need to know what my work had to do with evolution, your quest for the Pyramidions, and why I'm hiding in the vacuous vortex of a literal nowhere instead of working a high-level job for the ultimate somewhere. So, anyway, are you familiar with the Origins Program?"

Branch answered, "I think it involves NASA's goal to discover evidence for the origin of mankind."

"Almost right. *Discover* isn't the correct word. *Create* evidence for man's origin is what they intend. I was working on a virtual reality program, which would do just that. Suddenly, we'd have proof of alien life forms in outer space, with no more need to prove earth-sired evolution. The new gospel being that mankind was dropped here as full-fledged human beings. We could assume they did all their evolving elsewhere.

"As the pseudosciences of Einstein, Copernicus, and Darwin come crashing down, the evolutionists would have themselves covered."

"Wait a minute, you said Copernicus? Didn't he—?"

"Give us the heliocentric model of the universe which replaced the belief in the geocentric model? Yes, but Copernicus was wrong. The Earth doesn't move; doesn't rotate; doesn't revolve around the sun. So Earth isn't a planet in the true sense of the word, and, in fact, the sun and all the rest of creation revolve around the Earth."

Branch stared at Wilson for a long moment. *I came all the way out here to talk to this wing nut?* He looked at his watch. "I don't want to take up any more of your time."

Wilson laughed. "Ah, now, Mr. Nichols, don't give up on me so quickly. Hear me out. I just might be able to prove to your satisfaction that Copernicus was a fraud. Whose work was accepted only because of the work of another fraud, Albert Einstein. Both were accepted to protect another fraud, Charles Darwin. I can prove with non-theoretical—as in real—science that the biblical model for the universe was right all along."

"Look, I'm not gonna argue against your religion or worldview or anything like that. You have the right to believe whatever you wish, but I can't accept that all the best scientists in the world could be so wrong."

"You shouldn't assume that all the best scientists are in agreement. Your skepticism is natural. You've had the heliocentric model drilled into you since kindergarten. Are you afraid to find out you've been believing a lie for almost forty years?"

"No, I'm not afraid. I just need to go."

"Come on, Branch. Have you got the guts to realize the truth about the universe you live in, or are you chicken?" the scrawny little nerd said.

Branch sat back in the thickly padded chair, studying his challenger. He smiled, ever so slightly. "All right, dazzle me."

Roddy was reasonably sure he hadn't left Earth, but his jet lag verged on interplanetary magnitude. And it wouldn't have been a consolation knowing Branch was having the same experience nine thousand miles away. He all but stumbled through Trabzon airport and was glad to find his old friend, Brick Majors.

They shook hands and started to walk. Majors was in his late forties, and nearly as solid as he was in his twenties.

"I did some investigating," Majors said. "Seems the boy and his family disappeared. I have a contact familiar with the boy's village. He'll meet us."

He scrutinized Roddy. "Are you okay?"

"I don't usually get jet lag this bad. I can tough it out and no one even notices. I think I got hold of some bad food on the plane. So, now, I'm dealing with a double whammy."

"Bad news, then. We'll be flying to our destination in a beat-up old twin-engine."

"What's the boy's name?" Roddy asked.

"We don't know. People refer to him as the boy who found the ape-man."

They headed for a town on the eastern edge of Turkey near the border of Iran. They landed near a jeep with a young Turk sitting in the back.

The man wore a t-shirt and blue jeans indicative of the western influence in Turkey, but his head was covered by the traditional red fez.

"Where are we?" Roddy said to Brick.

"Doğubeyazıt."

Roddy blinked. "That's easy for you to say. How 'bout we just call the city 'dog biscuit'?"

The young man in the backseat said, "Try being a Turk and learn English."

"I'm sorry. I forgot my manners," Roddy said, as he turned with a smile. "I'm Roddy."

"Alp. In English, the name means courageous." They shook hands.

"Good. You may need to be."

"I'm well aware. Your reputation precedes you."

Roddy smiled and turned to gaze ahead. "Mountains. Are we near Little Ararat?"

"This town is surrounded by some of the highest peaks in Turkey," Alp said. "Including Mount Ararat and Little Ararat."

Brick shifted into gear and started to drive. "The boy lives in the countryside. Only a little further, Roddy, and we can stretch our legs."

It was late afternoon when they reached the outer limits of town. They had also reached the outer limits of poverty. Stopping the car, Brick said, "He lives there."

"Where?" said Roddy. "I don't see a house."

Brick pointed.

Roddy adjusted his gaze and realized Brick was pointing at a mud hut. He shook his head. "I haven't seen one of those since Cairo."

"People here are desperate," Alp said. "They would do almost anything for money."

"Especially a large amount of money," said Brick.

They talked to the neighbors. Brick understood enough of what they said, but Alp had to translate for Roddy. The people in the village didn't know where the family went. But the boy's little sister had claimed her brother was rich, and they were going to a new home.

"What is the boy's name?" Roddy asked one of the men.

"Chisisi."

"Interesting," Alp said.

"Why?" said Roddy.

"Chisisi means 'a secret.'"

Linda had enjoyed a good sleep and a tasty breakfast. She was now sitting on the porch with Jeremiah, each savoring a mug of hazelnut coffee.

"Are you ready for today's class?" Jeremiah said.

"Yes, and I promise to be your best student. Albeit, your only student."

"All right, then," he said with a laugh. "Let's look at what we know so far: the universe contains a set amount of heat, with never more or less than what already exists. When something is hot, the heat is organized. But heat is always trying to disorganize, move to a colder place, spread itself around.

"Entropy is the measure of this disorganization, this spreading out. One thing to remember is no natural process can ever break these laws. Okay so far?"

"Yes."

"Good. Now, the reason anything happens in the physical world is because of heat, or rather the flow of heat. When this happens, entropy—or disorganization—is added to the universe. We could put this the opposite way and say organization is subtracted from the universe.

"Important to understand is that while heat and energy aren't the same thing, all forms of energy can be viewed as a similarly designated quantity of heat. So, chemical, kinetic, nuclear, and even potential energy can all be recorded as a corresponding sum of heat."

"Sorry to interrupt," Linda said. "But how do the evolutionists get away with ignoring this?"

"They don't. Instead, they try to explain it away. This is where I need to contain my ire as I discuss the infamous—and truly stupid—snowflake response to entropy and the second law of thermodynamics.

"Some evolutionists claim the Second Law doesn't apply because snowflakes are complicated formations spontaneously built from disarranged pieces. They make the same claim about mineral crystals.

"But here is the truth: the sun sends heat to the ocean where the heat dissipates. This scattering is an increase in entropy. The resulting vapor rises, and as it reaches colder air, heat leaves the vapor. Entropy again. This forms into water droplets, with the release of even more heat.

"The air gets colder and the droplet becomes solid, forming snowflakes. At every step, heat decreases, meaning entropy increases. We see the same with mineral crystals. Mineralization occurs only because heat escapes to a cooler place, thus adding to the entropy of the universe.

"Whether discussing a mineral or a drop of water, evolutionists say crystallization happens contrary to thermodynamics. They are demonstrating ignorance of the fact that entropy increases during the process. And they err regarding evolution, in that crystal formation isn't even related to the source of life on Earth or to DNA coding."

Linda's Android rang. "Excuse me, Jeremiah."

"Go right ahead. I'll get us some more coffee."

He rose, took her mug, and left. Linda opened her purse and pulled out her phone. "Look who it is," she said to no one and hit the send button. "Mr. Eckstein, my day is made."

"Part of my job, Miss Eckstein," Hanley said.

"And you're bothering me, why?"

"I've got the MacGuffin."

She sat bolt upright. "You do? Oh, wonderful, Warren. I take back every rotten thing I've said about you... Well, most of them, anyway."

"We need to get together since you're carrying the fifth piece."

"When I leave here, I'll have the sixth, as well."

"Hey, good work. Are you still in Michigan?"

"Yes. Let's meet at the airport in Muskegon."

"Already have a ticket. Whadda-you-know? We had the same idea, as if sharing our thoughts."

"That's a stretch."

"My plane comes in at three, this afternoon."

"See you then."

"Looking forward."

"Breathless."

"Bye."

After a minute, Jeremiah returned with two full coffee mugs.

He gave one to Linda and set his down on an end table and left. Jeremiah returned with a snack tray and some blocks. He set the tray on the floor in front of them and stacked five blocks, one on top of another and sat down.

"Let's call these the building blocks of life," he said. "They did not build themselves randomly. I had to stack them. Currently the blocks represent potential energy or localized heat. When I shake the tray..." He shook it and the blocks fell. They lay scattered on the tray. "I produced kinetic energy or energy in motion. The result is entropy and chaos.

"If I shake the tray..." He shook it. "The blocks don't reassemble themselves. According to the evolutionists, though, if I sit here and shake the tray for a billion years, they'll eventually stack themselves up. Ridiculous. The same is true for DNA molecules. They can't assemble *themselves*. They can only break down. The Second Law is never violated in nature.

"Take green plants for instance. They make amino acids, along with proteins and sugars. This happens through the process of heat coming from a hot place, the sun, and moving to a colder place, the plant. Entropy in action. Now here's the irony. The machinery used by the plant to do this was constructed from amino acids, proteins, and sugars. Those are produced by the plant.

"So, to make a green plant, you need a green plant to start with.

"In conclusion, the Second Law insures neither a stack of blocks, nor any living thing, can just happen helter-skelter, a.k.a. evolution. Everything has to be preassembled in full."

Harlan and Branch were drinking water taken from the spring near Harlan's hut. Harlan began, "The story starts with a Renaissance figure, a Polish astronomer named Nicolaus Copernicus. Well, not actually, since Nick ripped off Greek astronomers. Anyway, it was the fifteenth century. Everyone believed the earth was the center of the universe and that everything else revolved around it.

"The accepted scientific explanation came from Ptolemy, a Roman citizen of Egypt. He was a second century astronomer and mathematician. Ptolemy based his work on that of Hipparchus, probably the greatest of the Greek astronomers.

"While at university, Copernicus began to have doubts about Ptolemy's explanation for how the universe worked. Over many years, he reworked the heliocentric model. That model had been the work of Aristarchus and Pythagoras over one and a half millennia earlier. Copernicus then claimed the model as his own. He wrote a book, and just before publication, he removed the two pages in which he'd given recognition to the Greek astronomers. You have to wonder about a scientist who doesn't give credit. His book, *On the Revolutions of the Celestial Spheres*, was published in 1543. One of the first copies was handed to him as he lay on his deathbed.

"But, along came Tycho Brahe, born three years after publication of *Celestial Spheres*. He was a Danish astronomer who rejected heliocentricity and embraced geocentricity. In fact, the model proposed by Brahe is still utilized today in applied science to predict eclipses. It's also employed by NASA in the launching of satellites. Of course, no one talks about that.

"Next came the traitor, Johannes Kepler. He worked as Brahe's assistant. Brahe's astronomical records were the most definitive of the sixteenth century. He demonstrated how the sun revolved around the Earth, and the planets revolved around the sun. The word planet means wanderer, so the Earth isn't a planet since it doesn't go anywhere.

"Brahe became worried Kepler would take all his work and misuse it. That he would claim the sun was at the center and the Earth just another planet. Before Brahe could do anything about it, he ate something that made him ill. After a couple of weeks, he died—suspiciously—at the age of fifty-four.

"Anyway, the battle was on. Galileo supported Kepler and Copernicanism. Astronomer Giovanni Riccioli opposed him.

Francis Bacon blasted sun-centered pseudo-science as unproven and awkward. Especially since the Earth was required to be moving three different ways at once. We now know it requires the Earth to be moving four different ways, and at incredible speeds.

"Finally, a physicist named A.A. Michelson and chemist E.W. Morley came up with an interesting device. It was in the 1880s and they called it an interferometer. The unexpected result was that the Earth was not moving. Scientists all over the world performed the experiment with the same result.

"After more than 200 attempts, they all gave up. The Earth wouldn't budge. The Copernicans struck back, claiming that since the apparatus was on the earth it was involved in the Earth's motion. Few were willing to accept such lame reasoning. The helio-nuts were in a quandary for two decades. Until their savior arrived. Enter the greatest thief of ideas and pseudo-science magician of all time: Albert Einstein.

Bullets careened off the car as Brick weaved it back and forth. A woman threw a basket of clothes at them as she turned to run for safety. With laundry on the windshield, Brick turned on the wipers.

"Duster Darkster," Alp said. "The body style and matte black finish are quite ominous."

"Look at the shape of the chrome on that bumper," Brick said. "Like a shark's mouth."

Alp yanked down the middle of the back seat and crawled into the trunk up to his waist. He backed out holding two AK-47s.

He handed one to Roddy between the front seats.

The rear window had been shot out, and Alp used the opening to return fire, forcing the driver behind them to swerve.

Roddy lowered his window, leaned out, and began shooting.

Brick said, "Okay, Roddy, tell me who your friends are."

"I don't think we've been introduced."

A bullet zipped over Alp's head as he ducked. It hit a Saint Christopher medal dangling from the rearview mirror and passed through the windshield, leaving a tiny hole surrounded by a web of faint cracks.

"There's adding insult to injury," Brick said, looking at the wounded image of Saint Chris. "Guardian of travelers? Huh!"

Alp sent a barrage of bullets at their pursuer and hit the left front tire. The vehicle was already swerving, and the sudden flat caused it to jerk out of control and off the road. The Darkster smashed into a loan Turkey Oak.

A second car was right behind. At a turn in the road, they saw yet another one following.

Alp said, "I knew the guy with the binoculars was suspicious."

Roddy said, "It was the one with the high-powered rifle and the telescopic sight that did it for me."

Brick said, "You mean the one who shot my hat off as I started to bend over to tie my shoe? Brand new hat! My shoe is still untied."

"What a crew we are," said Roddy. "So much for stealth and cunning."

"We did get caught with our trousers at half-mast, didn't we," Brick said. "But how could we know they'd be so fanatical about protecting the whereabouts of this boy."

"Which begs the question," Roddy said.

"You mean, why didn't they just kill him and his whole family?" Brick said. "And then bury them in the desert somewhere."

Alp leaned between the seats. "Unless they don't know where he is either."

"Right," said Roddy. "They're afraid we'll find him first."

The next car was closing in on them as Alp looked out the back window. "Here they come again."

Brick said, "We need a new plan."

"I'm open to suggestions," Roddy said.

"I was hoping you'd make one," said Brick.

Pointing, Alp said, "Turn right, up ahead. We're getting close to the city, and we need to lead these guys away from it."

"I agree," said Brick, and he made a hard right.

Their pursuers made the turn as well, though the first car skidded wildly. They drove north with the two cars hanging back, apparently not sure what to do next, and waiting for the best moment to attack.

Roddy and company came upon a scattering of urban ruins.

"This is Ani," Alp said. "Called the *City of 1001 Churches*. It once had a population between one-hundred and two-hundred thousand people. It was a prominent trading hub, but it's been abandoned for the last three centuries."

Roddy said, "You'd make a great tour guide."

"Thank you."

Brick said, "You'd think there'd be more buildings in a city that size."

"It's been subjected to earthquakes, army target practice, vandalism, excavations, and so on. Ani is on the border with Armenia. We don't get along with Armenia that well. Today Ani is a Turkish military zone."

"Is this a bad thing?" said Roddy.

"The city is also a tourist site."

"Is this a good thing?"

"You need to go to Kars to get a permit. A lengthy process."

"Do we have time?"

Alp looked behind at the two cars following them and turned back toward the front. "No."

Brick said, "Then we'll go in without one. By the way, we're low on gas, and we don't have time to stop for that either."

Roddy said, "We'll need cover, a place to hold them off. Slow down."

"Why?" asked Brick.

"I have a plan."

Brick slowed the car down to about twenty miles per hour. The two carloads of assassins slowed too and didn't come any closer. After they'd driven a little ways, Roddy said, "Let's separate in a hurry."

Brick pressed the gas pedal to the floor and the car darted away from the two following.

Roddy pointed. "Stop at the building up ahead. We'll take our chances there." Parts of the front of the stone edifice still stood with debris piled in places against the walls. The most complete part of the structure was a three-storey tower, the size of a corn silo rising behind what was left of the front. The building sat next to a gully with a stream flowing.

The car skidded to a stop and Brick popped open the trunk. The three jumped out, ran to the rear of the car, and grabbed all the firepower and ammo they could carry.

Roddy said, "You got a small arsenal in here."

Brick looked up at the two vehicles roaring at them. "I think we're gonna need every bit."

The three ran into the building.

Chapter Twelve

Linda had finished her visit with Jeremiah Daniels and was waiting by the front door. Jeremiah came back from his study holding the next piece to the pyramid.

"Here, Linda," he said. "Do you have the platform?"

"A friend does. He had to steal the thing back from someone."

"Oh, good heavens. Do be careful and don't let the key fall into the wrong hands again. You must hold onto it so you can unlock the potential."

"The potential what?"

He shrugged. "I don't know. You'll need all nine pieces to the pyramid to find out."

"So who's my next contact?"

"Oh, this one will surprise you. Unlike others you've met, who practice real science, this one is an exobiologist named Alexander Quigley."

"Don't they believe in life from outer space?"

"Yes, exactly."

"How'd he get to be a Pyramidion?"

"He was originally a physicist who kept his creation-design orientation a secret. Now he works with NASA in an attempt to discover what sort of chicanery they have planned."

"So he's undercover? A spy?"

Jeremiah became excited. "Yes. Don't you just love cloak and dagger stuff?"

Linda gave him her best smile. "Yes, Jeremiah. I do."

"You'll find Dr. Quigley at Ames Research Center in California."

"Thank you for everything."

"I bid you a safe journey."

She waved goodbye as she walked down the driveway to the sidewalk. She checked her watch. She might still get to the airport before Hanley arrived.

Harlan was not surprised at Branch's reaction.

"I thought Albert Einstein was the greatest scientist, the number one genius of the twentieth century," Branch said. "Or any century, for that matter."

"He was anointed as such, and we must give him credit for putting one over on most of the world with his relativistic physics. But he used daydreams that weren't science but fanciful imaginings. And his alleged proof was referred to as theoretical mathematics. What I call fantasy-math."

"You said he was a thief."

"Yes. For starters, Einstein didn't dream up curved space. The blame goes to a nineteenth century German mathematician named Bernhard Riemann. From W.K. Clifford, English mathematician and philosopher, we get the absurd notion that in curved space matter would wrinkle. Of all things.

"From Irish physicist George F. FitzGerald, Einstein latched onto the inane idea of objects contracting if they go too fast. From a Dutch physicist named Hendrik Lorentz, he absconded with the view that, in a vacuum, the speed of light would be constant.

"Another German mathematician, Hermann Minkowski supplied him with his space-time concept. Even the name, the principal of relativity was not Albert's. It was coined by Jules Henri Poincaré, a French mathematician, theoretical physicist, and philosopher of science.

"And physicist and mathematician Sir Joseph Larmor gets credit for the belief that a clock in motion will run slower."

"$E=mc^2$. That was Einstein's wasn't it?"

"J.J. Thompson, an English physicist developed the equation $E=3/4mc^2$. Einie added another quarter and made the equation his own. Doesn't matter. Neither one is true, which many physicists have always been aware of. Nothing of any consequence to Einstein's fame and glory was his. Everything he was famous for was illogical, wrought with mistakes, and even downright juvenile.

"Asked to give a talk on quantum theory, he said he couldn't comprehend it. Contrary to popular belief, Einstein didn't give us the atomic age. In fact, he thought the whole notion of atomic energy was ridiculous.

"He fumbled together a bunch of off-the-wall ideas from other scientists. He created a couple of theories allegedly provable through the use of theoretical mathematics. Keyword theoretical, meaning: might be true, might not. One notable scientist said the new math was nothing but 'flummadiddles.'

"However, his brave new fantasy seemed to negate the Michelson-Morley experiment. That saved, first, Copernicanism and second, Darwinism. This made him the most heralded scientist of all time. Giving new meaning to the word travesty.

"What's worse is that his despicable legacy goes beyond science. He claimed space and time are not absolute but relative. He said the motion of a thing in space isn't absolute but dependent on the view from each separate location. So motion isn't the same for an observer at one point as for the observer at another point. How retarded is that?

"This inanity spilled over into the culture. Now, truth is considered relative, being also in motion and changing from one opinion to the next. However, the statement 'there is no absolute truth' begs the question, 'are you *absolutely* sure'?

"The statement negates itself. So in reality, there is absolute truth, but good luck trying to get a relativist to comprehend the obvious."

Harlan appeared almost spent. He'd vented his frustration with so-called modern science. Branch was sure Harlan was satisfied he'd made his point, but Branch still had a question.

"My understanding is the geocentric model is more complicated than the heliocentric in explaining the orbits of the planets around the sun. Which in turn orbits around the Earth. Also, that when one theory is simpler than another, it makes more scientific sense to choose the less complicated of the two."

"The Principle of Simplicity. Often a pragmatic choice, but with no guarantee of being the right one. You want complicated versus simple. How about this? The Earth is supposedly rotating at over 1000 miles per hour at the equator while traveling around the sun at about 67,000 miles per hour. At the same time, we're told, our solar system moves around the Milky Way Galaxy at an estimated half-million miles per hour. On top of all that, we're expected to swallow the notion that the galaxy is whipping around the universe at something like 1,340,000 miles per hour. As I said earlier, you have the Earth moving in four different ways at unbelievable speeds.

"With the geocentric model, the Earth is at the center while everything else goes around it. Now, which one adheres to the Principle of Simplicity?"

"Yes, but you've still got the planets revolving around the sun as it revolves around the Earth."

"Minor complication compared to the alternative."

"But Harlan. The entire universe going around the Earth? How many billions of times the speed of light would the stars be traveling?"

"Quite a few, if the universe was billions of light years across, as we've been told. I would estimate the diameter of the universe is only about one light day. Meaning that from the Earth to the edge of the universe, in any direction, is only one-half light day."

Branch stared at Harlan. "You're serious."

"You're the eternal skeptic, aren't you?"

"Perhaps, but I'll think about what you said."

"It's essential that you do. Modern science, which is modern but not science, has given us the hopeless culture we live in today. It gives the appearance of legitimacy to the humanist religion and socialist politics spreading their tentacles around the Earth. This monster will one day squeeze the life out of mankind."

Linda drove into the parking lot soon after the arrival time for Hanley's flight. She went to the baggage claim area and spotted Hanley waiting for his luggage to come around on the carousel.

"See anything you like?" she said, as she sidled up next to him.

"I'm not concerned yet, but they seem to be out of stuff to send down."

Linda glanced at the other people, then leaned in toward Hanley. Standing on her toes, and in a surreptitious voice, she said, "Are you carrying the you-know-what?"

"Sure."

"Good."

"In my suitcase."

"Not good." She rubbed her fingertips across her forehead. "I can't believe you'd trust the airlines with something so important."

"I have no explanation for this lapse in judgment. I do remember a plane exactly like ours, with only one digit difference in the flight number, headed for Antarctica."

"Oh no, Hanley, you can't be serious. This is panic time. We've gotta get the MacGuffin back. What are we gonna do?"

He reached over to the carousel, grabbed a leather suitcase on the way by, and lifted the bag to his side. "Leave."

She stared at him for several seconds, glanced at the bag in Hanley's hand, and then back at him. "I saw that one sail by once already."

He grinned. "Good memory."

"I hate you," she said, trying not to smile. She turned and walked away.

Hanley trailed after her. "I hope this doesn't affect our relationship."

Over her shoulder, she said, "Can't affect what exists only in the mind of just one of us."

Arriving at the car, Linda sat in the driver's seat and Hanley got in next to her with his leather bag on his lap. He opened it and took out the partially constructed pyramid. Linda opened her purse, and as soon as she did so, pieces five and six jumped out and onto the MacGuffin.

"Whoa," said Hanley, as he dropped the MacGuffin on the floor. "What just happened?"

"I forgot. You're a first timer."

"What a nifty surprise," he said, reaching to the floor to retrieve the now two-thirds completed pyramid.

"Only three more," Linda said. "We'll need to turn in this rental and get plane tickets."

"Where are we going?"

"California. Ames Research Center."

"Branch went to Ames already."

"On a different mission. Our next contact with, we hope, another piece to the pyramid is at the Center."

Brick sat by a doorway at the front of the building. Alp had taken a position at the rear, and Roddy was climbing the crumbling staircase of the tower behind Brick.

Brick yelled, "How are you doing, Roddy?"

"So far, not so bad, but if you hear a loud yell and a thump, not so good."

The eight gunmen fired shots into the building. They took cover behind the cars, and had the decaying stone structure surrounded.

"You all right, Alp?" Brick said.

"Don't worry. If I get killed, I'll let you know."

"That'll be my cue to surrender. I don't think I can hold them off from two directions at once."

Roddy yelled, "No surrendering. I have a plan, remember."

"Which is appropriate since your idea got us pinned down in here," Brick said.

Roddy continued his treacherous climb up the stairs. He moved slowly, figuring it was better to be careful than quick. Reaching the top, he breathed a sigh of relief.

He was carrying a rifle with a scope. The tower featured windows all around and Roddy picked one facing one of the cars. He called out, "Brick, you know what to do."

Brick peeked around the doorway and fired a steady wave of bullets at the car. He shot out the windows and tires, then stopped and ducked back inside.

His assault worked. The idea had been to draw their fire, and it triggered an immediate response. All four gunmen rose up from behind the car and began firing into the doorway.

Roddy stuck his rifle out the little window, took aim, and shot one of the men. He took aim again, fired, and another one went down. The two remaining gunmen opened fire on Roddy, who dropped below the window.

Brick started shooting again, and the two gunmen took cover behind the car.

Roddy moved to the other side of the tower. "All right, Alp. Your turn."

Alp started to shoot at the four, sometimes hitting the car, sometimes only the air. The gun wielding assassins were unaware of what transpired on the opposite side of the building and fell for the same trick. They rose up and pounded the disintegrating stone framework as Alp shrank back inside.

Roddy put his rifle through the window and took aim. He dropped one of the shooters and turned his aim toward another. These remaining three reacted more quickly than the others had, pointed their guns at him, and opened fire. Roddy barely vacated the window in time.

Alp opened fired and dropped a second man.

One of the two remaining fired a torrent of lead through the little upstairs window. The shots bounced off the wall behind Roddy, sending stone dust everywhere. The other guy sprayed Alp's position.

Roddy crouched, pleased with himself. Already, half the villains were down. *Maybe they'll surrender now.* He smiled, not taking himself seriously.

Brick yelled up to Roddy. "A new wrinkle is developing."

Roddy went back to the other side and peeked out the window, careful not to let himself be seen by the last two shooters. Another Duster Darkster pulled up. Two hulks with hard eyes got out and glared at the building. One loosened his collar and the other cracked his knuckles. They both moved to the rear of the car. Knuckles stood with his gaze rising to the window of Roddy's tower. Collar reached into the trunk.

Roddy watched, wondering until Collar pulled out a rocket launcher.

The goon took aim at the tower.

Roddy leapt into running mode with such speed and agility it left him wondering: *How'd I do that?* He didn't stop to think, though. He just ran for the stairs. They were falling apart, but he had no time for creeping. He jumped down the staircase, just as a rocket zipped through the window and exploded on the ceiling above.

Roddy slid down the crumbly steps, with stone fragments raining down on him. He winced as jagged stone scrapped against his left arm and leg. He was sure he'd have quite a bruise where he landed on his hip.

Roddy got to his feet and leaned against the wall as he moved down the stairs. He was limping, his arm and shoulder were injured, and he was covered in dust, coughing in the swirling of fine powder. The descent was slow and difficult, and Roddy was aware one miscalculated step could result in a quick trip to the bottom.

Brick had stayed alert making sure no one could sneak up on him while also trying not to become a target. He didn't like the sound at the top of the tower.

He called out to Roddy, "You okay, Amigo?"

Roddy yelled back, "Wonderful. I'm on my way down."

"What's your E.T.A.?"

"At the rate I'm going, we'll both be too old to remember why I went up. And buddy, be advised: they got a rocket launcher."

"Great," Brick said, under his breath.

He peeked out just as Collar was getting ready to fire. Right at him! Brick swung into the doorway and began firing at Collar. The man dropped down and the other three began shooting at Brick, who pulled away to avoid the torrent of hot lead.

A rocket whizzed by and struck the wall on the far side of the room. Bits of stone splattered everywhere as Brick crouched low trying to make himself small and covered his face with his arm.

Incensed and determined to make someone else miserable, Brick bolted to his knees, took quick aim, and fired. Collar cried out and dropped from sight.

Brick was pretty sure he'd only wounded the man.

Now the other gunmen opened fire and Brick took one in the shoulder. He dove back to safety.

Sitting on the floor, he tore off pieces of his shirt and made a tourniquet that went under his arm and over his shoulder.

Roddy finished slinking down the stairs and limped over to Brick. He took notice of Brick's makeshift bandage. "Altering your wardrobe at a time like this? A fashion statement it's not."

Brick frowned. "You watch, when this becomes all the rage, you'll regret your words."

Alp called to them in a sort of yelling whisper. "Guys, we need to get out of here before they bring the whole building down on us."

Brick looked up at Roddy. "What do you think? The three magic words?"

Roddy smiled. "Attack, attack, attack."

"Are they in for it now," Brick said, as he started to climb to his feet.

"That's what I like about you. You're a hopelessly naive optimist."

Roddy tried to help Brick get up but stumbled because of the pain in his leg.

"A cripple helping the wounded," Brick said. "What a pair we make."

They crossed the tower's stone floor and joined Alp.

"What's the plan?" Alp said.

"We're gonna make them pay," Brick said.

"You gonna send them a bill?"

"One of us needs to go out and draw their fire," Roddy said. "The two who stay behind will wait till they show themselves."

"And take them out?" Alp said.

Roddy shrugged. "That's the plan."

"I'll go," Brick said.

"You're wounded," said Roddy. "I'll go."

"You're limping."

"All right," Alp said. "I'll be the sacrificial lamb."

"I thought he'd never catch on," Brick said.

Roddy tapped Alp on the shoulder. "Know that we both strenuously object."

Alp grinned. "Yeah."

They all reloaded so they'd have full clips in their guns.

"Ready guys?" said Alp.

They both nodded.

Just then, another rocket zoomed in from outside the front of the building and blasted the wall behind.

"The neighbors are restless," Alp said. He charged out the door as Roddy and Brick positioned themselves on either side of the doorway. Alp fired in the direction of the black Duster.

The two men behind the car, rose up, and as they began shooting, Alp dove to the ground, rolled over several times and continued firing.

Roddy and Brick stepped into the open doorway and shot at the two assailants. Both dropped as if they'd been hit.

Roddy and Brick went outside and cautiously moved toward the bullet riddled car. Alp got to his feet. When the three reached the other side of the automobile, they saw the four men lying on the ground. They lay between the car and the gully, either dead or unconscious.

Alp, being the only uninjured one, got behind the steering wheel. Brick took shotgun, and Roddy climbed in the back. Alp started the engine, while Roddy and Brick lowered their windows.

"Ready to enter warp drive," Alp said.

"Make it so, number one," said Brick.

Alp floored the gas pedal, fish-tailed, and then gained control as he whipped the Darkster around the dilapidated building.

They were picking up speed in a hurry as they sailed past their own car, then the two cars of the assailants.

Roddy and Brick hung out the windows and shot at the surprised gunmen. The gunmen assaulted the air with expletives, returned fire, and dove for cover. Two dropped from wounds, while another panicked in his chaotic attempt to recover from the ambush.

The one with the rocket launcher was calm as he took aim at Roddy and company. Roddy shot and hit the man in the shoulder just as he was pulling the trigger. The impact of the bullet caused him to raise the gun slightly. The rocket launched into the air just missed the top of the car. It exploded on a distant hillside.

When Linda and Hanley arrived in San Francisco, they hired a rental and headed for Ames Research Center. They'd called ahead and had an appointment with Quigley. They found him in an elegant, spacious office.

After introducing themselves, Hanley said, "Appears exobiologists, in spite of the paucity of any real science, are treated well at NASA."

Quigley laughed. "Amazing, I agree, and people say ours is the only science without any data."

"What do you do all day?" Linda asked.

"Our field is generous with speculation, and poor in offering genuine science. So if you possess a lot of imagination, you can excel, and no one questions anything. They treat us as if we know what we're talking about."

"A friend of ours, Branch Nichols, was here recently," Linda said. "He met with a man named Smith Underwood."

Quigley's countenance turned sober. "Yes, I'm aware."

"What's up?" Hanley said.

"Underwood was found dead the day after he spoke with your friend."

Harlan Wilson went to the door of his little hut in the Australian desert and reached in his pocket.

"Here's the next piece to the pyramid," he said, handing it to Branch. "And I hope I've helped to convince you of the importance of your mission for the Pyramidions."

"I'm not sure I get the connection yet."

"You will."

"I'm also not sure what the mission is. Other than finding the rest of a key without knowing its use or even its true value."

"Things will come together."

"Before I leave, I want to show you something." From his shirt pocket, he removed the scrap of paper Wendy had given him. "You seem like the kind of guy who would be good with riddles. What do you think this means?"

Harlan took the paper. "NDDGMR 23. Add four of what Hebrew has not, two of one, plus two others, then reverse, and follow—in their proper places—with two of the only number not in Gregory's dates."

Harlan shook his head and handed the paper to Branch. "Sorry, too cryptic for me."

Harlan opened the door, but after a quick glance, slammed it and dove on Branch, knocking him to the floor.

Bullets tore through the door and sliced along the wall. Harlan rolled off Branch, who lay still for a moment before speaking.

"How could they find me? Underwood is the only person who knew, except Linda, but no one knew where she was. We used encrypted phones."

"Then we can assume Underwood is dead." Harlan got up on all fours and scuttled to the bedroom. "Come on."

Branch started getting to his hands and knees. "Nuts. I kind of liked him." He followed Harlan.

Bullets continued to pour in through the door and windows, tearing up the walls and furniture. Their drinking glasses exploded, and the Picasso dropped to the floor, shattering the protective glass.

Branch gave a quick glance. *Waste of a good frame.*

Harlan raised the bed up and part of the floor went with it. He descended a staircase and turned on a light.

Reaching the opening, Branch peered down. "Well, I'll be. Another secret door for escape." He crawled onto the stairs.

"One must always have an exit strategy," Harlan said.

Branch stopped. "I've heard that before. I hope you aren't gonna blow yourself up and take me with you? I'd sooner look at other options."

"Be sure to close the door behind you," Harlan said, as he hurried off.

Branch pulled on a cord, drawing the floor down, along with the bed. He followed Harlan, who ran down a corridor for about fifty yards. At the end was a bright, metallic green dune buggy.

"They'll never spot us in this," Branch quipped.

"Won't matter what they spot; we won't be around long; I've had the engine modified; they'll never catch us."

Outside, things took a more violent turn. Two men with rocket launchers fired into the building. Four others tossed grenades. The resulting ear-shattering explosions caused the ground to vibrate, and the near total collapse of the hut. The air was filled with the smell of smoke and powdered adobe.

The dune buggy roared up a ramp and onto the desert floor, racing away as Harlan went through the gears.

Branch glanced over his shoulder at the smoking ruins in the predawn light.

"Very serious people," said Harlan. "You know, if they'd started with the explosives instead of the bullets, they might've been more successful."

"The bad guys must be scrapping the sides of the barrel to find help. Got any binoculars?"

"Under the seat."

"Branch retrieved them, turned in his seat, and focused on the six attackers, who now scrambled to get back into their two cars."

"See any former acquaintances?" asked Harlan.

"No, these are new guys."

"What happened to the old guys?"

Branch turned forward in his seat. "Had to blow them up."

Harlan looked in his rearview mirror. "Tit for tat, I'd say."

Roddy and Brick nursed their wounds as Alp drove them across the Turkish plain, back toward civilization.

Brick turned his head toward Alp. "Just before those goons showed up, you had an extended conversation with a young boy. Did you find out anything?"

"He is a friend of the boy who found the ape-man."

"And?" Brick said.

Alp seemed hesitant. He adjusted the red fez, pulling it lower on his forehead. "Sounds like Muslim agents were hired to recruit the boy to take Barrows out to the cave. But when they learned the boy was slated to be killed, they decided it wasn't right for a Turk to be terminated by infidels."

"You got all that?"

"I pieced it together from what he told me, what we suspect about the ape-man hoax, and what I know about Islamics. After all, I've been Islamic all my life. Except for my conversion to

Christianity. Which I keep a secret, of course, because if anyone found out, I'd be toast."

"Alp, you're stalling," Brick said. "What are you not telling us?"

Alp kept his eyes fixed ahead. He was surrounded by silence. He glanced at Brick, who stared back at him, then at Roddy, who was also watching him from the back seat.

Alp cleared his throat. "I know where the boy is."

Brick raised one eyebrow. "Are you gonna tell us?"

Alp looked at Brick. "You're not gonna believe it." He looked at Roddy. "And you're not gonna like it."

Brick and Roddy stared in anticipation.

"All right," Alp said. "To find the boy, we have to go to the Vatican."

Brick rolled his eyes. "I've died and gone to purgatory. I'm now a character in a pop novel."

"Yeah, lots of people make claims the Catholic Church is involved in all kinds of conspiracies," Roddy said.

"The Vatican has been reaching out to Muslims for years," Alp said. "They want to bring Muslims, Catholics, Jews, Buddhists, and Hindus together under the same umbrella. Sort of a pagan's last stand against the spread of Christianity."

Brick said, "But what exactly makes you think the boy will be at the Vatican? And Catholics aren't pagans."

"The boy said his friend told him 'The pontiff will protect me.' And yes they are."

"What am I gonna tell my wife?" Roddy said. "That the pope's involved in clandestine sneakiness? And that we're really pagans?"

"Intelligence at our headquarters in Istanbul has known for some time the Vatican is mixed up in some kind of conspiracy," Alp said. "They believe it will have international consequences. It involves Islam, but something else is going on."

Roddy sighed and flopped back in his seat. "I can't tell Christine stuff like that."

"I wouldn't worry so much about that as I would about what happens when we all go to Rome looking for this kid," Alp said. "We'll be hip deep in Camel dung."

"Spare me the odiferous metaphors," Brick said. "And, by the way, with this wound, I'm afraid I won't be able to make the trip just yet. I'll try to catch up later."

Hanley and Linda exchanged concerned looks. Then Hanley said to Quigley, "I hope we're not putting you in any danger."

"Underwood knew he was being watched, and that his office was bugged. He took exceptional precautions, but not enough it seems."

Hanley said, "What about you?"

"I'm not under suspicion."

"You're sure?"

"No, but I do a sweep of my office for bugs every morning, and again when I come back from lunch."

Linda said, "Do you think whoever killed him might be looking for Branch?"

"Could be, and Underwood was not one who would endure torture. He would've told them whatever they wanted to know."

Linda took out her phone. "Call Branch." She waited, and on the third ring, Branch answered. Linda hit the speaker button.

"Branch, are you okay?"

"Sure. Taking a nice drive across the countryside."

"I hear a roaring. Must be the engine."

"Yeah, modified. It's in a majorly cool California dune buggy built in the sixties. Why did you call? You missed me, right?"

"Branch, Underwood is dead, murdered."

"Well, that explains things."

"What things?"

"You know. Business as usual."

"Anyone we're acquainted with?"

"No, and you be careful, all right?"

"You have nothing to worry about," said Hanley. "She's with me."

"Now that's a contradiction in statements," Branch said.

Hanley smiled and shook his head.

Linda grinned. "Warren has been a complete gentleman. So far."

"Hey, buddy," Hanley said, "I got the MacGuffin."

"And I added pieces five and six," Linda said.

"Good work team. I've got the seventh piece. Meet me in Molokai. I want to find a physics professor from my days at M.I.T."

"You studied physics?" Linda said.

"He was one of Warren's professors. Something he told us one day. After listening to Harlan's fulmination against the icons of science, it suddenly just clicked. And I thought, *what if?*"

"You're sure he's in Molokai?" Linda said.

"Not sure. Not even sure if he's alive, but he retired there while we were still in school."

Hanley said, "You've been in the Australian sun too long. I've told you that guy is a nut case."

"I always thought so, but I need to talk to him."

"Okay," Linda said. "We'll meet you."

They said goodbye and hung up. Linda looked at Hanley. "What is he talking about?"

Hanley shook his head with a look of disgust. "Big Bang."

"That's it? Everyone's heard of the so-called Big Bang."

"Not from his perspective." Hanley turned to Quigley. "So tell us, what is NASA's Origins Program up to?"

Benjamin Rydal was sitting in front of his Panasonic 152 inch plasma TV screen, watching the five o'clock news.

Male reporter: "Ararat man is the sensation of the scientific world. He's being called the death knell for biblical creationism. After he's made the rounds of museums in the U.S., he'll be on his way to tour the world. Red Barrows, the archeologist who discovered the ape man of the hour has become a celebrity. He's even appearing on late night talk shows."

Benjamin's android phone rang. He hit the mute button on the TV remote, checked the caller ID, and smiled.

He clicked send. "Hello, Jeffery. I'm glad FedEx found you at home."

"I was surprised to discover you'd sent me a phone, and with your number programmed in. Unusual gift, Benjamin. Are we… okay?"

"Our call is encrypted. We can talk. I had to find a way to communicate with you. You heard about Lyle Wentsler?"

"Yes, and it makes no sense. They were watching him, sure, but why kill him? Just doesn't add up."

"Perhaps, but we'd better be careful. I wanted to let you know Operation Bilderberg is on."

"You're going through with it, then."

"Have to. We need to learn what they're planning."

"All right. I'll begin the arrangements, and talk to you in a few days."

"Thanks Jeffery. I know I can count on you."

Chapter Thirteen

"Virtual Reality Technology came to NASA in the mid-eighties, but wasn't ready for prime time," Quigley said. He sat behind his desk as Linda and Hanley sat on a leather couch. "Twenty years later, it began making a comeback. Imagine being able to sit in the comfort of your space shuttle, wearing VR goggles and gloves. A Robonaut, a human-like robot goes out to explore a Martian crater. Robo takes all the chances while you, safe in your comfortable chair, experience the thrill of being there."

"Sounds like fun," Hanley said. "Makes me want to get back into the space program."

Looking amused, Quigley said, "Yeah, that's gonna happen."

Hanley gave an embarrassed smile. He glanced at Linda, who considered him with a supportive expression.

Quigley went on. "The plan—albeit a clandestine one—is to invent reality. Evolutionists have no choice but to abandon Darwinism, so they need a new source. They're looking to outer space, and either the concept of panspermia or exogenesis. The two are often used interchangeably, though they're not the same.

"Panspermia is the belief that certain microbial life forms, extremophile bacteria can survive on space debris. And that some made the trip to the earth and began evolving. Similarly, exogenesis says life began somewhere else and spread throughout the universe. Exogenesis includes both panspermia and fully formed humans."

"They'll have solved evolution's embarrassing problems by claiming humans were dropped here by aliens," Linda said. "Of course, they still must explain where the aliens came from."

"They'd walk around the problem," Quigley said. "They're good at that. They admit that evolution can't happen in an oxygenated atmosphere. So the evolutionists might claim the visitors from another world evolved in some other dimension devoid of oxygen. Then came here and miraculously adapted to an atmosphere that is more than 20-percent oxygen."

Linda laughed. "Sounds typical." She leaned toward him. "You said they plan to invent reality."

"Right. In December of 1999, the Hubble Telescope underwent repairs. It was given a new brain, a new computer to replace the old one. The most significant feature was preprogrammed simulated images, which is only a presage of things to come. The new generation version known as The James Webb Space Telescope contains a Virtual Reality generator. It's programmed to broadcast images of stars shaping planetary systems, as well as alleged visual evidence of life in deep space."

Linda leaned back on the couch. "They're willing to go that far? Spend billions of dollars to perpetrate a lie?"

Quigley nodded. "Whatever it takes to avoid accepting the reality of God and creation."

A horrifying thought struck Hanley, and he decided to ask the question for which he was sure he already knew the answer. "Dr. Quigley, as ominous as this all seems by itself, I have the dread suspicion an awful lot more is going on than what you've told us. Am I right?"

Linda was filled with a mixture of curiosity and distress.

Quigley placed his elbows on the desk and folded his hands together. "You're perceptive, Mr. Hanley. The answer to your question was foreshadowed by an address to the United Nations, by the president of the United States way back in the 1980s."

"Ronald Reagan?" Linda said.

"Whether knowingly or unwittingly, he was setting the stage for what is to come."

Quigley opened his laptop, and after a few clicks, he had a movie ready to play. He turned his computer around so they could watch.

The movie started, and Ronald Reagan, standing at a podium, spoke, "Perhaps we need some outside universal threat to recognize this common bond. I occasionally think how quickly our differences, worldwide, would vanish if we were facing an alien threat from outside this world."

Hanley nodded. He'd begun to suspect just such a scenario—orchestrated by powers unseen—since his discovery of the hideaway of flying saucers.

"First, they'll convince us life was brought here from another world," Quigley said. "That the aliens who brought our ancestors are waiting to become our masters, to conquer, and then use humanity for its own ends. Finally, they'll make us think these beings from another world have begun to invade."

"Using flying saucers," Hanley said.

Quigley was surprised. "You know?"

"I drove one."

"Pardon me."

"A long story, but what's important is the technology is obviously way ahead of NASA's."

"At least thirty years. Enough to scare people into accepting a one-world government. A socialist dictatorship."

"We need to tell others what's coming," Linda said.

"Who would believe you?" Quigley said. "They'd simply toss it in with the current potpourri of conspiracy theories. Besides, people don't want to be told anything that'll challenge them. They're too busy worrying about how to pay off their credit cards. Many have chosen to live like zombies watching an endless array of idiotic TV shows. Lots of Christians prefer just to sit in their pews, exulting in curious theology, waiting for the Rapture that will never come."

"When do you think the phony invasion will happen?" Linda asked.

"I don't know," Quigley answered. "But we're not too far away."

"At least we have one good thing to look forward to," Linda said. "Once you give us the eighth piece to the pyramid, we'll only need one more."

"I'm sorry," Quigley said. "I don't have the piece, never did. Who actually has the eighth piece has become confused. You'll be traveling to Rome."

Hanley said to Linda: "I'll take the MacGuffin and fly to Rome." To Quigley he said: "Who's our contact?"

"The contact will find you."

"How'll he know me?"

"The contact knows all of you."

Linda said, "You're going alone?"

"Sure. You *need* to go to Molokai."

"*Need*?"

"I saw how you lit up when you heard Branch's voice on the phone."

"I did *not*... You... That isn't... Stop saying those things."

Quigley tried to stifle a smile, but Hanley flashed an unabashed grin.

Red-faced, Linda rose and offered her hand to Quigley. "Thank you so much for meeting with us."

"My pleasure," he said, as he stood and took her hand.

Brick lay in an Istanbul hospital bed, with Roddy and Alp standing on either side.

"You weren't limping so badly today," said Brick.

"Good night's sleep was all I needed," Roddy said. "How long are they gonna keep you here?"

"They think I'll be in bed for a week. I plan on leaving in a couple days. Do you have a strategy for finding the boy?"

"I'll make it up as I go along."

"Typical. Look, start with the Vatican tunnels."

"Tunnels? Under the Vatican?"

"They wouldn't be on top of the Vatican, would they?"

Roddy grinned.

"Secret entrances abound," Brick said. "Alp knows someone who can get you in one of them."

Roddy and Alp went to the baggage claim at Leonardo da Vinci International Airport. As soon as Roddy grabbed his bag, he heard a familiar voice behind him.

"What are the odds?"

Roddy turned around. *Hanley.*

"What brings you here?" Roddy said.

"The eighth piece but I don't know who's got it. I did bring the MacGuffin." He patted the belt pack he wore above his left front trouser pocket. "You came here for the boy?"

"Yes, but I don't know where he is."

"Great, we're on a roll."

Alp came to Roddy's side. "We do have a place to start searching. I'm Alp."

"Warren Hanley." They shook hands. "You got a last name?"

"Yes, but no American can pronounce it."

"Good to meet you, Alp But-No-American-Can-Pronounce-It."

Alp smiled and said to Roddy, "I like this guy."

It was late in the day when they rented a car and drove to the Basilica di San Clemente, a short walk from the Colosseum. Unimpressive from outside, the entrance was barely visible to the casual passerby. It had a plain frontage, featuring a small door, surrounded by a bland wall. But when Roddy, Alp, and Hanley entered, they were greeted by a magnificent spectacle.

Roddy was sure, if the pews were removed, the room could accommodate a basketball game. He eyed massive, three-foot-thick columns, set on mosaic flooring. Roddy judged the ceiling to be about three stories up. With the air-conditioning on, Roddy decided his own electric bill wasn't so bad.

Beyond the pews was an open space and after that two sections of wall with a gate between them, and openings on either side of the walls. The cathedral was open for tourists. Roddy and his two companions followed some of them into the forward area where the main pews were.

When they reached the front, a priest approached them. Alp glanced around the room and then spoke to the clergyman.

"This cathedral stinks."

Roddy looked at him with horror, but before he had a chance to make explanations and apologies, the priest answered.

"Not nearly as awful as a camel, or worse yet, a Turk.

Roddy blinked hard and stared.

Alp and the priest both smiled, and shook hands vigorously.

"Good to see you again, Alp."

"You too, Gorman. These are my friends Roddy and Warren. This is Gorman Smith, a.k.a. Father Smith."

They all shook hands.

"Why the unusual greeting?" Roddy said.

"Our own private code," said Gorman. "In case one of us is being impersonated."

"So you're not a priest?"

"It's my day job. My hobby is working for a super secret international organization not affiliated with any government."

"Are you gonna be our tour guide?" Hanley said.

"I'll take you down to the netherworld and give you a map. Then you're on your own."

"We're looking for the Turkish boy who found Ararat Man," Alp said. "I don't suppose you know anything that'd help us find him."

"Actually, I can help. My sources believe he's being held captive, along with his family. Possible locations are marked on the map."

Gorman took them down a stairway. "We'll go down the same way the tourists do. It's quite fascinating, layers of history going back more than 2,000 years. This basilica was built in the twelfth-century over a well-preserved fourth-century church. It had been built beside a third-century Mithraic temple.

"This is significant since Mithraism was the original religion of Simon Magus. He combined it with Christianity, threw in a little Greek influence, and founded the Catholic Church. He was the first Bishop of Rome, the title of pope not coming into use until the third century."

"Simon Peter was the first pope," Roddy said.

"No historical evidence exists for Peter ever having been in Rome. Which isn't surprising since Peter's mission was to take the gospel to the circumcised. We're told this in the book of Galatians. There were descendants of Israel and Judah all around the Middle East and the Jews knew where they were. The book of James is addressed, 'To the twelve tribes in the Dispersion.' In Babylon alone, there were many more Jews than in Israel."

"I don't understand," Roddy said. "Why were so many Jews in Babylon?"

"When the Babylonian captivity ended, a lot of the Jewish people elected not to move to Israel. Most had been born and raised in Babylon. It was their home.

"Also, many Christians are unaware that everyone born in Babylon spoke Aramaic. That became the language of Israel when the Jews returned.

"Hebrew had become almost a dead language. That was probably a contributing factor in the Old Testament being translated to Greek in the fourth century B.C. Along with the fact that Greek was becoming the international language."

"Who's this other Simon?" Roddy said.

"Simon Magus was a Samaritan of Babylonian lineage. He's mentioned by Luke in the Book of Acts. Simon was a sorcerer who amazed people with his magic. According to chapter eight, verse ten of the Book of Acts, people said of him, 'This man is the power of God that is called Great.'

"Acts goes on to say that Simon heard Philip preach the gospel. Simon believed, was baptized, and continued to follow Philip. Peter and John came to Samaria from Jerusalem to lay hands on the people, and pray for them to receive the Holy

Spirit. Simon, realizing the power of the Holy Spirit had been given to them, wanted the power for himself. He asked Peter if he could buy it.

"Peter was outraged and said to Simon, '...you are in the gall of bitterness and in the bond of iniquity.' Gall of bitterness appears in Deuteronomy twenty-nine, verses sixteen to eighteen. It's a tendency to choose false gods and idols. So Peter's words were a prophecy that Simon would inaugurate pagan beliefs and graven images into Christianity.

"Simon left Philip and moved to Rome, where he wowed the people with his sorcery. He established a counterfeit version of Christianity. That's why, when the Apostles wrote about a false Church in their letters, they wrote about it as one that already existed."

Roddy had been listening to Gorman intently during their walk down. So he hardly noticed any of the frescoes Hanley and Alp had been admiring as they descended to the lower excavations. Roddy was a life-long Catholic. This revelation that the religion he'd been practicing might only be a pagan counterfeit was unsettling.

They stopped at a door.

"But Simon's church in Rome would have competed with Paul's," Roddy said. "And what about the churches started in other cities, in other countries?"

"Simon's church pressured the others for centuries to accept his as the central ruling church. Then the first *official* pope was enthroned.

"Think about it, Roddy. The church teaches you to pray to a lot of dead guys, the so-called saints, none of whom rose from the dead. Why would you pray to anyone else but God? You need to realize that whoever you choose to pray to becomes your God."

"Are you saying the Catholic Church is polytheistic?"

"Of course. Also, kneeling before and praying to statues in the church is a violation of the second commandment."

"This is all enormously interesting," said Hanley. "But we're on a mission."

"Certainly," Gorman said. "This way." Gorman took keys out of his pocket, selected one and inserted the key in the lock. "These tunnels are off limits to everyone except Vatican personnel. I'm not even supposed to have this key." He opened the door and led the others in before closing it.

They were in a tunnel made of stone, about five-feet wide and seven feet high. Light bulbs dotted the upper right corner of the tunnel connected by, what Hanley guessed to be, hundred year old wiring. Gorman took a map out of his pocket and handed it to Alp.

"I'm not sure if all the tunnels are on this map. I've never gone exploring."

"Thanks, Gorman," Alp said.

"Are you sure you can't come with us?" Roddy said.

"I would have trouble explaining my absence. I need to protect my cover. The main reason for my being here is to keep tabs on the pope; try to find out what he's up to."

"Thanks for your help," Hanley said, and they shook hands.

"The door opens from this side without a key when you're ready to escape. I mean leave. Good luck." Gorman opened the door and left.

"Escape?" Roddy said.

"Don't worry." said Alp. "That's just his sense of humor... I hope."

The three headed into the dank, dimly-lit tunnel.

Branch lay on his stomach and elbows, on the beach, under the warm, morning June sun, looking out at the ocean. He was feeling more relaxed than he'd felt in a long time as he sipped on a Coke while reading a Michael Creighton novel.

"There you are," a voice said from behind.

He looked over his shoulder and saw Linda standing. She was wearing a one-piece bathing suit with a sarong.

"The concierge at the hotel told me where to find you."

"You must've paid him more money than I paid him to keep quiet."

"Ha, ha." She laid her towel on the sand next to his and sat down. "I brought a Chandler Ross novel."

"Don't want to discuss what we've been doing since we parted company?"

"I got all your text messages. Did you get mine?"

"Yep"

"Then I'll read my book."

"You're not gonna critique this one, are you?"

"The author's a pain in the neck, so why shouldn't I be?"

"A certain logic, I suppose."

She opened the book and began reading. Branch went back to his novel.

A soft breeze caressed them as they sat together. They were absorbed in their stories, while still aware of each other's presence. The only sounds were the waves fondling the shore and children laughing on the beach, as they played in the sand.

But troublesome things were on Branch's mind. After a while, Branch laid his book down, staring out at the ocean and the blue Hawaiian sky. He was coming to a crossroads in his life, or maybe a fork in the road. Whatever metaphor was appropriate, he was reaching a time of discerning and decision making.

All he had learned in recent days couldn't be ignored. It seemed his ornery skepticism was being pummeled by what he could only describe as radical truth. Branch didn't enjoy his now discomfited feeling. His worldview was changing in spite of his habitual resistance.

"Penny for your thoughts," Linda said, as she lay on her tummy and elbows.

"My thoughts don't come so cheap."

"You'd try to profit from my curiosity?"

"Sure I would. Besides, my book sales have been down of late."

"I'm not surprised. Let me point out a few things..."

"Here we go."

Linda laughed. "I'm kidding. This is quite good. So far. I'll let you know if that changes."

"I'm sure I'll appreciate your candor, as always."

She laid the book down and leaned toward him on her elbow. "Any luck finding your professor acquaintance?"

"Roddy's friend, Brick is doing some research using company resources."

"You mean the CIA? Is that legal?"

"We're talking about the Central Intelligence Agency. What's legal got to do with it?" He leaned toward her on his elbow.

"You're no longer reading your book. Did I distract you?" Linda said.

"Much as I hate to admit it, you distract me a lot, and you're not reading your book either."

"I needed a break."

Branch inched his elbow, and with it the rest of him, closer to Linda.

For several seconds, they stared at each other until Linda inched her elbow closer, and her nose came within an inch of his.

They stared into each other's eyes.

"You're a major distraction, Linda Chapel."

"Speak for yourself, Branch Nichols."

"Why, Miss Chapel, are you admitting to being attracted to me?"

"I admit nothing, Mr. Nichols."

"You're clearly romantically affected by me, which you can't deny, can you."

"I want you to know how disconcerted I am by this."

"I disconcert you, do I? Well, you disconcert me. But I'm sure we can work out a solution to our mutual disconcertation."

"You talk too much. Shut up and kiss me."

Branch blinked and realized she meant it. He leaned in and their lips were just about to touch.

"Branch Nichols!" a voice yelled. "Telephone call."

Branch sat up and waved so the concierge could locate him. The excited young man ran to him with a phone in hand.

"Your call from Turkey finally came, Mr. Nichols."

"Thank you." Branch gave him a brand new twenty and took the phone. "All right if I drop this at the desk later?"

"Hold onto it as long as you like." The concierge left, holding the twenty up to the sunlight.

"How timely," Linda said. "Strange how a fabulous beach can affect a girl's good sense."

"I'll deal with you later." He raised the phone to his ear. "Brick, what have you got for me?"

"Good news and bad news. The good news is I found Professor Fink, and he lives in your current neighborhood. If you want to talk to him, though, you better be quick because the bad news is there's a contract on his life."

"Ridiculous. He's a retired physicist. Who could he be dangerous to?"

"His previous day job didn't get him in trouble, but his lifelong hobby did."

"You mean his interest in Kabbalah?"

"Exactly. He's always maintained a connection exists between the Kabbalah, Zionism, and modern pseudoscience. Now he plans to publish. Someone at the publishing house alerted certain people and now the Mossad has sent an agent to terminate him."

"The Israeli secret service? Is his book that much of a problem?"

"If it reflects badly on the New World Order, yes. It's one of those cat-out-of-the-bag things that make certain people nervous."

"New World Order?"

"You didn't hear it from me. Understand?"

"All right, tell me where he is."

"I bet we took a wrong turn," Hanley said.

"No, I think we're okay," said Roddy.

"Are you sure you're not holding the map upside down?" Alp said.

"This tunnel seems familiar, like we've been here before," Hanley said. "I bet we're gonna spend the rest of our lives down here."

"Bread crumbs," Roddy said. "I always forget the bread crumbs."

They heard a noise and froze. The sound of two voices grew louder as the three stared straight ahead. Hanley looked behind them, but the tunnel was straight for quite a distance, with too little time to run and hide.

As the three watched, two men passed in front of them, walking through an intersecting tunnel, and carrying two trays. They went out of sight, and the three relaxed.

"I smell food," Roddy said.

"Must be what's on those trays," said Alp.

"Let's follow," Hanley said.

The three crept along the stone wall of the curving tunnel, staying just out of sight of the two men. Roddy watched them stop at an iron door which had a small window with bars. One of the men set his tray down, took some keys off his belt, and opened the door, which let out a shrill squeak. He picked up the tray and the two entered.

Roddy and the others crept to the open door. They peered inside at the two men taking food off the trays and putting it on a table. Seated at the table were a man, woman, boy, and a girl.

"See?" Roddy whispered. "I can read a map."

"I think you just got lucky," Hanley said. "I don't think this is where we were headed at all."

"Can we finish this rescue mission while I'm still young?" Alp said.

The three entered the room. The family at the table watched them come in, which caused the two tray guys to turn around. They appeared concerned, even scared. Tray Guy One said something in Italian.

Roddy said, "I don't speak Latin."

"Neither do they," Hanley said. "I'm pretty rusty, but I think he wants to know who we are."

Tray-Guy Two said, "We just work here, and we are not armed."

Alp spoke to the family in Turkish.

The boy replied in near-perfect English: "Is this about the ape-man? They promised to protect us, but now we are prisoners."

Hanley smiled with admiration. "Where did you learn such good English?"

"From many tourists," the boy replied.

"We're taking you out of here," Roddy said.

The boy told his family. They looked at the food.

"Take some," Roddy said.

They all grabbed some food and headed for the door. Roddy held out his hand to Tray Guy One, who handed him the keys. Everyone but the two Italians left the room. Roddy locked the door and dropped the keys on the floor.

They found their way through the tunnels, to where they'd started. They went up the stairs to the level with the fourth-century church and stood in an open area.

"So what's the plan, now?" Hanley said to Alp.

"Brick will meet me. We'll take the family to America. We're going to get them U.S. visas."

"Sounds like a good plan," Hanley said. "Now I need to complete my mission, find the eighth piece. I just wish I had a place to start."

The sound of a gun cocking caused them all to suspend breathing.

"Don't anyone move," a female voice said.

Without looking, Hanley said, "Hello, Midnight."

Roddy turned. "Of all the people on the planet to show up here."

"Hi, Roddy," she said.

Hanley turned and started moving toward her.

"I need you all to cooperate," Midnight said. "Especially you, Warren."

He kept walking until his forehead was against the barrel of her gun.

"You stood me up," Hanley said. "We had a date."

She smiled. "And I've regretted it ever since."

"You shoot me and you'll regret that even more."

"Perhaps."

"I won't," came a burly voice from the shadows.

Hanley turned and a saw a large man holding a gun. He had a bandage on his face and a cast on his foot.

"I don't believe it," Roddy said. "Brussel. Haven't seen you since the Grand Canyon. How'd you—?"

"Survive?" Wallach said, as he too stepped into the light, a bandage around his head, and his left arm in a sling. "You tried to blow us up you son-of-a—.'

"Hey, we got a woman and children here," said Roddy. "And what about the grenade in Switzerland? I was buried in debris."

"You blew a boat out from under us on Lake Michigan," Wallach said.

"We were in that boat. We could've drowned."

"You should've, and don't think I forgot about the palm tree you dropped on my car in the Bahamas."

"You locked us in the mummy room at the California museum."

"How *did* you get out, anyway?"

Roddy grinned. "Never figured that one out, huh?"

"You guys sure get around," Alp said.

"Enough of the tearful reunion," Brussel said.

Hanley looked at Midnight, a striking brunette, who was—he couldn't help noticing—as beautiful as ever. "Did you come for the boy?"

"He's a bonus."

"Then what did you come for, and how'd you find me?"

Midnight released the hammer on her gun and put it in her purse. She opened Hanley's belt pack and took out the MacGuffin. "Here's what we came for."

She flipped the partially finished pyramid over to bottom-side-up. "Here's how we found you." With her finger nail, she peeled an almost indiscernible circle off the bottom.

"A tracking device," said Hanley. "Transparent and paper thin."

"The professor at M.I.T. was collateral damage. The idea was to make you think you were being pursued, so you wouldn't suspect you were being tracked."

Midnight put the MacGuffin in her purse.

"Let's go," Brussel said.

They all went up the stairs.

When they reached the cathedral, they were ushered into a room where Darkin sat. Two more henchmen stood nearby.

"Ah, Mr. Rodriguez," Darkin said. "Where are the inestimable Mr. Nichols and the charming Miss Chapel?"

"Far away," Roddy said.

"I'm sure, but we'll meet again. And look who it is. The irrepressible Mr. Hanley."

"Nice wallpaper."

"You did extensive damage to my house."

"Talk to your goon squad. And I'm curious. Why the room-in-a-time-warp motif?"

"Not that my home is any of your business, but I kept the room as it was when my parents were killed in an auto accident. When my life became real."

"Real? You teach evolution."

"As long as we control the class rooms and the scientific community, Darwinism will remain an indisputable scientific fact."

"Haven't you heard?" Hanley said, a mischievous twinkle in his eye. "Darwinism is being dumped in favor of exogenesis."

Darkin's countenance became grim and his eyes burned. "Aliens seeding the planet? I'll destroy those people just as I've worked to destroy Christianity."

"A riff between evolutionists. I like it. Anyway, evolution, whether explained by Darwin or aliens, is so stupid and unsupportable, why don't you just give up."

Darkin stood, his fists clenched. "And look a complete fool for having taught a myth as science for the last thirty years?" Darkin went to Midnight. "Have you got the key?"

She opened her purse, took out the MacGuffin, and handed the little pyramid to Darkin.

"Wonderful," he said. "Only two more pieces to go." He turned to Roddy. "I don't suppose you're gonna tell me who the next contact is?"

"Not even if I knew."

Darkin put the MacGuffin in a briefcase and handed it to Midnight. "Put this in my car, then drive yours to the airport and go to Turkey. Find Brick Majors and kill him. I don't want any loose ends."

Alp started after Darkin, but Hanley and Roddy held him back.

Midnight glanced toward Hanley. "I guess I forgot to say goodbye last time. So I won't this time either, Warren, sweetie."

"I'm all broke up, too," Hanley said.

She turned and left.

"Can I kill them now?" said Wallach.

"We should keep them alive," Darkin said, "until we find out where the rest of the pieces are. If Branch Nichols knows, he'll tell us to save his friends. Time for you to hunt him down, Mr. Wallach."

"My pleasure."

Darkin went out the door with Wallach right behind him, leaving Brussel and the other two.

"You two," Brussel said, "tie them up." He turned to his captives. "There'll be no escaping this time."

When everyone was tied up, Brussel said, "Stay here and don't let them move around. I'll be back." Brussel left, and the two henchmen stood by the door.

Roddy said, "I can't believe Midnight turned out so bad."

"Not at all," Hanley said. "She's amazing."

"What do you mean?" Alp said. "She's gonna kill Brick."

Hanley leaned in and whispered, "No, she's not."

"She's one of them," Roddy said. "She gave Darkin the MacGuffin."

"Roddy, you lost count, didn't you?" Hanley whispered.

"What's going on?" one of the gunmen said.

Hanley replied, "Just counting the seconds before you and I switch places."

The two goons glanced at each other.

The door burst open, and Gorman entered. "I'm sorry," he said, "I believe I left my reading glasses in here." He went past the two guards, who traded confused looks. They stiffened at the sound of two gun hammers being cocked immediately behind their ears. They turned their heads just enough to see Midnight holding the guns.

Gorman disarmed both of them. "Sit against the wall you two."

They did as they were told while Midnight went to the captives. She untied their ropes and gave the guns to Alp and Roddy, who began to tie up and gag the hapless gunmen.

When everyone was free, Hanley put his arms around Midnight and embraced her.

"You're good at this," he said.

"As long as I don't have to shoot anyone."

Hanley smiled, "I knew you couldn't." They hugged again.

Roddy and Alp finished securing their two prisoners.

"We've gotta get after Darkin," Roddy said, "so we can retrieve the MacGuffin. Again."

"No need," Hanley said. "Show him, Midnight."

She opened her purse and pulled out the little pyramid. Roddy studied it. "Only two pieces missing. You were right. I miscounted. We had six when we came here, not counting the one Branch has, which makes seven."

"And Midnight had the eighth," Hanley said.

"Seventh," said Midnight. "The eighth and ninth ones are the top pieces. Mine attached itself to the pyramid when I put it in my purse. Fortunately, Darkin didn't know how many pieces you'd recovered."

"Is this why you were at M.I.T.?" Hanley said.

"Yes, I was there to get acquainted with Branch. Darkin suspected he was pivotal to the Pyramidions, and would be chosen to assemble the key. Although Darkin had infiltrated *us*, he never suspected I was a double agent, a Pyramidion."

Hanley said, "But we have the pyramid now and Branch isn't here."

"At his discretion, he can pass the pyramid along to anyone he trusts."

"You said Branch was your reason for being at M.I.T. What about me?"

She gave him an inviting smile. "You, I fell for. Against my will."

"Why did you leave and never contact me?"

"I had a mission. And you were a loose cannon. I thought it best to get away from you."

"What about now?"

"My mission is complete. Now I need an exit strategy."

"You're not getting away from me this time."

"Just try and get rid of me."

Alp said, "You two can make kissy-face later. Right now, we need to get out of here. Gorman?"

"My cover is blown," Gorman said. "I'm with you."

Chapter Fourteen

Branch and Linda walked along the beach holding hands. Brick had given them his best guess on where to find Dr. Fink if he were still alive. They looked for a thatch hut in a secluded area, on the other side of the island. They had to park their car at the end of a dirt road.

"So tell me about this guy," Linda said. "Warren thinks you want to ask him about the Big Bang."

"Among other things. Professor Fink once told me and Hanley something about the Big Bang. He said a lot of so-called modern science had its origin in an ancient mystical, religious writing known as the Kabbalah."

"I'm somewhat familiar with Kabbalah. It's an esoteric rendering of Hebrew Scripture which had its beginning at least as early as the twelfth century."

"Quite a bit earlier."

Branch looked up as they walked and saw a rustic hut, nestled in the palm trees, situated ten feet above the ground.

"We may have found him." Branch said.

Standing near the seaside shanty, it looked to be twenty feet by twenty feet. Underneath was a noisy structure of about 150 cubic feet. A wire ran up to the hut. Linda and Branch couldn't see a stairway.

"I think this must be the wrong place," Linda said. "Unless we're looking for Tarzan."

"Professor Fink," Branch yelled. "Are you home, Dr. Fink?"

A voice from inside yelled, "No one by that name here."

"Professor, it's Branch Nichols. I was a student at M.I.T. many years ago."

Part of the wall, which turned out to be a concealed door, opened into the hut. A man, who looked like Robinson Crusoe at his grungiest, stuck his hairy head out. "Nichols, I remember you. Hung around with that intrepid rapscallion, Warren Hanley."

"Yes, sir."

Fink disappeared and a moment later a rope ladder dropped down.

"After you," Branch said, and Linda started to climb. When she reached the top, Fink took her hand and helped her up. Branch came in right behind her.

The furnishings were built from the same indigenous growth as the hut itself. They all sat on the rustic furniture. He offered them something to drink, and they accepted lemonade, with ice cubes.

"You have a freezer?" Linda said.

"The generator underneath us supplies all my electricity. I haven't gone entirely native."

"What is it with retired scientists?" Branch said. "I found one living in an out-of-the-way spot in New Mexico and one living in a black hole in Australia. You live here, on a beach, in a tree house."

"Some of us have a short history ahead of us. Especially if we're deemed to be influential, with a proclivity for speaking out against the international religion."

"Then perhaps you're aware some exceedingly rude people are looking for you, and you might want to think about relocating."

"Yes, I am but thank you for the heads-up, anyway."

"I'm a little surprised you still remember me after all these years. Especially since I never sat in one of your classes, although Warren did."

"Who could forget Hanley. To paraphrase Dickens, he was the best student I ever had. He was the worst student I ever had."

Linda laughed. A reaction not lost on Branch, since it appeared, to him, to be an affectionate laugh.

"Now, what occasioned your visit?" Fink said.

"Well, Dr. Fink—" Branch began.

"Please, no titles. I've always thought titles pretentious. My name is Hezekiah Fink. Just call me Hezy."

"All right, Hezy. I wanted to ask you about the Kabbalah and its connection to modern science."

"Modern, yes. Science, no."

"You're not the first to tell me that."

"Today, all you need to be a cutting edge scientist is a vivid imagination and a talent for creating elegant mathematical theories. At their simplest, two plus two can equal five, or any other number you happen to need. Einstein's the one who started the trend.

"But Einstein's relativity, Copernicus' heliocentricity, and Lemaître's Big Bang have one thing in common. They all go back to ancient mysticism known as Kabbalah. Nechunya ben HaKanah, a Kabbalist lived in the first century. He claimed the universe was over fifteen billion years old just as the modern day astrophysicists do. Coincidence? No.

"Indeed, Kabbalism is at the heart of the occult. It looks for hidden meanings in Hebrew scripture, using Gematria, numbers. Kabbalah has been used to justify evolution and Zionism. Many Christians think they are supposed to support Israel, believing its existence and future is part of God's plan. It's like this modern-day mindless fascination with the Rapture. Interpreting, or rather forcing, bone-head theology into the Scriptures has become all the rage."

"You also mentioned the Freemasons," Branch said.

"The 32nd and 33rd degree Freemasons have been used to create wars and depressions. They orchestrate the affairs of nations. Their politics is socialism and their religion is Kabbalistic Humanism. They intend to control the world, create a new world order."

Linda said, "I've noticed a trend in movies to portray the Freemasons as the good guys."

"Freemasons own most of Hollywood, as well as the public school system, and both major political parties. Which is why it doesn't matter which candidate you vote for for president. Unless you voted for Trump of course. A true outsider."

Hezy stood and started pacing.

"Tell me: do you want to uncover what goes on in the world regarding the power elite, and what the insidious influence of evolution has done to this world? Do you wish to understand the importance of the pyramid? If so, you need to talk to my old friend Isaiah Arcane. How's that for a name? He's worked in banking and government and knows where all the bodies are buried."

"The importance of the pyramid?" Branch said.

"Yes. You've seen it on the dollar bill with the all-seeing eye. The pyramid was hijacked, and its Godly significance distorted, by the Freemasons. The greatest theft in history. Many Christians think it's an occult symbol."

Hezy stopped pacing and peered through a window. "Trouble." He flipped open a chest and pulled out two Jackhammer Machine Shotguns. "Here." He tossed one to Branch.

"Again?" Linda said. "Can't we go anywhere and just have a nice time?"

Hezy went back to the window. "Rocket Launcher." He surveyed the room. "Under the couch," he said.

Branch and Hezy grabbed the corners to turn the couch over, and all three got underneath. An explosion shook the hutch. The floor dropped, but only six feet, landing them on the generator. The roof collapsed on top of the couch. They heard the sound of crashing debris all around them.

Linda said, "This is the third time I've been saved by a couch."

"Pardon me?" Hezy said.

"Long story," said Branch.

"Ready?" Hezy said.

"Let's go," said Branch.

They threw the couch off, along with a section of the roof, and came up shooting. Bullets pinged off the trees as the attacker turned and fled.

Branch hopped off the generator, set his gun down, and helped Linda.

Hezy jumped off and started in the direction of the sniper. "You two go back the way you came. I'll take care of our guest."

"Where will you live now?" Linda said.

"Back-up hideout in the jungle, or if you're politically correct, rainforest."

"I never do politically correct," said Linda.

Hezy stopped and turned. "Hey, all I know about Isaiah's whereabouts is that he's somewhere in Costa Rica."

"Thanks," Branch said.

Hezy nodded and jogged away.

Back at the car, Linda received a text message. "It's Roddy. He's leaving Rome and wants to know where he can meet us."

"Tell him Costa Rica."

Branch and Linda sat in the wide-body jet as it landed at Juan Santamaría International Airport, twelve and a half miles from San José, Costa Rica. They expected to meet Roddy, whose flight was supposed to land not long before theirs. On their way to the baggage claim, they spotted him talking to another man.

Linda ran to Roddy and kissed him on the cheek.

"Nice to see you again, too," Roddy said. He gave Linda a hug. "Hey, Amigo," he said, as Branch approached.

"Looks like the Pyramid Gang's all here," said Branch.

Roddy said, "Too bad Warren and Midnight couldn't come, but they decided to drop off the grid."

"How is Midnight?" Branch said.

Linda watched Branch for any sign that he still cared for his enigmatic old flame.

"No different," said Roddy. "Unless you count being more beautiful than ever."

"No kidding," Branch said, with a smile.

Linda bristled.

Roddy opened a travel bag hanging from his shoulder. "I brought the MacGuffin," he said as he took the tiny pyramid out.

The eighth piece, resting in Branch's shirt pocket, leapt out and onto the pyramid.

"One more to go," Roddy said with a smile. He handed the MacGuffin to Linda who put it in her purse.

The man whom Roddy had been talking to nudged him.

"I'm sorry," Roddy said. "This is Mr. Isaiah Arcane. Brick found him for me."

"Call me Isaiah." He had a ruddy complexion, a vigorous look in his eyes, and white hair.

"Brick told me you want to know what makes the world go," Isaiah said. "Said my old buddy, Hezekiah sent you."

"We're hoping you can shed some light on the nature of our mission to recover all the pieces to the little pyramid you just saw." Branch said.

"I'll do more. I'll give you an unconventional tour of history, and an understanding of the present-day world that'll scare the socks off you. Do you think you have the courage to find out how the world works? I mean, *really* works?"

Roddy and Linda looked at Branch, waiting for him to answer.

A faint smile appeared. "Sure. Do your scariest."

"Oh, I will."

They left the airport in Isaiah's SUV and drove into the area known as Central Valley, where 70 percent of Costa Ricans live. Isaiah's two-story house was all but buried in the plush green tropical growth.

Upon arriving, Isaiah said, "I know you're all tired from your trips. So if you'd rather wait—"

"No," Branch said. "I'm eager to hear what you have to say."

"Me too," Linda said. "You've piqued my curiosity."

"Sit down and I'll begin by telling you a story. This is to give background for the present day, and how things came to be as they are."

"Terrific," Roddy said. "I love stories."

"I will admit, though, I'm gonna leave out a pertinent piece of information until the end. Saving my thunder, you might say." He leaned back in an over-stuffed chair. He rested his elbows on the arms of the chair and folded his fingers together. "All right then, we begin in 1743, with the birth of Mayer Amschel Bauer.

"His father, a money-lender, taught him everything about the business. During the 1760s, Mayer began laying the groundwork for unbridled acquisition of wealth. He'd become associated with William of Hanau-Hesse. This one man, Hesse became the key to the future.

"Bauer married in 1770. He fathered five boys and five girls. His third son, Nathan was particularly brilliant and a most prominent figure in the unfolding of this story.

"In 1776, Mayer created the Illuminati and appointed Johann Adam Weishaupt head of the organization. Weishaupt infiltrated the Masons so Bauer could use them to help write history. Years later, Bauer would create an unprecedented explosion of wealth, even printing the money itself.

"In 1790, Bauer said, 'Let me issue and control a nation's money, and I care not who writes the laws.' The realization of his bold statement has dictated the course of history for more than two centuries.

"In 1806, Hesse fled to Denmark to escape the French. He left three million dollars in the care of Mayer Bauer. He embezzled the money and sent it to his son Nathan in London to open a merchant bank.

"Then in 1815, the future of England, indeed Europe, would be decided by a single three-day battle, in present day Belgium. The Bauers had spies at Waterloo, and when the battle was over, one of them raced back to England. The next morning, he met with Nathan at Folkstone.

"Knowing the true outcome, Nathan had his brokers begin selling. The more they sold, the more sure others were that the wily banker had advanced knowledge of Wellington's defeat. In a panic, everyone started dumping their stocks.

"When stocks were selling for five cents on the dollar, Nathan's agents bought hand-over-fist until Nathan virtually owned the country. When the real news arrived that Wellington had won, the market soared. Nathan had multiplied his already massive wealth by twenty times.

"The Bauer family had financed both sides in the war, putting both countries deep in debt, and then conquered England in one day. Without firing a shot.

"Nathan's brothers, Karl and James pulled off a similar financial takeover in France three years later. They manipulated the bond market, which supported a faltering French economy. More coups d'états were performed in other countries."

Isaiah stopped for a moment. His audience stared with rapt attention. He enjoyed imparting and shocking people with the truth. In the present world, truth had become the scarcest and most shocking story of all. Now confident he had his three listeners in his verbal grasp, he continued.

"Next, they turned their eye toward the United States, which was way too prosperous for their liking. Its constitution said that only Congress could print money. That meant the country would never be in debt to the banks as the European countries now were. America's uniqueness would attract the brains and wealth of the world. The Bauer Dynasty had to destroy the competition.

"They'd already had a twenty-year charter for a central bank from 1791 to 1811. This had come about through their agent, Alexander Hamilton. But congress refused to renew their charter. Nathan decided to punish the fledgling nation and caused Britain to declare war. What we now call the War of 1812.

"A second charter, approved in 1816, gave the Dynasty control of the American money supply. However, in 1833, Andrew Jackson, probably the only president who actually did balance the budget, was determined to take back control of the money for his country. He began withdrawing government deposits from the Second Bank of the United States and putting the money in democratically controlled banks.

"In retaliation, the Dynasty contracted the money supply and caused a depression. Jackson called them thieves and vipers and said he would rout them out. The Dynasty sent an assassin, who brought two one-shot pistols. Miraculously, both of them misfired. In 1836, the bank folded when the charter was not renewed.

"In 1841, the Dynasty tried again, but President John Tyler vetoed the move.

"Enraged, the Dynasty decided to destroy the country. They sent hoards of British agents into the southern states, spreading propaganda, fomenting rebellion."

"Wait a minute," Roddy said. "Wasn't the Civil War fought over slavery?"

"Yes and no. Agents of the Bauers conducted the slave trade in a deliberate attempt to divide the country. But it was more complex.

"The South was afraid an all-powerful federal government would force them to abdicate their states' rights. This was what led to the rebellion, not slavery. Most of the soldiers in the southern army didn't own slaves, and they weren't willing to fight for the alleged right of the rich few who did. And while slavery was abhorred by a majority in the North, there weren't enough people willing to go to war over it.

"The freeing of the slaves was an important outcome of the war, especially when you consider the addition of 200,000 black men into the Union Army. Without them the North might not have won. Ironically, blacks, who were brought here to divide the Union, may have saved it. But another hundred years were needed for them to, finally, begin to be fully integrated.

"Anyway, getting back to the subject at hand, in 1861, Lincoln went to the banks in New York to get a loan to finance the war. Of course, they were under the influence of the Dynasty. So the banks said they'd charge Lincoln 24-percent to 36-percent interest. Hopping mad, Lincoln decided to print his own money.

"The Dynasty didn't give up. Violating the Monroe Doctrine, British, French, and Spanish troops swept into Mexico. Things looked pretty bleak. But Lincoln discovered the Russian czar had also been fighting the Dynasty's attempts to set up a central bank in his country. So Lincoln asked for help.

"The czar said that if England or France got involved, Russia would declare war on them. The countries backed off, but the Dynasty would get its revenge on the czar's descendants many years later. In 1917, having financed the Bolshevik revolution, the Dynasty ordered the execution of the czar and his family.

"Revenge against Lincoln came more swiftly. Izola Forrester, granddaughter of John Wilkes Booth said in her book *This One Mad Act* that some rather cryptic Europeans had contacted Booth. She said that he went to Europe at least once before the assassination, and that he was also helped in his escape, living quietly for many years after.

"But the Dynasty still didn't have a central bank, and with it, control of the American currency. Almost five more decades were needed to realize this goal. James Garfield stood against them and was assassinated. William McKinley barred the door, and he, too, was eliminated.

"In 1907, a Dynasty representative in the U.S., Jacob Schiff warned that without a central bank, the country would experience a devastating money panic. In the creatively engineered monetary crisis that followed, tens of thousands of people were financially wiped out. The bankers made billions.

"Banking conspirators met secretly on Jekyll Island near the coast of Georgia in 1908 to plan America's financial future. The Dynasty convinced a gullible Congress to pass the Federal Reserve Act. A naive President Wilson signed the Central Bank into being in 1913.

"Not all had been fooled, though. Congressman Charles Lindbergh said, 'The invisible government of the monetary power will be legalized...' Years later, when Wilson realized his mistake, he said, 'I have unwittingly ruined my country.'

"Then began the bloodiest century in world history. The Dynasty intended to construct a New World Order out of the ashes and chaos of a world that would nearly destroy itself. The plan, laid out in 1871 by Albert Pike, a Scottish Freemason, declared three world wars would be necessary.

"The first one would eliminate the czarist control of Russia, and place the country under Illuminati control. The second would expand the Russian domain, making them the monster in the closet for the world to fear. The war would also be used to create a Zionist stronghold in Israel.

"The final war will be brought on by antagonism between Arabs and Zionists, through the efforts of the Illuminati. Russia, China, and India are being groomed for participation, as are the U.S. and the European Union. All religions, especially Christianity and atheism, will be seen as failures. From the ruins of civilization, the world will be turned toward Lucifer as the god of the human race."

"Lucifer?" Roddy said. "Did I miss something? How'd he get into this?"

"I need to go back to the patriarch of the Dynasty, Mayer Amschel Bauer. He used to get into long discussions with his rabbi about the Talmud, which is at the center of the Jewish culture. It's more valuable to Jews than the Hebrew Bible. The Kabbalah is a Talmudic philosophy of spiritual matters, full of pseudo-science and witchcraft.

"Kabbalah is embraced by the higher level Masons and Illuminati. It's the basis for Theosophy, Mormonism, and Rosicrucianism. Albert Pike, who I already mentioned, said, 'Lucifer, the Son of the Morning! Is it he who bears the Light... Doubt it not!' Now consider what the prophet Isaiah said: 'How art thou fallen from heaven, O Lucifer, son of the morning! How art thou cut down to the ground, which didst weaken the nations!'

"Study of Kabbalah ultimately leads to Lucifer, the son of the morning. He's the god of this world, which connects to something interesting about the United Nations. I'll get to that in a little bit.

"For now, be aware that Freemasonry includes many occult symbols taken from the Kabbalah. The Star of David is a mystic symbol that has nothing to do with King David. The Star originated with Kabbalists in about the thirteenth century.

"The all-seeing eye. Lucifer told Adam and Eve, 'For God doth know that in the day ye eat thereof, then your eyes shall be opened, and ye shall be as gods...' But the Hebrew word `ayin is actually the singular, eye. That is, the all-seeing eye.

"Lucifer is seen as the one who brings freedom, both noetically and spiritually."

"Noetically?" Roddy said.

"Perception, learning, reasoning."

"Oh. I thought maybe it was some kind of code word." He shrugged as he gave an embarrassed smile to Linda and Branch.

"I wanted to mention, once more, the central bank of the United States. We call it the Federal Reserve, though it's not federal and there's no reserve. It's a printing press. The fifth president to be targeted was John Kennedy, a boy scout, in way over his head. He had no idea of the forces he was dealing with. And it wasn't just the bank.

"Kennedy wanted not only to destroy the Federal Reserve. He signed Executive Order 11110, which gave back to the government the power to print money, bypassing the Fed. He also wanted to break up the CIA. He wanted to bring troops home from Vietnam, and he opposed Zionism. Signing the nuclear test ban treaty didn't help his cause either. Then, throw in his brother's war on the mob and you can see why a whole lot of people wanted him terminated.

"The war in Vietnam helped create the illusion of enemies at our doorstep. It created profits for some, and increased our debt to the Federal Reserve. The CIA meddled in foreign affairs, and this may or may not have been before they became an international drug cartel. Zionism was the spark that could ignite the entire Middle East. The mafia had helped Kennedy get elected and they felt betrayed.

"The CIA wanted him eliminated, as did the Mossad, the mafia, and the Federal Reserve bankers. The Illuminati-Freemason banking Dynasty gave the short straw to the CIA. Harvey Oswald was chosen as the fall guy, even though he couldn't shoot straight. I mean, his first shot missed the entire automobile and bounced off the curb on the far side of the street. The two kill shots came from a man on a grassy knoll. Not sure who the shooter was, but Howard Hunt, on his death bed, confessed he had managed the entire event for the CIA.

"When Nixon didn't obey his puppet masters, he was driven out of office. Again, Howard Hunt was involved. A Freemason FBI associate director, famously known as Deep Throat, fed a couple of journalists—Hardy Boy wannabes—just enough clues to get the job done. Meanwhile, Henry Kissinger controlled the information Nixon received. He kept Nixon under stress—and in a state of confusion."

Roddy said, "But he worked for President Nixon."

"His first allegiance was to the Dynasty. Kissinger was the first person known to say that billions of people will need to be terminated in preparation for the New World Order."

"You can't be serious," Linda said.

"Oh, yes. And they've been doing a good job of population control for a long time. One of the affects of war is to eliminate people, which leaves fewer people to make babies. Currently, they are starving millions of people to death. And the whole reason for making DDT illegal was population control."

"What?" Linda said. "I thought DDT was poisonous to humans."

"Not at all. A 500-plus-page report concluded that it was not dangerous to humans. But it killed mosquitoes, and malaria carrying mosquitoes were seen as a way to decrease the number of 'useless' people."

Linda shook her head in dismay.

Isaiah went on: "DDT was supposedly killing birds, and the bald eagle was said to be in danger of extinction. The claim was erroneous. In fact, Professor Kenneth Mellanby, for forty years, was known to eat DDT in front of his students to show how harmless the stuff was.

"The anti-DDT people claimed the insecticide was losing its effectiveness against bedbugs. But with the current epidemic in the United States, I'm sure plenty of people would love a chance to prove them wrong.

"Some third world countries still use it, while others do not, and usually, the alternatives are too expensive.

"Now I'd like to shock you with the real story of HIV, which was created in a lab at Fort Detrick, in Frederick, Maryland. Back in the seventies, the Dynasty, the secret world government, determined to exterminate the black population of Africa. For years we were told AIDS came from green monkeys, but we now know they have the wrong DNA. Turns out, the virus was spread through smallpox vaccinations, and the people most susceptible to the virus are blacks. Making HIV a serious problem in the U.S. as well."

"Can you corroborate all this?" Branch said. "I mean you're telling us some pretty fantastic stuff."

"I've worked in banking and government. I've seen and heard things, and I've studied real history. Not the pseudo-history you learn in school.

"This is all available. You can do your own research. There are books, the Net, and documentaries. Be sure to test your sources, making sure they're reliable, not just opinionated, or merely copied from what someone else wrote. Also, that they aren't simply conspiracy theorists or social gadflies who just like to rock the boat and draw attention.

"You've heard the maxim that truth is stranger than fiction. Well, truth is also scarier than theory. The widely held belief that the 9/11 attack on the Twin Towers was a false flag conspiracy is no theory, but the fingers are all pointing in the wrong directions. Come on, Bush needed help tying his own shoe. Can the Mossad manipulate Arabs to such a degree? No, the shadow government, controlled by the Dynasty, was responsible.

"They needed something to replace the Cold War. Hitler said it well: 'Terrorism is the best political weapon, for nothing drives people harder than a fear of sudden death.' Terrorism and increasing socialism are being used to drive up the debt to the central bank, the Federal Reserve.

"The invisible government, as Lindbergh called it, is determined to destroy this country. Their greatest weapon is the Fed, a reincarnation of the bank Andrew Jackson put out of business in the 1830s. It's been controlling our country for 100 years.

"Before he managed to put the central bank out of business, Jackson said, 'If the people only understood the rank injustice of our money and banking system, there would be a revolution before morning.' What he said is truer today than it was then.

"Of course that's not as insidious as the drive to depopulate the world. They intend to decrease the population of the U.S., as well. U.N. troops are already entering and engaging in marshal law drills. F.E.M.A. is building detention centers capable of housing millions. Many will only be temporarily housed, if you know what I mean."

"Such a thing can happen in the United States?" Linda said.

"You bet. If they are ever successful in disarming the public, it will only be a matter of time. A short time."

"I'm still waiting for you to make the connection between all this and evolution," Branch said.

"And I will. For starters, you wouldn't be in favor of mass genocide as Hitler was, if you thought you'd someday have to answer to an almighty God. Yet, there are dunderheads who say when Hitler talked about evolution, he was referring to social evolution.

"But Hitler said, 'The first step which visibly brought mankind away from the animal world was that which led to the first invention.' Now how can separation from the animal world be construed as social evolution? I guess some people will believe only what they want.

"Then there was Stalin, who murdered tens of millions of his own people, as did Mao in China. Both, by the way, were financed by the Dynasty. And of course, as I've told you, we have an engineered disease, AIDS. We have the banning of a harmless substance, DDT, which could save millions of lives. And last, but most devastating of all, we have forced starvation.

"If you're only practicing animal control, like deer hunting season, what's the harm? It's a good thing, right? And when it comes to the most destitute on our planet, devising means for their extinction is comparable to cleaning out the rats in your city's sewer system.

"Morality is just a word with no significant meaning if there's no God."

Linda said, "You promised to tell us more about Lucifer and his connection to the U.N."

"Yes, and this is something many people would find difficult to believe, but as someone said, he doesn't care what you believe. He being Lucifer.

"It started with Alice and Foster Bailey. Foster was a 32nd degree Mason, and Alice was a disciple of Helena Blavatsky, founder of the Theosophical Society in 1875. The society's logo includes the Star of David. It also includes the swastika, which she considered to be a symbol of the Aryan race, an esoteric symbol. In fact, she believed it to be the most powerful one of them all.

"Alice incorporated Lucifer Publishing in 1920 to publish her books, but changed the name to Lucis Publishing in 1925. Now known as Lucis Trust, it includes a correspondence school based on her teachings. It's the publishing house that prints and distributes United Nations material, and among other things, World Goodwill, founded in 1932.

"That particular arm of the Lucis Trust, a member of the U.N. Economic and Social Council, has the ignominious responsibility of getting the world ready for the second coming.

Not Christ's, but Lucifer's. They believe—and you can read this at the Lucis Trust website—that Lucifer was a superior being who came down, with his brethren from Venus, eons ago. A human at the time was just a man-animal, and Lucifer brought the 'principle of mind' to give man's evolution a jump-start. This, in Theosophical teaching, was not a fall from grace, but an enormous sacrifice.

"Thus saith the publication and dissemination center for the United Nations, steeped in New Age and pagan philosophy."

"This is all scary, to say the least," Linda said. "But I'm not sure how everything ties in. Zionists, the Catholic Church, nefarious bankers being an invisible government. And who's Bauer? I've never heard of him."

"Ah, remember I said I would leave out one essential detail, saving my proverbial thunder till near the end. What I left out was the name change. The patriarch of the banking Dynasty Mayer Amschel Bauer changed his name to Red Shield."

He watched them as they hung on every word, the showman in him being inspired. "In German the words are Rotes Schild, which in English becomes Rothschild."

Their eyes showed their recognition of one of the most famous names on Earth.

"The Rothschild family, known as The House of Rothschild, along with a dozen other families is the elite. They are the puppet masters of the world's invisible government, and the planners of the New World Order. No one knows for sure how much money they have. Estimates for the Rothschild's worth ranges from 100 trillion to 900 trillion. The wealth of the other families, mostly oil and banking, isn't as vast but still fantastic. The Rockefellers, for instance, are worth tens of trillions.

"Of course, you won't find any of this in *Forbes*. And you won't hear a lot said against them either. They created the Anti-defamation League to convince people an attack on the Rothschilds is an attack on all Jews.

"Now I must tell you more about how they plan to bring the world to its knees. Their motto is *Ordo ab Chao*, which is Latin for order out of chaos.

"The shadow government of international banking elite produces fiscal disasters like stock crashes, recessions, and depressions. They employ more socialist programs as the answer, calling them stimulus packages. This adds to their stranglehold on the poor by increasing their dependence and destroying the middle class with increased inflation and taxation.

"They create false flag episodes like 9/11 and then use it to enact new legislation. The Patriot Act, for example, has further eroded our freedom, moving us ever closer to a police state."

"How do we fight something visible like a bank or corporate entity, but not visible as a manipulator of world events?" Branch said.

"The would-be masters of the New World Order do have a visible strategic arm, one you can point to and say there they are, plotting again. They are known as the Bilderbergs."

The silence that followed those words shook the air. Branch's posture stiffened as his muscles went rigid. He shared an incredulous glance with Linda and Roddy.

"You've heard of them," Isaiah said.

"Yes," said Branch.

"What do you think Benjamin is into?" Roddy said.

"We better find out," answered Branch.

Chapter Fifteen

Benjamin read his mail—which he more than suspected had already been read by Homeland Security—at the direction of the Bilderbergs. Nothing was marked as it normally would be, but Benjamin knew. He was not being taken for granted, not by the richest, most powerful men on the planet. They needed to be sure he was not a mole.

In recent years, leaks had sprung. Sensitive information about their clandestine meetings had fallen into the hands of whistleblowers. They were courageous people who wrote books and built websites. They were people who did not want the human race to become the slaves of the few.

Contact between the world's elite had always been sporadic. But in 1954, international financiers held their first annual meeting at the Bilderberg Hotel in Oosterbeek, Netherlands. The core of the group had thirty-nine members. Various other powerful individuals in fields such as industry, politics, and media were also invited. Never more than about a hundred people attended. Each year a different five-star hotel in a different country was chosen. At these meetings, they'd attempt to decide the fate of the planet.

Benjamin was invited this year—a rare occurrence for a black man. He'd become influential enough that he was now considered someone who would further the goal of creating a global government regime. Benjamin was also liked by the elite because of his ability to stay under the radar. The size of his wealth was not public knowledge, and few people had ever heard of him.

Benjamin's Android rang. He picked it up and smiled when he saw who was calling.

"Jeffrey, are things moving along according to plan?"

"Yes, Benjamin. Our gear is better than state-of-the-art. You wouldn't believe the stuff we've been able to acquire. Your every word and the voices of everyone within twenty feet of you will be picked up. Speeches will be audible and recorded with near-perfect clarity at a remote location outside the hotel. Tiny cameras, hidden on you and your wheel chair, will be sending us their images in high definition. And you'll be able to record remote conversations from anywhere in the building."

"Wonderful, but I hope you were careful about where, and from whom, you got your equipment."

"You worry too much, Benjamin. We'll be fine. The day after the meetings, many hours of recordings will be on the Internet for everyone to see and listen to. The world's elite will be condemning themselves with their own words."

"I look forward to our next and only meeting, when I get wired up. Until then, watch your back."

The Hanleys sat together on the balcony of their cozy seaside home in Hallstatt, Austria. They stared out over the Hallstätter See, and the surrounding Dachstein mountains. It's considered by many to be the loveliest of all lakeside villages in the world. Hallstatt graces countless business calendars and computer desktops. It has inspired poets, painters, and at least one composer. According to legend, Hallstatt's breathtaking beauty stirred Richard Wagner to write *Parsifal* while he hid from his creditors.

Though the view was grand, Midnight was admiring the rings on her third finger, left hand.

Warren stopped reading his Robert Ludlum novel and said, "You keep staring, you're gonna wear them out."

"Don't be silly. Oh, listen to me, telling you not to be silly."

"Ha, ha. I'm glad you like your rings."

"Such a gorgeous engagement ring. I bet ours was the shortest engagement in history."

"Yeah, only a few hours."

"Three hours, nineteen-and-a-half minutes."

"You know exactly?"

"Well, I rounded off. I'm not positive it was exactly thirty seconds. About thirty, give or take." She caught sight of his bewildered stare. "What?"

He shook his head and went back to his novel.

Midnight said, "Do you realize our first anniversary will be in just 364 days, 1 hour, and 7 minutes."

Without looking up from his book, Warren said, "Not even gonna comment."

"I'm amazed we were engaged, married, and moved into this wonderful spot, virtually overnight. You had this romantic paradise of a place sitting here, waiting."

"Family heirloom."

She gazed at the lake, and the mountains, and the waterfalls. "Even my family doesn't have one this remote, or this beautiful."

"No matter where we are, I just want to make the most of the forty to fifty years we have left."

"You're optimistic."

"Not necessarily. Based on the actuarial tables of insurance companies—"

"Oh, shush. Quit trying to be romantic."

Outside the Hanley's home stood two seriously ugly men dressed in the traditional garb of the 1,100 locals, including lederhosen. But under their vests, each carried a Glock handgun. One of them glanced around to see that no one was watching, then nodded to the other. Their movements were silent and swift as they slithered toward the entrance.

"Did you know that after the war the Nazis threw all kinds of incriminating contraband into the water, along with valuables and firearms?" Warren said. "Divers have been pulling the stuff out for years. One guy found plates for printing counterfeit money."

She gave him a look. "You miss the old life, don't you? The adventure and all."

"Of course not. Do you realize artifact hunters have found everything from a Stone Age axe to a Roman sword. Imagine, for thousands of years, this has been a dumpsite for historical relics. You hungry? I'm going to a restaurant and get us some fish for carryout."

"Good idea. Especially since I haven't had a chance to do grocery shopping yet."

Warren got up and left the balcony, walked across the bedroom, and out to the hall.

Opening the front door, he found two men standing. "Hello. Can I help you?"

The men moved their vests aside and started to pull their Glocks.

Warren slammed the door, locked it, and ran.

Bullets pierced the dark mahogany. The two gunmen kicked the door open, together and stepped into the house.

Warren didn't run back to where Midnight was, but in another direction, to draw them away.

Midnight noticed a faint noise, like gunshots. She got up from her chair on the balcony and went into the bedroom. She listened but heard nothing.

Warren stood in the dark shadow of a nook across the hall from a doorway to a storage room. One of the men crept along the corridor. He peeked into the room, and Warren jumped him from behind. He grabbed the intruder's collar and shoved him forward, banging his head against the doorway. Then he yanked the guy back and tripped him, causing him to hit his head against the wall on the way down.

Warren picked up the gun.

Midnight stood by the door to the bedroom, not sure what to do. The door flew open, and a man wielding a gun entered. He closed the door behind him.

"Miss Jones," the man said. "Or perhaps I should say Mrs. Hanley."

"How'd you find us?"

"You ought to know, but I can't tell. You'd have to beat it out of me."

"That can be arranged." She swung her right foot up and kicked the gun out of his hand."

The surprised gunman blinked at her.

She smiled and said, "I'm your worst nightmare." She shot her foot out hitting him in the chest and knocked him against the door.

She turned and jabbed her other foot into his stomach. He let out a grunt, but he was still standing, and didn't seem particularly fazed.

She whirled half way around, swinging her leg up in her best roundhouse kick, going for the side of his head right above the ear.

He put his arm up and deflected her.

She brought her foot back to the floor and stood in a ready position.

"Come on," he said. "You're a woman, and I'm twice your size."

"This stuff always works in the movies."

He started to laugh. He laughed so hard he threw his head back. At that moment, the door opened, smacking him in the back of the head and knocking him down. He banged his forehead on the wood floor and went unconscious.

Warren stepped in, holding a Glock. "Mrs. Hanley, are you all right?"

"Why yes, Mr., Hanley." She glanced down at the man. "Boy, he's ugly."

"Think so? You should see the other one."

"I hope that's all of them," Midnight said. "I'm so sorry. I'm sure my former colleagues sent these two after me. I know too much about their operations."

He reached in his shirt pocket and pulled out a photograph. "Here's what I found on the other guy."

"Picture of you. Not a particularly good one. Is this a flying saucer behind you?"

"No doubt taken by a surveillance camera. Appears I know too much, as well."

"Good. I don't need to be sorry," she said, with a smile. "How do you think they found us? And so soon after leaving Rome? This guy said I should know."

"Did he, now?" Warren grabbed her purse from the bureau and emptied the contents on the bed. He sifted through all the stuff.

"What are you doing?" Midnight said.

He opened her purse wide and peered inside. Warren stuck his hand in and peeled something off the bottom. He held the suspicious peel up to the light.

"Tracking device," she said. "Like the one on the little pyramid."

He threw it down and handed her the purse. "Put your stuff back. We're getting out of Austria." Warren retrieved a suitcase from the closet and started throwing clothes in.

Midnight shoveled everything back into her purse. She slid her shoe off and examined her foot.

When Warren finished packing, he said, "You okay?"

"I think I broke a nail."

"You'll live. Though your quality of life may be wretched."

She put her shoe on. "Quiet, or I'll give you what I gave him." She hurried out the door.

He smiled and went after her.

Isaiah said, "The Bilderberg meetings may change locations, but the incendiaries of worldwide tyranny also have a permanent address. They can be found in the City of London."

"London, England?" Roddy said.

"Not London proper, but a small area in the heart of Greater London, comprising just over a square mile of land. About 8,000 people live in the City of London, and around 320,000 work there.

"It's a global financial center, with its own mayor and its own police. Within its borders is the London Stock Exchange, the insurance company known as Lloyd's of London. And of course, the infamous Bank of England, home of the Rothschilds.

"A lot of people are aware, although you won't hear about it in the conventional media. But no less scary than the City of London, regarding the fate of mankind, is the Tower of Babel."

"In the land of Shinar?" Linda said. "In Babylon?"

"No. In Strasbourg, France. At one of the European Parliament edifices, called the Louise Weiss Building, is an unfinished tower. It's meant to resemble the famous Tower of Babel painted in 1563 by a Renaissance Painter named Pieter Brueghel. The motto associated with the Tower is Europe: Many Tongues One Voice.

"The world has come full circle. And it was significant that the European Union constitution was signed in front of a bronze statue of Pope Innocent the Tenth. The Vatican is trying to unite Catholics, Protestants, Muslims, Buddhists, Hindus, and Jews into one religion. The church claims they all worship the same God, but from different points of view."

"Do you consider the pope to be the antichrist?" Branch said, sardonically.

"The pope is being used like the Zionists in Israel and the Freemasons. All tools. In the end, most of the people on the planet will need to be disposed of, and any tool no longer considered useful will be cast aside. The elite will rule, and everybody else will serve."

"You told us you'd help us understand our quest to find the key to the Great Pyramid," Branch said.

"I believe the Pyramid of Giza was built before the flood on instructions from God. Just like the Ark of the Covenant and Solomon's Temple. The Pyramid was never used. It was intended for mankind's benefit thousands of years after its construction, at a time when the technology for building it has been lost."

Linda said, "Do you think they were more advanced than us."

"Think about it. We can make computers, bombs that can destroy entire cities, and send men to the moon. But we can't build a decent pyramid. Certainly not one like Giza. If the antediluvians had the ability to construct the Great Pyramid, what else were they capable of?"

"Good point," Roddy said.

"How do you know this about the Pyramid?" Branch said.

"I'm a Pyramidion."

All three reacted with a start at this new revelation.

"I used to possess a piece to your pyramid. The last piece, I believe."

"Where is it now?" said Branch.

I passed it on to an engineer named Gordon Becker.

This time they were headed back to Florida. Becker met them at Miami International Airport, and they rode with him in his mini-van.

Branch said, "Isaiah didn't mention which field of engineering you're in."

"I'm an acoustical engineer with a knack for reverse engineering. I'll explain to you what I know about the Great Pyramid after I show you the work of someone who figured out how the thing was built."

"You mean someone built his own pyramid?" Roddy said.

"No, not a pyramid. Are you familiar with Coral Castle?" They returned head shakes and blank looks, so Becker went on. "A man named Edward Leedskalnin, a Latvian immigrated to America around 1916 or '17. He built a phenomenal monument out of megaton stones cut from a type of coral known as oolite, or oolitic limestone, which contains coral. At the castle, people call it coral stone.

"He kept his methods a secret, but it's believed that the process involved anti-gravity and the use of electromagnetism.

"Ed was an enigma, a man with a fourth-grade education who had advanced knowledge of engineering, and magnetics in particular. His book, entitled *Magnetic Current*, is still used in science classes today."

They arrived at Coral Castle in Homestead, Florida, after a thirty-three mile trip. Several cars were parked along an outer wall, and some tourists wandered about.

Within the stone walls, they marveled at the various stone cuttings. Under the bright, hot, Florida sun they sat on stone blocks placed around a heart shaped stone table with flowers planted in the center.

"The heaviest block here weighs thirty tons," Becker said. "Many are in the twenty-ton range. Ed quarried and cut the stones with hand tools and laid all the stones himself. Photos exist of Ed allegedly working with a tripod made out of telephone poles. Obviously a put-on, because they'd snap like toothpicks if used to raise a twenty-ton block.

"And Ed raising the block would require an awful lot of pulleys. Especially when you consider he was only five-feet tall, weighing a little over 100 pounds. Now how does a little stonecutter like Ed move all these stones into place without any help?"

Branch said, "You think Ed discovered what the Stonehenge and pyramid builders used, which was what? Levitation?"

"Right."

"I thought the mystery of the pyramid builders had been solved. I heard they created a mix in wooden forms, like mixing cement, then let the stuff harden, and removed the forms. This would also explain why the tolerances between the stones are so close. The guy who came up with the idea demonstrated his theory."

"I'm aware of the theory, but it hasn't yet been proven the pyramid stones are a result of polymerization, rather than having been quarried and cut. And it doesn't solve the Coral Castle mystery either.

"Ed worked on his creations for thirty years, until his death in 1951. However, many of these stones weren't here, originally. Ed started his project in Florida City. After thirteen years, he moved the entire complex to this location, ten miles north of the old one. He spent three years, using flatbed trucks. The only help he had was the truck driver.

"Which brings up an entertaining story. On the first day, Ed asked the driver to leave for a minute. The driver went outside the complex, and moments later he heard a loud crash. The driver ran back inside and found a giant stone sitting on his truck. Ed was standing by the block, dusting his hands off. Undoubtedly another put-on.

"When they arrived here, Ed asked the driver to leave and come back the next day. The driver did and when he returned, the stones were all on the ground, with no sign of anything Ed might have used to get them off the truck."

Roddy said, "Didn't anyone ever try to find out what his secret was?"

"Oh yes, but Ed did all his work between midnight and 6 AM to cut the risk of being seen. However, people still tried to sneak a peek. Unfortunately, Ed was hard to sneak up on, and he'd stop working until they left. One time, some teenagers claimed they were successful. They said he was floating the stones around like hydrogen balloons."

"Gordon, I'm wondering what motivated him to do all this," Linda said.

"Ah, you'll appreciate the story behind Coral Castle. At age twenty-six, Ed was still living in Latvia, where he fell in love with a sixteen-year-old girl, named Agnes Scuffs. They were gonna be married, but the day before the wedding, Agnes broke it off. Several years later, the heartbroken Edward Leedskalnin came to America.

"He said he built all this for his 'Sweet Sixteen,' as he called her. He always claimed she'd one day come here and join him. This table we're sitting at is a permanent valentine he built for her, and those flowers in the center were planted over sixty years ago. Just for her."

"Oh, how romantic, and so sad," Linda said. "I love that story."

Branch and Roddy exchanged looks.

Without even glancing at the two, Linda said, "Of course, I wouldn't expect either of my travelling companions to appreciate it. But if they make fun, I'll hurt them."

"Hey, I'm romantic," Roddy said. "Just ask Christine."

He looked at Branch, who turned his head with a sarcastic smile.

"Or not," Roddy said.

"I've been sitting here yammering away," said Becker. "I should have asked if you all were hungry."

"Always," Roddy said.

"Let's get some lunch and I'll tell you what I think about what might be the purpose for the Great Pyramid. And while you're here, I also want to tell you about something, a modern day contraption, which may scare the socks off you."

Latter, they were back at their stone table eating bratwurst—Roddy had two—as Gordon began again.

"I spent twenty years reverse engineering the Pyramid of Giza. I determined that it's a giant machine, the largest one ever built. I believe the Pyramid is a power generator, a reservoir of endless energy the entire world may access.

"This belief of mine, that the Pyramid was constructed to generate energy, isn't new. I came up with a way of explaining why it might work, if not how.

"The Earth itself is believed to be a dynamo with convection currents running through the core of the Earth, made up of molten metal. This creates the Earth's magnetic field, which I believe both Edward Leedskalnin and the Pyramid builders used.

"Imagine using the vibrations the Earth generates along with the right resonator, the Pyramid. The energy producers of the world would be out of business. Since the oil magnates, along with the bankers who lend them money, pretty much run the world, you now should have a better idea who is behind the gunmen chasing you all over the globe."

"We thought the culprit was Roger Darkin," Roddy said.

"The millionaire biologist. He was convinced by operatives of the world's shadow government to track you down. He believes the inscriptions on the walls you took pictures of would destroy evolution. I believe he's right. And I believe the Shadow Swayers, as I call them, want the key to the Pyramid. Either to discover how they can use it to their own advantage or keep the key from ever being used at all.

"Anyway, getting back to the subject, the vibrations from the Earth have their own frequency, or notes, which comprise the F-sharp chord. The Egyptians claimed this was the Earth's harmonic. Acoustic data exists that indicates the Pyramid has the same resonant frequency. This would give the Pyramid the potential to be what is referred to as a coupled oscillator. It would draw energy from the planet and make it available to the Earth's people.

"Electromagnetics was Ed's thing. He said all matter was magnetic. When matter moved, whether through space or a tangible substance, it created things like magnetic attraction, electrical energy, and so on.

"Now I want to tell you about something in the field of electromagnetism that might have an enormous—though not necessarily beneficial—effect on us all. The technology is based on the early 1900s work of Nikola Tesla, for my money, the most remarkable scientist who ever lived.

"Are you aware of the Alaskan-based project called HAARP?"

"Yes," Branch said, but Linda shook her head.

Roddy nodded and said, "All I know about HAARP is you can't play it."

"Don't they plan to use it for research to improve surveillance and communications?" Branch said.

"That's the official explanation," Gordon said. "But the real reasons are much more nefarious." He looked at his watch. "I was hoping for another visitor to be here by now. Someone with more understanding who could lay this out for you."

"Who would that be?" Linda said.

"Me," a voice said, a voice they'd heard before.

They all turned.

Linda gasped.

"You're dead," Roddy said. "I mean, there was a kaboom, fire, ashes, pieces of the building dropping on our car."

Only Branch was not surprised at the appearance of Dr. Peter Reed, still tanned, contrasting his white hair.

"You don't look the least bit astounded, Mr. Nichols," Reed said, as he approached the table.

"I got enough hints from people I've met since then."

"I'm sorry, Miss Chapel if I upset you," he said, sitting down on one of the stone blocks.

"Why did you fake your death?" Linda said. "And how did you escape?"

"I knew they were watching from a distance. I was sure they would soon come after me, although what they wanted even more was to pick up your trail."

"They followed us to California, didn't they?" Branch said. "Brussel and Wallach."

"Yes. Wendy, my niece was aware they were coming, but she's resourceful. As to the how, I had an underground escape tunnel. After I was convinced my watchers were gone, I drove off across the desert."

"Just guessing, here," Branch said. "Was your escape vehicle a dune buggy?"

"Yes it was. How'd you guess?"

"That's how I escaped with your friend, Harlan Wilson, across an Australian desert."

"Green, I'll bet. He and I built our first dune buggy together when we were fourteen. Argued over the color."

"Fourteen?" Roddy said. "You weren't old enough to drive."

"Didn't stop us."

"Peter, would you tell these folks what HAARP is?" Gordon said.

"Sure, why should *they* sleep well at night? First, I must tell you about the ionosphere, which is on the outer edge of our Earth's atmosphere, forty to sixty miles up, and loaded with free electrons. HAARP can be used to punch it with an electromagnetic beam.

"The letters of HAARP stand for High-Frequency Active Auroral Research Program. Other ionospheric heaters in the world aren't considered dangerous, but this one is different. Through games with words, dissimulation, and flat-out lying, the military has once again played the public for fools."

"Dissimu-who?" Roddy said.

"I'm sorry. It means to employ deceit. Something they're really good at.

"Now, one of the things they might do with this technology is to create an electromagnetic pulse, EMP. It's the same thing that detonating a nuke in the upper atmosphere would produce."

"I understand what you're talking about," Branch said, "but I don't think Linda does."

Reed acknowledged her blank expression. "All right, let's say some terrorists got hold of an average-size nuke, twenty megatons. Next, they acquire the technology needed to get their payload up to 200 miles above Kansas. In theory, the EMP produced by the explosion would knock out everything electrical on the mainland of the United States."

"So EMP is like a lightning bolt?" Roddy said.

"No. That's a common, but mistaken, notion. EMP is more like an especially potent radio wave."

"This is scary stuff," said Linda.

Reed said, "Of course, another option is to drop an army on Gakona, or Poker Flat, or one of the other Alaskan sites, and use HAARP to attack us."

"How likely is any of this?" said Linda.

"Our military has looked into the possibility of bouncing a signal off the moon to hit far away targets, causing a nuclear-sized burst but with no radiation. And keep in mind that countries like Korea and China are convinced that someday we're gonna attack them. It would be sensible for them to move first. How safe does that make you feel?"

They all stared at him, trying to comprehend how mankind had gotten itself to this point, and what if anything could be done.

Then he dropped the real bombshell.

"What I've told you so far is nothing compared to the ultimate dangers of HAARP."

"It gets worse?" Roddy said.

"Oh, much. What I'm about to tell you involves the potential for nothing less than global vandalism. It's the kind of thing you might think could only happen in a sci-fi disaster movie. Except this is real. For starters, in geophysical warfare, weather modification might be used against an enemy.

"In Vietnam, the Department of Defense tried rainmaking, manipulating a hurricane, and creation of lightning. The code names for these endeavors were Project Stormfury and Project Skyfire. The military has studied ways to destroy ozone over the enemy, using lasers and chemicals. In the Prime Argus project, they examined the possibility of causing earthquakes.

"They might wind up affecting an entire hemisphere, causing damage impossible to repair. The ionosphere is susceptible to accelerated electrochemical reactions. One small change could have major consequences. One scientist compared the ionosphere to a soap bubble. Perforate the bubble with a large enough hole and it just might pop."

They all hung on the words of Dr. Peter Reed. This was a Pandora's box waiting to be opened by curious, perhaps irresponsible, arch meddlers seeking the power to manhandle nature.

Reed continued: "Another use and a bizarre one is to manipulate the minds of entire populations. Perceptual unhinging and confusion would be induced, along with physical disorders.

"Now, for the really scary stuff. Around 1970, Zbigniew Brzezinski, one of Jimmy Carter's evil cronies, made a horrifying revelation. He said we would one day have a 'more controlled and directed society,' involving the use of technology. He said they'd be governed by an elite entity.

"He prognosticated that the use of one social crisis after another, and the propaganda machine known as mass media, would convince the United States sheep to willingly accept it.

"Another way they want to use this technology, in their attempt to play god, is in heightening individual powers. They want to induce unnatural and remarkable evolutions. They think they can create super-beings."

"This is difficult to take in," said Linda. "As you said, this sounds like the stuff of outrageous sci-fi movies."

"If only it were," Reed said. "Gordon, do you want to share anything else with the intrepid Pyramid Gang before we send them on their way?"

"I've nothing to add," Gordon said. "Just need to tell you where to go to retrieve the next piece."

"You don't have it?" Branch said.

"No, I'm sorry. I guess this particular piece is pretty well-traveled."

"Why don't we just call first?" said Roddy. "In case the next guy passed it on to someone else."

"Waste of time," Gordon said. "No Pyramidion will even admit over the phone to having any knowledge of that little MacGuffin you're carrying around."

"Okay," Branch said. "Where to?"

"Skamania County, Washington. His name is Bart Schaeffer, a geologist. He'll meet you at Mount St. Helens."

Chapter Sixteen

Benjamin sat in his wheelchair in front of his giant plasma television screen watching the news. A young man with a smug smile sat at a news desk in front of a video screen.

Broadcaster: "The evolution versus creation debate is being pronounced, by scientists, as over. Creationists, however, aren't giving up, and are picketing wherever the Ararat Man exhibit is shown. Live with us now is Candy Kane. Candy…"

On the video screen behind him, an extremely attractive girl stood in front of a museum with a microphone in her hand. She appeared young enough to be shopping for next year's prom dress.

Candy: "Hello, Todd. I'm here with Red Barrows who made the momentous discovery that may finally launch us out of the dark ages and into a new age of welcomed enlightenment."

The camera angle widened to include Barrows.

Candy: "Dr. Barrows, how sure can we be that this find is genuine?"

Barrows: "Oh, you can be as sure of this as you can of anything. We've carbon dated A-man, as we like to call him, to around 300,000 years. This means the final, full transition to human came rather swiftly, as we now know to be the case."

Candy: "How about the accusation from creationists. They say the DNA test to prove whether the apelike bones and human bones belonged together was a fraud?"

Barrows: "Lies and fairytales. What else do the creationists have, really?"

Candy, looking solemn: "I'm sure you mourn the tragic and sudden death of the lab technician who did the actual testing. What about claims from creationists who say he called them. That he said he would show them proof the bones came from two separate life forms, one a man and the other an ape?"

Barrows, also looking solemn: "Yes, his death was tragic and sudden. I can't say whether the poor man was pushed out of the window as some are saying. Perhaps he jumped as a result of constant harassment from creationists." He shook his head. "For them to make this up the day after his death... I feel bad for his family."

The Carol of the Bells ring-tone emanated from the side pocket of Benjamin's wheelchair. He turned off the television and took his phone out. After checking caller ID, he answered the call.

"Hello, Jeffrey. Are we all ready to go with Operation Bilderberg?"

"They hit us, Benjamin. They hit us hard. Everyone's dead." Jeffrey started coughing.

"Jeffrey, are you all right?"

"No, I'm not, but don't worry. Nothing can connect you with us. We were putting together all the equipment we would need to act on your plan. Someone in our group may have been under surveillance, and I think we got some of our gear from the wrong people." He coughed again. "Pawns working for the shadow government. Everyone, including our attackers, were killed in the shootout. I'm the only one left."

"Jeffrey, hold on. I'll send help."

"Too late. Just for the record, though. I believe the plan would've worked, but now I think you should forget..."

Benjamin sat, stunned, unable to speak until, finally, "Jeffrey... Jeffrey!"

Branch, Roddy, and Linda arrived in Washington State the next afternoon. They drove to the Johnston Ridge Observatory, just five and a half miles from the north face of the volcano, where Schaeffer was supposed to meet them. They walked across the deck, toward the railing, with a spectacular view of Mount St. Helens.

Many tourists hugged the railing. The Pyramid Gang approached a man with his back turned wearing a gray fishing hat, which they'd been told to look for.

"Bart Schaeffer?" Branch said.

The man turned around, displaying a beard that matched the color of his hat.

"The Pyramid Gang. I'm so happy to meet you. Come, stand by the rail, and gaze with me at the aftermath of nature's most explosive—pun intended—event."

They joined him, and Roddy said, "Who's this observatory named after?"

"David Johnston," Schaeffer said. "He was a volcanologist who was sitting right here on the ridge in May of 1980, watching the volcano burst forth. Before the blast, he was in radio contact with a Geological Survey base in Vancouver, Washington. His final words were, 'Vancouver! Vancouver! This is it!' His body was never found.

"Thanks to Johnston's efforts in keeping the area closed, only fifty-seven people, including him, were killed. Not the thousands that would have been. The blast was 33,000 times more powerful than the bomb dropped on Hiroshima. And it did incredible things to the surrounding environment. The once scenic landscape is more like the moon's surface.

"From a positive perspective, the eruption of Mount St. Helens gave evolution a slug on the face, a punch in the gut, a kick to the groin... Well, you get the idea.

"In school, we were taught the Grand Canyon took millions of years to form. A resulting mudflow from St. Helens carved out a canyon about one-fortieth the size of nature's stupendous wonder. Now a river flows through what is called Little Grand Canyon. Imagine an evolutionist discovering it thousands of years from now. If he didn't know about the St. Helens eructation, he might assume the canyon had been carved out over eons by that little river.

"Erosion of the canyon revealed a deposit measuring twenty-five-feet high, with thousands of layers. The piling up didn't take millions of years, as the evolutionists claim similar layers at the Grand Canyon required. It didn't even take one full day. Most geologists now admit the Grand Canyon was gouged out quickly and by an awful lot of water.

"Evidence at St. Helens gives credence to the possibility of Noah's Flood. Genesis 7:11 says 'all the fountains of the great deep burst forth.' Did you know the Pacific Ocean has 20,000 volcanoes? Imagine if they all blew at once."

"Is it possible such a thing could ever happen?" Roddy said.

"Are you aware of HAARP?"

"Yes, we are," Branch said.

"Foolish boys with amazing toys is what I call them," Schaeffer said. "The antediluvians, no doubt, were far more advanced than we are. Imagine the toys they may have had."

"You're not the first person to tell us that," Roddy said. "But how could they be so far ahead of us."

"According to the laws of thermodynamics, all of nature is breaking down, and that includes us. This degeneration or devolution will continue, and unless God intervenes, the human race will become extinct. In fact, all geneticists agree that each new generation has hundreds of mutations the previous generation didn't have."

"Many of them still believe in evolution?" Linda said.

"Yes. Talk about living in denial," said Schaeffer. "Anyway, let's backtrack to the first and second millenniums of human existence. Back when man was still close to the perfect creations of Adam and Eve. Before devolution really got rolling. No doubt, people were intellectually and physically superior, far superior to us, and they lived hundreds of years. They would've been able to continue learning for such an extraordinary length of time. The amount of knowledge they could accumulate is so astounding we can't even begin to fathom how far ahead of us they were."

"If we can accept such long life spans, what you say is staggering," Branch said. "Tell us more about the St. Helens explosion."

"An intriguing feature of the aftermath is what's gone on at Spirit Lake, which received around a million trees. Becoming waterlogged, they began sinking to the bottom, landing on their roots. Those roots are becoming covered by sedimentation. If you found them a thousand years from now, and didn't know the truth, you'd think they grew and died there.

"You can observe the same formation at Yellowstone National Park, at a place called Specimen Ridge. A sign posted at the Ridge used to read: 'Buried within the volcanic rocks that compose the mountain are twenty-seven distinct layers of fossil forest that flourished 50 million years ago.' Thanks to Spirit Lake, we know that isn't true. The sign was removed.

"Then there's the lava on the dome of the volcano. A fifteen-pound sample of volcanic rock known as dacite was extracted and sent to Geochron Laboratories in Cambridge, Massachusetts, for potassium-argon testing. They weren't told where the rock came from and proceeded to embarrass themselves. The analysis of the rock and various minerals contained within revealed ages ranging from 350,000 years, to 2.8 million years. From a ten-year-old chunk of lava.

"Of course the evolutionists fought back with the usual labyrinth of reasoning. When examined, it's filled with vacuous suppositions and a lot of misdirection. They never refuted the finding, but got away with preaching to the choir."

"Thank you for your insights, Dr. Schaeffer," Branch said. "And now, if you could give us the last piece to the pyramid..."

"Sadly, I passed the piece on to someone else."

Linda's shoulders dropped, Roddy threw his hands in the air, and Branch shook his head. How many more stops would they need to make to finish their mission?

Schaeffer went on. "I gave the piece to a young lady named Midnight Jones. Her background is in philosophy."

The three glanced at one another.

"I'm sorry," Schaeffer said. "You all appear downright crestfallen. What is it?"

"We've already retrieved Midnight's piece," Linda said.

"And you're still short one?"

"Yeah, and now the trail's gone cold again," Branch said.

"I'm sorry I can't help you."

"What's our next move?" Roddy said.

Branch thought for a moment. "Back to Pennsylvania. I want to talk to Benjamin about this Bilderberg thing. Find out what he's up to."

The next morning, they arrived in Pennsylvania and were picked up by Benjamin's chauffeur. Benjamin greeted them at the mansion. He was cordial, and they could see he was glad at their arrival but he was not himself.

They sat in the same room as before. Branch said, "Something's changed since we were here last. Something to do with the Bilderbergs? Should we be concerned?"

"You've been informed about our world's shadow government," Benjamin said, "so, I'll tell you everything. Doesn't matter now, but I had a plan to infiltrate. It's taken me decades to become a billionaire, being involved in all forms of media, including publishing."

He turned toward Linda. "I publish Branch's Chandler Ross novels." He glanced at Branch. "By the way, your last novel wasn't up to par."

"I know," said Linda. "The ending was not quite satisfying."

"Nor the beginning," Benjamin said. "Or the middle."

Branch rolled his eyes.

"I liked it," Roddy said. "Could've had more action, though."

Benjamin hinted a smile. "Well, anyway, moving on. I convinced the right people I'm a diehard socialist. They believe I could be instrumental in helping to control what the public thinks by exercising my media muscles.

"I was invited to an annual Bilderberg meeting. This year they are going to be at the Tiara Chateau Hotel Mont Royal, in Chantilly, France. I wanted to go as a spy, with state-of-the-art audio and video equipment and with infiltrators on the hotel staff." Benjamin stopped, looking pensive.

"Something went wrong?" Branch said.

"My team was wiped out. If I go, I can only take notes. I was hoping to have video footage for the internet, to let the world see and hear what the elite are planning for them."

Branch looked at Linda and Roddy. "What do you think, team?"

"When do we leave?" Roddy said.

"It's beautiful there," said Linda. "Of course I'm in."

"Now wait," said Benjamin. "None of you has any experience in this kind of thing."

"Think of our participation as on the job training," Branch said.

"I can be your chauffeur," said Roddy.

"I can be... your nurse," said Linda.

"Guess I'll be in the van," Branch said. "Making sure everything gets recorded."

"I don't suppose I'm gonna be able to talk the three of you out of this, am I?"

"Not a chance," Linda said.

"All right, but I think we should leave the MacGuffin here for safekeeping."

Linda opened her purse and handed the little unfinished pyramid to Benjamin. He put it on his lap and used the controls to move his wheelchair to a bookcase against the wall. Benjamin reached behind some books, and the bottom part of the bookcase started moving to the right. In front of an open wall a safe appeared. Benjamin punched in the code, opened the safe, and put the MacGuffin in.

After he closed the safe and replaced the bookcase, he rode his wheelchair back to his original spot. "Now it's put away, and we'll deal with it later."

"I just wish we knew where to pick up the trail to the last piece," Branch said.

"I'm sure a trail will present itself in due time," said Benjamin. "Now we need to work out our strategy. Our biggest problem is none of us knows what we're doing."

"My friend Brick does," Roddy said. "He'll help."

"All right, let's begin making plans to put one over on the most powerful men in the world."

Fifteen minutes from modern-day Charles de Gaulle Airport, and thirty-five minutes from Paris, sat the Tiara Chateau. The hotel was a hundred-years elegant, maintaining an old world quality with its early twentieth century architecture.

Benjamin's long white limo, which he'd flown in, eased up behind a black limo. The occupants were talking with the security personal at the gateway to the Tiara Chateau. Roddy put the car in neutral and left his foot on the brake.

Linda peered through the windshield from the back seat. "Those are some pretty serious-looking security men."

"Don't worry," Benjamin said. "They're gonna believe they are protecting us from the outsiders."

She looked through tinted windows. "You mean these evil press people who just want to find out the truth?"

The car in front moved on, and the security men signaled them forward. Roddy moved the car up, stopped, and shifted into park. "Here we go," Roddy said, and he lowered the window.

"Identification and invitation, please," the man said.

Roddy handed him his ID and invitation.

Reading, the man said, "Chico Rodriguez."

"I'm the chauffeur," Roddy said, smiling.

"Yes, thank you." He handed the stuff back to Roddy and moved to the back window.

Benjamin lowered the window and handed invitations and IDs for himself and Linda to the man. Linda stopped breathing and fidgeted with her hands.

The security man returned everything to Benjamin. "All right, go ahead." He walked back to his original post.

Benjamin observed Branch standing by a van with the words "Free Press" written on the side. Neither of them gave any sign of recognition.

Linda caught sight of Branch and said, "Oh, there's—"

"Linda," Benjamin said, "You don't know anyone outside this car. Remember that."

"Right. I'm sorry." She turned and stared in the opposite direction.

Benjamin raised his window as Roddy pulled forward onto the driveway that went around the hotel. The Tiara Chateau, three stories tall was a white building with over 100 rooms.

Roddy stopped near an entrance, and security men opened the doors for Benjamin and Linda. Roddy took in a deep breath and exhaled slowly. Being more concerned for his two passengers than for himself, he wondered if they were gonna pull this off.

Branch climbed into the van where Brick and Alp sat in front of two monitors, recording decks, and control panel.

"The fox is in the hen house," Branch said.

"Oh, come on," Brick said. "Just because we're CIA, you don't have to use code names."

"I can tell you're not gonna be any fun at all. By the way, I don't suppose the CIA knows you're here."

"Officially, I'm on leave. Recovering from my wounds."

"I'm on vacation," Alp said.

"Here's your earpiece, Branch," said Brick. "You'll be able to listen to what anyone of the others is saying."

"What if they all talk at once?"

"You can turn anyone of them off by hitting one of those buttons. Each one is marked with a name."

"Wonderful. I can turn Roddy off any time I like."

"I heard that," Roddy said.

"Ah good, the earpiece is working. Just checking, buddy."

"Let's all be professional," Benjamin said.

"You may want professionals," said Branch. "But you've got the motley crew."

"Tell me about it," said Alp.

Benjamin entered the building with Linda just ahead of him as a doorman showed them in. The concierge called a bellboy who took them to their rooms. As she walked, Linda took hold of herself thinking about the fact that they were in a building with the most powerful people on Earth.

"This is your room, Monsieur Rydal," the bellhop said, as he opened the door. "Would you like me to show the lady to hers, now?"

"Yes, please," Benjamin replied. "Linda, come back as soon as you're settled in."

"All right," she said, as the door closed behind Benjamin.

"The servant's quarters are this way," the bellboy said.

Roddy had parked the car and struck up a conversation with some of the chauffeurs, who all spoke English. At the same time he was forced to listen to Branch on his earpiece. "Tell them about your boat, Roddy.... Remember in high school when you got up enough courage to talk to Christine for the first time. You blurted out, 'My name is Cheeky Rodriguez.' I bet they'd love that."

Linda had been given a key to Benjamin's room. When she entered, her mouth fell open at the sight of the spacious, impeccably decorated lodging.

"Nice digs, Mr. Rydal."

"Thank you, Miss Chapel. It'll do."

Linda sat on a couch. Benjamin was by a window, gazing out at the Chantilly forest surrounding the hotel.

"So," Linda said, examining the room. "Tell me about the history of this whole Bilderberg thing. Is this the real life version of Big Brother?"

"This is a major arm of Big Brother," he said, continuing to gaze out the window. "The European Union was engineered at these meetings, as were plans to unite Canada, the U.S., and Mexico. They're working toward control of all world governments by the United Nations. A socialist, totalitarian empire, run by bankers. Sounds bizarre when I say the words. Even to me. But I know it to be true."

Benjamin's cell phone rang with the theme from Mission Impossible.

"New ring tone. How appropriate," said Linda.

"Hello," Benjamin said. "All right, thank you. I'll come at once." He put the phone back in the arm-pocket of his wheelchair. "I have a meeting with some other media moguls and a representative of the inner thirty-nine core Bilderberg members."

"What should *I* do? They have a pool, you know."

Benjamin was amused. "Sounds wonderful but don't forget we're here to work."

"Okay, Mr. Workaholic."

"Now you have a taste of what I've been putting up with," Branch said from the van.

"Excuse me," Linda said. "This is a private conversation."

Benjamin laughed, and then: "Linda, I'd like you to find any group of people talking together and sit nearby. Ignore small talk and move on. Keep trying until you find a group saying anything provocative. They shouldn't pay you any notice since you're one of the invited.

"You guys in the van ready to record?"

Branch replied, "We're getting every word of Roddy's dynamic repartee with the chauffeurs."

"Why can't we hear him?" said Linda.

Brick said, "I cut him off from you and Benjamin since you don't need that extra chatter."

"Let's go," Benjamin said. He powered his wheelchair across the room.

Linda took in a deep breath, and slowly let it out. Then she put her shoulders back and walked to the door.

Benjamin had been with the group for over an hour and hadn't learned anything from Cross, the inner-core representative. He seemed more interested in pumping the media moguls for information than in sharing any.

Finally, once Cross seemed satisfied with what he'd gotten out of them, Benjamin decided to ask him a question.

"What can you tell us about the NAFTA superhighways from Mexico to Canada?"

Cross was taken aback since this was not only the first question he'd been asked, but was a departure from the subject at hand. He appeared reluctant to talk about the matter, and Benjamin realized he would have to give him a reason.

"I ask because the highway is so essential to uniting the three countries. I'd like to know how to publicize the construction, convince the public to give their support."

"We'd rather this type of thing wasn't in the media. The less the American people know the better, although we do get some help already from the media. The *National Post*, for instance, went so far as to say the whole thing is an urban myth. We also get away with subterfuge by disguising the true nature of any new construction."

"Yes, but with the opposition to eminent domain in Texas, and Arizona resisting—"

"This isn't a media issue for you to concern yourself with," Cross said. "Just stick to promoting a benign global union as the idea to save the world."

"I understand. Make it vague, distant to Americans. So they're not yet cognizant of the reality that they'll have to give up their freedom." As soon as the words left his mouth, Benjamin knew he'd been too direct. His question lacked savvy. He'd let his emotions have too much influence, and it was too late to take it back.

Cross stared at him. This was not the type of conversation he expected from someone who was not a core member. It sounded more like the words of rabble-rousers.

"Talk of a North American Union would be perceived as an immediate threat. That's why we bypassed Congress in our plans to build the superhighways joining Mexico to Canada."

"So I assume strategies for getting the superhighways constructed are on a need-to-know basis. And we don't need to know," Benjamin said, with his most affable smile.

Cross rose to his feet, and in a cold whisper he said, "No, you don't." Cross turned and left.

From the van, Branch said, "Sounds like you burned a bridge."

Linda spent her time roaming, listening, and sometimes talking to other guests. They were mostly men and the fact that she wasn't a person of importance was rendered irrelevant by her attractiveness. However, when Linda asked about plans for globalization, answers were vague and non-revealing.

She met with Benjamin near the banquet room. Linda said, "If the tape in the van was rolling, it recorded four different fake phone numbers I gave out. Beyond that the conversations get pretty dull."

"You're doing better than I am. At least people here like you. I've had talks with several people. I'm probably being blacklisted as we speak. I won't be able to have contact with anyone in the core thirty-nine, and quite-a-few others besides. I may have done more harm to our cause than good. I'm just a better business man than I am a diplomat."

A voice nearby said, "You have to bug their main meeting." Linda and Benjamin turned in the direction of the voice and recognized the speaker. "Where all the heavy stuff goes down." Warren Hanley was dressed as a workman and carried tools.

Benjamin winced as his earpiece swelled at the sound of Branch yelling, "How'd that bum get in?"

"Why are you here?" Benjamin said to Warren. "And, more intriguing, how are you here?"

"As to why, we were run out of Austria by some nasty characters. Having a pretty good idea who's responsible, we decided on some payback. As to how—"

Another familiar voice said, "He's just the sneakiest man I've ever known."

"Midnight, you too?" Benjamin said to her as she peeked from behind Warren.

She was dressed as a maid. "I go where my hubby goes."

"Hubby?"

Midnight peeled off a white cleaning glove from her left hand and held out her hand to show the rings.

"Congratulations," Linda said. She took Midnight's hand to get a close look at the rings. "I'm Linda Chapel, by the way."

"Midnight Hanley"

"I don't believe it," Benjamin said to Warren. "I work for years, decades to get in here, and you show up on a whim."

They heard voices as a group of men walked down the hallway toward the banquet room. Warren looked over his shoulder and then back at Benjamin.

"Jenaro Batista of Spain. We're pretty sure he's at the top of the organization that Midnight worked for when she was undercover. A real snake."

"I read a book many years ago claiming he was the antichrist," Benjamin said.

"No kidding."

"The author also said Jesus would come back in 1979."

"Oops."

"I bought the book through the author's ministry in 1981."

"He was still selling the book?" Linda said.

"Too lazy to revise, I guess."

Jenaro Batista and the other men went into the banquet room. Two guards stayed posted at the doors.

"Now that's where we need to be," Benjamin said. "I'm pretty sure all those men are part of the inner thirty-nine."

"I just came from there," Hanley said. "Put several bugs under the tables."

"You *are* sneaky," said Benjamin.

"Uh, oh," Hanley said. "I think you're about to have a close encounter with the Grinch who stole the world, or at least one of his representatives."

Benjamin looked over his shoulder, down the hall. He spotted Cross approaching with a swarm of security people.

"Come on, Midnight. Let's disappear." Warren and Midnight walked, in no great hurry, away from Cross and company.

"Nice to see you again, Mr. Rydal," Cross said.

Benjamin smiled and nodded.

"Seems your nurse, if that's what she is, has been wandering about without purpose other than to get close to ongoing conversations."

"Can't help myself," Linda said. "I like to keep up on all the international gossip."

"How droll," he said to Linda. Then he turned his attention back to Benjamin. "We've picked up communication from an alleged news van."

One of the security men waved a counter surveillance tool at the wheelchair. "He's on the air," the man said.

"Admirable attempt." Cross said. To his security: "Take Mr. Rydal and his accomplice to his suite for now. We'll transport them later."

"Can't you just let us leave?"

"We have interesting plans for you."

"At least let the girl go."

He shook his head. "I believe you'll be much more cooperative if we hang on to her."

Branch leaned back in his chair, stunned. They'd been caught, and so quickly. What to do now?

Brick said, "I'm sure you're not gonna do anything rash."

Branch jumped out of the chair and flung the side door open.

"Forgot who I was talking to," Brick said.

"Rash or not, I've gotta do something."

"Security won't let you in. You'd either have to go over them or sneak in under them."

"Got a convenient tunnel handy?"

"No. You'll have to go over them."

"Pardon me."

Brick went to the back of the van, opened a door in the floor, and removed a box. He flipped it open.

Branch stepped closer. "A jet-pack? Are you kidding?"

"Not at all," Brick took the pack out of the box.

"What kind of fuel does this thing burn and how unsafe is it?"

"Nothing actually burns. It uses hydrogen peroxide, which is relatively stable."

"Relative to what? Nitro glycerin?"

"When silver comes in contact, you get decomposition. That's followed by five times the original volume in the form of superheated steam and oxygen. You control the jet nozzles for releasing the pressure. And it's up, up, and away."

Brick handed him a strange-looking helmet, a holster, and gun and jumped out of the van with the jet pack under his arm. Branch was tentative, but started to go after him.

Alp said, "Hey, Branch."

Branch stopped, "What?"

"It's been an honor working with you."

"Why does that sound like a final goodbye?"

"Gotta get back to work." Alp put his headphones on.

Branch followed Brick into the trees.

Brick put the jet-pack on Branch's back, and began fastening the hooks. "The distinct advantage of this type over, say, the turbojet is that they are much simpler to build."

"And disadvantages?"

"For one thing, your fuel lasts for only forty seconds... Or less."

"How much less?"

Brick shrugged.

"You said, for one thing. Is there more?"

"Very expensive stuff."

"And?"

"Well, the absolute difficulty of learning to fly with one of these. Takes time."

"Time?"

Brick put the helmet on Branch. "And you have nothing but this if the darn contraption malfunctions."

"Malfunctions?"

"Stop blabbering on. You have a mission to fulfill."

Brick strapped the holster on Branch. "Tranquillizer gun." He pulled down two extensions that stuck out the length of Branch's forearms, and pointed at the controls. "Press this to go up, and like this to go down. Use this to change direction."

"Seems simple enough."

Brick tried to smile. "Yes, doesn't it." Brick flipped a switch and the pack came on. Brick hurried away and stood behind a tree.

Branch raised his hands and grabbed hold of the controls. He lifted gently off the ground. "Hey, this is exciting." He started drifting. Brick ducked behind his tree just before Branch crashed, chest bumping the tree. He was still several feet above ground, but he was being pressed into the bark.

Brick peaked around the tree. "You okay?"

"Having trouble breathing," was all he could manage to squeak out.

"Better get going. Remember, your flight ends in forty seconds."

Branch got his foot against the tree and pushed himself away.

"Or less," Brick added.

Branch turned his body away from the tree, hit the thrusters, and shot up into the air.

"Branch, watch out for the..."

Branch hurtled through the branches, sending a spray of splinters and leaves to the ground. He broke into the open, leveling off just above the trees.

"Branches," Brick finished.

Branch started moving toward the chateau. He noticed security men pointing at him. They began running and shouting.

The side of the building was coming up fast. He turned before hitting it, but kept moving, scraping his right hand as he went.

He took his right hand off the control and spun around 180 degrees. Now his left hand scraped.

Branch let go and grabbed the other control with his right.

He could no longer remember which control did what, but he stopped moving.

Branch slipped his left hand between the control and the wall and turned himself so that the jet pack was against the side of the building.

He adjusted the controls and started to go up. Branch's head met with an overhang and he had to lean forward, plant his feet and push away.

Branch cleared the overhang, went up higher and coasted over the rooftop. He let out a sigh of relief.

In his earpiece, Brick heard Branch say, "How much time do you think I have left?" The jet pack went silent, and Branch dropped fifteen feet onto the green rooftop.

"None," Brick said.

"Thanks for the heads-up." Branch groaned as he struggled to his knees. "The eagle has landed."

"The eagle better hide quick," said Brick. "That roof will be crawling with security long before said bird can build a nest."

Branch removed the helmet, tossed it, and watched the only thing that had stood between him and a massive headache roll off the roof. Unfastening the jet pack, he let it fall off his back, then stood, and ran along the rooftop.

Someone yelled, "You, stop!" Branch turned. A security guy climbed onto the roof holding a gun. Branch went to the edge and looked down. The green roof angled sharply downward with a row of circular windows.

Branch lay down, dropped his legs, and kicked at a window, opening it. "Not locked. I get a break." As he started to climb down, he slipped and fell. Branch grabbed the bottom of the window and hung on. "So much for getting a break." He climbed up and through the opening just as the security guy peeked over the edge.

Branch stood up. He was in the chateau's garret, which appeared to be a storage area for hotel supplies.

"Benjamin, can you hear me?"

Benjamin's voice came back to Branch's earpiece. "Yes. Linda and I are sequestered at the north end, on the second floor. Suite 219."

"On my way."

Brick returned to the van. "Let's pack up, Alp."

"Are we leaving?"

"Not yet. They're gonna need help getting out." Brick sat at the console and hit a button. "Roddy, get to the limo and wait for us."

"Already in the driver's seat."

"Good man."

Branch crept down a stairway, taking a quick glance at his grazed hands. He opened a door on the third floor, peeked out, and when he saw no one, he entered the hall. He ran to the elevator, pushed the down button, and pulled out his tranq-gun.

After a few moments the doors opened. Two security men stood inside. For a moment, they just stared, then blinked and went for their guns.

Branch shot them each in the thigh with a tranquilizer dart.

They aimed their guns at Branch. "Don't moo...," one of them said, as his eyes glazed over and he fell to the floor.

The other one watched his partner fall, then looked at Branch and cocked his gun.

Why is he still standing?

"Nuts," the guard said as he too collapsed.

Branch stepped inside and hit the button for the second floor.

Linda sat on the couch near Benjamin. Three stoned-faced security men stood between them and the door.

"I would like to give the three of you the chance to surrender," Benjamin said.

The two nearest glanced sidelong and evinced a hint of a smile.

"All right," Benjamin said. "I feel better that I at least gave you the opportunity."

A knock on the door sounded. The third security man went to answer while the other two kept their backs to him.

The guard opened the door and was met by a dart to the shoulder. Before he hit the floor, Branch shot the other two in the thighs, and they dropped.

Alp sat behind the wheel of the van and Brick rode shotgun.

"Okay, Alp, are you ready to do this?"

"Can you say Turkish invasion?" He took his foot off the brake and eased forward. As they got closer to the entrance, two men began waving for them to stop.

Alp hit the gas and roared ahead, knocking down a barrier as they swept past the guards.

Branch and Linda strolled down the hall of the first floor. Benjamin was right ahead of them in his chair.

"You're hurt," Linda said, noticing one of his scraped hands.

"I'm fine."

Two security men entered the hall. Branch glanced behind and saw another. He'd gotten rid of the holster and hid the gun.

One of the guards ahead of them said, "Would you please stop? Aren't two of you supposed to be detained?"

Branch started to fake a severe cough. He bent over at a ninety degree angle and took the gun out of the pouch on the back of the chair. He stooped down, out of sight of the two ahead of them, turned and shot the one behind.

He stepped out and away from Benjamin to get him out of the line of fire.

The two guards went for their guns.

Branch shot and dropped them with two tranquilizer darts.

Benjamin and Linda proceeded.

Two more men came running across a room, to the side of the hall, with its double doors wide open. They had their guns drawn.

Branch dove to his right as the two opened fire. He shot back, and both of the security men stumbled and fell.

Alp and Brick skidded to a stop alongside the limo. They grabbed tapes, recorders, as much stuff as they could, and started dumping it in the open sun roof.

Roddy lowered his window.

"Do we know where they'll be exiting the building?"

"Oh, yeah" Brick said to Alp. "Don't forget we'll need a doorway."

"A door?" Roddy said. "What are you gonna do with a door?"

"A door*way*," Brick said.

"Yeah, we got time to cut open a doorway. I've got some tools in the trunk."

Branch, Linda, and Benjamin went through a pair of French doors. They entered into a circular room measuring ninety feet across. Branch closed and locked the doors behind them.

Roddy drove to the end of the building as Brick instructed. It featured a one story circular attachment, with a sundeck on top. Roddy saw a few sunbathers strolling about.

A throng of security men were spread around the limo. Some of them were on one knee, some were standing, and all had their guns drawn. No one was getting in or out of the building.

"Now what," Roddy said.

"Doorway time," said Brick.

Brick and Alp popped up through the open sunroof with rocket launchers.

"Open sesame," said Alp.

They both fired. Flames, mortar, and glass filled the surrounding air. When the smoke cleared, a sizeable hole appeared. Alp and Brick dropped back out of sight as an avalanche of bullets smothered the bulletproof limo.

Roddy knew what to do, and sped toward the improvised doorway and into the circular room.

He slammed on the brakes and skidded to a stop.

Letting down the window, he said, "Anyone here need a ride?"

"I don't believe you guys," Benjamin said, with mock anger. "You think they're ever going let me come back?" He sped his wheelchair toward the rear door. "I'll be lucky if I'm not banned from every five-star hotel on the planet."

Branch got Benjamin and his wheelchair into the car. Linda jumped in with Benjamin, and Branch got in front with Roddy.

"Okay," Branch said. "You want to get us out of here?"

Roddy looked in his rearview mirror. A horde of well-armed security men approached the hole in the wall. Nine of them dove to the ground just outside Brick and Alp's fresh doorway. Eight more dropped to one knee behind them and a dozen more stood at the rear. All aiming their guns at the limo.

"Not going out the way we came. Hey, guys. We need a new doorway."

"Coming up," Brick said.

Brick and Alp rose up through the open sunroof with their rocket launchers.

"Open sesame," Alp said, and they both fired.

The sound of the blast inside the building was deafening.

Brick and Alp dropped down as the twenty-nine men behind them opened fire.

As the smoke cleared, it was displaced by sunlight. Roddy floored the gas pedal and drove through the gaping hole, across a short stretch of grass, and onto the hotel's drive.

They sped toward the entrance, which now had two black Hummers blocking the way. Security men sent a steady wave of bullets that pinged off the sleek white limo.

"Hang on," Roddy said.

The security men scattered when they realized Roddy wasn't even gonna slow down, let alone stop.

The formidable limo smashed against the two tank-like cars. The limo knocked them to either side and sped off down the highway.

Moments later, a tiny, pink and gray Smart Car wended between the mauled Hummers. From inside, Warren and Midnight smiled and waved at the security men, who were holstering their guns.

The little automobile then crept along the road and into the green Chantilly Forest.

At the landing strip, the limo was being loaded onto a cargo plane as its former occupants huddled near Benjamin's private jet.

"What I don't understand," Roddy said, "is why the police didn't come after us."

"The police would ask questions," Benjamin said. "Many of the Bilderbergs could find themselves subpoenaed. They don't want anything that goes on there to become public. Better just to let us escape."

"What about the destruction at the hotel? I think someone will notice."

"They'll pay all employees to be quiet. And the reconstruction will be done quietly and quickly. To the rest of the world, it never happened."

"Company," Alp said, pointing at an approaching pink and gray Smart Car.

When it stopped, the doors opened, and Warren and Midnight got out. Warren was carrying a box. "Thought you might like to have the recordings we got." He handed the box to Benjamin.

"Thank you, Warren," Benjamin said.

Branch was staring at the car. "Say uh, Hanley—"

"Not one word about the car, Nichols."

"I picked it out," Midnight said.

"I like your car," said Linda.

"Thank you."

Roddy said, "So what are you two gonna do now?"

"I had a private conversation with Jenaro Batista," Warren said. "I assured him I know where he lives, and that others would visit him if anything happened to me or my wife. He promised to leave me and Midnight alone."

"We're gonna stay off the grid, anyway," Midnight said.

"We're buying a house in Switzerland," said Warren. "Belonged to the late Dr. Von Brunner."

"No kidding," Roddy said.

"We've been there," said Branch.

"Ah," Warren said. "That would explain the wreckage. Lot of sweeping up to do, bullet holes to patch."

"Did you find the secret stairway?" Roddy asked.

"The what?" said Midnight.

"Come on," Linda said. "I'll tell you how to find it while you show me the interior of this cute little car."

They said their goodbyes. The Hanleys drove away, and the others boarded Benjamin's private jet. On board, Benjamin asked Alp and Brick if they'd be flying with them to Pennsylvania, or if he should drop them somewhere.

"We'll go with you," Brick said. "And then we're heading to Chicago."

"Yeah," said Alp. "We're gonna make a surprise visit to the Field Museum of Natural History."

Chapter Seventeen

Branch and Linda sat side by side on the couch in Benjamin's study. Linda twisted a Rubik's Cube. Roddy played with the train set. Benjamin wheeled into the room.

"I've been listening to some of the recordings we got in France," Benjamin said. "Some provocative stuff. I have people putting together tracks of material, and we'll begin disseminating it soon.

"Don't know if we collected enough to change the world. But it will give people something to think about, something to get mad about."

"I heard from Brick," Roddy said. "We're supposed to watch a live broadcast on cable in about..."—he checked his wristwatch—"now."

Benjamin clicked on his giant-screen TV.

"Seventy-seven," Roddy said.

Benjamin clicked the channel buttons.

A young reporter stood in front of a crowd. "Hi, I'm Mandy Barnes, here at the Field Museum of Natural History. Today, we say goodbye to Ararat Man as he leaves on a tour of the country, and then the world. In a moment, we'll be hearing from Dr. Red Barrows, Ararat's discoverer. And here he comes now."

The audience applauded as Barrows approached the stage with a self-assured gait. His head was tipped forward in mock humility, and his tight smile was full of smugness. Each long, confident stride was propelled by the realization of the glory he basked in.

After Barrows climbed the steps to the Ararat exhibit, he turned to the audience and tipped his head a little more. He raised his hand in a self-aggrandizing manner as if begging his admirers to stop piling on so much adulation.

The applause faded and he lifted his head. "Friends, we're witnessing the end of the age of superstition. This is the beginning of the age of full acceptance of science as the true source of reality."

The onlookers applauded and cheered. Barrows nodded his appreciation for several seconds before holding up his hand.

The audience quieted and Barrows began again. "I want to say... Oh, what's this?" He was looking toward the steps. Chisisi, wearing a mixture of American and Turkish garb, was climbing them.

"This is unexpected but wonderful," Barrows said. "Here is the boy who led me to the discovery."

Everyone clapped. Barrows smiled.

After a few moments, the crowd stopped applauding, and Chisisi spoke.

"This skeleton is a fake." He pointed at Darkin standing off to the side. "That man gave me the bones and told me to hide them in the cave."

"This is ridiculous," Darkin said. He started toward the stairs, but before he could get to them, Brick cut him off.

Barrows resembled a man whose child had just been insulted. He glared at Chisisi. "Who put you up to this?" He was about to make a move toward the boy when Alp shot up the stairs, and stood between the two.

Chisisi pointed at Darkin again. "He gave me a picture showing how to lay the bones. He paid me money."

"This is preposterous," said Darkin.

"No," Brick said, and he indicated Ararat Man. "That's preposterous."

"Mandy Barnes here," she shouted from the back of the crowd. "This doesn't change anything, does it? I mean, this is only one exhibit. The museum has many others."

"And they're lies too," Alp said. "Don't you get it? Without lies, they have nothing." He motioned toward Ararat Man. "Some lies are just bolder than others."

The crowd was silent. Barrows appeared as though he was going to cry. Darkin looked ready to explode.

The camera focused in on Mandy. "Well that's it here at the Field Museum of Natural History after an odd turn of events. Now, back to you Brent *and* Connie," she said with a perky smile. "With today's salacious celebrity tidbit."

Benjamin clicked off the TV.

Linda set the Rubik's Cube down on Branch's lap.

His eyebrows rose as he realized each of the sides was now a single color.

"I feel sorry for Dr. Barrows." Linda said. "He appears to be an innocent dupe in all this."

"A dupe, perhaps," Benjamin said. "But innocent? I think he found what he wanted to find, which is why he was so easy to manipulate."

"So what's our next move?" said Roddy.

"Mine is to continue figuring out this riddle," Branch said. He took the paper out of his pocket.

"Read it again," Roddy said. "Maybe I can figure this thing out."

"NDDGMR 23. Add four of what Hebrew has not, two of one, plus two others, then reverse, and follow—in their proper places—with two of the only number not in Gregory's dates."

Roddy was deep in thought, his brow furrowed, his eyes squinted, and his nose scrunched. After several seconds his facial muscles relaxed. "Nope. Sorry. No idea." He turned back to the train.

Branch frowned. "Thanks, Roddy."

"Maybe I can help," Benjamin said. "I've given the riddle a lot of thought."

"You know the answer?" said Linda.

"Perhaps, but I need to give you some historical background. From a biblical perspective. Many scholars believe the creation occurred in 4004 B.C. and that exactly 4000 years later, Jesus was born. That would be 4 B.C. He lived 33 years, dying in A.D. 30.

"Jesus walked the Earth for forty days after the Resurrection. Ten days after his ascension, on the day of Pentecost, the End Times, or last days, began."

Linda said, "You believe the End Times began at Pentecost?"

"Yes. The apostles, who were all together inside a building, were filled with the Holy Spirit, burst outside, and spoke to the crowd. People from several countries were present. Each heard the apostles speaking in the hearer's own language.

"Peter explained that this phenomenon was a sign of what the prophet Joel had written: 'And in the last days it shall be...' So no matter what pop theology you hear from your favorite author or TV evangelist, the Bible says the End Times started on the Day of Pentecost."

"One thing puzzles me," Roddy said. "You told us Jesus was born in 4 B.C. and died in 30 A.D., but you said he was thirty-three years old. Isn't that thirty-four years?"

"Good observation, Roddy. By the way, it's A.D. 30, not the other way around. The A.D. comes before the number, even though we see it written improperly all the time.

"As to your question, the reason for the seeming error stems from the fact that the Gregorian calendar has no year zero. The time between 1 B.C. and A.D. 1 is a span of only one year, not two."

"How come?"

"The western calendar was conceived in 1582, when the number zero had not yet been accepted in the West."

"Ten has a zero," Roddy said. "A hundred has two zeros."

"Numerical digits, placeholders. Ten has value—one more than nine, one less than eleven—but as a number by itself, zero was unacceptable. Zero means nothing and, therefore, was not considered to have any value. Using it in the calendar would have been tantamount to mathematical heresy."

"Eureka," Branch said. "Gregory's dates. Dates are on a calendar. The western calendar was created by Pope Gregory. Zero is the missing number, but it must hold a place, become a place holder, a part of a larger number."

Linda said, "So the zeros join the two and the three."

"2030," said Roddy.

"Good," Branch said. "Next we have the letters. All consonants. No vowels."

"Oh, I'm such a dunce," Linda said. "Hebrew doesn't use vowels, only consonants."

"That's crazy," Roddy said. "How could you read Hebrew without vowels?"

"The vowel sounds for each word were known," Linda said. "But not written down. At least not until around A.D. 600. But ancient Hebrew didn't have written vowels so Gazanfer left them out."

"We need to figure out the vowels for this word," said Branch.

"Two of one and two others," said Linda. "So one of the vowels is repeated."

"I keep staring at this, and I'm not getting anything," Branch said.

Roddy was adjusting the wheels on one of the train cars. Without looking up, he said, "Noddegamra."

"What?" Branch said.

"N O D D E G A M R A. Noddegamra."

"That's not a word," Branch said.

"You're a genius, Roddy," Benjamin said.

Roddy looked up from the train set. "I am?"

Benjamin looked at Linda and Branch. "What is Noddegamra spelled backwards?"

Branch and Linda thought for a moment, then shared a glance and together they said, "Armageddon."

"Would the Bilderbergs start another world war?" Linda said.

"You bet they would," said Benjamin. "They can decrease the population, and they hope to convince the survivors of the need for a one-world government."

"So is that when the world is gonna end?" Roddy said.

"No," said Benjamin. "Armageddon and the Great Tribulation weren't about the end of the world, just the end of the Old Covenant. The 'last days' was a forty-year period that extended from A.D. 30, the beginning of Jesus' ministry, to A.D. 70."

"I thought Jesus' ministry ended in A.D. 30," Linda said.

"The most recent, and certainly the most reliable evidence, convinces me that he was born in 1 B.C. Pope Gregory had it right all along."

"So what are you saying about the riddle?" Roddy asked.

"It's a fake. Who knows where it really came from or how it got in the hands of a Pyramidion. But it's one more clever ruse meant to lead Christians away from the truth. Not surprisingly, the idea of a rapture also came from a monk. He lived in the 18th century. His name was Manuel Lacunza. His rapture theory didn't take hold until it was discovered by John Nelson Darby in the early nineteenth century. It was popularized by the Scofield Bible in the early 20th century and sensationalized by books and movies in recent years."

"The rapture theory," said Linda, "*has* kept many Christians inactive. Rather than oppose evil, they'd rather escape."

"Yes," said Benjamin, "and it's significant that Lacunza was a Jesuit."

"Why's that?" said Roddy.

"The Jesuits are a nefarious bunch. Kicked out of numerous countries. And they've controlled the Catholic Church for hundreds of years."

"Then we just need to put the riddle aside and finish what we started," said Branch.

"If we only knew where to search for the last piece," Linda said.

"Would you bring me the MacGuffin?" Benjamin said to Branch. "You know the combination."

Branch set the Rubik's Cube on the couch. He went to the wall, hit the button that caused the bookcase to slide away, and punched in the code to the safe. He reached in and pulled out the pyramid.

"I don't believe this." Branch looked over his shoulder at Benjamin, who sat with a Cheshire Cat grin. "You."

"What is it?" Linda said.

Branch turned around and held out the pyramid. The fully assembled pyramid.

Roddy said, "Where did the last piece come from?"

"The ninth piece was in the safe all along," said Branch, as he took the MacGuffin to Benjamin.

"You're a Pyramidion?" Linda said.

"Yes. My job was to start the process of retrieving all the pieces."

Roddy said, "Why not just have everyone mail them in?"

"I couldn't, since I had no knowledge of their identities. All I had was the ninth piece and my contact in Egypt."

Branch sat next to the cube and said, "The question now is, what is this thing for?"

"To find the pyramidion," Benjamin said.

"We found lots of Pyramidions," said Roddy.

"I'm not talking about them. Didn't any of you consult a dictionary to find out what a pyramidion is?"

The three of them glanced at one another, and then back at Benjamin, like children who've been caught without their homework.

"A pyramidion is the capstone that goes on top of a pyramid."

"And you believe this will lead us to it," Branch said.

Benjamin nodded.

"Why is the capstone so important?" Roddy said.

"Let me tell you a story which might help explain," said Benjamin. "In the nineteenth century, a German-born inventor, named Charles William Siemens, climbed the Great Pyramid. At the top he found a flat surface with each of the four sides measuring sixty feet.

"One of his Arab guides informed him that when he spread his fingers and raised his hand, he heard a ringing sound. When Siemens held up his index finger, he experienced a tingling sensation.

"Pondering this, he sat down and opened a bottle of wine. As he started to drink, he was subjected to an electric shock. His scientific curiosity aroused, he enclosed the wine bottle in wet newspaper, creating a Leyden jar, an old-fashioned capacitor."

"Old-fashioned what?" Linda said.

"An independent electronic unit capable of containing an electric charge. Holding it above his head, the makeshift capacitor became electrically charged. The bottle gave off sparks.

"Believing Siemens was practicing some form of witchcraft, a guide tried to grab Siemens' companion. Siemens noticed him in time and aimed the bottle at the Arab, who was zapped by a shock that knocked him down and unconscious."

Linda said. "What is it about the Pyramid that would cause such a thing?"

"Don't know, but putting the pyramidion atop the Great Pyramid might turn it on, making the Pyramid a powerful source of energy."

"Guess we're headed back to Egypt," Roddy said.

"They'll be waiting for you," said Benjamin. "Brussel and Wallach, and a host of others."

"Why do you say that?" said Linda.

"By now they've given up on getting the little pyramid back before you complete it. If they guess what the MacGuffin is for, they'll have someone watching for you."

Branch nodded and looked away. At nothing, for several moments. Finally, he turned toward Linda.

She read his concern for her in his eyes. "Oh no, you're not leaving me behind."

"Linda, we've put you in enough danger enough times, and I feel guiltier each time. They're gonna be more than ready for us."

"You're going after the greatest archeological find in the history of mankind. This tops the Ark of the Covenant, Noah's Ark, and Atlantis. I'm coming along."

"No," Branch said. "Not this time. You can't come. I'm sorry."

Linda picked up the Rubik's Cube and stood. "All right, fine." She charged from the room.

Branch could swear she left a trail of hot fumes in her wake.

He got the pyramid from Benjamin, took it to his room, and put it in his black Rolfs top-zip travel kit.

Branch slept fitfully. The next morning, he and Roddy left early. Branch checked the backseat and even the trunk. Roddy couldn't stop laughing, but Branch was determined Linda wouldn't sneak her way to Egypt with them.

On the plane Branch got up to search three times, but no Linda.

"Give it up," Roddy said. "She isn't on the plane. That means she stayed behind."

Branch sat, sullen. "Couldn't be this easy." After a few moments: "We did the right thing, though. Didn't we?"

"You miss her, don't you?"

"What makes you say that?"

"I've known you since kindergarten. I still remember the day when our teacher, Miss Nancy, didn't come. You had that same look."

"What are you talking about?"

"You remember the crush you had on Miss Nancy."

Branch stared at him a moment; then jammed a pair of headphones on his head. "Should've left you behind."

In Cairo, they met a man who gave them the keys to a bright lime green dune buggy, with roll-bars instead of a roof.

"Who did you say got us this dune buggy?" Roddy said, from the passenger seat.

"My friend Harlan in Australia. He built it for this guy in Cairo and convinced the guy to let us borrow the buggy. If we have to make a run, this'll be ideal on the sand."

"No choice about the color, though, huh?"

"Don't complain. One of these already helped save my life."

"Maybe if I put on dark glasses." He put his shades on. "A little better."

Arriving at Giza well into the night, they stopped where the access road intersects with another road. It was the one they parked on the first time they were here, not far from one corner of the Great Pyramid.

"Sure looks different than last time," said Roddy, taking off his sunglasses. "We can see stuff."

"Yeah, with a full moon reflecting off the sand, we have near daylight without the glare.

An all-too-familiar voice said, "How amazingly coincidental is this? You guys came to Egypt; I came to Egypt."

Branch and Roddy turned to find Linda standing next to a car.

She sauntered over to the dune buggy.

"Nice to see you, Missy," said Roddy.

Branch glared at him, then back at Linda.

"How'd you get here ahead of us?" Branch said.

"Took an earlier flight."

"Well, take an early flight back. Is that your rental?"

"Sort of. They were all out of rentals, but said I could have this cute little Chery Car for free."

"Why's that?"

"Bullet holes and no windows."

Branch and Roddy exchanged a quick glance, recognizing the car as the one they'd driven here the night this all began.

"So, you want me to hop in back?" Linda said.

"No," Branch said. "You are not coming, and please don't beg. Begging is unseemly."

"You'll want me to come."

"Why would I want...?" Branch became suspicious. He reached into the back seat, grabbed his travel bag, and unzipped it. Instead of the pyramid, he found the Rubik's Cube.

He looked at Linda, who took the pyramid out of her purse.

"And please don't you beg," Linda said. "Begging is unmanly."

Branch shoved the cube back in the bag, zipped it, and tossed it in the back seat. He put both hands on the steering wheel and stared straight ahead.

Roddy opened the door and got out. "You can sit in front. I'll jump in back."

Linda hurried around the front of the car, and got in next to Branch while Roddy jumped in the backseat.

"All right," Roddy said. "How do we search for this thing?"

"We'll start by driving around and looking for any anomalies, things people might have missed, but that could give us a clue."

"In other words, you have no idea."

"We're gonna play it by ear."

Linda said, "Maybe we should go underground to look for clues."

"We might have to," Branch said. "But we could end up trapped if our friends show up. If they don't show, we'll consider going down."

"I just wish I knew what we were looking for," Linda said.

"Anomalies," Roddy said. "We're looking for anomalies. Hey, Branch, what's an anomalies."

"Like Christine saying something complementary about me."

"Gotcha."

They drove out onto the sand and began to cruise past the Pyramid of Khafre. They hadn't gone far when Roddy glanced over his shoulder at the road to Cairo.

"Would you call four black Road Rangers driving at high speed an anomaly?"

Branch took a look. "I'd call it bad news." Branch hit the gas and turned left, onto a causeway, in the direction of the Sphinx.

Two of the Rangers followed them, while the other two went left, past the Great Pyramid, and toward the opposite side of the Sphinx.

Roddy flipped open a cargo hold behind the back seat. "Good thing we planned ahead this time." He drew out an automatic weapon and held it out to Linda.

"No thanks. I'll just scream at them as usual."

Roddy pulled a big handgun out and handed it to Branch, who continued driving with one hand.

"Lotta rock things around here," Roddy said.

"Doing my best to avoid them," said Branch.

"Take a right," Linda said. "We'll swing around the Southern Cemetery."

"You know where you're going?" Branch said.

"I've done enough archeology articles on Giza that I kind of know my way around."

They were on sand now as they swung around the east end of the Southern Cemetery. Arriving at the other side, Branch slammed on the brakes. One of the Road Rangers was coming straight at them.

"Oops! Sorry," said Linda.

Branch took a sharp left and drove over a hill of sand and then over a bigger hill of sand. Coming down the hill, they encountered another Ranger approaching them from their left.

They were nearing the road and saw the other Rangers stop. Eight men got out and drew their guns.

Branch, Roddy, and Linda ducked as they drove through a hail of bullets.

"Keep going," Linda said. "Past the Mohammedan Cemetery and the Coptic Cemetery."

"Lot of cemeteries," Roddy said.

"This whole area is a necropolis."

"A what?"

"Burial ground."

"The irony is amusing," Branch said. "I hope you have a plan to get us out of here."

"Plan?" Linda said.

"Oh, nuts," Branch said as he shot around the last cemetery and into open sand. "Now we'll be easier targets for them."

"Hey, Branch," Roddy said. "Do you think they'd send a helicopter after us?"

"Why?"

"We got one at six o'clock headed this way."

Branch peeked over his shoulder and spotted the helicopter. Which opened fire, using machine guns mounted underneath.

He swerved out of the path of the two streams of pursuing lead, and the copter swept by them.

Branch drove as fast as he could across the desert sand in the direction of four smaller pyramids on the right. Two of the black Road Rangers were side-by-side, in pursuit. The helicopter had slowed, and was turning to face them.

Roddy opened fire on the Rangers.

Guns came out the side windows of the two vehicles and fired back.

A man stood in the open sunroof of one of the cars and aimed a grenade launcher.

"Incoming," Roddy said.

Branch glanced in his rearview mirror and spotted the approaching projectile. He swerved left, and the grenade exploded harmlessly forty yards in front of them.

Now the helicopter pilot was taking aim.

Branch whipped to the right, nearly rolling the car, and avoided the fresh spray of bullets from their overhead tormentor.

They were driving under the copter when the ground began to shake.

"Earthquake?" Roddy said.

After several moments, the shaking stopped, and they continued on.

"Better get rid of the aerial pursuit, Roddy."

"Right." Roddy reached into the trunk behind the seat and pulled out a rocket launcher.

"Mess with Chico Rodriguez, and you pay the price."

"Speak louder," Branch said. "I don't think they heard you."

Roddy took aim, and the copter's pilot, seeing Roddy about to shoot him out of the sky, took off the other way.

Roddy fired and hit one of the landing rails. The explosion shook the helicopter, but the pilot righted his craft and kept going.

"Wow, I got him good," Roddy said.

"You got him?" said Branch.

"Shot off one of his landing rails."

"Is that all? A landing rail?"

"He's gonna land crooked."

"What? Are you kidding me?"

"I wouldn't want to land crooked." He looked to Linda—crouched on the floor—for help. "You wouldn't want to land crooked, would you?"

"You did fine, Roddy," Linda said. "You scared him away."

"Thank you."

They continued on across the sand.

Linda popped up and glanced around. "On our right, we have the Pyramid of Menkaure," Linda said. "Just before it is the Funerary Temple, and these three smaller ones are the Pyramids of Queens."

"What are you, a tour guide?" Branch said.

"Better pay attention; this is all gonna be on the test."

"Incoming," Roddy said.

In his rearview mirror, Branch spotted a launched grenade coming at them. He veered to the right to avoid being hit.

This one exploded near enough on the sand to cause the dune buggy to shake. They each held on tight to whatever part of the buggy they could. They were pelted by a shower of sand impacting their faces like hundreds of tiny needles.

They kept on rolling.

As they rounded the three small pyramids next to Menkaure, they noticed the road ahead.

"Maybe we can escape now," said Linda.

"I don't think so," Branch said.

One of the Road Rangers sped around the bend near the corner of the Khafre Pyramid and came barreling toward them.

"Surrounded again," said Roddy.

Branch angled around Menkaure and away from the road. They broke into the open sand again, experiencing a light warm breeze.

The two Rangers that had followed them across the sand had turned around at the Queens Pyramids and were now trying to cut them off.

"These guys are good," said Roddy.

"Gets worse," Branch said. "Look."

The helicopter was dead ahead and coming straight at them. The whirl of the blades grew louder.

"Sure looks dumb with only one rail," Roddy said.

Branch glanced over his shoulder and frowned.

"Well, it does," said Roddy.

Roddy loaded up his launcher, but before he could shoot, the occupants of all three pursuing vehicles opened fire.

The hapless targets ducked. When the shooting let up, Roddy came up fast and fired his rocket launcher at the copter bearing down on them.

The pilot nimbly jerked his craft away from the projectile.

The dune buggy sped across the sand. At the same spot as before, the ground started to shake.

"I think we found another Bermuda Triangle," Roddy said.

They curved left and headed toward the road, near the Sphinx. The fourth black Ranger was waiting for them. The vehicle burst onto the sand and headed straight toward them.

The other three Rangers had spread out. One stayed directly behind them, with the other two hanging back and off to either side.

And the helicopter was coming up fast behind them.

"Roddy," Branch said. "Forget the rocket launcher. Shoot the pilot."

Roddy reached into the trunk and took out a high-powered rifle.

"Will the bullet pierce the tempered glass in front of the cockpit?" Branch said.

"I'm using armor-piercing bullets," Roddy said.

"All right. Fire on my signal."

The Ranger ahead was getting closer, as was the pursuing helicopter.

Linda cringed on the floor in front. "I hope you know what you're doing, Mr. Nichols."

"Don't worry, Miss Chapel. I have everything under control."

He glanced back at Roddy, who rolled his eyes and shook his head.

The men in the approaching auto opened fire, and bullets pinged off the lime green paint as Branch and Roddy ducked low. The copter behind them commenced firing its guns, but the pilot was dipping the front so low the bullets merely trailed the dune buggy.

"You wanta give that signal yet, buddy?" Roddy said.

"Wait for it... Now."

Roddy rose up, took aim, and fired three quick shots, hitting the pilot each time.

He fell forward on the stick, and the copter picked up speed, moving lower and lower to the ground.

The Ranger ahead was still coming hard. Automatic weapons, hung out the windows, kept up a steady pummeling of the buggy.

Branch jerked hard on the wheel and they sailed off to the right, just missed by the copter as it zipped by. Heading straight for the oncoming Ranger.

With nowhere to go, and no time to react, all the driver could do was smack head-on into the helicopter.

A massive explosion followed with flames and smoke hurling into the air.

Branch did the unexpected, turning the car 180 degrees and heading back toward their pursuers.

"Shouldn't we be trying to get away?" Linda said.

"We gotta get back to the Bermuda Triangle."

The first car was coming toward them, but not straight at them. They'd pass within thirty feet of each other.

A grenade launcher came out the back window, even as Roddy loaded his rocket launcher.

Roddy took aim. He waited, waited, and fired as the other guy also fired. The two projectiles passed by each other.

The grenade whizzed just inches above the buggy.

Roddy's rocket went in one back window and out the other.

"Bet you couldn't do that again if you tried," Branch said.

"Not surprised," Roddy said. "Did you notice who was in the car?"

"The duo with nine lives."

The other two cars turned in, angling toward the center in an apparent attempt to cut them off.

Linda came up from the floor to get a look. "Do you have a smoke bomb, Roddy?"

"Sure."

"You're kidding," Branch said.

"Can you launch it?" said Linda.

Branch said, "Will you leave guns and bomb stuff to us?"

"I can make a sling," said Roddy.

He fashioned a makeshift sling with some rope, put the smoke bomb in one end, and grabbed hold of a knot at the other.

"You know what to do, Roddy?" Linda said.

"You bet."

"Is this cordial, albeit meaningless conversation going anywhere?" said Branch.

"Watch and learn," Roddy said. "First, you gotta slow down."

"You sure?"

"Trust me."

Branch slowed. The two black Rangers adjusted their angle so they'd still be headed straight at them.

Roddy stood on the back seat and swung the sling, with its cargo, overhead. After several rotations, he let the load fly, sling and all.

The bomb landed well in front of them, and smoke billowed up, blotting out their view of the two approaching Rangers.

The buggy shot into the smoke and immediately after, the two Rangers, coming at angles, headed into the smoke, as well.

"I get it," said Branch, and he hit the gas. The buggy jumped forward, and they sped out of the smoke.

The big black vehicles crashed into each other as the dune buggy continued on.

"No way that should work," Branch said.

"And you wanted to leave me behind," Linda said.

Branch gave her a quizzical stare. "All right, you can come."

The remaining Road Ranger had turned around and was once again in pursuit.

"Linda, give me the MacGuffin," said Branch.

"What are you gonna do?" Linda said, as she took the little pyramid out of her purse and handed it to him.

He held it in his hand. The pyramid lit up, and the ground shook. After several moments, the tremors stopped, and the MacGuffin ceased glowing.

"Never did that before," said Roddy.

Branch hit the brakes, cocked the wheel, and did a one-eighty. Now they were sitting still, facing the on-coming Ranger.

They could see men staggering from the two wrecked autos as a soft Egyptian wind blew the smoke away, with the fire from the copter raging. The last car still coming.

"A little closer," Branch said. "Yeah, that's good."

As if they could hear Branch, they stopped the car right where he wanted them to. The doors opened. Brussel, Wallach, and two others got out. The two in back aimed their guns at the buggy.

Brussel yelled, "Give us the pyramid and we'll let you live."

Branch opened the door and got out.

"What are you gonna do?" Linda said.

Branch stepped away from the car and threw the pyramid toward the Ranger. The MacGuffin glowed as it sailed through the air, and the ground beneath the Ranger shook. The tiny pyramid landed about thirty yards short, with a now-pulsating glow.

The ground under the car shook more violently. All four men got back in.

The earth under them began to rise. They were on a pinnacle of sand, rising higher and higher.

The sand at the top started to fall away, revealing a gold pyramidion.

Up, higher and higher, went the pyramidion reaching a height of sixty feet, sand caving around it, filling in the hole beneath.

The car teetered, precariously.

"Don't anyone sneeze," Roddy said.

Finally, the Ranger fell, and rolled over and over, till the car landed on its wheels, at the bottom. No one in the car was visible.

"Hope they had safety belts on," Linda said.

"I don't," said Branch.

Brussel and Wallach sat up and stared for a moment. Then Brussel turned the car around and drove away.

Epilogue

Six months later, the original three members of the Pyramid Gang gathered with Benjamin in his study. Christine was present too.

Branch said, "Do you think they'll ever put the pyramidion on top of Giza?"

Benjamin said, "As soon as the Egyptians discovered tourists would pay money to touch it, they built a fence and started collecting."

"I take that as a probably not."

Benjamin continued: "In 1998, the Freemasons built a gold *covered* capstone for the Pyramid. That would've rendered the Pyramid useless because the capstone was not solid gold. They convinced the Egyptians to put the fake one on, but at the eleventh hour, the Egyptians changed their minds. Now they're trying to decide what to do with the real one."

Benjamin's cell phone rang, and he checked the caller ID. "Dr. Meir."

"Uncle Dagan?" Linda said.

"Hello... Yes, all right. I'll turn the screen on."

Benjamin opened a conference call on the internet. Dr. Dagan Meir appeared on the screen.

"Hi, Uncle Dagan."

"Hello, Linda. Ah, I'm glad you're all present. I've something to show you. I've been deciphering the writing you photographed on the wall of the underground chamber at the Grand Canyon Pyramid.

"I've learned much about the antediluvian world. But the one thing that stood out was the measurements of the speed of light over the first 1,000 years of man's existence.

"You'll notice on this chart because the line is going almost straight up, that light was traveling near infinity at the moment of creation. The speed couldn't be measured. This was the day without any yesterdays.

"Now, by placing dots on the chart for each new measurement, every 100 years, we find that the speed slowed quickly at first but more gradually over time.

"By extending the line for a total of 6,000 years, the velocity reaches the current speed of light. This matches the chart derived from light speed measurements over the last 300 years as Dr. Von Brunner demonstrated. This has the potential to destroy evolution since it shows the shortness of the universe's existence."

"I agree," Benjamin said. "Though they won't give in easily. They'll fight back with the usual evasiveness, distortions of facts, lateral reasoning, and outright lies. But for all who care about truth, this is a banner discovery."

"I agree, and I congratulate the Pyramid Gang on this finding. I hope my niece hasn't been too much of a bother for you two young fellows."

Branch deadpanned his response. "Bother? Let me count the ways."

"Just keep it up, mister," Linda said, with a hint of a smile.

"I'll talk with you later," Benjamin said.

"All right. Bye for now," said Meir.

"Bye, Uncle Dagan."

The image on the screen vanished.

Branch whispered to Linda, "Come outside. I need to talk to you."

They got up and started to leave.

"Don't run off anywhere, Linda," Christine said. "We have a lunch date, remember."

"Lunch?" Branch said.

"Christine has known you since childhood, hasn't she?" said Linda.

"Yeah."

"So, now I'm gonna find out all about you."

Branch glanced at Christine, then back at Linda.

"I'll deny everything."

Christine and Linda laughed.

Outside the mansion, Branch and Linda came out wearing jackets against the brisk December air. A light snowfall embraced them.

"There's something I've wanted to ask you," Branch said.

"Is it important?" she said, with a coy smile.

"Yeah... Will you marry me?"

"After all the times you tried to get rid of me?"

"Uh, maybe this is a bad time."

"Of course I will, you big dope."

"You will? Great. Because ever since I met you, you've been driving me crazy. In a good way, I mean. And I just—"

"Shut up and kiss me."

He stared down at her and smiled, but not his usual mocking smile. This time it was different. She couldn't say how but she would, from that day forward, insist that it was the first time she saw *I love you* in his eyes.

He bent his head down as she stood on her toes and he gave her a long, passionate kiss.

End of Story

"There's a plot in this country to enslave every man, woman, and child. Before I leave this high and noble office, I intend to expose this plot."

President John F. Kennedy
Seven days before his assassination